This book is a gift from

The Friends of the
Carmel Valley Library

# THE
# HERETIC

# THE
# HERETIC

## MIGUEL DELIBES

**THE OVERLOOK PRESS**
WOODSTOCK . NEW YORK

First published in the United States in 2006 by
The Overlook Press, Peter Mayer Publishers, Inc.
Woodstock and New York

NEW YORK:
141 Wooster Street
New York, NY 10012

WOODSTOCK:
One Overlook Drive
Woodstock, NY 12498
www.overlookpress.com
[for individual orders, bulk and special sales, contact our Woodstock office]

This work has been published with a subsidy from the General Director of Books, Archives,
and Libraries of the Cultural Ministry of Spain

∞ The paper used in this book meets the requirements for paper
permanence as described in the ANSI Z39.48-1992 standard.

Cataloging-in-Publication Data is available from the Library of Congress

*Book design and type formatting by Bernard Schleifer*
Manufactured in the United States of America
FIRST EDITION
ISBN 1-58567-570-9
9 8 7 6 5 4 3 2 1

*To Valladolid,*
*my city*

# CONTENTS

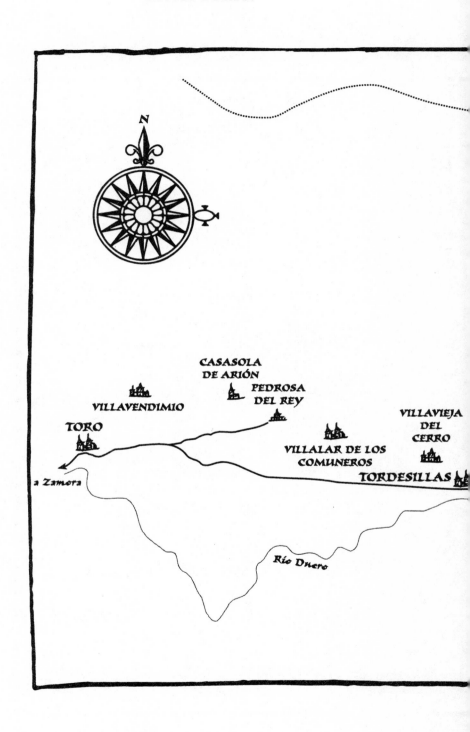

El Páramo

a Burgos
y Santander

LA MUDARRA

Itinerario de las colinas

Río Pisuerga

VILLANUBLA

El Cabildo

SANTOVENIA
DE PISUERGA

ZARATÁN

La Judería

Río Esgueva

Puente Mayor

VALLADOLID

ARROYO

TUDELA
DE DUERO

SIMANCAS

GERIA

Puente Romano

Río Duero

HERRERA
DE DUERO

PUENTE
DUERO

a Segovia

Tierra de
Pinares

a Madrid

0        5        10 km

S. Gregorio

La Rutigua

Colegiata

VALLADOLID
(hacia 1600)

How can we remain silent about so many kinds of violence per-petrated in the name of faith? Wars of religion, the courts of the Inquisition, and other mechanisms whereby the rights of indi-viduals were violated . . . It is necessary that the Church, in accord with Vatican Council II, take the initiative in reviewing the darker aspects of its history, judging them in the light of the principles enunciated in the Gospels.

(John Paul II to the cardinals, 1994)

# PRELUDE

❧⸘❧

T HE *Hamburg*, a trim galliass, slowly passed out of the river's mouth and entered the open sea just as the sun came up. It was early October, 1557. The calm surface of the sea and the steadiness of the ship promised fair weather, a tranquil, probably hot voyage, with bright sun and mild northerly winds. The *Hamburg* was a small cargo ship with a crew of fifty-two, and during fair weather, her captain, Heinrich Berger, a man with a keen eye for profit, would erect two small tents on the poop deck where, for a modest sum, he would lodge up to four trustworthy passengers.

The first tent, walking from the prow, housed a well-turned-out man of modest stature with a short beard cut in the style of Valladolid, his hometown. His hat, breeches, doublet, and shirt, however, were made in Segovia. Leaning on the handrail, he was gazing through a telescope back at the port they'd just left. A flock of sea gulls screeching raucously over the *Hamburg*'s wake was preparing to return to land. Ahead, beyond the bow and above the outline of the land, the fog was beginning to fade. Through the tattered mist appeared patches of the blue sky promised by the dead calm of dawn. The man's small, nervous hand hunted around in the purse under his jacket and pulled out the folded paper a sailor had handed him as he came aboard. He reread the brief message it contained: "Welcome aboard. I hope to have the pleasure of your company at lunch in my cabin at one o'clock. Captain Berger."

Back in Valladolid, the Doctor had spoken affectionately of the captain. Although they hadn't seen each other for a long time, they shared a long-standing friendship. The Doctor had so much confidence in the captain that he wouldn't authorize his fellow protestant Cipriano Salcedo's voyage to Germany until he was certain the captain would be returning to Spain in the fall. The small man contemplated the sea as he mentally reconstructed the image of the Doctor: he'd recently become extremely silent and fearful, always warning him of the risks of traveling in Europe. True enough, the recent law against crossing borders applied only to clerics and students, but everyone knew that any traveler who passed through Germany would be subjected to *discreet scrutiny*. The Doctor had said *discreet scrutiny*, but Cipriano Salcedo deduced from his tone of voice that the scrutiny would be close and threatening. That explained the precautions Salcedo took over the course of his journey: sudden changes of means of transportation, extreme care in choosing inns or  meeting places, vigilance even in visits to booksellers.

Cipriano Salcedo was proud that the Doctor had chosen him for such a delicate mission. His decision freed him from old complexes, allowed him to think he could still be useful to someone, that there was at least one being in the world who had confidence in him and who would put himself in his hands. And the fact that this being was a wise, intelligent, and prudent man like the Doctor satisfied his incipient vanity. Now Salcedo, out on the deck, was thinking that he was on the verge of ending his journey, that during this next-to-last stage aboard the *Hamburg*, under the command of Captain Berger, he could sleep peacefully, and that the orders of Doctor Cazalla had been carried out.

He heard voices on deck and turned, the telescope still in his small, hairy hand. Half a dozen barefoot sailors were carrying planks toward the stern along with the cables needed to join them. Behind them, another three were carrying a wooden structure designed to fit on the stern. On it, in large, gold letters: *Dante Alighieri*. In a few minutes, with an efficiency that revealed habitual practice, the team arranged the boards along the stern and fastened the dangling rope ends that held them together to the mizzen mast. Then two sailors jumped into the boatswain's chair while the others used cords to hang up the huge sign those below placed over the name *Hamburg*. Up on the hanging scaffold they used nails and marlinespikes to make fast the structure with the new name. In barely half an hour, the galliass was prudently rebaptized.

Two hours later, in his cabin, while a cabin boy served them lunch, Captain Berger explained that the change of name was merely a precaution they practiced whenever the ship docked in countries hostile to Luther's Reform. But since Cipriano Salcedo seemed hesitant, Captain Berger, who always spoke with his eyes half-closed, as if he were forever scrutinizing the horizon, added, with the worm-eaten, hoarse voice common among men who lived on the sea: "We can easily avoid risky situations. The *Hamburg* is registered in both Hamburg and Venice. Both names, therefore, are legitimate. Using one or the other depends on what's advantageous to us."

They'd just taken their places around the table when Salcedo suddenly noticed the third dinner guest, his neighbor in the other tent on the poop deck. The captain had introduced him as Don Isidoro Tellería, from Sevilla, a tall, thin, clean-shaven man, dressed completely in black, who said he'd spent the last half year in Geneva. When the captain began the conversation, Tellería remained silent, only raising his eyes when the captain asked Salcedo about the *Doktor*.

Salcedo cleared his throat. He always hesitated before speaking. It was a remnant of his fear of his father: his icy stare, his reproaches, and his spasmodic coughing on winter mornings. It wasn't that Cipriano stuttered; rather, it was a slight tripping over the first syllable, like an insignificant vacillation: "Th . . . the Doctor is in good health, captain. Perhaps a bit thinner and more disillusioned. Things are not going well there. He's afraid the Council of Trent will return the problem to its origin, that we won't get a thing. That's the reason for my trip: to get information. To find out what the real situation is in Germany, to interview Philipp Melanchthon, and to buy books . . ."

"What kind of books?"

"All kinds, especially the most recent. For a long time no books have entered Spain. The Holy Office has intensified its vigilance. Even now, they're revising the Index of Prohibited Books. Reading those texts, selling them, or circulating them are all serious crimes."

Salcedo stopped, thinking that the captain would not be satisfied with his vague answer, and in view of his silence he added: "Now, the

Doctor's mother did die. We buried her in the Convent of San Benedict in rather grand style, respecting all forms properly. Even so, there was muttering and protest at the funeral."

"Doña Leonor de Vivero?" asked the captain.

"Doña Leonor de Vivero, exactly. In a certain sense, she at times was the soul of the enterprise in Valladolid."

Smiling, Captain Berger shook his head in the negative. He was perhaps twelve or fifteen years older than Salcedo, with a red goatee and very blond, almost albino white hair, more like that of a Scandinavian than a German. He went on observing Salcedo's small hands with avid curiosity, his eyes half closed. Slowly he raised his eyes to Salcedo's face, which was also small, as were his well-proportioned features, dominated by somber and deep-set eyes. To side-step Salcedo's suggestion, he drank half a glass of Bordeaux out of a clay jug at the center of the table, raised his eyes and stated: "I think the soul of the enterprise in Valladolid was always the *Doktor*. His mother was one of his supporters. Perhaps the one who embraced the doctrine of justification with the greatest enthusiasm. I met the *Doktor* in Germany, in Erfurt, when he was still an exasperated follower of Erasmus. By the time he returned to Valladolid, he was already carrying the *leprosy*."

Salcedo coiled uncomfortably. It always happened when he thought he'd said something improper, perhaps another reminiscence of his childhood fears: "What I actually meant," he clarified, "is that Doña Leonor was the strong woman who sustained the Doctor during his low moments and gave life and meaning to the small groups who believe as we do."

Captain Berger went on as if he hadn't heard him: "I didn't see the *Doktor* again until eight years later. That was an unforgettable visit to Valladolid. I had the honor to attend a group meeting presided over by the *Doktor* together with his mother, Doña Leonor de Vivero. There can be no doubt that she had a clear vision of things, an unequivocal idea of the essential things, though in her manner she was a bit authoritarian."

The blue line of the sea rose and fell in the porthole, following the mild rocking of the ship. The constant creaking of the wooden bulkhead that separated the small dinning room from the captain's cabin was a kind of accompaniment to the men at table. Cipriano Salcedo agreed:

"All her children venerate her. Her faith comforted them. One of them, Pedro, the parish priest of Pedrosa, shared with her Luther's affection for music because he understood that truth and culture—to be worthy of the name—must march forward together."

The young cabin boy was now serving them a plate of meat; when he was finished, he placed another jug of wine on the table and excused himself. The captain poured wine into Salcedo's glass. Tellería still hadn't tasted his and continued to observe Berger with the curiosity of an entomologist, as he packed the bowl of his clay Indian pipe, the kind the smugglers who worked on the galleons introduced into Sevilla along with tobacco, whose consumption was beginning to spread among the people despite the Inquisition's hostility to it. The captain waited until the cabin boy closed the sliding door to say: "When we talk about Sevilla, we shouldn't forget a key man, Don Carlos de Seso, the perfect incarnation of Veronese manhood: elegant, strong, intelligent, and conceited. As I see it, Don Carlos de Seso is an absolutely essential figure in the awakening of Castilian Lutheranism."

Cipriano Salcedo ruffled his short beard. He nodded in a mechanical, slightly forced way: "Don Carlos de Seso is an interesting, very well-read man, but there is something obscure surrounding his person: Why did he leave Verona? Why did he end up in Spain? Was he perhaps fleeing something or was it simply enthusiasm for the mission?"

Captain Berger hid not a single detail that could be taken as ignorance of Lutheran reality: "In principle, the papists accept Seso, count on him. They even sent him to Trent, to the Council, accompanying the bishop of Calahorra. Some ill-intentioned person actually said that he was going along only as an interpreter, but that's not true. The bishop himself told Carranza as he was preparing for the return trip to Spain that when he was with Don Carlos de Seso he was well-accompanied, that Don Carlos was an affable and well-educated gentleman about whom people spoke with satisfaction, that there was no scandal attached to him in any intellectual circle. Besides, there was his famous interview with the great theologian Carranza in Valladolid, even though no one knows for sure what happened there."

The galliass began to pitch lightly, and Tellería, who'd just taken a deep puff of his pipe, glanced toward the porthole in surprise, as if he'd been playing cards and had suddenly discovered he was being cheated. For his part, Cipriano observed the man from Sevilla with intense suspicion, this hieratic man dressed in mourning who smoked his pipe without getting involved in the conversation. But Captain Berger's open attitude toward him, the ironic disdain in his eye when he glanced at him, dissipated all distrust instantly. His gray eyes, so aware and responsible, seemed to say: Speak freely, Salcedo my friend. Our guest, Don Isidoro Tellería, has more reasons than we do to keep silent. Nevertheless, the captain looked at Tellería before laconically clarifying: "We've entered the Channel."

He removed the empty jug and replaced it with a full one. Isidoro Tellería, who had yet to taste the wine, observed his companions with a mix of astonishment and skepticism. By contrast, Captain Berger became more and more loquacious with every glass he drank: "Your excellency's journey interests me," he said to Salcedo. "Buying books, looking for support, visiting Melanchthon, you say those were your objectives. Were you able to carry them through? How did you travel through the country? What cities did you visit?"

"On April 13th I left Valladolid. Except for our contact with Sevilla, which was becoming more and more difficult every day, we'd been in isolation for months. After long discussions, the Doctor admitted we needed first-hand information. With Luther dead, he'd become very interested in Melanchthon's thinking, but he didn't know exactly where he was going."

"And how did you arrange matters?"

"It was," Salcedo admitted, still suspicious of Tellería, "a delicate affair." The Holy Office had just prohibited clerics and intellectuals from leaving Spain. I traveled on horseback to Pamplona, where a guide helped me cross the Pyrenees. Then I made use of every imaginable sort of transport: coaches, boats, horses—I even walked. It was prudent not to travel in a straight line and to change lodging and means of transportation frequently. So I went through southern France: Bordeaux, Toulouse, all the way to Lausanne. France has good roads despite the heavy traffic."

The captain was impatient: "And, in Germany?"

"I maintained my precautions. People said there were spies everywhere, so I showed myself as little as possible. I made contact in the important cities. I visited Hamburg, Erfurt, Eisleben, and Wittenberg —the heart of lutheranism—with frequent side trips to the country. But it was in Wittenberg where I bought books and where I was finally able to speak with Philipp Melanchthon."

Captain Berger's narrowed eyes spurred Salcedo on: "What surprised me in Wittenberg was the sheer quantity of publishing. There were printing houses and bookstores everywhere. After a walk through the city, I understood that saying "Luther was the child of the printing press," because, all things considered, that's where his strength lay. He was the first heretic who had such an efficient, powerful, and swift means of communication at his disposal. I noticed that most of the typographers were followers of his, and, like faithful disciples, were diligent with the texts that interested the reformer and, conversely, worked slowly with the works of his adversaries, filling them with typographical errors. It was there, in Wittenberg, where I could leaf through *Passionate*, that antipapist libel filled with coarse texts and vulgar illustrations, like the one in which the Pope is pictured as an ass defecated by the devil."

Tellería finished smoking his pipe and was knocking the ashes into a bowl. Captain Berger suddenly interrupted Salcedo: "Those scurrilous writings are not the Reformation, so you shouldn't judge the Reformation by them. In any revolution there are excesses. It's inevitable. In revolutionary criticism, there are never nuances."

Salcedo, unfazed, had warmed to his subject and was going on without the slightest hesitation, dispassionately, as if he were judging something alien to his own ideas, something completely obvious: "No, Captain, they aren't the Reformation, but they do work against it. Seeing these things, the foreign visitor in Germany gets the impression that Luther went too far. He rightly thought to print a divine invention, but I suspect he would not have approved of the bad use it's being put to now that he's dead as is the case with his first books *Babylonian Captivity* and *The Papacy Founded by the Devil*, which were hardly fairy tales."

"But remember his *Bible*, don't forget the fundamental thing."

"I know, Captain. The German *Bible*, a monument, isn't it? According to some Spanish intellectuals, that book alone justifies the celebrated saying "God has spoken in German." It's so beautiful, so pleasing to the ear. Luther and his *Bible* are making the German language, now touched by the sacred, universal. That much is clear."

The rocking of the *Hamburg* became more pronounced, and Don Isidoro Tellería clasped his head between his hands as if he were afraid it would fly off his shoulders with the shifting of the sea. The cabin boy, who'd removed the dishes, swept the crumbs from the table onto a tray, and when he finished, served glasses of brandy. Captain Berger stared compassionately at Isidoro Tellería and waited until the boy had closed the sliding door behind him before adding: "It's significant that Luther made use of music and printing. That speaks better of him than his wild outbursts. At least these things are more convincing. And when he says, "I don't want to retract anything because it isn't honorable to act against one's conscience," he's talking about his theses, not about his mockery and insults."

Captain Berger's fixed, scrutinizing gaze disconcerted Salcedo. It reminded him of his father's frigid stare as he stood before Don Alvaro Cabeza de Vaca, who betrayed him: "He's missing; I can't find him, Mister Salcedo."

"But," he pointed out scratching his beard, "in *Babylonian Captivity*, Luther asserts that Our Lord only instituted two sacraments: baptism and communion. That's probably the only thing he intended to say, but he takes advantage of the moment to berate, reproach, and insult. Something similar happens in *The Roman Papacy*."

The captain raised his right hand: "Please allow me one word. The jokes the papists make about those books and about his having married a nun are even more pitiless than Luther's jokes about them."

It was a verbal duel, which Salcedo prolonged in order to sound out the captain, to see how far he'd let him go, to put Lutheran flexibility to the test. He didn't answer him, but he did see there was something the captain had yet to say. He stared fixedly at the tip of the captain's nose, which, as Father Arnaldo at the Foundlings always said, was what you had to do with the wicked in order to make them vomit everything they were hiding. Captain Berger said: "I insist that we simply have to use a different scale to weigh the reformer's sensibility, his love for the fine arts, and his use of music in the liturgy. But let me say that the hymn "A Mighty Fortress is Our God" caused a greater stir in Central Europe than the *Te Deum*."

Captain Berger's voice began to tremble, like the voices of the new preachers. He was becoming excited. Salcedo deliberately softened his tone: "Luther should take responsibility for everything, including the lutherans and their outrages. Captain, I've accepted the doctrine of justification by faith, as has the entire Valladolid group, because I think faith is the essential thing and that Christ's sacrifice has a greater value as far as my redemption is concerned than my good works, no matter how altruistic they may be."

Like a hound following a trail, Cipriano Salcedo did not raise his nose from the ground. One track might separate from another, but Salcedo found a rare pleasure in flushing out one rabbit before starting on the next. There was no question that his denunciations derived from a single source, but he delighted in dividing them up, ascribing them to different motives, pushing the captain out of the mental processes he usually followed in his normal discussions: "Another thing, captain. The fury of the Thuringian peasants. Twenty years after the *Zwickau Prophets*, violence was still smoldering. They don't understand religious change unless it involves social change. The bad example came from the princes when they appropriated church property. For the peasants, religious change without money is of no interest."

Captain Berger placed his glass on the table: "Religion inevitably has a social aspect," he said, carefully choosing his words, as if desiring to put things in their proper order. "The *Zwickau Prophets* were the reformers of the Reformation. They smashed sacred images and wanted money above anything else. They were human. They hoped religion would redeem them and fought for a practical religion. That's why they provoked a war. Franz von Siecbingen, with all his prestige, made himself their leader, but Luther was more powerful and defeated them. And not because he thought their aspirations were paltry but because they hadn't chosen the proper path to reach them."

"I don't approve of that path either."

"Everything is human and understandable. The peasants, the artisans, and the miners had no great thinkers among them. They only had four simple ideas, but those were more then enough to inflame them,

and their movement spread through Alsatia. The most important idea
was Divine Right, they said. But that Right was supposed to prevail over
the servants of the nobility, the privilege of hunting, or the *jus primae
noctis* . . . in sum, over all the abuses practiced by the nobility. And, at
the same time, they wanted to elect their parish priests, to modify the
taxes imposed on them by their Church, and to live an evangelical life.
For them, everything was religion."

　　Cipriano Salcedo did not disagree, but he took a certain pleasure
in knocking down the captain's assertions: "Until that point, things were
fine, but later on politics predominated."

　　"Are you referring to their plan to create a Parliament of
Peasants? Does that dream of the disinherited seem excessive to you?
Don't you think it's a Christian dream? Thomas Múntzer, thinking he
was one of the illuminati, decided to found a theocracy, but he was anni-
hilated at Frankenhausen. More than a hundred thousand dead, a
slaughter. And there are still those who go around saying Luther signed
pamphlets "against the thieving, murderous hordes of peasants," even
though it's never been proved. Luther detested disorder, but he loved
justice."

　　"The case of the anabaptists was rather similar."

　　"What made the anabaptists unpopular was the fact that they postponed the baptism of children. People were terrified the souls of
unbaptized children would end in limbo. Besides, the anabaptists were
idealists who waved anarchism around like a flag. Hubmaier brought
anarchism to Thuringia. In addition to the elimination of the State, they
also wanted to suppress the Church, the hierarchy, the sacraments, and
private property. It was a completely revolutionary program.
Remember that Hutter was burned in Austria during those years for
doing exactly the same thing. Finally, it was the people who rose up,
Catholics and protestants together, and defeated them in Münster.
After all that blood, how can you be surprised that there are still traces
of violence in Thuringia?"

　　Berger's tattered voice grew more vehement. "There are times
when he resembles a majestic canon," the Doctor said in jest in one of
their conversations before the journey. "A good man, fundamentally
good, and educated," he immediately added, fearing he was giving a false

impression of his friend. Salcedo could see that the captain knew every detail of recent German history, the pros and cons of Luther's revolution, and that, probably, he thought him, Salcedo, a poor intruder, an ignorant novice. The small ship continued to pitch, sometimes violently, but Don Isidoro Tellería imperturbably filled his pipe again.

Cipriano Salcedo paused, looked into Berger's light eyes, and went on: "Things like that heightened my desire to meet Melanchthon. He and Luther did not always agree, but their followers now recognize him as the head of protestantism. Finally I managed to be received in Wittenberg. He was affable and understanding with me. He spoke about Luther in terms of exalted devotion, with the affection of a son. He spoke about Luther the reformer and about the cloistered Luther, faithful husband and loving father. He expressed interest in Lutheran groups in Spain and gave me a greeting to take back to them. Then he meekly submitted to my questioning, a long interrogation that began with the 1521 War of the Bonfires and ended with the defeat of the Emperor in Innsbruck and the splitting of Europe into two armed camps: Catholics and protestants."

"Did he speak about his own actions?"

"Of course he did. Melanchthon recognized that he himself urged the students in Wittenberg to burn the papal bull and alluded to his later differences with Luther at the diets of Worms and Spira, diets that heightened the tension between the two groups. On both occasions, Melanchthon showed himself to be a humanist and a conciliator, but Luther disapproved of his attitude. What he expressly said, with a touch of nostalgia, was that Rome and the Reform were on the verge of mutual understanding, even in very delicate matters such as matrimony for clerics and communion in the two senses, but neither Luther nor the princes accepted those proposals."

"What about his role in systematizing the new faith?"

"He talked about that as well. With Luther he brought up the need to create codes of faith and conduct. Luther himself, with a clear vision of the problem, wrote out two catechisms: one for preachers, on a very elevated plane, and the other for the people, a much simpler version. Both were extremely effective. He also created a baptismal blessing and a nuptial blessing to take the place of the sacraments of baptism and marriage, neither of which caused alarm among the simple people, who at first thought that with the new liturgy married couples and children would be left spiritually adrift, like animals devoid of souls. *Personally*—he said to me—*"in order to participate in the organization of the system, I wrote the book Common Homes, which was well received."* Dogmatic education was elementary: only Christ, only the Scriptures, only grace. Faith is sufficient. Lutheranism failed at the moment of making the Church an invisible entity, with no structure. Such a thing was impossible, and in that aspect both Zwingli and Calvin went too far with it."

Isidoro Tellería coughed twice, two dry, harsh coughs after a deep puff. Until then his silence had been so hermetic that Captain Berger spun around to look at him. He'd completely forgotten Tellería was there, and now his dark, deep voice, as overpowering as his black costume, thundered in the small cabin:

"I agree," he said, toying with his lit pipe, fully aware he was going to surprise the other two. "Luther created a Church in the air; Calvin has been more practical: he's turned Geneva into a church-city. During the past months I've been traveling through Geneva, Basil, and Paris, but it was in a Parisian community, listening to the psalm *Raise Your Heart, Open Your Ears*, when I felt myself touched by grace. I left Sevilla a Lutheran, and I return a Calvinist."

Captain Berger, in order not to stare impolitely into Tellería's eyes, turned to look at Salcedo's small, nervous hands tapping on the table:

"Do you believe in absolute power?" he asked.

"I love discipline. Calvin accepts the benefit of the faith and supplies us with an order, a Church, and an austere lifestyle discretely scrutinized by the consistory."

"And don't you see in that *discreet scrutiny* a replica of the Inquisition?"

Isidoro Tellería had learned his lessons well: "Faith alone is not enough," he said. "It must be served. In that aspect, I disagree with Luther. Calvinism has a missionary spirit, something Lutheranism lacks, and it creates a concept of Church that is a bit overwrought and radical."

"Exactly that: overwrought and radical."

"Please understand, I'm not referring so much to the norms in themselves as to the absolute need they be obeyed: Calvin threatens with excommunication anyone who won't accept the norms. Does that seem excessive? Perhaps it is, but a man has to be very sure of what he's saying before adopting a measure like that. I think the matter certainly deserves some reflection. And Calvin voluntarily submitted to such reflection in Strasbourg, where he stayed for three years as chaplain to the French community. At the same time, he took advantage of the situation to start writing *Christian Institution*, which is as long as it is edifying. In Strasbourg, Calvin's position is passive, a waiting game."

"Do you think he was waiting for the call from the citizens of Geneva?"

"Whether he was waiting for it or not, the call came. Geneva put itself in his hands and submitted to the experiment. Its citizens were remorseful about having expelled him. Then Calvin began the formation of a Church. That was essential. To belong to it, to belong to that Church, was something like what faith is for you, a guarantee of salvation. Calvin organized a genuine theocracy, the government of God. Beginning at that moment, practically nothing worked in Geneva except preaching and sacraments. The believer must be devout. The world is a vale of tears, and we should accommodate life to a religious idea and to an attitude of service."

"And he went even further. Anything that does not appear in the Bible is superfluous and prohibited."

"True, but that rigor, distanced from Lutheran frivolities, is what attracted me in principle to Calvinism. A short time later, in Paris, my conversion took place. When I returned to Geneva, the city edified me. It was like a gigantic temple in contrast to Lutheran cities: The children had biblical names, there was catechism, study, prayer, sermons . . . Gambling was declared to be damned, and young people were forbidden to sing and dance. The spirit of sacrifice was imposed on them. Naturally, there were protests, but finally reason prevailed: The world was not created for pleasure, and the people joyfully accepted Calvin's authority."

The light coming through the porthole was fading. Cipriano Salcedo regarded Don Isidoro Tellería with remote pity. His childhood scruples were gnawing away at his mind, as were his risk-filled spiritual life and his incipient pessimism. Tellería's dark words had abstracted him to such a degree that he had to make an effort to reintegrate himself into reality, to become aware once again of the rocking of the ship, the creaking of the midship frame and the bulkhead. In a vague way he became aware that in one fashion or another all of them there at that strange meeting on the high seas were seeking God. He felt the need to intervene: "But in France," he said, recalling his travels there, "the Huguenots secretly baptize their children Catholic and secretly attend Catholic mass. So Calvin's doctrine, even though he's French and French is his language, hasn't managed to make France a nation with one religion and one religion alone."

Whenever someone contradicted him, Tellería's dark voice would become more opaque and foggy, the result of his excitement.

"It's not the same thing." He smiled rigidly with half his mouth. "A small city like Geneva is not the same thing as an entire kingdom like France. France is a vast world to be conquered, and Calvin has accepted that challenge. He's sent large contingents of missionaries there. That's one more thing in his favor. In this way, little by little, Calvinism is making a place for itself: France, Scotland, the Netherlands . . . It's the intellectuals, educated at the Geneva Academy, who have catechized in those countries. I've just come from Geneva; I spent six months there and can assure you that the city is an example of religious spirit for anyone who knows how to view it without prejudices."

Isidoro Tellería had become pale, and Captain Berger's squinting, tightly focused gaze fixed on him with obvious skepticism. He looked sorry he'd allowed him on his ship. He suddenly turned his eyes toward the porthole and announced that the discussion, which had begun to annoy him immensely, was over: "Gentlemen, it's getting dark."

He stood up awkwardly. His stool, screwed to the deck, obliged him to flex his legs in order to leave the table. Cipriano Salcedo imitated him. When Isidoro Tellería attempted the same maneuver, he slipped, clutched the table, and raised his right hand to his sweaty brow: "This boat rocks a lot. I'm a little sick."

Captain Berger put his back to the bulkhead in order to allow his guest to pass: "It's stuffy in here. And your pipe. Tobacco is more harm-

ful to your head than the sea. Why this eagerness to imitate the
Indians?" Salcedo helped a trembling Tellería to climb out on deck
through the prow hatch. Silhouetted against the sky they could see a
motionless sailor standing watch. On the port side, they could make out
the tenuous outline of the French coast. Tellería took a deep breath of
fresh air and shook his head from one side to another. "Below deck it
smelled intensely of pitch," he complained, "it smelled of pitch as if
they'd just caulked the ship."

Because of his seasickness, Tellería had lost his austere bearing.
When they came upon a coil of rope on the deck, Salcedo urged him to
sit down, to rest before making his way to his tent up on the poop deck.
Cipriano Salcedo's small, hairy, lively hands held on to his traveling
companion's arm. Up above, in the tinted clouds, a waning moon gave
off a faded glow devoid of contrasts. A loose strip of canvas beat against
the mainmast with intermittent violence. Tellería refused to sit down.
The change of position would have increased his feeling of instability:
"I can make it to my tent," he said. "I'd rather go to bed."

It had cooled off, and when they reached Tellería's tent, he
slipped in and tumbled into his hammock without even taking off his
shoes. At his side, piled up, was all his luggage. Salcedo sat down on the
chest, which, along with the hammock, was the only furniture in the
tent. The wind carried in the voice of a sailor singing somewhere far off.
In the light of the candle, and in stark contrast to his funeral clothing,
Tellería was green, his features distorted. Salcedo stood up and bent
over him: "Would you like me to bring you something to eat?"

Tellería shook his head: "I shouldn't eat. In my condition, it
wouldn't be a good idea."

He pulled up the blanket over his stomach. Salcedo whispered:
"I'll let you rest and come back in a while."

He left the tent and went into his own. In the corner, he spied the
sack of books and, almost hiding it, the three sacks containing his baggage. He'd spent several months in this state of uncomfortable provi-
sionality, with his clothing packed up, moving from inn to inn. He
dreamed of seeing himself firmly established in a house, his clothing
clean and pressed, perfumed, properly arranged in a large armoir. In
just over thirty hours, they would reach port, and he was certain that

Vicente, his servant, would not miss the meeting arranged four months earlier.

If Vicente had followed his orders, he would have a room in Laredo in the Monk's Inn, a horse, and a mule for the trip to Valladolid. For a moment he considered getting into the hammock, as Tellería had, but he finally decided against it and again stepped out on deck. He verified that it was indeed the sailor on watch who was singing to himself and that the strip of sail was still beating against the mainmast while two young men scrambled barefoot along the rigging in order to repair the small tear. He took a deep breath, and the sea air ventilated his lungs.

He strolled slowly across the deck thinking about his colleagues in Valladolid, his house, the tailor shop in the Ghetto, his property in Pedrosa, where his friend Pedro Cazalla, the parish priest, every afternoon set up a blind at the entrance to La Gallarita so they could hunt using decoys. This association of ideas led him to think about the Doctor, about his brother, so cowardly and beaten down of late, as if he sensed an imminent tragedy, about his zeal in proposing this trip and his exaggerated precautions.

That winter, Salcedo had been involved with a thousand matters, but the Doctor's confidence moved him, the fact that he chose him over other members of the group who'd joined earlier. Then the Doctor revealed his fear that the Inquisition had come to suspect the group's existence. For a long time, the Doctor had been upset about the activities of Cristóbal de Padilla, the servant of the marquises of Alcañices, and his clumsy proselytizing in Toro and Zamora.

Generally speaking, the Doctor was satisfied with the group, with its high intellectual level, its social position, its discretion, but he had no confidence in the lower-class people, in a few poor illiterates who, he said, had infiltrated it. "What can we hope," he said to Salcedo days before his journey, "from that impenitent gossip's proselytizing?" In his Erfurt letter he'd returned to the same subject. In a certain sense, Salcedo shared the Doctor's fear, but he was even more distrustful of Paula Rupérez, the wife of Juan García the jeweler, even though she didn't belong to the group. That led him to think about Teo, his own wife, about the strange failure of their marriage, the physical disparity between them, his inability to make her a mother, and the final collapse of their relationship.

Teo lacked the maternal warmth he'd erroneously ascribed to her when they met. Salcedo's loneliness had actually grown with marriage. He hadn't flinched at their sleeping in separate beds, in separate rooms, having separate lives. One day he spoke to Pedro Cazalla, the parish priest of Pedrosa, about the matter: Not only did he not love his wife—he felt contempt for her. It was a serious sin, and Our Lord would take account of it. Something similar had taken place in the life of his father, Don Bernardo. Was it the case, then, that certain beings were born only to hate? It was then that Pedro Cazalla told him to put his confidence in the merits of Christ and not to give so much importance to his own feelings.

A new light appeared on his narrow horizon. So all wasn't lost, the Passion of Christ was worth more than Salcedo's works, his paltry feelings. After that came Don Carlos de Seso and after him came the Doctor, who went even more deeply into that idea: Purgatory, therefore, was unnecessary. The sect provided him with a fraternity he hadn't known before. He gave himself over to it with fruition, with enthusiasm. The journey to Germany was a part of that self-yielding.

But now, as he strolled the deck of the *Hamburg* in the dark, the tender memory of Ana Enríquez could not keep him from feeling alone and insignificant. They were sailing along the French coast, and from time to time a hesitant, faint light would wink from land, pointing out the diffuse border between land and sea. The ship was approaching the coast, where they expected to find an ocean pressed as flat as a sheet, but despite all their efforts the *Hamburg* would not stop rocking. Salcedo remembered Tellería and went to the galley. A heavy-set, pink cabin boy naked from the waist up, with reddish nipples, gave him two apples for "the Spanish passenger who felt ill." Without peeling them, Isidoro Tellería, still in his hammock and visible in the light of the candle, wolfed both down in huge bites. He looked better than he had during the afternoon, and when he'd finished, he blew out the candle, wrapped himself up in the blanket and slept until the next morning.

Salcedo was up early. The first thing he noticed was that the French coast had disappeared and a chaotic land breeze was frenetically shaking the sails. It was cold. Except for a long blue strip in the west, the gray nimbus clouds sealed the sky. Half a dozen barefoot sailors were cleaning the starboard side of the deck with pails of water, brushes, and mops, and every so often they would suddenly empty their pails, and the water would bubble in the gutters before flowing into the sea. He strode along the deck to stretch his legs and, after a while, he passed through the galley, where the cabin boy with the red nipples handed him a cup of hot herb tea for Don Isidoro Tellería.

He found Tellería awake and in better form but still refusing to get up. The same thing occurred at lunch—broth and two apples—and Salcedo deduced that even if the trip lasted a month the man from Sevilla would remain stretched out in his hammock, not moving a muscle. Salcedo stayed with him for a while, sitting on the chest, where, by chance, he discovered next to the candle Pérez de Pineda's New Testament, Tellería's bedside reading.

Salcedo spent the afternoon looking over the various sections of the small ship: the lowest deck, the orlop deck, where the rowers sat, empty now; the bilge, where the cargo was stored; the dunnage; the bridge; the storeroom; the castle; the captain's headquarters . . . He barely rested a few minutes during lunch. He'd had a bad night, and was feeling uneasy and nervous. Unfounded fears plagued him, fears that grew the more he turned them over in his mind. For example, he suspected that his servant Vicente would not be there on the dock to meet him the next day, that he'd be all alone at the ship with no means of transportation and a sack of prohibited books in his hand. After dinner, he calmed down by contemplating the sunset, still refusing to admit that this brilliant, moist star sinking into the sea was the same one Pedro Cazalla and he would watch from the Pedrosa hills as it disappeared behind the blazing hot fields after harvest time. When night had fallen, he leaned over the poop deck, distractedly watching the shapes thrown up by the wake as it divided the sea. Captain Berger approached noiselessly, and Salcedo suddenly saw him materialize at his side, his wide hands on the handrail, inquiring in a mocking tone: "And is our friend, the illustrious Calvinist, resting?"

Cipriano pointed to the silent tent. Then he again leaned on the handrail and told the captain why his was nervous. He was disturbed that his servant might possibly have misunderstood his instructions and wouldn't be waiting for him at the port. He was also upset by the fact that during his absence the Holy Office had established new laws to impede the circulation of dangerous books. These two things were deeply troubling.

Captain Berger did not seem to take his fears seriously. The guards and constables of the Holy Office checked the cargo of ships, opened barrels or parcels if they seemed suspicious, but they usually left travelers in peace. When he finished, he asked if Salcedo were carrying many. "Books?" "Books, yes, of course." "Nineteen," answered Salcedo, and holding his hands before him, he enumerated: "A small satchel . . . but the risky part is the content: Luther, Melanchthon, Erasmus, two Bibles, and a complete collection of the Passionate." A thought suddenly came into his head, and he added very quickly: "Did you know that the censure of Bibles in Valladolid three years ago ended up bringing in over one hundred different editions of the book of books, most of them by protestant authors?"

Captain Berger's teeth glistened in the darkness when he smiled: "We ship captains are experts in that field. We've lived through the past twenty years in a state of perpetual fear. One of the Bibles you're talking about: I introduced two hundred copies of it through the port of Santoña in 1528 in two barrels. Nothing happened. At that time, barrels were innocent things. Today, if you stick a book into a cask it's as if you were manufacturing explosives."

"When did things change?"

In 1530, ten large casks of books came to the port of Valencia in three Venetian ships. They were intercepted, and the discovery put the Holy Office on guard. Luther's most caustic work, everything he wrote in Wartburg, dozens of copies. The Inquisition staged a real *auto-da-fé*. The three captains were imprisoned, and in the main square of Valencia hundreds of books burned in a gigantic pyre, all with the screaming enthusiasm of the illiterate masses. The Holy Office always loves to capture huge amounts of contraband material so it can make a public show of it."

The calm night with its brilliant stars invited confidences. Salcedo didn't move. He expected Captain Berger to go on. He was sure he would and waited, staring at the space between his brows: "Book burnings have become normal pastimes in Spain," he finally said. "People still talk about the one in Salamanca. The most cultured city in the world burning the vehicles of culture; it doesn't make sense. Two years later there was another showy burning in San Sebastián . . . But don't think that Spain has exclusive rights in that business. Thousands of copies of

*The Christian's Freedom*, translated into Spanish, were burned in Antwerp, with all pomp and circumstance. I was there; I lived through the event."

Salcedo smiled weakly: "The Inquisition is growing more intolerant every day. Now they're demanding that confessors require the penitent to turn in anyone hiding prohibited books. And anyone who refuses is to be denied absolution. Neither bishops nor the king himself are exempt from that measure."

Captain Berger, who'd been leaning against the handrail, turned and rested his elbows on it: "I understand that whenever the Inquisition condemns someone because of a book, that book is prohibited. And I'm not referring only to anti-Christian works. Six years ago, the *Louvain Catalogue* prohibited the Bible and the New Testament translated into Spanish. It's taken for granted that the Spanish people are destined never to know the book of books."

Cipriano Salcedo looked at the captain out of the corner of his eye before making this observation: "Love of reading is now so suspect that illiteracy has become desirable and honorable. If you're illiterate, it's easy to prove you're uncontaminated and belong to the enviable class of old Christians."

A silence opened between the two men that made the faint whisper of the wake perceptible. Captain Berger did not fail to notice Salcedo's gesture of bringing his watch up to his eyes. "It's late," he said before Salcedo could speak. "Almost two, captain. A very good time to go to bed.

The new day broke with fog. From his tent, Salcedo could make out Tellería on deck smoking his pipe. He was no longer in mourning. He was wearing sheepskin half boots and a heavy woolen duster over his wrinkled shirt and doublet. Inexplicably, he seemed taller and thinner than he did wearing black, perhaps because of his extremely tight breeches or because he'd actually lost weight thanks to his spartan diet during the passage. Salcedo walked over to him and said hello. He'd slept well, he said. His symptoms had disappeared, and he was fully recovered. He wouldn't be leaving the ship at Laredo but would instead go on to Sevilla.

The mist was rising, and the coast, visible once more and now very close, took on life and relief under a weak sun. Along the slight undulations of the landscape there appeared small villages scattered here and there, hemmed in by forests of beech and ash trees, with cows and mares grazing in the neighboring meadows. The horizon line stopped at the cliffs and, just beyond, at the vast, golden beach away from which spread the town, with its smoking chimneys.

The *Hamburg* veered to port, and its prow cut the waters of the bay, with the jetty in the distance. A team of sailors struck the sails, and the ship slid smoothly over the surface only to stop minutes later at the mouth of the harbor next to the pier. Isidoro Tellería and Cipriano Salcedo walked over to the bridge, where the captain was shouting orders. Suddenly, the gangway bell clanged, the ship stopped, and a sailor hung a rope ladder over the side. The pilot who would take charge of the tiller climbed aboard. Both sides of the *Hamburg* were bristling with oars that moved rhythmically the instant Captain Berger gave the order through his megaphone. The ship slowly advanced to the docking area. The captain came over to Salcedo and pointed out an empty space in the docks beyond, where the wool warehouses were located. "That's where we anchor."

Now the ship was parallel to the dock. Captain Berger looked over the scene with his spyglass, while two small boats pushed the boat against the dock and four sailors tossed protective devices down the sides of the ship. The oars were retracted while the ship was tied to the mooring post. The captain stopped looking and smiled to Salcedo as he handed him the telescope: "I don't see any problems."

Salcedo concentrated on the docking area and checked the dry docks: dismantled sailing ships, then the town, a train of mules along the beach road. When his gaze came to the small forest of beeches, it returned slowly along the line of docked galliasses, the dock, the warehouses, and then, suddenly, he discovered him: a small, emaciated man standing before door number 2, dressed in a poor smock and wearing rope sandals was staring unblinkingly at the newly docked ship. He was holding the bridles of two horses and behind him, tied to a ring in the warehouse wall, a mule impatiently stamped the cobblestones.

Salcedo pointed toward him: "There he is," he said again and again staring at the captain. "That boy with the horses at the door of the warehouse is Vicente, my servant. Could he come aboard to take charge of my baggage?"

# BOOK I
# THE EARLY YEARS

## I

ETWEEN the Pisuerga and Esgueva rivers, Valladolid in the 1560s
had a population of twenty-eight thousand. It was a service-economy
city, and the presence of the Royal Chancellery and the nobility
(always susceptible to the flirtation of the Court) graced it with an obvious social prominence. The Duero, the Pisuerga, and the Esgueva—
before it divided into its three urban branches—sheltered the pleasure
houses of the aristocracy and also constituted a kind of natural wall
against the periodic onslaughts of plague.

The actual urban area was surrounded by gardens and orchards
(almond, apple, hawthorn trees), which in turn were surrounded by a
wider circle of vineyards that extended in rows over the hills and plains.
These vineyards stretched so far that the avenues of vines, covered with
leaves and tendrils during summer, marked the horizon line visible from
Saint Christopher Hill to La Maruquesa Mountain. On the left side of
the Duero, advancing westward, the new stands of pine trees were rapidly proliferating, while on the other side of the gray hills, northward, a
wide band of wheat linked the valley with the Páramo, a large area of
pasturage and holly trees inhabited by shepherds and their wool-bear-
ing sheep.

This location provided abundant food to the city, which preferred
bread and wine: The young grape vines closest to town yielded a thin
red wine, then jolly light reds in the Cigales and Fuensaldaña zone, and
extraordinary white wines in Rueda, Serrada, and La Seca. According to
the bylaws of the Guild of Wine Heirs, which monopolized wine production, wine produced elsewhere could not be sold until local supplies

were exhausted. A green branch at the tavern door announced a new barrel, and, in such cases, the servants from great houses, the maids from middling houses, and the poorest citizens of Valladolid stood in long lines at the door of the establishment to cast a vote about the quality of the new stock. Grand consumers of wine, the people of Valladolid in the sixteenth century, people with refined palates, could easily tell good wine from bad even though they liked both. This was so true that the per-capita consumption reached one hundred and five liters, which, subtracting women (usually light drinkers), children, the abstemious, and the poor, was a very respectable figure.

Hemmed in by the two rivers, the town of small dimensions (as people in those days said: if bread became dear in Valladolid, there is hunger in Spain) was a rectangle with several access points: the large bridge, the Puente Mayor, to the north; the Del Campo bridge to the south; the Tudela bridge to the east; and La Rinconada bridge to the west. And except for the very heart of town, gray with cobblestone streets, with an open sewer ditch running down the middle of every street, the place was dusty and arid in summer, cold and muddy in winter, and filthy and stinking in all seasons. At the same time, in the very place where your nose would be offended, your eyes would be delighted with monuments like Saint Gregory, the Antigua, and Santa Cruz or the massive convents of Saint Paul and Saint Benedict. Narrow streets flanked by arcades, two- or three-story buildings without balconies, with businesses or guild-owned shops on the ground floor. Valladolid at that time, with its lively traffic of coaches, horses, and mules presented an almost blooming aspect of manifest prosperity.

Before the Court arrived, on the night of October 30, 1517, the coach occupied by the business man and property owner, Don Bernardo Salcedo, and his beautiful wife, Doña Catalina de Bustamante, stopped outside number 5, Corredera de San Pablo. They'd just spent the evening at the house of Don Ignacio, Bernardo's brother, a blond and hairless judge in the Royal Chancery, and just as they were leaving, Catalina had discreetly confided to her husband that she had pains in her kidneys. Now, outside their own house, she again brought her lips to her husband's ear to whisper that she also noted moistness in her buttocks. Bernardo Salcedo, with little knowledge of these matters, a beginner at the age of forty, ordered his servant Juan Dueñas, who was holding open the coach door, to dash over to the house of Doctor Almenara, on Cárcava Street, and tell him that Mrs. Salcedo was ill and required his attention.

Bernardo Salcedo considered the child announced by this indisposition to be a genuine miracle. His wife's pregnancy came as a complete surprise to both of them; after all, they'd been married for ten years. The Salcedos did not often stoop to such vulgarities; it was Doña Catalina, intrigued by the sterility of her husband, who put herself in the hands of Don Francisco Almenara, the most prestigious doctor specializing in women in the region. Authorized to practice medicine in 1505 by the Royal Tribunal of Medicine after acquitting himself brilliantly on examinations, Dr. Almenara worked with the highly respected doctor Don Diego de Leza, thereby confirming the great promise he'd shown early in his career.

Doctor Almenara's fame had spread far beyond Valladolid, and the most famous merchants of Burgos habitually appeared in his offices. Even so, Doña Catalina Bustamante wept over her decision. How could she show her pudenda to a stranger, no matter how eminent he might be? How could she consult with anyone about a problem as intimate as those concerning her fruitless sexual relations with her husband? Her curiosity finally overwhelmed her modesty. Even though she was not grieving over not having a child, she was a solidly pragmatic woman and wanted to know why her conduct, comparable to that of so many women, was not yielding the same results.

Some days after deciding to see him, her scruples were completely obliterated by the noble figure of Doctor Almenara wrapped in his velvet robe, by the ruby hanging from his collar, by his long, pointy beard, and by the outsized emerald that adorned his right thumb. Her acceptance of the doctor was facilitated by his excellent manners, his soft, barely whispered words, the delicacy with which he sought access to the most intimate parts of her body, and the contacts, minimal but upsetting, he required to complete his task. The long period in which Catalina and Bernardo were in his hands erased all suspicion in her soul and opened her heart to a loyal friendship. But before that took place, she had to go through terrible tests, like that of garlic, in order to ascer-

tain whether it was she or her husband who was the cause of their matrimonial sterility. To that end, Don Francisco Almenara introduced a
carefully peeled clove of garlic into Doña Catalina's vagina before he
put her to bed with a warning: "Do not get up before I get here. I must
be the first to smell it."

Bernardo was up at dawn. He vaguely intuited that something
serious related to his masculinity was in question. For hours, he wandered around the house, and then, at about nine o'clock, hearing the
sound of the doctor's mule, he pushed aside the window curtain with
obvious nervousness. The doctor's servant, leading the mule by the bridle, helped the doctor to dismount and tied the bridle to the ring on the
column outside the door. Everything that happened after that was dis-
concerting and confusing for Bernardo. Don Francisco ordered
Catalina, just as she was, in her night dress, to get out of bed and led
her by the hand to the wash basin. There he cheerfully asked to smell
her breath: "What?" Catalina was visibly shaken.

"Your breath, madam. Exhale toward me," the doctor insisted,
leaning over his patient's face. She finally obeyed. "Once again, if you
don't mind."

She wife exhaled at the nose of Don Francisco, who somberly
wrinkled his brow. Immediately, wearing an expression of extreme
gravity, Doctor Almenara entered Bernardo's office, sat down at his
desk, and stared at him in an unusually cold fashion:

"I regret having to tell you that your wife's passages are open," he
said simply.

"What do you mean, doctor?"

"I mean that your wife is capable of conceiving."

Bernardo's heart sank: "Are you trying to suggest . . ." he began,
incapable of finishing his question.

"I'm suggesting nothing, Mr. Salcedo. I categorically state that your
wife's breath smells of garlic. What does that mean? Simply that the
receptive channels of her body are open and not obstructed. Conception
would be normal after a well-timed insemination."

Bernardo had begun to sweat, and his movements became awkward and resigned: "This means I'm the cause of our matrimonial
failure."

Almenara looked him up and down with a slight touch of disdain: "In medicine, two and two are not always four, Mr. Salcedo. I mean that these are not mathematical proofs. There is the possibility that both of you are capable of procreating and that for some reason your respective contributions cannot agree with each other."

"Meaning that my wife and I don't just don't get along."

"Call it whatever you like."

Salcedo maintained a cautious silence. Doctor Almenara's knowledge, his spectacular successes with the most distinguished families in the city, and his lucidity were convincing enough for him. It was also common knowledge that there were three hundred and twelve volumes in his library, not as many as there were in his brother Ignacio's, but enough to give an idea of the level of his learning. There was no reason to throw a tantrum for such an insignificant reason. Nevertheless, he asked: "And doesn't science have another test, let's say one that wouldn't be so humiliating, one that's more delicate?"

"We could subject your wife to the urine test, but it's a disgusting operation and as lacking in certitude as the garlic test."

"Well, what do we do?"

Almenara got up from the desk slowly. Wrapped in his velvet robe, he looked like a giant. His pointy beard reached the third button. He lightly took Bernardo by the elbow: "Tell me the truth now, Mr. Salcedo, What would be more depressing, that fact that you have no children or having to recognize in the presence of your wife that it's your fault?"

Salcedo cleared his throat: "I see you're also a specialist in men."

"Anyone who knows women well ends up knowing men. They are complementary fields."

Bernardo raised empty, strangely opaque eyes: "Wouldn't it be sufficient, doctor, to communicate to my wife that our organisms don't rhyme, that our respective contributions, as you say, cannot agree with each other?"

"That's good advice," he smiled. "Let's do what you say. And you're not even asking me to lie."

Doctor Almenara's concession saved the harmony of the marriage and the friendship between the two men. But, eight years later, and even though there had been no radical change in their matrimonial life but the simple passage of time, Bernardo and Doña Catalina returned to his offices, informing him that the lady had missed two periods. Doctor Almenara congratulated himself on his discretion. He asked Doña Catalina to lie down on the examination table and carefully took her pulse. Then he placed the palm of his right hand on her left breast, above her heart, and when he felt his patient grow nervous, he whispered: be calm, madam, be calm, you don't have any fever. He turned toward his friend and repeated: she has no fever, Mister Salcedo. Then he bent at the waist, applied his ear to the woman's chest and listened to the rapid beating of her heart. When he finished, his expert hand opened a space between her bodice and her skirt and explored her abdomen, the hardness of her spleen and liver, the most elusive organs. But his hand went even lower. Doña Catalina was losing her breath; she was on the point of fainting because it was his right hand, the one with the emerald on the thumb, and at times she could feel its smooth edges on her pubis. Doctor Almenara was acting with excessive audacity that morning. Finally, he removed his hand and washed it off at the washbasin. As he dried himself, he spoke: "Missed periods are almost always a conclusive sign of pregnancy," he observed, "but in such a short time it is impossible to detect anything by touch."

He looked at Salcedo and added, as if he were picking up the subject they'd discussed eight years earlier. "These things happen in medicine. Your respective contributions, which did not seem to agree, have suddenly decided to collaborate. Let's celebrate the event. I'll see you both here in eight weeks."

The couple returned to the office two months later, but by then Doña Catalina was experiencing morning sickness regularly, and on two occasions, she'd gagged and vomited. She told this to the doctor before lying down on the table. The doctor patiently listened to the sounds of her body, as soon as he began touching her abdomen, his mouth stretched into a smile. "Here we have the head of the young Salcedo," he said grinning even more widely. "You two have done it!"

Month after month, Doña Catalina, accompanied by her husband, would visit Doctor Almenara. It had to be a matter of pride to hear from his mouth the periodic confirmation of the approaching delivery. Even so, in the eighth month of the pregnancy, the doctor asked an unpleasant question: "Are you two sure you've kept an accurate count?" Bernardo became angry: "The missed periods are not errors, doctor. The first time we visited you, she'd missed two, and now it's eight, exactly eight." "The head is very small," commented the doctor, "no larger than an apple."

The next month, the doctor confirmed that all was going well except for the size of the fetus, which was too puny, but there was nothing else to do but wait. Finally, as if he were asking the most innocent question in the world, Bernardo inquired if they had a birthstool at home. Bernardo Salcedo nodded with satisfaction. He felt happy to be able to please Doctor Almenara even in that minor detail. He went into detail about the wool fleet and the foresight of Don Néstor Maluenda, the well-known Burgos merchant, who years earlier had made a gift of one to Doña Catalina the moment they appeared for the first time in the Flanders markets. "They invented the birthstool," smiled the doctor. But again he adopted a scornful tone to add: "In any case, given his size, the young Salcedo won't need help to burst into this world."

Now Doña Catalina would wait for the doctor walking around in the sitting room. From time to time, she'd grab the console table with both hands, grimace, and blush without saying a word. "Again?" Bernardo would solicitously ask, consulting his watch. She would nod. "They're coming more frequently, barely a couple of minutes since the last, perhaps less."

In his heart, Salcedo was puffed up with pride at the thought of having provoked this disturbance. The immodesty of the stud animal rather than the father was pounding in his veins. After so many mischances, he'd succeeded. He admired his wife's serenity and was struck by her discreet manner of dressing, given the circumstances—a farthingale-supported skirt, billowed out to dissimulate her pregnancy, a blouse with a round décolletage and a suggestive off-the-shoulder cut. He smiled inwardly. The day she first wore that blouse he didn't have the patience to undress her. Sometimes these intemperate impulses came over him without his being able to explain their cause. They depended more on his carnal desires than his wife's clothing. Even so, that provocative blouse, those white, fragile shoulders competing with the silk had always aroused him.

Once again, his wife grimaced clutching the console, and, once the pain passed, Doña Catalina nervously rang the silver bell. Blasa, the old cook, wearing a skirt of coarse cloth with a hair net on her head, appeared grumbling, dragging her slippers along. At the age of five, Blasa began working in the house of Doña Catalina's grandmother to amuse her recently born mother. She was there when Doña Catalina was born. She was an institution in the house. Even so, she said nothing when her mistress told her the baby was on the way, that she should prepare the room, and heat up water in the kitchen. It was probably better to say nothing to Modesta, the maid. She should go to bed. It was not a good idea that she get involved in these nerve wracking situations at her tender age. Regarding Juan Dueñas, the servant who'd gone to fetch the doctor, he'd have to be at the ready, prepared for any eventuality during the night. Right now, he was to get the birthstool out of the storeroom where it had been locked up for ten years. Blasa nodded and nodded again with her heavy head, her swollen eyelids, totally impassive in the face of the commotion to come. She looked at her mistress out of tired eyes: "Anything else, madam?"

But Doña Catalina was listening to her husband, who was advising her in a didactic tone to get into more comfortable clothes, that she shouldn't think of giving birth wearing a hoop skirt and blouse. What with her nervousness and her contractions, Doña Catalina hadn't even thought about what the right clothes might be. Bernardo became specific: "Night dress, loose, and, naturally, open."

A carriage was approaching. Salcedo knew every pothole, every misaligned cobblestone on the street, and the special creaking of his old coach as it bounced over them: "Be quick now. The doctor is here."

Doña Catalina escaped from the room by a side door while Don Franciso de Almenara, wearing his dark velvet robe and holding his satchel in his emerald-adorned hand, passed through the front door. He knew how important a showy entrance was. The doctor or the midwife in a house where the first child was being born was a kind of god. Bernardo met him, full of a strange nervousness: "The thing has begun, doctor."

"Is she feeling pains?"

"For more than an hour now. Every two minutes."

Don Francisco de Almenara looked around and noted the absence of the midwife. Bernardo apologized: He had had no idea she was indispensable. The doctor wrote two names and two addresses down on a piece of paper, and Salcedo summoned Juan Dueñas. "Get the first one. Get the second only if the other is not at home." Then he led the doctor to the bedroom, but, a solidly jealous man, he knocked before entering. Doña Catalina invited them in with a stifled voice. She was in bed, leaning back on two woolen pillows and wearing the night-gown she'd used on her wedding night along with a loose robe over her shoulders. The doctor held the door and said, with some delicacy, to Bernardo: "It's better you wait outside."

Salcedo took a step back, humiliated. What did this veteran doctor think he was going to do alone with his wife? The minutes passed with exasperating slowness. With the thick oak door blocking the way, he could barely hear faint murmuring, and when the doctor let him in he rushed into the sanctuary—the term he used for the conjugal bedroom from the day of his marriage. Doctor Almenara stopped him: "Everything normal. The dilation has begun."

The midwife arrived, a small, hard woman with skin like parchment, wearing an old skirt and with her head covered with a wimple. "Good evening, Victoria," said the doctor. "Things are moving along correctly, but this is no time to rest. Prepare an artemisia infusion for the lady."

Modesta, with her bouncy walk, was right behind the midwife, but Bernardo stopped her. "You'd better go to bed. Blasa will take care of the mistress." He turned to Juan Dueñas, who stared at him, immobile from the door. "You wait below, Juan. We still don't know if we're going to need you."

Doña Catalina meekly drank the concoction which brought about no apparent change in things. Nevertheless, the dilation increased. The midwife was constantly running in and out of the room: "Doctor, the dilation is sufficient, but I see no signs of any desire to participate. She's passive."

"Give her rhubarb."

The patient moved her bowels thanks to the rhubarb. She buried her face in the pillows with each contraction, but she made no effort herself.

"Squeeze," said the doctor.

"Squeeze? Where?"

"When the pain comes, make a push."

The doctor sat down on the boot jack. When he heard the midwife complain, he turned his face toward Doña Catalina:

"Squeeze!"

"I can't, doctor."

He got up. The head is there, its' small, but why the devil won't it come out? Half an hour passed, and nothing changed. The dilation was virtually complete, but Doña Catalina was still not doing her part.

"Victoria!" shouted the doctor energetically. "The birthstool, please!"

Bernardo himself helped bring it into the bedroom. It was made of wood and leather, the seat much lower than the leg supports, and two loops on the arms where the patient was to hold on while pushing. The midwife and Blasa helped Doña Catalina settle into the chair. Emaciated, with her legs raised and spread, and her backside resting on the black leather seat, presented an awkward and ridiculous spectacle. A pain hit her, and the doctor said, "Push," and she grimaced, but when the pain passed, she began to lose her temper and in no uncertain terms ordered her husband to leave the room and wait in the sitting room. It annoyed her that he was witnessing her degradation. Bernardo never imagined that the birth of a child involved such a prolonged and humiliating process.

At two-thirty in the morning on October 31, 1517, the dilation was reaching its maximum, but the child was not emerging. Doña Catalina was shouting, but she went on without pushing herself to bring the process to its proper conclusion. It was at that moment when the prestigious Doctor Almenara spoke a sentence that was to become popular in Valladolid: "This child is stuck." Just then, something unimaginable took place: The baby's head disappeared and in its place materialized a tiny arm with its hand open and waving, as if it were either saying good-by or hello. And there the arm remained, limp and fallen like a penis between the lady's spread legs.

"This devil has turned around," said the doctor losing his head. "Look to her, quickly."

The midwife opened her basket and pulled out a flask of dill oil and a small box of lard, smeared the dangling little arm with both substances and with a rapid movement, very professionally and wisely executed, put it back in Doña Catalina's womb. The patient meekly allowed herself to be manipulated, and, when she noticed that doctor was taking the huge emerald ring off his thumb and putting it on the dressing table she felt as helpless as if he'd unscrewed his hand and placed all responsibility on her. But in an unforeseen way, the exact opposite occurred. She instantly felt his power in her womb. The doctor grasped the baby's shoulder with his slender fingers and very skillfully rotated it so the small head would again be lined up with the vulva. Doña Catalina, forgetting her manners, berated and insulted everyone there, again felt a concentration of energies in her pelvis. She shrieked, squeezed with all her strength while the midwife urged her on: "That's it, that's it," and suddenly, as if it were a cannonball, a bloody piece of pink meat shot out. The doctor moved his head back to avoid the impact, and the child landed on the white towel the midwife was holding in her arms just behind him. She stared at the baby in shock: "A boy! How small he is, he looks like a kitten."

Bernardo rushed in, and Doctor Almenara, who was washing his hands in the basin, fixed his eyes on him, saying: "Here's your son, Mr. Salcedo. Are you two certain you counted correctly? Judging by his size, I'd say he was premature, a seven-month baby."

But the effort, the vertigo, the tension of Doña Catalina, who for the first time in her life had performed a personal chore by herself, without having recourse to paid hands, felt its painful consequences. She felt exhausted and pulled to pieces, and the next morning, when the child was brought in so she could feed him, the little boy thrashed his head away from the nipple, beset with a convulsive fit of tears. Doctor Almenara, who'd witnessed the newborn's reaction, patiently auscultated Catalina, placed his ring hand on the sick woman's left breast, turned to Bernardo and his brothers, who had unexpectedly appeared, and made another of his lapidary statements: "The new mother has a fever. Summon a wet nurse."

The influence of the Salcedo family extended beyond the town to the neighboring villages. Ignacio, judge in the chancery, where this morning the reception for the king was in preparation, spread the word among the subaltern personnel: He needed a young wet nurse, with milk for several days, healthy, and willing to live in the house of the new parents. The wool agents in the Páramo received the same message from Don Bernardo: Needed: a Wet Nurse. The Salcedo family urgently needs a wet nurse. At twelve o'clock the next day, a girl, almost a child, appeared. She came from Santovenia, an unwed mother who'd been lactating for four days, who'd lost her baby giving birth. Catalina, still not overwhelmed by fever, liked the young woman, who was tall, slender, tender, and had an attractive smile.

She gave the sensation of being a jolly girl despite her grief. And when once the baby curled up in her lap, remaining motionless for an entire hour sucking on her nipple, and then fell asleep, Catalina was deeply moved. The *maternal fervor* of the girl was obvious in her touch, in her meticulous care in putting the child to bed, in the communion between the two when she fed him. Much taken by her good disposition, Catalina hired her with no hesitation and praised her unreservedly. In this hasty fashion, Minervina Capa, a native of Santovenia, fifteen years of age, frustrated mother, became a member of the Salcedo family's serving staff in number 5 Corredera de San Pablo.

Minervina met with no resistance in the kitchen, where the cook Blasa, in principle a tough nut to crack, presided. Before Minervina appeared, she'd given the child two doses of donkey milk diluted with water and heavily sugared, as she'd seen her mother do on several occasions, and Catalina feared the girl would receive a hostile welcome. But Blasa was intrigued by Minervina's origins, and the moment she found herself alone with her asked if, back in her village, she knew a certain Pedro Lanuza, the father of two presentable but scatterbrained lads. Even before she'd finished asking the question, Minervina burst out laughing: "A family of illuminati, Mrs. Blasa."

"And what do you mean by that?"

"Exactly what I said, Mrs. Blasa, illuminati, those who say Our Lord would rather see a man and woman in bed than in church praying in Latin."

"Is that what they say in your town? That family was always a little strange."

Minervina tried hard to remember more things to indulge Mrs. Blasa, to get on her good side: "They also say that Our Lord comes to them without their having to do anything but sit down and wait. That all they have to do is stay still and wait for the Lord to illuminate them. That's why they're also called *negligent*."

Blasa nodded: "That word describes Pedro Lanuza better than the other word you used. Never in my life did I see a lazier or neglectful man."

"Now if you'd like to see them, on Saturdays they come down to Valladolid on the donkey. They go to the house of a certain Francisca Hernández and priest who's called Don Francisco."

Blasa opened her eyes wide: "Tell me child, where does this Francisca Hernández live?"

"I don't remember that, Mrs. Blasa, but if you're interested I can ask the first day I get to go into town."

And thus it was that Minervina took possession of Blasa's dominions. Modesta, short and timid, but silly, also accepted the happy girl. Used to the old woman, she found youth in her new companion, some points of view more like her own, and fluid conversation, uncommon in a village girl.

Doña Catalina passed the day in peace. The arrival of Minervina, as clean as she was obedient, had calmed her down. To add to her sense of well-being, her sister-in-law Doña Gabriela walked in at midday to report on the festivities underway in the city: the forty thousand foreigners who'd arrived to receive the King, the packed streets, the gaily decorated wooden arches at the corners, the painted panels and tapestries adorning the most noble houses. And then the military parade along Nuevo Espolón, the prince Don Fernando, flanked by the cardinal of Tortosa, the archbishop of Zaragoza, followed by heralds, governors, ushers, and mace-bearers. The mob shouted itself hoarse cheering the king when Don Carlos appeared on the pavement, alone, elegant, in the center of the roadway, marching to the rhythm of the kettledrums, the diamonds sewn to his suit glittering in the November sun. He was preceded by a band of trumpets and snare drums and guarding him from behind were five hundred harquebusiers, four hundred Germans and one hundred Spaniards. Behind them came the King's sister Doña Leonor with the ladies of the entourage attended by nobles. And closing the procession, a company of archers caracoling their horses and cheering Castile and the King. Doña Catalina, an excitable woman, began to tremble under the eiderdown, so Doña Gabriela, noticing her agitation, changed the subject and talked instead about the huge elephant positioned at the Plaza del Mercado for the amusement of children and adults.

The next day, for no apparent reason, Doña Catalina's condition worsened. Her fever grew higher, and Doctor Almenara admitted that it could be a fit of hysteria, so in order to gain time, he ordered the barber-surgeon Gaspar Laguna, who on a memorable occasion had restored to life the president of the Chancery in a seemingly hopeless situation, to bleed the patient, which he did with admirable skill. But since Doña Catalina continued in the same state the next day, Don Francisco Almenara blazed a new trail to hope by having recourse to theriaca: "We've got to give it to her. There's no other choice."

The midwife nodded. Bernardo resignedly dug some coins out of the pockets in his outer shirt, but the doctor, noticing his gesture, told him this was an expensive medicine. "How expensive?," asked Salcedo. "Twelve ducats," said the doctor precisely. "Twelve ducats!," exploded Bernardo. The doctor explained the reasons for such a price: "Just realize that it's only made in Venice, and that its preparation involves more than fifty different elements." While Modesta went down to Custodio's pharmacy, troops of cavalry could be heard passing in the street followed immediately by a *long live the king* followed in turn by the noise of halberdiers marching to the beat of a drum.

Suddenly, as if a soprano on the stage were answering a powerful baritone voice, a small bell tinkled amid the military roar. Bernardo pushed away the window curtain. He'd ordered the mass of the Five Wounds from the Convent of Saint Paul for the health of his sick wife along with the holy oils if things went seriously wrong. On his right he saw Brother Hernando coming with the covered chalice, an altar boy at his side ringing the bell. People kneeled as he went by, and as they rose, vigorously shook the dust off their breeches or skirts. On the stairs, the altar boy's bell became seemed sharper, more musical, and imperative.

Bernardo approached Brother Hernando: "Father, the oil is all we need. She isn't conscious."

Just as the priest was initiating the rite, Doña Catalina's chin fell onto her bosom. She was motionless, her mouth wide open. The doctor came to her, took her pulse, and placed the hand adorned by the emerald over her heart. He turned to those assisting him: "She's dead."

A quarter of an hour later, Modesta, with the theriaca in her hand, collided with Juan Dueñas at the entryway. Dueñas laconically muttered: "Doña Catalina's dead."

Modesta sobbed. She walked up the stair slowly, hanging onto the balustrade. The dead filled her with fear, and she hoped to delay entering the house. Through the half-open door, she could make out Bernardo, his brother, Blasa, and the wet nurse moving the furniture in the vestibule, making room. She stood still, without entering. Minutes later, the professional mourners arrived to set up the funeral chapel in the office. Modesta took advantage of the temporary confusion to go to the kitchen. Minervina, weeping her heart out while seated on a stool, was feeding the baby, while Blasa, impassive, tended to the fire with that indifference characteristic of people prematurely torn from their place of origin, who've seen everything. Modesta joined the domestic work. She delivered the medicine to the master of the house. Bernardo grumbled: "Twelve ducats thrown out the window." Modesta spoke in an inaudible voice: "I'm sorry for you, Mr. Bernardo. God rest her soul."

But the hustle and bustle of visits—the knocks at the door, the flowers—was already beginning, and she joined in the work immediately. People came in small groups and passed into the sitting room, where Bernardo and his brother received them. Once, when he happened to pass opposite the open door of the office, Bernardo glanced in and saw his wife on a table, her eyes and mouth closed, pale, indifferent, and tranquil. The visits went on all afternoon. People would arrive downcast and walk out relieved, having discharged a painful obligation. Bouquets of flowers would arrive, and Modesta would carry them to the office, her eyes half-closed. She was terrified of seeing the mistress again.

Alongside the body, Doña Gabriela, the deceased's sister-in-law, directed the prayers of the group. Late that same night, when their friends were gone and they were left alone, Bernardo and his brother, the executor, sat down together at the feet of the dead woman—an old family custom—to read her last will and testament. Catalina's first wish was to be buried in the atrium of the Convent of Saint Paul and not inside the church, as she explained, because the burials within had produced disagreeable stenches "that inhibited devotion." Twelve poor young women were to accompany her to her final resting place. They were to be dressed blue and white and were to carry burning candles. Bernardo was to give each a copper *real* in payment. The burial was to take place after a requiem mass in the church, to be followed, on successive days during the first nine days of mourning, by sung masses with deacons and subdeacons, and other masses in each church in the city on the eighth day after her death.

Bernardo read these directions out in a faltering voice, not so much out of affliction but because he knew the financial liberality of his wife, which he feared would manifest itself again and again. And his trembling voice completely broke when, in her idiosyncratic, pointy handwriting, the dead woman ordered, in terms that allowed for no interpretations, that a permanent donation be established in her name for the Convent of Saint Paul, that it be, at the very least, two thousand six hundred and fifty *maravedíes* per annum. When he could finally bring himself to read this out, Bernardo paused, peered at his brother over the paper, and said in a dry tone: "Catalina was born to be a princess."

He thought about his shop in the Ghetto, his farms in Pedrosa, and about Benjamín, his tenant farmer: "A donation like this is going to cost me the profit from more than one farm."

His brother Ignacio, blond and clean-shaven with short hair, became annoyed. He wrinkled his nose as if sensing a foul smell: "This is a valid will. You can pay for that donation easily."

The two brothers had always been extremely close, despite the fact that when it came to money they had very different opinions. Standing opposite the feet of the deceased Doña Catalina, they argued amid the dizzying aroma of the flowers. Bernardo called his wife a spendthrift, but Ignacio discreetly terminated the conversation, telling his brother it simply wasn't the right moment to be making statements like that.

The next day, the body was seated in the coach, tied in place, and driven by Juan Dueñas. Presided over by Bernardo and Ignacio Salcedo, services for the deceased took place. Twelve girls, almost children, with seraphic faces, dressed in blue and white, flanked the coach, intoning religious canticles with nasal voices. In double file later, in the central nave of the church, escorting the body, their juvenile faces softened the solemnity of the occasion. Then the remains of Doña Catalina Bustamante were received into the earth in the atrium, and the girls paraded past the brothers, holding out their hands, wishing them peace or showering them with words of consolation. Once the final condolences were expressed, in the presence of the grieving friends, the young widower distributed to the young women the twelve copper *reales* stipulated by his wife's will.

When they'd returned home, Gabriela, accompanied by the two men, went to the ironing room to see the infant Cipriano. Looking at him, apparently asleep, she shed two untimely tears. Don Bernardo, on the other hand, contemplated the baby with an impassive face. At the head of his little cradle, the young Minervina had tied a black taffeta ribbon. Don Bernardo's eyes hardened.

"What can this little parricide be thinking while he sleeps?"

Ignacio took him by the shoulder: "Please, no more nonsense, Bernardo. The Lord might punish you."

Bernardo shook his head from side to side sobbing: "Could there be a punishment greater than the one I'm already suffering?"

# II

CATALINA'S death reordered the house on Corredera de San Pablo. Cipriano became part of the servants's world in the wooden attics on the top floor, while Bernardo remained lord and master of the main floor. The only significant alteration he made was to change the site of the conjugal sanctuary, which was now located —having ceased to be a sanctuary—in the office he'd used his entire life.

Naturally, the baby was totally attached to his nurse. He was at her breast every three hours, spent the day twittering in the ironing room, and slept with her in one of the tiny rooms in the attic, near the stairway. Life on the street level of the house suffered not the slightest alteration. Juan Dueñas, the male servant, went on living in the small chamber next to the stable housing the two horses and two mules, adjacent to the small coach house.

While none of these matters changed Bernardo's life in the slightest, he seemed to have entered a phase of defeated passivity. He stopped going to the wool warehouse in the old Ghetto, and completely forgot about Benjamín Martín, his tenant farmer out in Pedrosa. He even stopped amusing himself with his friends in Dámaso Garabito's tavern, drinking Dámaso's select white wines. He first spent a few days in the sitting room armchair looking through the window curtains, watching how the light came and left. He barely moved until Modesta told him dinner was served, when he would grudgingly get up and sit down at the table. But he didn't eat. He simply moved the food around to fool himself, and in the process, made the servants nervous.

Internally, he'd decided on a week of mourning, but seven days later, he found his simulation of grief was so convincing that he began to enjoy the honey of compassion. As a child, Bernardo had imposed his will on his parents, so as a man he was an authoritarian prig at home who recognized no authority but his own. Once he married, he subjected Catalina to harsh discipline. Perhaps that explained why he was suffering now: He had no one to order around, no one on whom to exercise his power.

Modesta, the maid, when she served him his meals, revealed her affliction with two little tears. One day, she could no longer contain herself and called him to order: Don't let yourself go, sir. You have nothing to regret. These simple words made Bernardo see that there were other subtle pleasures in the world beside those derived from authority: being pitied, arousing compassion. To emanate a feeling of grief so strong that it appeared no one in the world had ever felt the like was another way of seeming important. He became a master of affectation. He spent the day in front of the mirror practicing expressions and poses that would show his sorrow. He made the display of affliction his goal, so just as he pretended not to eat when Modesta served him, he also declared he'd lost the ability to sleep. He groaned about long nights when he never slept a wink, telling everyone his insomnia was irremediable.

Of course, when the house was dark and silent, Don Bernardo would light a little lamp and ransack the cupboard and the pantry for some appetizing dish to compensate for his daytime diet, which he observed so scrupulously. When he finished, he would walk from one part of the house to another, making noise deliberately to awaken the servants and confirm his own sleeplessness. Compassion for the suffering widower spread. From the servants, it spread to his brother and sister-in-law, Ignacio and Gabriela; from Ignacio it spread to Dionisio Manrique, the head of the warehouse; from the head of the warehouse to Estacio del Valle, the agent in the Páramo; and from Estacio del Valle to the other agents in Castile and to his friends in Dámaso Garabito's tavern.

Don Bernardo wasn't eating or sleeping, and did nothing more, people said, than give his servant Juan Dueñas instructions every morning and chat for a couple of hours in the afternoon with his brother, the judge. The only change in the first fortnight of his widowerhood was that he began strolling around the sitting room, taking solemn walks with no objective when he tired of resting in the armchair. He would stand up automatically every half hour and stride around the room with his eyes on the floor, his hands behind his back, his mind focussed on his own progress as an actor.

Minervina noticed something striking about those strolls. As soon as the master began to move and his footsteps began to ring out on the parquet floor, the child would wake up. And something else would happen whenever Bernardo went upstairs, not so much to see the baby as to have the nurse see him downcast and weepy. It almost seemed as if the child could feel the cutting edge of his father's gaze on his closed eyelids, an annoying sensation of intrusion that instantly woke him up. He would stretch his wrinkled little turtle neck, open his eyes, and slowly turn his head to look all around the room before bursting into tears.

Minervina was not at all pleased when Bernardo came upstairs without warning to stare at the baby with those cold, bloodshot, eyes full of reproaches: "He doesn't love the boy, Blasa. All you have to see is how he looks at him," she would say. Every time Bernardo came up to watch him sleep, the baby became uncomfortable for the rest of the day, uneasy, crying intermittently for no reason at all. Minervina understood perfectly: The baby wept because his father terrified him; he was horrified by his father's eyes, his mourning, his somber consternation. And once night fell and it was time for the baby's bath, Minervina would recite the news of the day to the other servants while the baby played in the round, brass bathtub, splashing with his little hands. And every time the nurse squeezed the sponge against his eyes and little streams of water ran down his cheeks, he felt angry and happy. When the bath was over, she would lay him on the towel in her lap, perfume him carefully, and dress him. It was then, as they studied Cipriano's pink little body, when the women would talk about his size, when Blasa would grumble that the baby was small but not thin, because his bones were like those of a fish.

Bernardo's false grief and the real way he distanced himself brought the girl closer to the child and made her sympathy for him increase. Minervina enjoyed watching the eagerness with which the boy sucked on her pink nipples, the movements of his little hands, his inarticulate gurgling, his confidant dependency. Holding him in her arms, she sometimes thought that her own child hadn't died, that he was resting securely in her lap, and that she had to protect him. "What a fool I am!," she would immediately say. "Was I thinking the baby was mine?"

Setting aside the permanent care the baby required and the comments he aroused, the only thing that broke the daily monotony during those days was the evening visit of Ignacio and Gabriela. Gabriela's beauty and elegance dazzled Modesta and Minervina, and the splendor of her clothes amazed them. She never wore the same style twice, but whatever she wore emphasized her bosom and the flexibility of her waist. French skirts, open brocaded mantles, slashed sleeves that gave a glimpse of her white chemise—all of it provided the girls with topics of conversation.

But there was also Doña Gabriela's way of walking: very lively and elegant, weightless, as if her body had the privilege of floating, of escaping gravity. Modesta and Minervina stayed with her whenever she came up to the attic to visit the baby. Gabriela never mentioned the baby's size; she liked him that way, and she was greatly moved by his having lost his mother. Using tricks of all sorts, she tried to find out about what the feelings of the boy's father were. She became upset whenever Minervina told her about his brusqueness and was on the verge of fainting when Minervina told her Bernardo referred to the infant as a *small parricide*. Given her brother-in-law's aversion toward his son and with the infertility of her own marriage confirmed, Gabriela, during one of those silent, confidential afternoons of Don Bernardo's early widowerhood, broached, in a trembling voice, the magnanimous possibility of taking charge of the baby. Not legally, with no plan for adoption, simply to take care of him until he reached a reasonable age, his father would stipulate.

Bernardo blinked until he felt the warmth of tears in his eyes, and said categorically: "The child is mine; this is his house." Skillfully, Doña Gabriela pointed out that the boy, far from consoling him, aroused *tortuous memories* in him, to which Bernardo retorted that while that was certainly the case, it was no reason for him to wash his hands of his paternal obligations. His eyes were shining, and he blinked to simulate sorrow, but Ignacio, always attentive to the afflictive reactions of his brother, spoke to him in a discreet fashion about how much sense it made to provide the baby with an *artificial mother*, linked to him by family ties, to which Bernardo replied that there was no need of such ties, that the young Minervina, with her small but efficient breasts and her tenderness, played that role to the satisfaction of all concerned. There was nothing in this brotherly difference of opinion to suggest tenseness, no improper language. Don Bernardo simply declined the offer.

On some afternoons when his brother was visiting, the widower would remain silent, as if hypnotized, staring at the curtain of the darkened window. This was one of his best stage effects, but his brother would grow nervous, ask him things, tell him gossip all to draw him out of his passivity. Bernardo was overjoyed at Ignacio's disquiet because Ignacio was the intellectual, the family eminence. The happiness he felt at being pitied he experienced most fully in regard to his brother, the number one, the discreet gentleman.

Unaware of his brother's playacting, Ignacio nervously kept track of Bernardo's strange actions. "You should set yourself a task, Bernardo," he would say, "something to distract you, to absorb you. You can't go on living this way, idle, with this sadness weighing on you." Bernardo replied that things were going along on their own and it was better to let them, that the secret of life resided in setting things in motion and then letting them move forward at their own speed. But Ignacio argued that he'd completely neglected the warehouse and that Dionisio Manrique lacked the brains to take over. The same thing was happening with Benjamín Martín, the Pedrosa tenant farmer to whom he owed a visit, if only to formalize Doña Catalina's testament.

On principle, Bernardo did not follow his brother's advice. Only after a few months, when he began to grow bored with his role as inconsolable widower and when he'd begun to miss the wines over in Garabito's tavern, did he admit to himself that the pleasure of being pitied was not enough to fill a life. It was then that he began to appear softer and more receptive to his brother who, for his part, had reached the conclusion that only an unexpected event, a shock, could lift Bernardo out of his prostration. And the shock came, in the form of an urgent letter, one afternoon when Ignacio, as usual, was urging his brother to change his life.

The letter was from Burgos, from Néstor Maluenda, the merchant who'd once upon a time thought it appropriate to give his wife the birthstool of such bitter memory. For Bernardo, who respected the merchant deeply, that letter announcing the departure date from Bilbao of the wool fleet signified a liberating piece of news. The fleece had been in storage in the Ghetto since August, and the wool of all Castile—except Burgos and Segovia—was rotting there without his being able to do anything with it. He sent the messenger back to Néstor Maluenda, begging his pardon for the delay and announcing that the Castilian shipment would leave for Burgos on March 2, that it would arrive in three days by forced march, and that he personally would lead the caravan.

The next morning, from Argimiro Rodicio, he hired five teams of eight mules each and five huge wagons, all to be ready for the second of the month. He also advised Dionisio Manrique and Juan Dueñas that they should be ready for the journey. He himself would drive the first wagon. He'd only done it once in his life, but now he needed to show Néstor Maluenda what kind of man he was. At the same time, he intuited that driving eight mules at high speed over a long distance, wielding a whip, would give him the physical release he needed. So at dawn on the second day of the month, once the sacks were loaded, Bernardo put on work clothes, including a hat and sheepskin jacket, and crossed the bridge, the Puente Mayor, leading his expedition. Behind him came Dionisio, the man in charge of the warehouse, driving another wagon pulled by eight mules, then another two blaspheming drivers he'd just hired, and, bringing up the rear, the faithful Juan, whom Bernardo had trained in all sorts of work.

On the road, full of potholes and ruts, Bernardo whipped his lead mules, forcing numerous horsemen, mule drivers, and carts coming in the opposite direction to take refuge in the ditches. Salcedo's lead mules, Chestnut and Moor, were his own property, and jumped when he shouted or whipped them, keeping up a fast trot or canter which, to those facing them, looked like a devastating cavalry charge. Little by little, Bernardo, a pacific and tranquil man by nature, grew bolder and began to gallop his animals at full speed, with the result that sunset sur-

prised them in the village of Cohorcos. There Salcedo changed four
mules at the Moral Inn and another four at the Villamanco post, where
he slept the second night. Rufino, the innkeeper, an old acquaintance,
waited on him with country amiability: "And just where are you going
in such a hurry? The mules are covered with harness sores." Bernardo
smiled a sour half-smile: "We've all got to do our duty, Rufino. The lead
mules are mine, so don't worry about the animals."

Liberated from his play-acting, he instantly fell asleep, for the first
time since the death of his wife. Even so, the next morning, he was clear-
headed, but every bone in his body ached. Every time the wagon shook,
he felt it, just as he felt every pothole and every change in speed. But on
the third day, before sunset, the caravan was entering Burgos through
the Wagon Gate. The din and the shouts of the drivers were such that
passersby stopped on the sides of the streets to watch them proceed. The
wheels of the carts and the hooves of the mules, which struck sparks
from the cobblestones, produced a deafening roar: "Salcedo's caravan is
late this year," commented one citizen. Opposite the Las Huelgas
Monastery rose Néstor Maluenda's enormous warehouse, which
received, in two annual deliveries, half the fleece of Spain. Dionisio
Manrique and Juan Dueñas stayed behind with the carts, watching over
the unloading process, while Bernardo Salcedo booked a room at Pedro
Luaces's inn, where he always stayed, and put on fresh clothes suitable
for dining in the most luxurious establishments in the city.

Néstor gave him a friendly greeting. But Néstor's presence—he
was so refined, such a gentleman, so much the master of his domain—
had always inhibited Bernardo: He was much more relaxed face-to-face
with the prince than with Néstor Maluenda. Everything about the old
man impressed him: his fortune; the fact that he was tall and svelte
despite his age; his impeccably shaven, pale cheeks; that short haircut
in the Flemish style, and his clothes: the long cassock worn under a
jacket, the square neckline of his shirt allowing a glimpse of his under-
garment, his slashed doublet, which would be next year's fashion.

As always, Néstor was welcoming and showed Bernardo his latest
acquisitions: the large mirror in the gilt frame hanging in the vestibule,
the matched set of Venetian *cassoni*, artistically facing each other in the
sitting room. Bernardo devoutly walked over the rugs, devoutly admired

the thick curtains hanging to the floor that sealed the windows. Inevitably, voices became velvety in a mansion so luxuriously appointed. Néstor became visibly upset when Bernardo told him his wife had died and that it was her death and the foreseeable consequences that had been the cause of his delay: "It was my first child," he said, his eyes shining.

"The child died as well?"

"No, the child did not die, Don Néstor. He's alive, but at what a price!"

It was also inevitable that the subject of the birthstool would come up, and Bernardo, despite his sad memories, acknowledged how useful it had been: "It was a breech birth, but the chair made it easier to extract him. Unfortunately, it couldn't stave off Catalina's fever or her subsequent demise."

Néstor had seated him between two candelabra and then blinked in frustration, lamenting that not even the Flemish chair had been able to avoid the tragedy. But, good businessman that he was, he immediately found the appropriate solution: "Salcedo my friend, everything you've told me is very moving, but Our Lord, with His divine foresight, has arranged things so that there is a solution to all the evils of this life. A man cannot live without a woman and, if you look at things objectively, a woman, as far as a man is concerned, is nothing more that a replacement part. You should remarry."

Bernardo was thankful for this intimate chat with the great Castilian merchant, but the subject they were discussing could only be a source of mortification and tension for him: "Time will tell, Don Néstor," he said in a mournful voice.

"Why not take charge of the matter yourself instead of leaving it to time? Life is short, and sitting back and waiting is not the right way to go about it. We've got no business twiddling our thumbs. Just look at me: three marriages in thirty years, and all of them gave me children. The wool business with Flanders is guaranteed for three generations."

In no apparent order, several subjects came into Salcedo's mind: the problem of his heir, the humiliating garlic test, Doña Catalina's bequests. So he only managed to blurt out in a tiny voice: "I'm afraid I'm a one-woman man."

When he smiled, Néstor's makeup-covered face aged ten years:

"There is no such thing, my dear friend. That's a fallacy. Especially now, when you're in a superb place to find someone. In Burgos just last month, a woman married with a hundred-thousand-ducat dowry. Many great fortunes were founded exactly that way, with a marriage of convenience."

Bernardo lowered his eyes. After months of reclusion and isolation, this conversation in such a softly cushioned space with a man this wise and prudent seemed like a dream to him: "I'll think it over, Don Néstor. I'll think about it. And if I some day change my mind, I'll come straight to you. I promise."

Néstor served him a glass of wine from Rueda and thanked him for taking personal charge of delivering the skins. We saved a day, said Bernardo with a surge of pride. Then Maluenda confided to him that this was an exceptional year, that the mules were going to the port at Bilbao in teams of twelve or fifteen and that more than seventy thousand *quintales*, at one hundred pounds each, were already stored on the Basque docks. This year he'd be sending more than eighty thousand mules, something unseen in Castile since 1509. His mouth watered with all these huge figures, and he ended his economic dissertation on a fatuous note: "Today, right now, Salcedo, I could lend money to the Crown."

As they sat there, at opposite ends of the grand walnut table, staring at each other like the Venetian *cassoni* in the sitting room, Bernardo thought that, even though Néstor had been married three times, he'd never met any of his wives: "They're nothing more than interchangeable parts," he thought. He never included them in his business meetings. It was his opinion that a woman should only adorn her husband in social gatherings. That was her job. The black servant brought them chicken soup. Bernardo became flustered when he noticed the man's race, but he said nothing until the servant was gone. Even then he said not a word but looked questioningly at his host: "Damián," said Néstor, "is a slave from Mozambique. Five years ago the Count of Ribadavia made a gift of him to me. He could just as easily have given me a Christian Moor, but that would have been vulgar. The favor was too great for such a meager response. Nowadays, a slave from Mozambique is a luxury only the aristocracy can afford. When he was fifteen, I had him baptized, and today he serves me with exemplary faithfulness."

Bernardo was becoming more and more intimidated. Néstor's display could not be more dazzling for a poor bourgeois like him. Néstor's fortune was perhaps comparable to that of the Count of Benavente. And for Bernardo money had a singular importance. After the chicken soup, the servant brought trout and an excellent Bordeaux. He moved silently, never allowing the silver dishes to grate against the table service, never allowing the Bohemian crystal goblets to touch the lip of the wine pitcher. The slave moved like a ghost, lifting his thighs to avoid having his slippers rub the carpeting. While he was out of the room, Néstor finished telling his story and what plans he had for the slave: "He's lazy and would run away if given half a chance, but he's faithful. I've chosen him as my personal manservant, but the other servants are jealous of him. As far as I'm concerned, Salcedo, he's another member of my family. He may be black, but his soul is as white as ours, equally capable of being saved. For the time being, however, what I refuse to allow him to do is marry. Just imagine a breeding bull like that set loose in this house. Disgusting. However, when he turns forty, I'll set him free. That will be a way of thanking him for his service."

The trip to Burgos, the evening with Néstor Maluenda, all did Salcedo a great deal of good. He forgot his negligence, his simulation; he finally rid himself of Catalina's corpse. As soon as he reached his house, without taking off his boots or wool jacket, he went up to the attic, where Cipriano was napping and stood stock still at the foot of his little bed, staring fixedly at him. The child, as usual, woke up, opened his eyes, and just stared at his father unblinkingly, frightened. But contrary to all expectation, Bernardo did not change his attitude because of the baby's tender stare: "What can the clever little parricide be cooking up?," he again muttered through his teeth.

His gaze was icy, and this time, without stretching out his tiny turtle neck and scaning the horizon, the child burst disconsolately into tears. Minervina came running in, her body swaying. "You've frightened him out of his wits, sir," she said, picking the child up and soothing him.

Bernardo pointed out that a male child of this age should be hardier and bolder, but he instantly began staring at the graceful figure of the girl with the baby in her arms, saying something that would have shocked Néstor Maluenda: "How is it possible, my dear girl, that with a face that beautiful and a body that slim you waste you time with job as prosaic as being a wet nurse?"

Bernardo Salcedo was ashamed of his own audacity. That afternoon, his brother Ignacio, the judge, joyfully hugged him, as if he'd just come back from a voyage to the Americas. He found Bernardo changed, ready to take on the whole world. Thanks to his trip to Burgos, Bernardo had, in effect, begun a phase of febrile recovery. A week later, stimulated by the livestock fair at Rioseco, he faced up to another of the tasks he'd left undone since the year '16: He had to travel up to the Páramo to visit and reorganize his agents in Torozos.

In point of fact, all of Valladolid's sheep had taken refuge there, as in the vicinity of the city there was no grazing land. Large vegetable gardens took up that space; then came the vineyards and the wheat fields. Only the highlands were left, where grassland alternated with scrub oak. The town fathers limited the right to graze sheep and goats to nonarable land, allowing only one male per herd, since, as they said, female sheep are unimportant and merely annoy everyone. But then the wool suppliers and the sheepskin jacket manufacturers fought for their meat and skins. Everything in that stupid but very gentle animal was useful. In other words, sheep were more important than the town fathers thought. When the city passed a regulation prohibiting the herds from grazing at less than two leagues from Valladolid, their displacement to the Páramo was inevitable and definitive. Then they not only occupied the lands around Torozos, specifically the properties of Peñaflor, Rioseco, Mazariegos, Torrelobatón, Wamba, Ciguñuela, Villanubla, and others, but their owners had to rent pasturage even further off, in territories like Villalpando and Benavente.

Bernardo Salcedo knew the itinerary by heart. On the way to Rioseco, he thought about the inns, hostels, taverns, and boarding houses run by widows that awaited him on the way. He thought of Widow Pellica de Castrodeza, at whose inn he used to sleep on an iron bed with two mattresses and two pillows, got three meals a day, and boarded his horse all for eight *maravedíes* per diem. The nature of the trip obliged him to change bed every night and travel two or three leagues every day. Bernardo was sure he could cross the Páramo from east to west in a couple of weeks and come back down to the plains at Toro, then stop over in Pedrosa, where he had his hacienda.

Breathing in the fine air of the hillsides, he thought of his agents as he made out in the distance the first stone houses in Villanubla. On his right hand, without his even having to leave the highway, was the hostelry of Florencio, who welcomed him as usual with good manners and few words. The laconic character of the people of the Páramo was proverbial. He'd often talked about these men with his brother Ignacio, and they reached rather optimistic conclusions: The men of Torozos were rough, concise, and sententious but hard-working and determined. In Villanubla, except for half a dozen people who had concrete professions, most people survived doing agricultural work: a few ploughmen, ten or so farm hands and day laborers who got occasional jobs from those who were more established. They were in general underprivileged, poor folk who lived in bare adobe hovels with floors of pounded earth.

Bernardo stopped over in Florencio's inn and spent the afternoon chatting with Estacio del Valle, his representative in the Páramo. Things were not going badly, or at least not as badly as they'd gone the year before. The herds owned by the common had grown to twelve hundred head of sheep, and the last grazing period had been favorable. Two shepherds working for independent farmers had emigrated and their places had been taken by two inexperienced hands who were, nevertheless, skillful shearers. One thing could make up for the other. The only serious matter in the area was the tendency among the landless farmhands, who were unemployed during the long highland winter and who only had occasional, badly-paid jobs in harvesting and threshing, to emigrate.

Taking a long view of things, it was entirely possible that in the near future Villanubla could be a problem if emigration continued at its current rate. The life of the poor, relegated to an unchanging diet of vegetables and pork, was monotonous, unhealthy, and stupefying. Estacio del Valle, an unambitious overseer, with his linen breeches and his sandals was dressed with a kind of elegance compared to the boys crossing the muddy streets, barefoot and wearing filthy knee-length trousers. This was the fate of the men of the Páramo, where social class began at the calf: bare, covered by breeches, or with buttoned trousers like those of the shepherds.

Bernardo left Villanubla the next day. Life deep in these highlands varied little, but even so he found the Rioseco fair unusually lively. In visible terms, there was nothing especially new in the town except its growth in comparison to the rest of the villages in the Páramo. The number of sheep was steady, and the shearers were preparing their equipment for the month of June. The reserve stock of wood and grass was fine, and Salcedo passed a tranquil night despite the bedbugs infesting Evencio Reglero's inn.

The trip through the Páramo did present him with a few surprises. One positive surprise: the growth of the flocks in Peñaflor de Hornija, where the census exceeded ten thousand head, and two negative: Widow Pellica had died, and Hernando Acebes, Bernardo's agent in Torrelobatón, had suffered an attack of apoplexy. Even though the barber in Villanubla bled him twice, he didn't recover, and there he was sitting up all day in a wicker armchair placed at the entry way to his house, a useless thing. Hernando Acebes, penniless, wiped away his own tears when he gave Bernardo the names and addresses of those who could take his place.

Just as he'd planned, Bernardo left the Páramo at the start of May, following the highway to Toro. It was a mild day, the sun was bright, and the crickets were raising a deafening din along the side of the road. The autumn and spring rains had fallen steadily, and the shoots announced a dense crop of seedlings. Even the skeletal vineyards looked healthy, and unless the sun beat down on them too hard, the grapes would mature in their time, and, unlike last year, there would be a good harvest. From the low hills of La Voluta, Salcedo could make out the Picado peak and, at its base, the village of Pedrosa, set among vineyards, crammed into the space to the left of the church. The day was so clear that from Mota del Niño he could see the Duero woodlands, with poplars and elms still only half covered with leaves. Beyond the Duero, he saw the dark green of the pines that were planted in the sandy soil when the century had just begun.

Bernardo skirted a mound covered with sheets of crystallized limestone, and two rabbits ran this way and that to take shelter in their warren. Benjamín, his tenant farmer, was waiting for him. He was a pudgy man, as were almost all the men of the zone as well as their sons —prematurely bald, with puffy, negroid features that were so typical that Salcedo could have picked him out of a crowd of a thousand. He wore a short cape that hung low, made of rough cloth, and sailcloth

breeches to the knee, which exposed his short, hairy legs—his perenni-
al uniform. Benjamín was one of the few men in that era of conspicu-
ous consumption who liked to give the impression that he was less than
he was. His income and social standing as a tenant farmer—after all, the
livelihood of the day laborers depended on him—gave him the right to
another physical image, one he and his family scorned.

Both Lucrecia del Toro, his wife, and his sons, Martín, Antonio,
and Judas Thaddeas, wore smocks and short brown capes that had been
woven and rewoven, clothing in which Lucrecia had invested more
stitches than all the weavers of Segovia. Benjamín confirmed the good
signs to Bernardo: The wheat and barley were coming along nicely, and
although any statement about the vineyards would be premature, if
nothing unforeseen came up, the grape crop could be a fifth larger than
it was the previous year. They could hear the impatient whinnies of
Lucero, Bernardo's horse tied up at the door of the hovel; inside, in the
hall, where they were talking, it was cool and smelled of aloe. Bernardo
was sitting up straight and stiff on a long bench, while Benjamín rested
on a short one, next to the chest where Lucrecia stored the sheets and
bed clothes in fragrant herbs. The house was rudimentary and earthy.
There was little furniture, no adornment of any sort, which is why the
family went to great lengths to protect a hanging that depicted the
Nativity as well as the embossed leather canopy over the bed where
Benjamín and Lucrecia had slept for the past twenty-five years.

Benjamín emanated the same austerity sitting on his worn-out
mule, using a blanket in place of a saddle, along with his son Martín, his
first-born, who rode a nondescript burro with one haunch higher than
the other when they went out with Bernardo to inspect the land. Behind
the little hill, Bernardo noticed that Benjamín had replaced a barley
field with a vineyard: "It's grapes that bring in the money, Bernardo, we
have to be realistic"—that was all he gave by way of explanation. But
what Bernardo was interested in knowing was which were the acres that
yielded the least: "The land around La Mambla," Benjamín answered
without the slightest hesitation. They inspected those vineyards, which
looked fine, and only yielded little at harvest time. "These are the poorest?," insisted Bernardo. "By far, Mr. Salcedo, fewer grapes and much
more sour, who knows why."

Only on their return did Bernardo, sitting on his horse, communicate to Benjamín Martín and Martín Martín, his first-born, that Catalina had died. Benjamín, on his mule, removed his hat and made the Sign of the Cross: "May God grant you health, sir, to pray for her soul," he said in a low voice, while Martín Martín, the boy, more ashamed than sad, simply bowed his head.

Lucrecia gave Bernardo his midday meal in the kitchen, on the pine table around which the family sat on benches. Opposite the table was the cupboard, crammed with cooking pots and casseroles, flanked by two clay water pots. Whenever Bernardo hadn't visited for a long time, Lucrecia paid him this honor, preparing him dinner without telling him, without prior invitation. It was an accepted event, and when Bernardo sat down at the table, in the heart of the family, Benjamín was already eating. He chewed ferociously, his hat pulled down to his ears, and after eight or ten mouthfuls, he brought his hand to his mouth and belched, making no attempt to cover it up.

Between belches, he reported all the news, especially items that affected his income. Wages were constantly rising. Today it was impossible to hire someone to harvest grapes for less then twenty *maravedíes*; laborers wouldn't take less than forty, and a vine pruner, sixty. In that sense, things were going badly. And as if that weren't enough, the last harvest was very scanty, and as a result, as Bernardo may have noticed, he hadn't paid his Easter rent. Bernardo pointed out that bad times out here affected him as much as they did his tenant and that holding back the rent was far from a solution: "You're going to end up in the hands of moneylenders, Benjamín," he declared, pointing his index finger at him.

But Benjamín reserved the major issue for after dinner, when the thick Toro wine had produced its effects. Primitive as he was, Benjamín was intelligent, and instead of directly broaching the matter of substituting mules for oxen, he began with a lateral matter, the leaving of fields fallow, which he considered old fashioned and useless. Bernardo had a superficial knowledge of the land, but he mitigated his ignorance with the experience of his friends in Garabito's tavern on Orates Street. He answered that to soften and air the soil, they would have to plant something else, millet for example, which was little done in Castile. Benjamín stared at Bernardo and argued that fertilizer was preferable to a change of crop, that in Toro, people had been using fertilizer for two years and that the yield was twice as great.

Martín Martín, like a puppy trained to be submissive, supported his father with his eyes, but Bernardo, irritated by the untruthful argumentation of both father and son, asked them where they thought they were going to find fertilizer in Toro, since in Castile, the only thing that gets bigger is the number of sheep, but that what the land needs is manure, not sheep turds, and that the little manure they do have is used in vegetable gardening. The conversation had followed the lines foreseen by Benjamín, who alleged, with regard to manure, that the most modern development in agriculture involved substituting mules for oxen. They eat less, they're lighter, faster, and they save time, especially in plowing.

Bernardo, asphyxiated by the argument and the wine, argued that mules lacked strength and barely scratched the surface of the earth while oxen, thanks to their strength, plowed deep furrows, which protected the seeds. To this the tenant retorted that oxen ate more, that the grass they ate was hard to grow and expensive, but Bernardo, far from giving in, tried to make him see that the decline of agriculture in other parts of Spain derived precisely from the fact that mules were now doing the work of oxen. More pragmatic, Benjamín Martín pointed out that in Villanubla only two farmers were still plowing with oxen, but Bernardo interrupted to ask, quite sensibly, if it wasn't the case that Villanubla was the only village in decay in the whole Páramo. The tenant admitted this to be the case, but pointed out a new difficulty: the high degree to which land was parcelled out required the rapid movement of plowing teams, and that from oxen you could expect anything but speed.

The clay mugs of thick Toro wine were disappearing from the table, and Bernardo, his elbows resting ont he table, his ears red, and his eyes glazed, finally adopted a Salomonic solution. They could try it out; innovations require experimentation. That's how knowledge advances. They could, for example, exchange the oxen in one team for mules but leave the other two teams as they were. The harvest would tell if the agility and feeding of mules compensated for the greater work carried out by oxen, or if oxen were still superior to the supposed virtues of mules.

Bernardo was tired. He'd spent too many days tangled up in foolish arguments, and foolish arguments he found especially tiring. Besides, talking with illiterates drove him mad. Night was falling when he left his tenants' house, his head heavy and foggy. He took Lucero's horse and walked him to the house of widow Baruque, where, as was his custom, he thought he'd spend the night. There wasn't a soul on the street, and the widow came to the door carrying a candle. They lodged Lucero in the stable, and she asked Salcedo what he wanted for dinner. He preferred not eating at all. The midday meal, made up of pork and pinto beans, left him feeling stuffed; he had indigestion.

When he stripped off his encumbering clothes and stretched out naked on the ironed sheets, he sighed with pleasure. He'd spent two weeks changing food and lodging every day. Very early in the morning he paid the widow, and using the Vivero shortcut, he entered the Zamora highway. At the crossroad, a hare leapt out of the vineyard and ran a hundred zigzagging meters right in front of the horse. Bernardo then spurred his horse and cantered toward Tordesillas. His methodical and routine-bound personality would not allow him to change routes. For a few seconds, he thought about his son and about the elegance of Minervina with the boy in her arms. He smiled. He passed by Tordesillas, put the spurs to Lucero, crossed the Villamarciel and Geria lands, went by Simancas, crossed the river on the Roman bridge, and, at midday, entered Valladolid by the Puerta del Campo, passing on the right the town brothel.

# III

ALMOST without realizing it, Bernardo found himself once again caught up in routine. Months back, he actually began to believe he might die of boredom, but now, as if all that had been nothing but a passing cloud on a sunny day, he realized his fears were unfounded. He'd overcome his *entrance into melancholy*, as he pompously referred to his months of idleness, and here he was firmly in charge of his household and his business affairs.

In the morning, after one of Modesta's lavish breakfasts, he would make his way to the warehouse in the old Ghetto, close by the Puente Mayor, and meet with his faithful assistant Dionisio Manrique, who just a few months ago had come to the conclusion that his employer was dying and that the warehouse would have to close. He imagined himself jobless, penniless, destitute, begging among the tumor-covered children who filled the streets of the town winter and summer. But Mr. Salcedo, for no good or bad reason, was suddenly back among the living, fully in command of the situation.

The trip to Burgos started his master's revival. In the office, Manrique would take his place at a Soria-pine table opposite his master's and keep an account of the mule teams that came down from the Páramo and of the fleeces stored in the immense hall of the Ghetto. Attila, the ferocious mastiff Manrique had owned since he was a pup, charged around, barking in the space between the building and the adobe wall around it. The dog slept out in the guard house at the entrance, apparently with one eye open. He also possessed very good hearing and a mean temper. At night, especially when there was a full moon, he'd howl from one end of the hall to the other. He'd never actually bitten anyone, but both Bernardo and Dionisio were sure no one had carried off so much a single fleece since Attila began guarding the warehouse.

Manrique, with no other help than Federico, a fifteen-year-old ragamuffin mute from birth, was the soul of the establishment. Office, table, the oversleeves he wore working on the accounts: These were the limits of his prosaic activities. On the one hand, Dionisio noted the fleece that came in and went out, and on the other he lent a useful, workmanlike hand wherever one was needed. For example, when there was either a delivery or a shipment, Dionisio and Federico would go out to the loading area, almost always a sea of mud, and the two of them along with the mule driver would unload the sacks without hiring any extra hands. Then they'd stack the skins in orderly fashion. In the same way, Dionisio, if there was any need for haste as there was in the last trip to Burgos, wouldn't hesitate to pick up his sheepskin jacket and whip and personally drive a wagon to Néstor Maluenda's establishment in Las Huelgas or anywhere else. Once he got started, nothing would stop him: He'd eat at the counter with the mule drivers or sleep in the collective bedrooms at inns, all in order to save his master a few *maravedíes*.

With regard to the small business Bernardo Salcedo had with the Camilo Dorado and his sheepskin jacket factory in Segovia: It was Manrique himself who hired the mule teams and drove them through the mountains, taking stony shortcuts only he knew. Bernardo, who knew all about Dionisio's versatility and his handiness, defined his employee in a peculiar fashion, one not devoid of contempt, as a man lacking perspective.

The first days of summer were frantic at the warehouse, and the boundless activity into which Bernardo threw himself cured him of the glut caused by his gastronomic excesses. No doubt his recovery was aided by Gaspar Laguna, who bled him. In the past, he'd uselessly done the same for his wife, but Salcedo never bore grudges. He hated shoddy work, but he valued work done well even if it was unsuccessful. If he had confidence in a person, he wouldn't stop believing in him because of a mistake. Bernardo based his view of the world on human imperfection, when he summoned the barber-surgeon he showed he bore him no ill will, even if, when he arrived, Salcedo welcomed him with these words: "Laguna my friend, let's see if we have better luck than we did with Doña Catalina, may she rest in peace." All of which obliged the barber to use all his knowledge and ability.

At twelve noon, Bernardo left the warehouse. These were weeks of heat, and the streets stank of garbage and trash. Children, their little faces covered with tumors and cysts, surrounded him, begging for money, but he paid no attention. "They've got my brother," he thought. "Is there anyone in Valladolid who does more for his fellow man than Ignacio?" He was walking slowly, avoiding open sewers, listening carefully for the shout of "Watch out below!," which meant someone was emptying a chamber pot out a window, until he reached Orates Street and Garabito's tavern, whose sign, as usual, was set out a leafy branch. It was there that three or four friends habitually met to taste the white wines of Rueda.

The first time he walked in after his long absence, everyone present told him how much they'd missed him. They were all of that class of circumstantial friends, the kind you meet in places like Garabito's, timid men who attended Catalina's funeral, as was only proper, but who didn't dare set foot in Bernardo's house. Catalina called them his "pals," and could find no better expression to define them. But the pals celebrated Bernardo's reintegration into their morning gatherings by hoisting a few glasses. He told them about his *entrance into melancholy*, and even though none of them knew exactly what that malady might be, they asked him, repeatedly, as is the custom among drunks, how he'd managed to shake it. Bernardo, given to verbal ingenuity, looked over his pals one by one and made the revelation he'd prepared two weeks earlier at home: "I was cured by an urgent letter from Burgos." The pals laughed, slapped him on the back, and told other pals, and all agreed that the contents of the wineskin from La Seca that Dámaso Garabito had just opened would finish the cure.

There in the tavern Bernardo abandoned his social norms and hypocrisy: He cursed, used obscene language, and laughed at dirty jokes. Excesses like that brightened his mood and enabled him to face the afternoon tasks in town in better spirits. It also happened that from

time to time he would ask advice in Garabito's place, as he did in the
case of Teófilo Roldán, a farmer from Tudela, who, along with his horse,
crossed the Duero river twice a week on Herrera's ferry to tend his
fields. Teófilo drank out of a clay pot because in his opinion white wine
drunk from clear glass lost a good part of its flavor.

He listened to Bernardo's story of his tenant, and when Bernardo
asked him whether he thought it better to have his tenant working by
share or on a fixed salary, Teófilo, inspired by the wine, answered with
crushing logic that it depended on the size of the share. For once,
Bernardo responded honestly: "Let's say a third of the harvest." Teófilo
instantly retorted: "In Tudela we give more." Salcedo blushed slightly;
he had soft skin which blushed easily: "let's not compare. Tudela is a
prosperous town while Pedrosa just barely survives." Then he pointed
out that with a third a family in his town could get out of debt and even
make a profit, but that it was a different matter if the tenant was illiterate, couldn't do basic arithmetic, and farted all the time right in front of
his master.

"It's impossible to get him to give up any idea that takes root in his
brain." Teófilo Roldán drank without pause. He'd reached that point
where we forget the weight of our body and feel ourselves floating.
"What idea? What idea are you talking about, Salcedo?" "Specifically,"
said Bernardo, trying to persuade him without resorting to numbers,
"that using a team of oxen is more profitable than using mules." Roldán
leaned toward him until their heads almost touched: "Do you really
believe that?" Bernardo was taken aback: "Don't you? It all depends,"
said Teófilo, "on the amount of work and the land." Bernardo, for no
reason except that he too was drinking a lot, began to feel optimistic.
Suddenly the oxen, the mules, and the profitability of either stopped
mattering to him; all he cared about was hearing his own voice, feeling
alive, and savoring the good wine of La Seca: "Plowing," he said, "that's
what I'm talking about. Mules don't plow, they scratch the earth and let
the pigeons and crows eat all the seed." "All birds eat seed," stammered
Roldán, putting a hand on Bernardo's shoulder. Bernardo smiled, shaking his head: "Not always, my friend. The oxen allow the plow to go
deep, and that defends the seed." Teófilo's eyes grew cloudy: "Bu . . . bu
. . . but do you have so much authority that you can give orders to your

tenant?" "He allows me that privilege." Salcedo clarified: "He yields that power to me spontaneously because he doesn't understand anything about papers."

Bernardo actually liked being enmeshed in his old routines. He would turn up every day at the tavern on Orates Street, next to the madhouse that gave it its name, or, for that matter, at any other where a green branch was draped over the establishment's sign. It was significant because, without ever agreeing on it, the pals always met in the tavern that was opening a new barrel or wineskin that day. Usually they were wines that entered the city at one of two gates, at the Puente Mayor or at Santiesteban, wines that had yet to ferment the five months after the harvest as was prescribed, but which were entered in the registry in order to determine the fluctuations of consumption. The reds were usually thin, half finished, and not popular, but the connoisseur was always on the look-out for pleasant surprises.

After sampling it, the aficionados would comment the virtues and defects of the new vintage. And from time to time, another old friend would turn up, one less attentive to wines than the others, but who had heard something about Bernardo's illness and would ask about his recovery. Salcedo, who considered his answer one of the wittiest of the century, would burst out laughing and say: "An urgent letter from Burgos cured me, even if you find that hard to believe." And the old pal would laugh with him, slapping him fervently on the back, because the new wines had a higher alcohol content than was expected, and four glasses usually clouded the drinker's brain.

At two, Bernardo would return home in the good humor provided by Garabito's tavern. Modesta, as she served him his lunch, would chatter on about the baby's newest tricks. She could not understand how a father could be indifferent to the progress of his own son, but the fact is that Salcedo barely listened to her and asked himself a thousand times just what it was, really, that he felt for the child. On his return from Pedrosa, Bernardo imagined that his feelings swung back and forth between attraction and repulsion. Even so, some afternoons, when he'd walk up to the attic to visit his son, he would recognize he never felt any love for him, at most he felt a zoological curiosity. Then a week could go by without his visiting again.

After a week, he would again feel that vague attraction and make a surprise visit. Minervina would be doing the ironing or changing the baby's diapers, accompanying herself with whispered songs or tender chatter. Bernard stared at the girl fixedly: He was convinced that vegetables and pork, the unchanging diet of the people, produced wide and short people. Which is why the young woman from Santovenia surprised him: She was tall and delicate, a woman who revealed a new charm every day—her long, fragile neck, her sharp little breasts under the coarse smock, her small but prominent behind, which he observed whenever she leaned over the ironing board. She was all beauty and harmony, a kind of vision.

A month later, he realized something else: The baby did not inspire both attraction and rejection—it was just rejection. The attraction came from Minervina. It was then he altered the confidence uttered to Néstor Maluenda in the sense that he was not a one-woman man: He was a man for whom there could be only one wife. As time passed, his elemental erotic feelings grew stronger each time he saw the girl. But she seemed so unreceptive, so indifferent to his gazes, so, at times, recriminating that he never dared go beyond mere contemplation. Nevertheless, one blazing summer day he suggested to her that she sleep on the ground floor, where the heat was more bearable.

"What about the baby?" she said defensively.

"With the baby, of course. I only suggested it thinking about the child's health."

Minervina looked him up and down with her transparent violet eyes, shadowed by thick eyelashes, then glanced over at the child. She then shook her head as if to underline her refusal: "We're just fine right here, sir."

After that puerile encounter, the image of the wet nurse never left his mind. Under the spell of her charms, he spied on her day and night. Knowing the baby nursed every three hours, he tried to know when the last session took place so he could surprise her during the next with her breast bare. Each time he tried this maneuver, he would climb the steps on tiptoe, his hands trembling, and his heart pounding. But if before he opened the door next to the stairway, he heard laughter and love-play in the next room, he would instantly return to the sitting room without making an appearance. It happened as well that Minervina took her own precautions, given the frequency of Salcedo's visits, but one afternoon, when she least expected it, he peeked through the narrow space where the door had been left ajar, and caught her with the baby on her lap, her right arm outside her smock, and her small, hard, pointy breast with its pink nipple waiting for the child to seize it. "My God," muttered Bernardo, dazzled by so much beauty, gluing his eye to the crack. "Don't you want it today, darling?" said the girl.

Then she smiled with her young, full lips. Seeing the child's lack of interest, she took her breast between two fingers and traced the baby's lips with her nipple. After such direct stimulation, he took hold of the breast with the eagerness of the trout who swallows the worm the fisherman dangles before him. Bernardo, unable to control his own panting, stepped back from the door, and ran down the stairs, fearful someone would catch him. He repeated the trip upstairs on the following afternoons. The memory of that little breast innocently offered drove him insane. In the warehouse, he couldn't concentrate, worked little, and delegated most of the chores to Manrique. Then in Garabito's he would get drunk tasting wines, and when he reached home would get instantly into bed, claiming he had a headache. The alcoholic mists would fade, but in their place the image of that naked little breast would reenter his mind. He calculated the feedings, and went upstairs at around six, the fourth feeding of the day. But one stifling afternoon at the end of September, when the doors of the attic rooms were wide open, a blast of hot wind violently slammed Minervina's door. With no warning, Blasa appeared at the last door on the hall.

"Did you need something, sir?"

Bernardo was ashamed of himself: "I was coming up to see the baby. I haven't seen him for days."

Blasa instantly went into Minervina's room and instantly came out again: "He's nursing. Minervina will bring him down to you as soon as he's finished."

He slowly slinked down the stairs like a sensitive thief caught red-handed. But that night, during a visit to his brother Ignacio, he confessed: "Now I'm wondering if I spoke the truth to Néstor Maluenda, Ignacio. Don't you think you can be husband to one and only one wife but a man for more than one woman? My body is demanding satisfaction, Ignacio, pressuring me. There are days when I think of nothing else. It seems to me I need a woman at my side."

He waited for his brother, eight years younger but upright and just, to give him some wise advice or, perhaps, to give him the chance to tell him about his growing passion for Minervina. But Ignacio nipped his illusions in the bud: "Who told you that you're a man who could have only one wife, Bernardo? You need a new wife. That's all. Why don't you tell Brother Hernando to help you find one?"

Bernardo was disconcerted. This was not a matter of speaking to Brother Hernando, but of convincing Minervina that between feedings she should amuse herself a while with him in the attic bed. Their problem had nothing to do with arranging a wedding but in gaining access to the girl's quarters and being able to release his carnal pressures with her. Brother Hernando would never approve that. Nor would his brother Ignacio, who was so proper, so proper. To whom could he turn?

One afternoon, Modesta startled him, shouting that the baby was walking. He'd just turned ten months old, but he barely weighed fifteen pounds. Even so, he'd given many proofs of his agility. Sometimes he'd practically stand on his head in Minervina's bed so she would laugh. Others he'd jump over the rail around his cradle with notable dexterity and stand upright a while without moving, without holding on to anything, observing, as he usually did when he opened his eyes, the objects around him.

Now Bernardo, jolted out of a doze, did not waste the opportunity to see the girl again. He strode heavily up the stairs. In the corridor, he ran into his son, walking by himself toward the stairs while Minervina, smiling, followed him bent over, her arms open behind him, protecting him. Behind her walked, Modesta and Blasa with expressions of satisfaction on their faces: "Do you realize, sir, that the boy is walking by himself?" exploded the cook.

Bernardo, projecting an anger he did not really feel, took advantage of the situation to castigate Minervina for her carelessness, to reprimand her sharply. You can't allow a child nine months of age to walk around unless you want his legs to be bowed for the rest of his life. A baby's legs were like gelatine, unable to bear the body's weight without bending. He went on raising his voice, and when he saw that Minervina's lilac eyes were flooded with tears, he experienced a strange pleasure, as if he'd whipped the girl's naked back.

In spite of his apparent indignation, it was impossible from that afternoon on to keep Cipriano in his cradle. He got out of it with shocking ease and dashed around the hallway like a two or three-year-old. That is, Cipriano not only walked but ran, as if he'd spent his life trying to do so, and if anyone tried to stop him, he'd wriggle out of their arms and dash off again. You'd almost say that the icy stares of his father had left their mark on the boy, when that chill feeling would wake him up and he'd feel the need to escape.

Some afternoons, his aunt and uncle, Gabriela and Ignacio, would climb the stairs to see him. At first, the child's dexterity was like a circus performance. But Gabriela did not hide her fear: Wasn't the baby too young? She wasn't referring to his age but to his size, but Minervina, who all the while was going into ecstasies over the clasps and wrist ruffs on Gabriela's dress, made a spirited defense of the boy: "Don't believe a word of it, madam, Cipriano's not a weakling, he's got strength to spare." And then, when the novelty wore off, Gabriela and Ignacio began to make fewer and fewer visits, and Bernardo began increasing his to Santiago Street. Wound up in his routine, he took care of his obligations, but he never forgot Minervina. The sudden appearance of the cook when he was sneaking up to the girl's room did, however, restrain his initial impulses.

At night, he would mull things over in bed, excited about the possibilities a rich man had to sleep with a poor woman from a tiny hamlet, who was, in any case, barely fifteen. He thought he had lots of possibilities, but he lacked the aggressivity of a rich man, and Minervina did not correspond to the image of the submissive poor woman. The girl, never using grand words or melodramatic gestures, had kept him in check until that moment. But, convinced that all the advantages were his, Bernardo one day made a virile decision: He would make a frontal attack and show the girl what a need he had for her favors.

He put his plan into practice one night toward the end of September. Carrying a lamp, barefoot, he made his way up the stairs to the servants's quarters, wearing only his night shirt, trying to keep the

stairs from squeaking. He stopped outside Minervina's door. His pounding heart was suffocating him. The image of the girl stretched out care-
lessly on the bed went right to his head. Lamp in hand, he slowly
opened the door, and in the shadows made out the baby asleep in his
cradle and Minervina next to him, also asleep, breathing slowly. When
he sat down on the bed, the girl instantly woke up. Her eyes, now very
round, were more surprised than indignant: "Sir, what are you doing
here in my room at this hour of night?"

Bernardo cleared his throat hypocritically: "I thought I heard the
baby crying."

Minervina covered her exposed bosom with the corner of the
sheet: "Since when have you been concerned about Cipriano's crying?"

With his free hand, Bernardo seized Minervina's, as if it were a
butterfly.

"I like you, girl, and I can't do anything about it. What could be
wrong if you and I were to spend some time together from time to
time? Can't you divide your tenderness so that father and son get equal
shares? You'd live like a queen, Minervina. You'd lack for nothing, I
swear. All I'm asking is that you set aside a little of your warmth for a
poor widower."

Minervina freed her captured hand. Indignation flamed in her lilac
eyes in the candle light: "Get-out-of-here-this-minute," she said, biting
her words. "Out of here, sir. I love this child more than my own life, but
I'll leave this house if you ever dare to set foot in this room again."

Bernardo, crushed, stood up to leave, and just then the baby woke
up in terror. Bernardo felt that Cipriano's eyes were unmasking him, so
he put the candle between himself and the crib, opened the door, and
walked into the hall. Strong words hadn't passed between them, not
even absurd posturing—none of which kept him from feeling like a
shallow teenager. That simply was not a situation proper to a man of his
age and estate. He got into bed, feeling disdain for himself, a disdain
that was not the result of complicated causes but which increased if he
thought about his brother Ignacio and Néstor Maluenda. What would
they have thought if they'd seen him humiliate himself that way with a
fifteen-year-old maid?

Even so, his sexual need continued to pressure him as he left the house the next day for the Ghetto. He decided to visit the town brothel next to the Puerta del Campo, where he hadn't set foot for almost twenty years. "This is a good deed," he said, to justify it. The brothel was linked to the Guild of Conception and Consolation and used its profits to maintain small hospitals to help the poor and sick in the town. If a brothel can be used for such purposes, he told himself, it must be holy.

On both sides of the street, as it was every day, there were poor little girls, four or five years old, their faces covered with tumors, begging. He distributed a handful of *maravedíes* among them, but hours later, while he was chatting with Candelas in the brothel, in her small and charming room, the sad eyes of the beggar girls, the purulent tumors on their faces filled his mind. When he found himself within those four walls, his lust, which had been so sharp, relented. He saw that Candelas was ready to put her seductive talents to work: "Don't bother," he said, "we're not going to do anything. I just came by to chat a while."

He eagerly sat down in an armchair, while she, surprised, sat at the foot of the bed. Bernardo felt obliged to clarify things: "It's syphilis, haven't you noticed? The whole town is rotten with syphilis, dying of syphilis. More than half the people have it. Haven't you seen the children on Santiago Street? They're all covered with running sores and tumors. Valladolid is the champion when it comes to disgusting diseases." Dejected, he leaned forward with his elbows on his knees. Candelas was still surprised. What had this gentleman come looking for in the town brothel?

She challenged him: "Why just Valladolid? The whole world is full of disgusting diseases. And what can we do about it?" He stretched and crossed his legs. He stared directly at her: "Aren't you afraid? All of you here expose yourselves every day, you have no protection . . . I have to have some way to make a living and feed the poor," she said by way of justification. Obsessed, Bernardo now saw beneath Candelas's makeup the same tumors he'd seen on the little girls: "I mean, if all of you can take advantage of the doctors who work for the Town Council, if the town is concerned both about your health and the health of your clients. . . ."

She laughed halfheartedly, shaking her head, and he stood up. He had the feeling that the cysts and tumors weren't in the women but in the place itself. He stretched his hand out to her: "I'm happy to have met you." He put a ducat in her white hand. "I'll visit again," he added. He bowed his head and furtively slipped out of the bordello without saying goodby to the madam.

On his way home, he thought about Dionisio Manrique, his factotum in the warehouse. Manrique was a bachelor, full of fun and lustful. He was religious but was reputed to be a lecher. He and Bernardo had never spoken a word on the subject to each other. Manrique, to Salcedo, seemed a timid young man, still of marriageable age and well-behaved. Salcedo seemed an honest man, the soul of propriety, reserved in the exercise of his authority. His astonishment was understandable when his master got up from his table that morning and walked over to his, his eyes flashing fire: "Manrique, last night I visited the bordello," he said without mincing words. "All men have needs, and I naively thought I could satisfy mine there. But have you seen how the streets of the town are filled with beggars covered with tumors and scrofula? Where do all these syphilitics come from? How can we keep that abominable sickness from killing us off?"

Dionisio Manrique, who had time to cover up his anxiety while Bernardo was speaking, looked directly at his master and saw he was at wits's end, clutching at straws. He tried to comfort him: "Don Bernardo, things are being done. And your brother is well aware of them. The heat cure is producing results. They're doing it in the San Lázaro Hospital— I have a niece there. The method couldn't be simpler: heat, heat, and more heat. To do it they seal doors and windows and flood the room in a haze of guaiacum vapors. Those infected are covered with blankets, and then stoves and braziers are lit next to their beds so they sweat as much as possible. They say that with heat and a light diet all they need is thirty days of treatment. The tumors disappear."

Dionisio sighed with relief, but he noticed that his answer was not the one Bernardo was hoping for: "Yes," said Bernardo. "I have no doubt that medicine is progressing, but how can anyone have a carnal relationship with a woman without risking his health in the process? I have no intention of remarrying, Manrique—I'm not the kind of man who likes to walk the same road twice—but how can I satisfy my physical needs without risk?"

Dionisio blinked, a sign he was thinking things over: "The security you're looking for can be found in only one place. You have to do it with a virgin and only with her. "

"And where do I find a virgin in this city of fornicators, Manrique?"

The employee's blinking became more rapid: "That's not hard, Don Bernardo. That's why there are go-betweens. The women in the Páramo are cheaper and more trustworthy, because they lead harder lives than the women in the lowlands. They do have one peculiarity: If they see that the client is a respectable person, they're fully capable of selling him their own daughter. If that's not a problem for you, I can put you in touch with one."

Three days later, María de las Casas, the hardest-working go-between in the Páramo, appeared at the warehouse. Officially she was an agent for maids, but she was actually a procuress. Dionisio stepped out of the office so his master could speak freely. María de las Casas was not tongue-tied. She spoke about three virgins up in the Páramo, two of them seventeen years old and a third who was sixteen. She described them minutely: They were all strong ("You know that for a baby to survive in the Páramo it has to be strong," she said) and obliging. "Clara Ribera is more full-figured than the others, but, on the other hand, Ana de Cevico is a better cook than a professional."

As he had in the town brothel, Bernardo Salcedo began to feel a repugnance toward himself. The conversation he had with María de las Casas was like those between livestock dealers before they make a deal. At the same time, the woman dizzied him with her chatter. He thought about Minervina's discretion; her image filled his mind, and he had to shake his head to clear it. "As far as being clean, super-clean, none of them is better than Máxima Antolín, from Castrodeza. Her house and her person sparkle." She concluded by saying, "I bet that with any one of them you'd have many good times, Señor Salcedo."

More intimidated than stimulated, Bernardo chose Clara Ribera. In bed he liked a lively, daring, even shameless girl. "If that's the case," María de las Casas added, "you'll be more than satisfied with Clara." Salcedo arranged with the procuress to wait for them the next Tuesday, but it had to be agreed that in principle there was no obligation on his part. Four days later, when María de las Casas turned up at the warehouse with the girl, Bernardo's spirits sank. Clara Ribera was decidedly cross-eyed and suffered a nervous tic in her mouth, like an intermittent frown on the left side. This distracted the would-be lover: How was he supposed to kiss her?

"This girl's not lively. She's nervous, María. Before anything, she needs treatment. Take her to a doctor."

María de las Casas lifted the girl's skirt and showed off a white, sausage-like thigh, too soft and colorless for such a young woman.

"Just look at this delightful flesh, Mister Salcedo. More than one man, more than two men would give a fortune to deflower her."

Clara Ribera looked up at the wall calendar, down at the brazier near her shoes, over at the small window opened onto the patio, but no matter how swiftly she was to look over the warehouse, her left eye could never focus. It seemed that nothing under discussion had anything to do with her. María de las Casas began to grow impatient: "The first thing you've got to do, sir, is speak frankly in this matter: Do you want a girl to fool around with a couple of times a week or do you want a woman to keep?"

The question seemed to offend Bernardo Salcedo: "I want a woman I can keep, but I thought Dionisio had told you that. I've got a house all ready for her. I'm a serious person."

María de las Casas's attitude changed. Bernardo's answer opened new perspectives. She thought about Tita, over in Torrelobatón; about the gypsy beauty of Agustina, in Cañizares; about Eleuteria, who lived in Villanubla. She stared excitedly at Bernardo: "That being the case, things are more easily done, but I can't spend my life going up and down. It would be better if you came up and chose."

"Came up where, María?"

"Up to the Páramo, Don Bernardo. The best-looking girls in these parts are in the Páramo. If they could appear in taverns and inns, you could be sure there wouldn't be a virgin left. You also have to see the girl they call "Exquisita," in Mazariegos. She's out of this world."

"I'd rather they didn't have nicknames, María. Less well-known girls who've spent their lives close to home. Nicknames, let's be clear on this subject, are not a good sign for women in this kind of life."

The next day, Bernardo saddled up Lucero, and, for the second time in half a year, he rode up to the Páramo along the Villanubla road. María de las Casas had agreed to meet him in Castrodeza, and from there they would make their way to the other hamlets. However, in Castrodeza, Bernardo made the acquaintance of Petra Gregorio, a timid girl with blue, malicious eyes, and a flexible body. She was dressed modestly, with carefully arranged braids that set her apart from the austere furnishings of the house. Bernardo liked the family, and arranged with María de las Casas that he would see to the house over the course of the next week and come up for Petra the following week.

It was toward the end of November when Bernardo rode up to Castrodeza. An hour after he arrived, now with Petra Gregorio holding a sack with her poor belongings on her lap, riding behind him, he was heading back to Valladolid, trying to get there before nightfall. The sheep were moving back toward the commons, and barely a league outside of Ciguñuela, a flock of crows took off from a broom field. Bernardo made three unsuccessful attempts to get Petra Gregorio to break her silence. The girl, a good rider, easily adapted to the movements of the horse, but from time to time she would sigh mournfully. By the time they reached Simancas, night had fallen, which is what Bernardo wanted, and as they crossed the bridge over the Pisuerga he asked the girl if she knew Valladolid. Her answer didn't surprise him: She'd never been there. Nor was he surprised when a short time later the girl confessed to being eighteen years old. Bernardo had finally managed to get her to talk, and when they dismounted in Plaza de San Juan and he showed her the house by candle light, the girl couldn't stop sighing. She wasn't afraid. She told him so with great resolution, and that relieved him.

Finally he sat her down on a bench and helped her out of the sheepskin coat she'd put on to make the trip. Bernardo had been trying to excite himself for a while, though until then he'd felt nothing for the girl but compassion. So docile, so silent, so resigned: Bernardo wondered what Petra Gregorio was feeling in those moments—sadness, homesickness, or disillusion. Her face betrayed no emotion, but when Bernardo pointed out that several families lived in the house, that she had people above, below, and on both sides, she smiled and

raised her shoulders. He made an awkward attempt to embrace her,
but her rigidity and a certain stench put him off. This experience led
him to show her where the brass bathtub was and to show her how to
use it. You'll have to bathe at least once a week, but you must wash
your feet and private parts every day. She nodded without interrupting
her sighs. Bernardo showed her the well-stocked food locker and left
her alone.

The next afternoon, he came back to see her. He imagined that by
then Petra Gregorio would have shed her nostalgia, but he found her
wearing the same clothes she was wearing the day before, sitting on a
kitchen stool disconsolate and sobbing. She hadn't eaten. The food in
the locker was intact. Salcedo encouraged her to walk around the neighborhood, but she wrapped herself up in her shawl like an old lady: "I'm
remembering my town, Don Bernardo. I can't help it."

He spoke seriously to her, saying they couldn't go on this way, that
she'd have to pull herself together, that the day she got her spirits up
they'd have good times together, but, when he came back the next day,
he found her weeping softly in the same spot. It was then he began to
admit he'd been wrong, that he'd have to send an urgent message to
María de las Casas to take the girl home.

But the next afternoon, he found Petra transformed. She'd
stopped her crying and answered his questions smartly. She'd met the
woman who lived next door, who was from Portillo and married to an
apprentice cabinet maker. Both told stories about their hometowns,
and the morning had gone by in the twinkling of an eye. Petra even
seemed less stiff and standoffish when Bernardo tired to caress her.
He again urged her to stroll through town, to visit shops, attend the
novenas at San Pablo, which were very lively. And, in a sudden
expression of tenderness, he put five shining ducats in her hand so
she could buy new clothes. That was the definitive argument. Petra
went down on her knees and began to kiss the beneficent hand again
and again.

Bernardo stood her up: "You should buy a new skirt, some pretty
bodices, and a cloak with a transparent ruff; then rings, bracelets,
necklaces, all to adorn your beautiful body". Petra Gregorio's eyes, the
same eyes Bernardo feared would melt away in sorrow, were shining.

In the last analysis, Bernardo concluded, Petra was like all women. At a certain moment, he found her so happy and full of spirit that he thought of carrying her to the big bed acquired for the new relationship, but then he decided it was better to wait until the next day. With new clothes and jewelry, she'd be more open and generous with her favors.

He found her wearing a simple dress, with a daring decollete her breasts revealed under the transparent ruff. She was embellished with a large necklace, cheap pendant earrings, and bracelets with bangles. Smiling, she opened her arms when she saw him come in, as if welcoming him. His old lust, absent for the last week, seemed to take control of Bernardo once again: "Are you well, my child?," he asked, handing her his short cape. He took her by the waist. "You look beautiful, Petra. You've dressed yourself up nicely." She asked him if he liked her and called him "sir." "Sir!," he said. "Forget that formality. You call me Bernardo." She smiled maliciously, and he then had a luminous idea: "What do you say if daddy teaches you to use the tub?" She said she'd bathed the previous afternoon. "It doesn't matter, doesn't matter at all, it's not even bad to bathe every day, my girl, whatever the doctors may say."

An arm around her waist, he guided her down the hall to the kitchen. He pointed to a large clay urn filled with water next to the cupboard, and told her to heat up a fourth of it. When the water was ready, Bernardo used a technique that in his youth had never failed him for undressing a girl. First, he slowly took off her jewelry, which he arranged on the stove, then the over-dress, her petticoat, and her bodice. He waited a moment before removing her underclothes.

He was treating her like a child, to the point of calling himself "daddy." "Daddy will take off your ruff now, but first you have to get into the tub." Petra stepped into the water, half fainting away. Before settling her in the tub, he kissed her now that she was naked and in his arms. As she sat, he kissed her again, harder. Her excitement grew, and she bit him, her arms wrapped around his neck. "Now you're going to be a good girl and let daddy wash you all over," he said in honeyed tones as he sponged her breasts, which fled through his fingers like fish. Their mouths madly hunted each other through the foam, and halfway through the bath, he took the girl out of the tub, sat her on the towel resting on his lap, and then lifted her up. He walked toward the bedroom with his precious burden, and when they were in bed together he asked if it was the first time she'd ever been to bed with a man. Petra Gregorio whispered that it was.

# IV

"I'M living a quiet life, that's a fact. What more could anyone want?" Bernardo Salcedo answered smilingly to the late-arriving pals who were yet to ask him about his health, to the sheep ranchers and agents who came down from the Páramo and found him  strolling around the town, or to his closer friends, those who attended the meetings at the Plaza del Mercado and the neighboring streets, who would come over to shake his hand. He'd gone on for weeks without any major problems, reasonably satisfied. Petra Gregorio, whose contract with the procuress María de las Casas was about to come to an end, had turned out to be a singular lover. Not only was she beautiful and slim, but seductive and proficient. The week she'd been so depressed and difficult after coming to Valladolid, when she was learning to adapt, was now ancient history.

Now he was seeing a Petra Gregorio who was frivolous, shameless, and ready for anything. She wasn't merely a submissive being, always ready to cater to the desires of her protector, but an impulsive, creative woman who often liked to take the initiative. The result was that even if Bernardo told his pals he was living a quiet life, the love nest he'd set up for Petra was quite a turbulent place. He visited her every afternoon, and it was a rare day when Petra didn't greet him with some surprise. Bernardo bragged about his ability as a teacher. In five days, he'd managed to transform a country mouse into a lustful panther.

Petra was much more than what he'd imagined her to be. She was a genuine prodigy in the amatory arts. One afternoon, she received him practically naked, just slightly covered by some sheer tulle, and the next she hid in the dark back room wearing only a minimum of lingerie, which she'd bought in the linen shop on Tovar street. She greeted him by mewing softly as soon as she heard his footsteps in the hall. She instantly stripped herself bare and ran around the house, hiding behind the furniture, agilely dodging her panting pursuer, who was begging her to stop. "You can't catch me, daddy, you're not going to catch me." She called him "daddy" just as he'd renamed himself the day he conquered her.

Welcome, daddy; bye-bye, daddy; daddy, why don't you buy your little girl a necklace of white beads? Always daddy. Salcedo became excited just hearing the word. There was natural wickedness in Petra, which she could turn into a disturbing seduction in the twinkling of an eye. And, once aroused, Bernardo showed himself to be generous. He handed over the ducats with a free hand, a surprising attitude in a man who was always so tightfisted when Catalina was alive. But Petra Gregorio made intelligent use of the money, actually managing it carefully. She dressed, decked herself out in jewelry, bought fine furniture, decorated the house with beautiful drapes and curtains. For Bernardo, she was the kept woman he'd always wanted to have.

Then one day, she asked him to change houses, "because this neighborhood is unworthy of you, daddy; only artisans and country people live here," she said. And he understood that Petra in such a neighborhood was like a rose on a dung hill. He moved her to Mantería street and a new apartment in a family house. Petra gained with this change not only in terms of status, but in space and prestige. It was a narrow street, of course, as were almost all the streets in town, but it was close to the center, paved, and with distinguished neighbors. Petra's seductive tricks multiplied in her new home. Salcedo spent whole afternoons chasing a doe in heat or running to the call of "Daddy, daddy, I'm lost!" The restful siestas he talked about in the tavern became genuine gymnastic exercises in which he indulged every afternoon.

Sometimes, alone in his house on Corredera de San Pablo, he took pleasure in remembering Petra's tricks, the twists and turns of her perverted imagination. He compared that image to the timid, modest girl he'd found in Castrodeza and concluded that he was a consummate teacher of the arts of lechery and she a brilliant student. That was the only way he could explain how the country bumpkin who eight months ago came down from the Páramo riding behind him on his horse and sighing the whole way, had achieved not only her current level of depravity but the natural elegance she knew how to reveal from time to time. Bernardo was so proud of himself that, unable any longer to leave his adventures and the salacious behavior of the girl in darkness, told his employee Dionisio Manrique all of it one morning in the warehouse.

Dionisio absorbed his master's confidences with the slightly slippery eagerness of the confirmed woman-chaser and never voiced his objections about Petra. In this way, Bernardo managed to extend his hours of pleasure by means of the easy trick of narrating every explicit detail. The mere mention of Petra's erotic pranks, which inevitably ended in bed, aroused his ardor once again, preparing him for the afternoon meeting. Meanwhile, Dionisio listened open-mouthed, drooling. Only Federico, the mute messenger, who took note of Manrique's lust, wondered just what it was those two were discussing, what subject could explain the wildness of their eyes and their awkward gestures.

To his brother Ignacio, with whom he met daily at nightfall, Bernardo never revealed those secrets. To the contrary, he made every effort, when with him, to behave with the decorum and respectability which had always been the pride of the Salcedo family. Ignacio was the mirror in which this Castilian town saw itself. Well-read and a chancery judge, and landowner, his titles and properties did not distance him from those in need. A member of the Mercy Guild, he each year gave five scholarships to orphans because he understood that helping the poor to learn was simply following the lesson of Our Savior.

But he did not limit himself to giving money to his fellow men. He also donated his personal efforts. Eight years younger than Bernardo, with a ruddy, hairless complexion, Ignacio visited local hospitals monthly and donated a day's rations to the sick. He made their beds, emptied their slop bowls, and took care of them for an entire night. In addition to that, he was the major patron of the Collegiate Hospital for Foundlings, which was held in high esteem in the town and only remained open thanks to donations from its citizens.

Not content with all this, not satisfied with his professional tasks in the chancery and his good works, Ignacio was also the best-informed citizen of Valladolid, not only about the smallest municipal events but about national and foreign affairs. Recently, there had been such a plethora of news that every time he strolled Mantería and Verdugo streets on his way to his brother's house that he would ask himself: What can have happened today? Doesn't it seem we're sitting inside a volcano? Ignacio was blunt when it came to making judgments, and never sugar-coated them. The result was that Bernardo, even though he was hardly interested in politics or social issues, was kept up to date on the lamentable state of Spanish reality. The growing disquiet of the towns, the hostility of the people toward the king's Flemish entourage, the lack of understanding between the king and his people: These were realities visible to all, facts that, like snowballs, were rolling along, growing in volume, and threatening to absorb everything in their path.

Suddenly one spring afternoon, one of those problems exploded, even though Ignacio reported the events in a calm voice: "Rodrigo de Tordesillas, the Procurator, was murdered in Sevilla. He was working hand-in-glove with the Flemings. Juan Bravo has taken command of the insurrection and is organizing Communities in Castilian towns. There are riots and disturbances everywhere. Cardinal Adriano wants to gather the Regency Council here in Valladolid, but the people are against it."

Bernardo was having some difficulty breathing. For weeks now, he'd been taking note of how a layer of fat was accumulating on his stomach. He looked at Ignacio, as if expecting a solution, but his brother had none to offer. The next afternoon, Ignacio showed him a poster he'd picked up at the San Pablo gate: NO SUBSIDIES. LET THE KING STAY AT HOME AND LET THE FLEMISH GO HOME. "Several sermons in different Valladolid churches had dwelled on the same problem: The king should stay in Spain, and the Flemish should return to their own country; the towns should continue to negotiate directly with the king without the mediation of priests and nobles. These are tough demands. Do you realize that, brother?"

Twenty-four hours later these strange new events had become realities, and Bernardo again found himself in Ignacio's house: "The royalists have burned Medina. In the Plaza Market, people were rioting this morning and shouting 'Long live freedom!' There are a few nobles with them, but most are professionals, lawyers, townspeople, and intellectuals. As usual, no one's bothered to ask the people what they think, but they're following the advice of those doing the shouting, and they're bursting with indignation."

That same night, the mob, ignorant and outraged, burned the houses of the town counselors who had approved the subsidies for the king. It was a night of great confusion and noise. Bernardo had gone out into the street just in time to see Rodrigo Postigo's mansion burn and Don Rodrigo escape out the rear entrance, galloping his horse and striking sparks from the cobblestones. At sunrise, his brother Ignacio and Miguel Zamora as well as other lawyers and professional men came to his house to borrow his horses because of the imminent struggle.

The Count of Benavente was enraged with the towns of Cigales and Fuensaldaña, and a confrontation was feared. Bernardo hesitated, dawdled. "Why should I send Lucero, my noble animal, into a mess like that?" "We've got to do something Bernardo. We can't just stand by and let ourselves be trampled into the dust." A bit ashamed of his cowardice, Bernardo finally allowed them the use of his horses. Lucero returned safe and sound that afternoon, but Valiente was killed in the Cigales vineyard. Ignacio rode back on Lucero with Miguel Zamora behind, and they joined Bernardo at his house to pluck up their spirits with a few glasses of Rueda. It had been impossible to hold back the people, because the only thing they'd understood were the Count of Benavente's threats. His rank, fortune, and authority had meant nothing. His Cigales castle was attacked by the mob and sacked. The paintings, the drapery, the valuable furniture was all burned in the commons by the enraged crowd. On the outskirts there had been an exchange of shots with a troop of horses sent by the Cardinal, and Valiente, true to his name, had fallen in the fight.

Bernardo listened to those stories, which touched him so closely, in a state of shock. He wasn't a brave man, and instead of arousing his ardor these disturbances simply depressed him. The next day, he told Petra Gregorio the latest news. When he came to the decisive moments, like the attack on the castle, the girl applauded as if she were witnessing a struggle between good and evil. She always declared herself against the Flemish. Surprised, Bernardo asked what she had against them. They want to take control here, even the stones know that. It was hardly edifying that Petra discoursed on these serious subjects with her breasts bare, covered only by the necklace of white beads, made from amber and galaxite. But the story went on unfailingly every single day in the two houses: Ignacio would load Bernardo with news and gossip, which he would in turn unload, more informally, at his lover's place.

Thus Bernardo found out about the expulsion of the nobles from Salamanca by Maldonado; about Avila's Holy Junta constitution, whose intent was to unite all the popular movements; about the private audience Padilla, Bravo, and Maldonado had with the Queen Mother in Tordesillas; and how warmly she greeted them. Slowly but surely, however, the news began taking on a less optimistic color: In Germany the king had refused to receive a commission sent by the rebels, and they had returned to Spain embarrassed and humiliated. The Communities were no longer united; those in Andalucía had even abandoned the struggle and placed themselves at the orders of the king . . .

Bernardo listened to his brother without changing expression, as Ignacio reflected: "Today, as always, there is a lack of organization; ideals are at odds with one another and badly defined. The towns have placed themselves in the hands of the lesser nobility, and the highest ranks have taken advantage of the fact. Did I sacrifice my noble stallion Valiente for that?" But Ignacio went on, implacably telling his story, giving all the details of the tragedy: The Junta, after presenting a list of grievances to the king, attempted to remove Queen Joan from Tordesillas and to hang the members of the Council in Medina. The Communes and the king had clashed in Villalar, with the defeat of the Communes. A tremendous massacre: more than a thousand dead. Padilla, Bravo, and Maldonado had been decapitated.

Life in Valladolid sank into sadness. The cavalrymen returned hungry on wounded horses, while the foot soldiers, disarmed and ragged, staggered along the Corredera toward San Pablo. They walked as if lost, adrift. The gathering of artisans in the Plaza del Mercado that afternoon was subdued, and people walked the streets downcast, not knowing who to blame for the defeat. Among them walked Bernardo Salcedo, saddened but satisfied that the situation had reached its crisis, that it was over. He found Petra Gregorio in a bizarre situation: standing in front of the door, dressed in a black underskirt and an overskirt open in front, a daring decollete, but no necklace. She had tears in her eyes when she said: "Daddy, we've lost."

Bernardo embraced her tenderly. Enveloped in his inexhaustible lubricity, Bernardo dissimulated a tenderness he rarely showed. He then took off his short cape and hung it over the back of a chair. He turned back to her: "Oh! Beautiful women shouldn't get mixed up in such filthy events." He embraced her again, and she took advantage of his nearness to extend her bare foot beyond her underskirt and place it between Salcedo's solid legs. Bernardo, surprised, asked: "What are you doing? What are you up to?"

She slipped out of his arms and slipped out of her overdress, pulling it over her head. She no underclothing on. She was naked. She untied the ribbon holding her underskirt in place, and it slid down to her feet. She burst into laughter as she quickly ran down the hall: "Daddy, that's how we should strip off our troubles. Can't you catch me?"

He ran awkwardly, tripping over the furniture, and even though he was overcome by a burning desire, he had to think about how changeable the girl was. Was she really crying, or was she just trying to excite him? Again, the doubts he'd had about Petra Gregorio's personality began gnawing at him again. Did he really know her well or did he only know that she was unfathomable? They were again playing hide and seek, and when at last he caught her in the dark room and stretched her out on the parquet floor among all the odds and ends, she yielded with no resistance.

The lust Petra aroused in him distracted Salcedo from his earlier fascination with Minervina. He saw little of her and even less of his son Cipriano, who was now three years old. But on May 15, 1521, a totally unforeseeable event took place in number 5 Corredera de San Pablo, an event that fortuitously renewed contact between him and the wet nurse. It seemed that young Minervina with the small breasts had suddenly stopped producing milk. The reason? Apparently, there was none. She slept well, ate what she always had, had experienced no physical strains. At the same time, the serious events taking place on the streets didn't affect her, nor had she experienced any deep emotions that might explain the phenomenon. The child refused the nipple, and when she squeezed her breast she saw that it was dry. Then she began to weep, prepared some milk sops for the child, gave them to him, washed her eyes at the basin, and faced up to her meeting with Bernardo: "I have something important to tell you, sir," she said humbly. "Just like that I've gone dry."

She knew that her milk had been, during the life of Bernardo's deceased spouse, the reason her contract existed. He was reading a new book, which he closed and placed on the table when he hear her voice: "Milk, milk, of course," he responded in bewilderment, "but I suppose there are other ways besides milk to nourish a child."

Minervina thought about the milk sops she'd just given him and said simply: "Certainly there are, and you should know, sir, that in my town no child ever died of hunger, even though there are no doctors or barbers to take care of them."

Bernardo picked up his book. The incident was closed as far as he was concerned. But, seeing the girl hanging on his every word, he raised his head, smiled, and added: "We've exchanged the wet nurse for a nanny. That settles the whole problem."

A radiant Minervina returned to the kitchen. Nothing had changed: "I'm not leaving, Blasa, I'm staying with the baby. The master understood things." She took the boy by the hands and moved him to the rhythm of a song she hummed. Then she leaned over and covered his face with noisy kisses. Thus Cipriano's life continued on course. During the morning, when the weather was fine, Minerva would carry the boy to the center of town to take a look at the vegetable market and the display cases in the shops in the gallery. Other times, they would pass along Espolón or the Prado de la Magdalena just to take the air. On Thursdays, in mid-morning, Jesús Revilla would carry them, along with other passengers, to Santovenia, and there they would spend the day with Minervina's parents. The boy loved riding in the wagon because it swayed and bounced, because of the heavy trot of the mules and the deep potholes they'd hit along the way, which would send him rolling and shouting for joy toward the net of woven grass at the rear. Occasionally a lady from town would watch him in terror, but Minervina would reassure her saying: "This child is a bit of a puppeteer." Then she'd laugh to show how trivial the incident was. Later, in the village, at Minervina's house, Cipriano would play with neighborhood children. He liked those one-story houses with pounded dirt floors. They were clean, with few pieces of furniture, at most two benches, a cupboard, a pine table where the family ate, and in the back rooms, black iron beds shared by all the members of the family when they slept.

On the first visit, Minervina's mother was surprised at the boy's size: "He's so skinny; he doesn't look as if he comes from a rich house." But Minervina stood her ground and defended him as if he were her own: "He isn't skinny, mother, what it is is that he's got fish bones instead of people bones, as the family cook says." Then, when Cipriano began to do tricks in the corners, Minervina, proud as could be, would repeat: "He's strong, mother. At five months, he would already bend all the way over to get my breast, and at nine months he was already walking. I never saw anything else like it."

Cipriano felt free and happy in the village. With friends his own age, he would run wild all over the place. Sometimes they would approach the house of Pedro Lanuza, painted yellow, and pound on pots, shouting "heretics" and "illuminati." And Pedro Lanuza's daughters, especially Olvido, would appear at the door with the mortar in their hands, threatening to pound them to pieces. After riding home on the wagon, the child and Minervina would tell all these things in the kitchen, and Blasa would ask: "Does Pedro Lanuza still come down to Francisca Hernández's place on Saturdays?" "So it seems, Blasa," Minervina would explain, "but, understand what I'm saying, it's not that they're bad, it's that that's the way their religion is." And Blasa would add: "One of these days I'm going over to where that lady lives and see what they're up to."

Weaning Cipriano, inevitably, had repercussions for Minervina's body. Her breasts, already small, became even smaller, tightened, while her body became even slimmer. Her arms and legs recovered the feline elasticity they'd lost while she was nursing. Accustomed now to sex, Bernardo did not overlook that slight metamorphosis. His eyes followed the girl whenever she happened to appear, and he took delight in keeping her in sight as long as he could. Sometimes, when she was carrying some delicate piece of china or porcelain, afraid she might spill its contents, her footsteps became tiny and her rhythm delightful, her hips undulating slightly.

The child followed her everywhere. Ever since he'd begun walking they spent as many hours in the attic, where they slept, as they did on the main floor. This multiplied the possibilities of his finding himself face to face with his father. Whenever that happened, he would hide behind his nanny's skirt as if he'd seen the devil. In the kitchen, she would ask him: "Don't you love your father?" "No, Mina, he makes me cold." "What things you say." "Very cold." And the child confessed that he felt as cold as when the Espolón fountain froze over and he climbed up on it to slide around.

The attraction Bernardo felt for the girl and his apathy toward his son ultimately began to grate on his sensibility. As time went on, he found his reaction at the time Minervina lost her milk unintelligent. He'd been indifferent, so he reacted in a bland fashion, not knowing how to derive any advantage from the situation. He'd been, he thought, too paternal and obliging. Which is why now, whenever he saw the child hidden behind the girl's skirt, he thought he ought to assert his authority as father and master over the two of them. The girl arrogated too much authority over the boy to herself. She'd have to be disciplined. His ill will strengthened by the grudges he had against her, Bernardo carefully considered what path to take. Cruel, as only a timid womanizer can be, he dreamed of a chimerical solution that would cause the girl pain. So, one morning while Minervina was changing the water of the flowers in the sitting room, the child clinging to her skirts, he adopted a grave attitude and asked her if she thought one of her obligations was to separate the boy from his father. Minervina placed the vase of flowers on the console and turned around in surprise: "What do you mean, sir? The child feels affection for the person who takes care of him. It's only natural."

Bernardo cleared his throat. He stared harshly at the girl, who was shielding the boy, and asked in an authoritarian tone: "Why do you work so hard at the atrocious task of distancing a son from his father? It's true the circumstances of his birth were not favorable to arousing my affection for him. In his own way, he killed his mother. But a father would be able to forget anything if his son made even the slightest attempt to show him some love. Why are you educating the child to be a small conspiracy against me?"

Even though she did not completely understand Salcedo's speech, Minervina felt her eyes cloud with tears. The boy, tired of her immobility, peeked out from behind her skirt. Then she said: "I think you're mistaken. I only want the best for the boy, but to my way of thinking, sir, you do nothing to attract him to you."

"Attract him? *I* should attract *him*? That fine action is no concern of mine. It's you who should instruct the child in the best way to orient his affections, explain to him what is good and what is evil. But all you've done is substitute milksops for your breast, and that is insufficient."

By now, Minerva was weeping openly. From the puffy cuff of her sleeve, she pulled a tiny handkerchief and dried her eyes with it. An intimate sensation of triumph was flowing into Bernardo. He bent over the girl without getting up from his armchair: "Have you ever tried to teach this good-for-nothing runt to honor his father? Do you think this little devil honors me very often with his attitude?"

Finally, he rose from his chair, feigning a fury he didn't feel and seized his son by the ear: "You come with me, my little gentleman," he said drawing him close.

The child, now outside his hiding place, saw Minervina crying, but as soon as he turned his eyes toward the bearded figure of his father, he became paralyzed, rigid, trembling. Minervina was staring back at the boy now, but she didn't dare do anything in his defense. Bernardo went on shaking the boy: "Well, are you going to tell me, my little gentleman, why you hate your father?"

The girl made an effort: "Don't torture him any more!" she shrieked. "The boy's afraid of you, sir. Why don't you try buying him a little toy?"

The simple question left Bernardo momentarily disarmed. In that instant of paternal vacillation, the boy ran to her. Minervina fell to her knees, and the two embraced in tears. Bernardo was helpless in the face of tears, melodramatic scenes got on his nerves, and words of forgiveness, especially when they diminished the tension of a scene he wanted to remain tense, repelled him. He opted for the spectacular finale. Without taking his eyes off the lovers kneeling on the rug, he crossed the room in two huge strides, entered his study, and slammed the door. Minervina went on hugging the child, mixing her tears with whispered

words in his ear: "Daddy's angry, Cipriano, you've got to love him a little. If you don't, he's going to throw us out of the house." The boy
clasped her neck with all his might: "Will we go to yours then? I want
to go to yours, Mina." She stood up with the boy in her arms. She whispered in his ear: "Mina's folks are poor, dearest, they couldn't feed us
every day."

Bernardo was satisfied with the scene he'd staged. Making the
eyes which had scorned him weep was something like revenge. But
when he told Ignacio he made no mention of vengeance, limiting himself to disguising his triumph as virtue: "With people like her, it does no
good to appeal to the fourth commandment." Ignacio, proper but rash,
alluded to the fact that Bernardo had been cold toward the child since
his birth, which prompted Bernardo to insist that whether his brother
liked it or not Cipriano was nothing more than a small parricide. Ignacio
again urged his brother not to tempt the Lord and added something
disturbing about which he'd never spoken, namely, that the fact little
Cipriano was born the same day as the Lutheran Reformation was not
exactly a good omen.

The religious controversies of which his countrymen were so fond
had barely any place in Bernardo's world. Dionisio Manrique in the
Ghetto warehouse, the pals over at Dámaso Garabito's tavern, his
agents in the Páramo, even Petra Gregorio in the soft love nest on
Mantería street: None of them was likely to bring up such lofty disqui-
sitions. For that reason, now that his brother had just made a reference
to Luther, he felt a burning need to talk about him: "Did you know that
Father Gamboa said on Sunday in San Gregorio church that the king
and Luther had come to an agreement?"

In talking with his older brother, Ignacio was more comfortable
dealing with these matters than those relevant to his nephew and his
nursemaid. Ignacio kept up to date about Luther's revolt and had contact with the intellectuals and soldiers who returned from Germany.
He read all kinds of books and pamphlets related to the Reformation. A
believer, a Catholic through and through, he became agitated whenever
he took up those subjects, his beardless face turning bright red: "They're
taking the land right out from under our feet, Bernardo. They're mocking what we consider most sacred. Luther became angry with the pope,

who gave the Dominicans the privilege of preaching indulgences, but what he really wants to tell us is that indulgences and the offerings people make to help those in purgatory are useless, that they can't speed anyone's salvation. According to Luther, the only thing that saves us is faith in Christ's sacrifice."

Bernardo listened with curiosity. He was intrigued by that incomprehensible world, about which he understood his brother to know much more than he would ever know. "The problem," he said, "of salvation has always been man's greatest problem."

Ignacio, leaning forward with his elbows on his knees so he could be closer to his brother, responded: "Luther skirts the controversy. His objective is to destroy, to eliminate the pope—he's called him an ass and a supplanter of Christ. Once the papacy is eliminated, he'll have the field open for himself and his followers. Lutheranism is already a considerable movement. The Eck attempt at reconciliation is a failure. Luther will retract nothing. He says that in order to debate he needs a pope who's better informed. Leo X has condemned his doctrines and excommunicated him. The Emperor has ratified that condemnation at Worms. Luther escaped to Wartberg and, hiding in the Prince's castle, never stops writing incendiary books that will spread this *leprosy* all over Europe."

Bernardo swallowed some Rueda wine. The afternoon visits to his brother had that advantage: He offered his guests the best wines in the nation. His wine cellar and his library—five hundred and forty three volumes—were the most highly esteemed in Valladolid. And, in addition to stocking fine wine, he served it in cups of the finest crystal. His sister-in-law Gabriela saw to it they were as spotless as her own costumes, which so bedazzled Modesta and Minervina. The childless marriage of Ignacio and Gabriela was the most stable and the best connected in social terms in the entire town. And even though Bernardo from time to time allowed himself the odd joke about his brother's religiosity, and even though he was eight years older, he felt for him and his opinions a physical, speculative, and deep respect. The result was that each time circumstances led them into conflict, Bernardo could never find any other argument than experience or age. That's how it fell out, for example, two months after their conversation about the Protestant Reformation, when Ignacio Salcedo, beside himself with rage, came to see him and greeted him with twisted, cryptic statement whose meaning eluded Bernardo, a statement that nevertheless, judging by Ignacio's gestures and tone of voice, contained a harsh censure: "Valladolid enjoys itself, and Bernardo Salcedo pays the piper. What do you think of that statement, which I hear every single day, wherever I go?"

Bernardo looked at him suspiciously, blushing lightly: "What's wrong with you? Are you out of your mind? What the devil do you mean by that?"

Ignacio had lost color, and both his hands and his wedding ring were shaking. As far as he could remember, their differences had never reached this level: "I mean that your sweetheart is cheating on you, cheating with the whole city. Everyone's talking about that little fortune hunter."

Suddenly Bernardo seemed to wake up: "How dare you talk to me that way? I could be your second father!"

"I wouldn't have said anything different to my first father, believe me, Bernardo. It isn't the two of us who are at stake here, it's our very name."

"And what's the source of these lying rumors?"

"In chancery, we don't have rumors, Bernardo. You can bank on what's said in chancery. Why don't you test it by visiting that slut at a time you're never at her place? Only after you've proven to yourself that what I'm saying is true will I discuss this disgusting subject with you."

When Bernardo opened the street door, he was already convinced that his brother was telling him the truth. Petra Gregorio had been playing with him since the first day. The logic of the idea grew stronger and stronger. He was far from being a master of amorous adventures, and she was far from being a brilliant student. What they were, simply, was a whore and a cuckold. Her behavior hadn't changed until the first ducats appeared. Later, the change of apartments, her wardrobe, the regal luxury of her new home. Why didn't he ever see that his allowance could never have covered so many excesses? María de las Casas had tricked him, and it was even possible that at this very moment his body was incubating a hideous illness. At the entryway, in the light of the lamp, he looked at the backs of his hands, which were trembling, and touched his cheeks. There were no tumors or hard spots. For the moment he could be calm.

Barely two hours earlier he'd said good-by to Petra, but he turned onto Verdugo street and went to her house. Her sexual depravity, he thought, did not spring up spontaneously, and they certainly didn't derive from recent lessons. His mistress had had a long amorous career before they met. The little girl who sighed again and again on Lucero's back the night he carried her down from the Páramo was not a naive girl but an accomplished actress. What should he do? How would he find her? How should a gentleman react to a trick like that? These were the thoughts that plagued Bernardo in the instant he was putting his key in the lock. Could there be any way of covering up his folly with no risk to his dignity?

He'd gone up the two flights of stairs quickly, and now he was panting on the little landing. But—he tried to calm himself—why believe Ignacio blindly? It was not true that the chancery only spoke proven truths. The chancery made mistakes like everyone else, and he was going to prove it. With a shaking hand, he opened the apartment door. The tentative light from the candles that reached the vestibule came from the back bedroom. Bernardo's slippers made no noise as he walked down the corridor. The growing silence of the house was alarming him more and more, but as he reached Petra's bedroom he spied Miguel Zamora, the lawyer, getting dressed on the rug, his unsteady legs exposed. The bedclothes were all tangled, but Petra wasn't there. Miguel Zamora, with his stockings in his hand, was horrified to see him, and blushed to the roots of his hair—more, it would seem, at being surprised in his underclothes than because of his betrayal: "What are you doing here at this hour, sir?"

"So this is why I lent you my horse, you son of a bitch?"

Miguel Zamora tried to slip his right foot into his stockings but without success. He stammered: "But Salcedo, one thing has nothing to with the other."

Bernardo seized him firmly by his embroidered doublet and raised him slightly off the floor. Zamora, on tiptoe with his hairy legs exposed, offered a grotesque spectacle:"I should kill you right here and now," said Bernardo, bringing his lips to the tip of Zamora's nose.

"Petra isn't your wife. You'd get no mercy from the court."

"But I would get the pleasure of killing you with my own hands, that I would get."

"That would be a punishable act, Salcedo. The law doesn't protect you in such cases."

They were speaking in low voices, inches apart, and when Bernardo derisively released him, he barely whispered, "Filthy shyster." Then more loudly, as he left the bedroom: "Both of us are just poor cuckolds who don't know where to hide our antlers."

He stepped into the hall just as Petra came through the kitchen door. She was carrying a huge silver platter of snacks and was striding along elegantly, but with Bernardo's solemn slap, everything flew noisily into the air, everything, that is, but Petra, who lost her balance and fell to the floor.

"Pack your traps," Bernardo said succinctly. "Tomorrow you're going back to the desert where you were born."

The next day, Dionisio Manrique arranged an interview between María de las Casas and Bernardo over at the warehouse: "You promised me a virgin, and you palmed off a whore on me. Does that sound fair to you?"

María de las Casas went down on her knees. She uselessly tried to kiss the hem of his coat: "I was just as taken in as you were, sir. I swear by everything holy."

She looked up at him imploringly, but Bernardo wasn't moved. He was too resentful: "Listen to me, María de las Casas. If tomorrow—and I hope to God this doesn't happen—I come down with syphilis because of you, I'm going to have you beaten to a pulp, and then I'll have you sent to jail until you rot. Remember, I've got a brother in chancery. Now get out of my sight."

V

ITHOUT knowing it, young Minervina was in conformity with the 1480 Synod of Alcalá de Henares and considered catechism and schooling to be one and the same thing. Her mother in Santovenia, twenty years earlier, also understood that learning to read and write was the equivalent of learning doctrine. Don Nicasio Celemín, the good-natured parish priest, collaborated in this endeavor. Every day at eleven o'clock, he had the church bell rung with an ambiguous intention that the citizens interpreted in their own way: "There's the school bell," some would say, while others, more pious, would give another explanation when they heard the pealing bells: "Don Nicasio is announcing catechism, start moving; it's the second call." In either case, the inhabitants of Santovenia, at the start of the century, identified instruction and indoctrination, and out of all that emerged a generation, of which Minervina was part, for whom speaking with God and learning were one and the same thing.

This idea was so ingrained in her that before Cipriano was seven, she was already setting aside one hour each morning for the boy's religious education. In principle, the child accepted this new idea as a pastime. Locked away in the attic where he slept, sitting at a table placed under the skylight, Minervina would begin the catechism. The first thing she taught him was to cross himself at his head, mouth, and heart, and also how to make the sign of the cross, religious gestures that cost Minervina immense labor twenty years earlier but which offered no difficulty to Cipriano: "You do this and this, and with your fingers you mark the two boards in the cross, do you see that?"

"Yes, the boards in the cross," said the boy smiling.

Cipriano understood the meaning of the sign perfectly, and when the girl told him that the cross he made on his forehead was to drive away evil thoughts, the cross over the mouth to avoid bad words, and the one over the chest to avoid bad desires, he understood, though he still didn't differentiate bad thoughts, bad words, or bad actions from good ones. After the signs of the good Christian, Minervina, following the example of Don Nicasio Celemín, who on the first day of classes had placed a huge stone tablet on a church cloth that said "Chart to Teach the Children to Read." And this he used to teach them prayers: the Our Father, the Holy Mary, the Credo, and the Salve. The girl sang them with the priest again and again as did Cipriano now, but he memorized them with surprising ease. Sometimes he would interrupt her: "I'm tired of this, Mina. Let's go play soldiers."

But she kept him at his lessons: "We've got to do these things even if we don't like them, my love. Without prayer no one can be saved, and Minervina will go to hell if she doesn't help you to save yourself."

She repeated Don Nicasio Celemín's key words, but she was completely certain in that moment that it was her fault if Cipriano didn't learn to pray, and that the child, and she along with him, would end up rotting in the flames of hell. It was a mixture of desire and fear that moved her: Going to heaven, the synthesis of all good things, was the objective, while hell represented for her and, in passing, for the child, eternal suffering, the sum of all evils, a danger to be avoided.

"And if I don't pray, will I go to hell, Mina?"

"Try to understand. You've got to begin by telling good from evil, and once you've done that, you'll be free to do whatever you like."

The child chanted, repeating the phrases Minervina pronounced. He obeyed her because he knew it was for his own good, that she was saving him, that she was doing for him the greatest thing one person could do for another. Even so, one morning, Cipriano, was so wound up in his games that there was no way of distracting him: "Later Mina. Right now I don't want to pray."

That night, he couldn't fall asleep. When he finally did, just before dawn, God the Father appeared to him, hovering above the sky, surrounded by clouds. It was an image he'd seen somewhere, perhaps in some book, but the one he was seeing now had exactly the same features as Bernardo Salcedo: full face, thick and straight beard and hair, a frozen, wounding gaze that for an instant met his own. Cipriano closed his eyes, curled up, and tried to disappear from the world, but Our Lord seized him by an ear and said: "Are you going to tell me, my little gentleman, why you don't want to pray?"

Cipriano woke up in horror. He spied, above him, the starry rectangle of the skylight, but he lacked even the strength to shout. His heart was making noise in his chest, and anguish had take possession of his stomach. He threw himself out of bed, kneeled on the floor, and began to whisper the prayers he'd omitted in the morning. He prayed and prayed until he fell asleep, collapsed against the bed. Minervina found him in that exact position at daybreak, got into bed with him, and warmed his chilled little body. In bits and pieces, the boy told her his experience: "And Our Lord came, but it was Daddy, Mina, and grabbed me by the ear and told me I always had to pray."

"Are you sure Daddy was Our Lord?"

"I'm sure, Mina. He had the same eyes and the same beard."

"And was he very angry?"

"Very angry, Mina. He grabbed me by the ear and called me 'little gentleman.'"

Bernardo did not look askance at the nanny's giving the boy religious instruction. He was surprised at Minervina's education and accepted Don Nicasio Celemín's method as a foundation. Even so, the girl's knowledge was very limited, and time went by without the boy's making much progress. After the ten commandments, Minervina taught him the articles of faith, the enemies of the soul, the theological virtues, and the eight beatitudes, but that was her limit. The "Chart to Teach the Children to Read" went no further, and neither did Don Nicasio Celemin's system of instruction. It was then Bernardo began to develop the idea of a tutor.

At that time, there were good tutors in the town, and the great families entrusted their children to them. Using a tutor supposed almost certain results in didactic terms, but, at the same time, it was also a sign of social distinction that would bring him closer to being a noble, Bernardo's secret lifelong dream. Bernardo knew that beyond the beatitudes, there was a much wider intellectual world that was wildly different from the one he knew: vowels and consonants, the possibility of syllabic union, Latin spelling and syntax. To read in Latin and write in Spanish, he secretly said to himself, that's the right road.

The boy was growing up, and it simply did not seem proper to leave his instruction in the hands of maids, especially when his social position was taken into account. Further down the road was the prospect, so defamed and untouchable, of the calculus tables which, despite the reticence of the era, he wanted Cipriano to learn. A tutor, therefore, was absolutely necessary, but should he live in the house? Bernardo was not in favor of allowing a veteran teacher into his house. The very idea inhibited him, and he feared that his ignorance, barely evident at this point for his brother Ignacio, would be obvious to a teacher who would share meals and after-dinner chats with him. So he reached the conclusion that he would hire a tutor who would come during the morning and leave the house at midday.

The presence of Álvaro Cabeza de Vaca, with his French-style but rather ragged outer robe down to his knees and his tight black stockings terrified Cipriano and did not bedazzle Bernardo. It was easy, nevertheless, to come to an agreement, although for the boy, the idea of moving to the main floor from the attic and exchanging his tiny room for another right next door to his father's, and to separate for the first time from Minervina, constituted a hard blow.

Don Álvaro, lean, severe, with prominent cheekbones and a thin beard, set himself, right on the first day, at a distance from his pupil. Nevertheless, the boy responded rapidly and intelligently, barely allowing his teacher to finish his question. And as long as they were going over the usual elementary subjects, things went along smoothly. Even so, Cipriano, frightened from the first day on, was horrified to see how close his father was, there in the next room. And every time he heard him clear his throat or slide his chair back, he went pale and stood stock still, his head empty, waiting for something to happen. Bernardo's seventeen consecutive sneezes in the first hours of the morning were proverbial. He never restrained himself, so each one was like a small explosion, making objects shake and the very foundation of the house tremble.

The idea that his father was nearby ultimately displaced all other considerations in Cipriano's mind. He lived constantly on the lookout for furtive noises, thick grunts, footsteps, and sneezes. Even when he was relaxing, Cipriano imagined his father's face, his icy stare, his oily beard, his cruel frown. Don Álvaro, nevertheless, did not notice the child's inattentiveness until he finished with the "Chart to Teach the Children to Read." While he felt no ill will toward his tutor, Cipriano resisted going down new paths. It wasn't a matter of refusing to learn: It was materially impossible for Cipriano to listen to the tutor's explanations, to hang his attention on his lips. The boy stared incessantly at his teacher's black calf, but his mind incessantly travelled to the other side of the partition. What was the meaning of Bernardo's authoritarian throat-clearing that he'd just heard? Why did he slide his chair back and stand up? Where was he going? All the fears of his infancy attacked him. Without Minervina at his side, he felt defenseless. In a slightly harsh voice, Don Álvaro droned on without stopping, his eyes deeply sunk behind his cheekbones. "Do you understand what I'm saying, Cipriano?" "Yes, sir."

Don Álvaro then went a bit further until he realized that Cipriano wasn't following him, that the child's mind was stuck on the "Chart to Teach the Children to Read." So, patiently, he started over from the beginning again and again. It was one of two things: either Don Álvaro had a blind faith in his intellectual capacities or the salary he'd agreed on with Bernardo was considerable. The fact is that the fiction prolonged itself for months and months, with Álvaro hoping his pupil would wake up, with Cipriano trying to know what was going on in the next room. So it was that the boy managed to read Latin with some ease, but tripped up when he had to decline nouns. His inability in that area was such that one fine day Don Álvaro, disillusioned, went to see Bernardo after class. The interview was short and pathetic: "We're not getting anything out of this, Don Bernardo. The boy's attention is on something else."

"On what else? The child hasn't known anything else, sir. It would be difficult for him to be focused on something else when he knows nothing else."

"He's just not there. I can't manage to get him to concentrate. That's all there is to it."

Bernardo, dressed to go to the warehouse, was clearly in a bad humor: "What you're suggesting then, sir, is that the boy is stupid."

"Please, Don Bernardo! The boy is as sharp as a tack, but teaching him is useless. He isn't with me, doesn't follow me, is not interested in what I can tell him."

Bernardo had to face facts and admit that the tutor was not the best means to educate his son, the little parricide. There were other solutions, but, spiteful man that he was, he quickly improvised his own: boarding school. A hard boarding school with no vacations. It was time to separate him from his nanny. Bernardo knew that in town there were no educational centers worthy of the name, but his brother Ignacio was the greatest patron of the most famous: the Foundling Hospital, managed by the Guild of Saint Joseph and Our Lady of O, dedicated to educating abandoned children.

The decision pained his brother: "That school is not for people of our class, Bernardo."

Bernardo was now flirting with the idea of teaching the aristocracy a lesson, opening its eyes: "People have spoken highly of it. There are twenty-eight beds for scholarship students, and my son could pay his board along with that of five other students if that's what it takes for the school to open its doors to him."

Ignacio clasped his head in his hands: "The Foundling Hospital survives because of charity, Bernardo. And you know that children abandoned by their parents are not usually recommendable people. It's a serious school because the Deputies of the Guild have worked hard to make it one, and we've hired a competent headmaster. When the bell tolls in the morning for religious instruction, children of all classes come, and some stay for the other lessons, because day students are allowed. Wouldn't it be better if Cipriano were a day student?"

Bernardo shook his head obstinately: "My son needs straightening out. His nanny spoiled him. But that's finished. I'll send him as a boarding student, and he won't even have vacation. But to get him into the Foundling Hospital I need your support. Are you willing to help?"

Intellectually, Ignacio was miles ahead of his brother, but he lacked the personality to dominate him. The next day, he visited the Guild that administered the school, and when he mentioned his brother's generous plan, he found nothing but words of praise, as he did in the deputies' meeting the following Thursday, at which Cipriano's admission was approved. By this means, and through the agreement of paying for the support of his son, supplying three scholarships, and generously donating to the charity fund, Cipriano was admitted into the school.

When she was told, Minervina wept until she had no more tears left, but for the first time, her crying did not spread to the child. His fear of his father outweighed any other argument, and the idea of moving away from his house and living with other boys seemed exciting and desirable. His father's decision not to see him *even in summer* enhanced his desire to distance himself from those piercing eyes that had cast a pall on his childhood. By the same token, the fact that Bernardo had talked about keeping Minervina on in her post gave him some security: His retreat was not irrevocably cut off. The girl again wept at the tannery, on the bank of the river, opposite the school. She kissed and hugged Cipriano several times before letting him escape, carrying a little bundle in each hand, only to disappear through the double doors. It was then she had the sensation she'd lost him forever.

The school building wasn't large, but it did have three big spaces: the chapel, the dormitory, and the play ground. As soon as he entered, Cipriano lost two basic things: his clothes and his name. He stopped wearing the elegant clothing Minervina so carefully laid out for him each week and instead wore the obligatory school uniform, which was of a decidedly rural character: heavy wool underclothes that went below the knee, a coarse overshirt, a short cape in winter, and open, tall sheepskin boots that were tightened around the calf with laces that ended in a bow. The second important thing Cipriano lost entering the school was his name. No one asked him what his name was, but just when the bell was rung summoning the students to religious instruction, a boy, known as the Charger, came over to him and said: "You ring it, Halfpint, you're the new boy."

The Charger was a tall boy with impetigo and disproportionately large hands and feet, whose body listed slightly to the left. He clearly held a preeminent position in the school. Cipriano eagerly shook the bell handle, the bell rang, while Tito Alba, with his round, astonished eyes and short eyelids, asked: "Are you a foundling too, Halfpint?"

"N . . . no."

"Are you poor?"

"N . . . no again."

"Then why the hell are you here?"

"To get an education. My father wants me to be educated like you."

"What an idea! You met the Charger?"

"He was the one who told me to ring the bell."

Cipriano was surprised at the hesitation in his voice when he answered the first questions. Contact with someone he didn't know made him nervous. He felt a strange emotion, a special fear of communicating. But once he overcame his initial resistance, his conversation ran along fluidly without snags. He thought about how he'd never noticed it before and concluded that his small world ended in the kitchen of his father's house and that during his short visits to Santovenia, his dealings with other children consisted of a game of mechanical questions and answers. Since there'd been no need for prior reflection, there'd been no reason for him to stutter.

In religious instruction class, they chanted the prayers, the questions, and the answers of the Hispanolatin catechism in the same monotonous singsong Minervina used, the same one Don Nicasio Celemín, the Santovenia parish priest, had used twenty years earlier. But when Don Lucio, "the Scribe," finished reciting the powers of the soul and asked the group of fifty-six boys if anyone knew the theological virtues, only Cipriano raised his hand: "F . . . faith, hope, and charity."

After religion, the next subject was usually Latin, then writing in Spanish, and the arithmetic tables. The change in Cipriano was strange to observe: his sudden eagerness to widen the horizon of his knowledge, his desire to learn, his growing pleasure in participating in the games his classmates played during recess.

At two-thirty, after eating in the noisy dining room at two large tables presided over from a dais by the Scribe, the foundlings took a walk accompanied by the inevitable tutor. It was a hygienic walk, but evidently the Council of Deputies that governed the school sought something more in that collective exercise. The Scribe made them take notice of street scenes, of what goods were on display, of the activities of the townspeople. He would ask them questions and then clarify their awkward or ambiguous answers: "Clemencio, what do you want to be when you leave this school?"

The Charger didn't hesitate: "A mule skinner."

"Where do mules come from?"

His friends whispered, "from mating donkeys and horses," but the big boy, perhaps because he didn't hear them or perhaps because of his innate urge to take the contrary point of view, instantly answered: "From male and female mules."

"You're going to have to learn something about mules if you really want to become a mule skinner."

They walked quickly, two by two, some draping an arm over a companion's shoulder, others walking apart. The people they passed viewed them with sympathy and whispered: "There go the foundlings." In fact, the townspeople contributed to the maintenance of the school and were very proud of it. The boys marched along Espolón Viejo and entered Espolón Nuevo, adjacent to the Puente Mayor. Once they'd crossed that bridge, they proceeded up to the hill called Cuesta de la Maruquesa, in whose caves and shacks lived very poor people. Along the Villanubla road they saw strings of mules coming down, beggars, and the odd gentleman in a hurry. As they came down from that isolated hill, Tito Alba, his partner in line, dug his elbow into Cipriano's side and said to him in hushed tones: "Look, there goes Charger jerking off again. He's always got to jerk off when we're out for a walk, the pig."

Cipriano stared at both boys innocently: "Wh . . . what is jerking off?" He was looking at Charger, bent over, his right hand shaking under his over shirt, red in the face.

Tito Alba explained. Cipriano paid attention with all his five senses, with a curiosity similar to that which he listened to the words of the Scribe. He was realizing that except for his brief contact with the children of Santovenia, he'd grown up in isolation and had no knowledge of life. Mina, with the best of intentions, had isolated him from the world. They were descending along Corredera de la Plaza Vieja, when the Scribe, who limped slightly on his right leg after only half a league, announced they were going to visit an old comrade of his.

The Guild did not wash its hands of the boys who'd passed

through its halls. In the small gallery on the ground floor of number 16 there was a carpenter's shop. Most of Cipriano's classmates, who knew exactly how far they could stray without getting into trouble, stood in groups around the fountain. The carpenter, with his long scruffy beard, was shaping a length of wood on a hand lathe being turned by a boy of about fifteen years of age. The place smelled of resin and sawdust. The carpenter courteously walked over to the Scribe, and after exchanging a few words with him, had the boy go into his office where he was joined by the Scribe. Through the window clogged by cobwebs it was possible to see a yard full of boards and piled up tree trunks. The teacher sat on the carpenter's stool and spoke to the boy in a low, confidential voice: "Are you behaving yourself, Eliseo?"

"I am, Don Lucio."

"Are you working as hard as you can, are you helping Don Moisés?"

"I think so, sir. He relies on me."

"Are you getting enough to eat?"

Eliseo smiled broadly: "You know me well enough, Don Lucio. I never get enough."

"And your allowance?"

"Always the right amount every Sunday."

"And are you learning? Do you think you're learning?"

"I am, sir. If I stick it out with Don Moisés, I'll be a carpenter in the year '29."

"That soon?"

"That's what he says."

Further along, on Tannery street, near the school, the Scribe visited another ex-student, an apprentice tanner. The street stank violently of dyes and leather. The interview was similar to the first except that in this case the apprentice recited a long list of complaints: He ate badly, his bed clothes were never changed, he was never given the agreed allowance. The Scribe mentally noted everything and said it would all be attended to, that he would speak to the Deputies of the Guild, who held a copy of the contract.

Within two months of entering the school, Cipriano was named alms-raiser for a week. For a school that lived on charity, the mission was arduous and complex. At dawn, Cipriano prepared the school cart; placed Blas, the little ass, between the poles; and set out with the Kid and Claudio, known as the Fatboy, to traverse the town. The Kid had caught Cipriano's attention from the start. He mentioned him to the Fatboy: "Th . . . the Kid has the face of a girl."

"He does have the face of a girl, but the Kid is a good guy."

He knew the city better than either of the other two, and each morning guided the cart from the school to the rear of the Mercy Hospital without the slightest hesitation. Miguel, "the Boy," who guarded the entrance and the morgue knew them well: "No corpses today, boys. You're on vacation," he said in his high pitched little voice.

Or he might say: "One poor man and one condemned man. Will you take both?"

Cipriano slung them over his shoulder effortlessly and tossed them on the bottom of the cart. He did the same with the picks, shovels, sawhorses, and timbers. Claudio, the Fatboy, was surprised at his strength: "You, Halfpint, where you get all that power? I never in my life saw anyone as skinny as you."

Cipriano poked a finger into Fatboy's potbelly: "I . . . if there were strength in fat, you'd be a champion. Look here."

He pulled up the sleeve of his robe and showed is flexed biceps, the well-formed muscle of an athlete.

"Look at the arm on this guy! Did you see that, Kid? This Halfpint's got muscles."

Often, Miguel, the Kid, would gently call them back to business: "Come on, boys. Stop yakking. Today the graves are in the San Juan atrium. Let's get cracking."

The Kid took the reins and the cart, bouncing along, went up to Imperial street, near the Ghetto. As soon as they got there, Cipriano jumped out of the cart, made a mound in the center of the street, and placed the two corpses on top of it. They had a technique, perfected by long practice, to stimulate the charity of the passersby, and Cipriano put it into practice with great skill: "Brothers and sisters: Here you see the bodies of two unfortunates who passed on to a better life without knowing the benefits of friendship. Please don't deny them now the right to holy ground. Our Lord ordered us to be brothers to the poor and the sinful, and only if we see in them Christ Himself will we know tomorrow the gift of glory. Help give a proper burial to these unfortunates."

A few people crossed the street and placed a few *maravedíes* on the plate next to the cart. The three students took turns imploring the citizens to be charitable. Sometimes, as occurred with Cipriano, they interpolated new sentences into the text, original phrases with pathetic effects: "They never knew the love of their fellow men." Or: "They never listened to the voice of the Lord." Or: "They lived abandoned like dogs."

Cipriano intuitively knew that this last sentence, which compared the dead with dogs moved the hearts of women before it touched those of men, and, conversely, that the men were moved most by the idea that the deceased had not had the chance to hear the voice of the Lord. From time to time, the Kid, Claudio, the Fatboy, and Cipriano, lined up behind the cart, would each add the litanies for the dead. Claudio, the Fatboy, would sing them and the other two would chime in with the responses:

*"Sancta Maria . . ."*
*"Ora pro nobis."*
*"Sancta Virgo Virginum."*
*"Ora pro nobis."*
*"Sancte Michael."*
*"Ora pro nobis."*

When they finished, they would stand silently for a time, line up behind the mound. If by chance Cipriano saw a group of women approaching, he would use his ventriloquist's voice and exclaim: "Brothers and sisters, some charity for these unfortunates who never knew the honey of friendship and lived abandoned like dogs."

The women immediately left off gossiping and deposited some well-worn coins on the plate. Seeing that, Claudio, the Fatboy, stimulated by the donation, would again start the chant: "Brothers and sisters, some charity for these unfortunates."

After a long hour in the first place, Cipriano would again place the corpses in the cart and, led by the Kid, they would set up the mound in Huelgas, Zurradores, and Espolón Vijo streets, where they would repeat the same ritual. At the end, they would bury the dead at the church indicated by the dwarf Miguel and, back at the school, would deposit the donations in the Charity Box.

The alms-raisers would finish their day well after nightfall, when the bells were rung for All Souls. The slow, melancholy tolling set all the bells of the city into motion, the time the faithful called "the hour of the dead."

Cipriano would usually fall into bed dead tired. The dormitory, a long room with two rows of narrow beds on each side, was lighted by a candle the Scribe would extinguish before going off to bed himself. The curtainless windows let in a milky glow from the river. And in winter, the cold was so intense that Claudio, the Fatboy, swore that when he awakened he had frost on his eyebrows. Except for the occasional howl from the Charger, the students went to bed so tired that once they'd put on their white nightgowns they would fall asleep the instant they were in bed. It was, therefore, with some surprise that Cipriano, on his last night as alms-raiser, heard a buzz at one end of the dormitory that was transmitted from bed to bed like some password: "Kid, the Charger needs you."

He heard Claudio, the Fatboy, sit up and repeat the message: "Kid, the Charger needs you."

A shadow crossed the dim clarity of the windows, heading toward the first whisper. Then in the corner the mattress on Charger's bed groaned, while all over the large room there were whispers and low laughs. After a while, the shadow again crossed the dormitory in the opposite direction, and everything was left in silence.

The next morning, Cipriano asked Tito Alba what the Charger was doing with the Kid in the dormitory. Tito stared at him with his saucer-shaped eyes: "Halfpint, are you from another world or are you just faking?" He wouldn't say another word, so Cipriano went to Claudio, the Fatboy: "You can figure it out for yourself. When the need comes over him, the Charger asks for the Kid. He's the boy most like a girl that we have in the school."

José, the Hick, gave him the rest of the information he needed. The Hick came from Tierra de Pinares and didn't know how to dissimulate his country nature or his stupidity. He was a primitive but open being who had trouble remembering the prayers and who could barely write four words of Spanish dictation. But as a friend, he was frank and informative.

Cipriano asked him why the Kid put up with the Charger's abuses. The Hick's face said everything: "He gives the orders. Haven't you noticed that after the Scribe, it's the Charger who says what goes here?"

During Latin class, the rumor circulated that the next day they wouldn't have religious instruction class because there was to be a funeral. The prayers of the foundlings were highly esteemed in the town. Their voices, now that they'd lost their childish tone but were yet to take on their adult pitch, had been well harmonized by the Scribe and constituted a desirable passport for many citizens on their deathbeds. Often, the final disposition of wills required the presence of the schoolboys at a funeral, for which they received contributions. And the uniformed boys, their sheepskin boots clean, lined up in two rows, all holding torches in their hands, accompanied the deceased to his final resting place.

This was the case at the funeral of a gentleman named Don Tomás de la Colina, whose testament begged the foundlings for their prayers in exchange for a fat purse destined for the school. The Scribe told the boys about the dead man's generous gift and urged them to behave with enthusiasm and propriety during the service. With a contrite air and with their torches lit, the boys accompanied the corpse, fervently listening to the psalmody of the clerics: the *Miserere* and the *De Profundis*. Once in the church, gathered around the body, they attended the funeral, and, when the epistle had been read, the Scribe raised his baton, and gave them the key to begin the *Dies irae:*

> *Dies irae, dies illa,*
> *Solvet saeclum in favilla:*
> *Teste David cum Sibylla.*
> *Quantus tremor est futurus,*
> *Quando Judex est venturus,*
> *Cuncta stricte discussurus!*
> *Per sepulcra regionum,*
> *Coget omnes ante thronum.*

When mass was over, as those gathered moved to the graveside, the boys, from the presbytery, intoned the intercession litanies of All Saints, guided by the nicely-toned voice of Tito Alba:

*Sancte Petre.*
*Ora pro nobis.*
*Sancte Paule.*
*Ora pro nobis.*
*Sancte Andrea.*
*Ora pro nobis.*
*Sancte Joannes.*
*Ora pro nobis.*
*Omnes Sancti Apostoli et Evangelistae.*
*Orate pro nobis.*

Those present then offered their condolences to the bereaved, while the foundlings finished their litany. In the church, there was a heavy stench, a mix of the sweat of the faithful and a whiff of the putrefaction of those buried there. But above all, the contralto voice of Tito Alba rang out:

*Ut omnibus benefactoribus nostris sempiterna bona retribuas.*
*Te rogamos audi nos.*
*Ut frutus terrae dare, et conservare digneris.*
*Te rogamos audi nos.*
*Ut omnibus fidelibus defunctis requiem aeternam donare*
    *digneris.*
*Te rogamos audi nos.*
*Ut nos exaudire digneris.*
*Te rogamos audi nos.*

The chanting of the students ended, and as a climax, the chorus and the sacristans intoned the final response:

*Libera me Domine de more aeterna, in die illa tremenda,*
*quando movendi sunt coeli et terra, dum veneris judicare*
*saeculum per ignen.*

Standing at the altar, the foundlings bowed deeply to Don Tomás de la Colina's relations before filing out of the church, one by one, carrying their torches over their heads. Cipriano didn't notice his uncle

Ignacio until he came to his side and felt his hand on his shoulder. The contact made him shudder. For him, Ignacio was a mute relative who never dared face his brother's eyes. He was affable, but nothing decisive was to be expected of him. Nevertheless, he did notice the exchange of glances between his uncle and the Scribe. And when his classmates extinguished their torches and formed ranks to return to the school, Cipriano followed them at a distance in the company of his uncle. Ignacio bent over him slightly: "Are you happy at the school? Do you like studying?"

Cipriano nodded silently to avoid stuttering. He saw no reason to confide in his uncle, who was in all likelihood sent by his father. Ignacio's voice became even more unctuous: "I don't know if you know that I preside over the board of trustees that administers the school and that I'm a member of the guild to which it belongs."

"Th . . . that's what people say, yes sir."

"But you don't know that in the last meeting of the Commission of Deputies I was given favorable reports about you. Top student in religious instruction, Latin, and writing, notable in arithmetic. Can you do better?"

The boy shrugged his shoulders. His uncle went on: "All that is important, Cipriano. Given your performance, I see no proper course of action except to speak with your father and describe the situation to him. Would you like to leave the school and return home?"

Ignacio was taken aback by the boy's decisiveness: "No. I like the school. I have friends here."

"That's what worries me, my boy. You schoolmates are boys without parents, without manners, without any proper upbringing. Besides, you already know what comes next. Another two years in class, and then you start working in the job you choose until you die. That's your future."

"But I can also enter the Parish Grammar School. It all depends on my record."

"That's quite true, Cipriano. I see you're well informed. And don't forget the Latin Center if you decide to become a priest. Would you like that?"

The boy waved his dead torch around a bit and then used it as a cane. First he shook his head and then said clearly:

"No."

"What about a law degree? You've got a good mind, you've learned Latin syntax, you write Spanish perfectly well . . . You could turn out to be a good lawyer one fine day. Your father will leave you a fortune and you will also inherit mine. But money must be ennobled. Money in itself is of no importance and even less so if it's money you haven't earned yourself."

They had emerged from Puerta del Campo and were walking down toward the new Tanneries neighborhood at the end of which stood the school. There was a stench of leather and dye and, between the city wall and the neighborhood, it was possible to see the Pisuerga river, swollen with rain. Cipriano looked up and contemplated the ruddy, hairless skin of his uncle, his uncertain eyes fixed on him.

"I don't know," he said at last. "There's a lot of time left. I'll have to think it over."

"That's fine. It's not wise to rush, but you should consider things carefully. Two years pass quickly, before you think about it, and when that time comes it would be good for you to have made a decision."

"One thing I will ask of you, Cipriano. Your father must not find out about our meeting or our conversation. He must not know anything about this. Does he write you?"

"No."

Ignacio hesitated before saying good-by. Cipriano was no longer a boy to be kissed; besides, for the boy he was almost a stranger. He clasped him by the shoulders, bowed a bit, then straightened up, released him, and held out his ring-covered hand. He'd changed his mind: "Good-by, Cipriano. Keep to your books. Take full advantage of Don Lucio's words. He's a great teacher. You'll never be sorry you did."

# VI

⚜

I N August, and for the second consecutive year since his arrival at the
school, Cipriano participated in the Ceremony of the Threshing Floor
along with two fellow students and two members of the Most Holy
Trinity Guild. The class, divided into groups, would visit the threshing
floors around the city and ask God for "a dense crop of sprouts and abundant grain." The boys enjoyed their contact with the peasants, threshing,
urging the mules on, riding young donkeys, and drinking from earthenware pitchers. Once the ritual Pater Noster and the litanies were sung,
the peasants gave the boys some sacks of grain, which they deposited in
the Charity Box back at the school. The next day, they transformed the
grain into cash in the market. Cipriano, along with Tito Alba and a new
classmate nicknamed Beggarbread, were just a bit below the group that
threshed most, but he was still praised by the Scribe when class began.

It was at about this time that Cipriano began to have qualms of
conscience. He paid close attention in doctrine and religion classes,
but he never derived spiritual tranquility from his efforts. Not only
that, he was of the opinion that his religious education left a great deal
to be desired. Father Arnaldo spoke to the students about oral and
mental prayer. He favored oral prayer, as long as the concentration of
the person who prayed was total. We must not leave Our Lord alone,
Father Arnaldo would say. You can use recess to pay Him a visit. Cipriano
began to visit the chapel during recess. It was an old custom that some
students observed. What Cipriano enjoyed was the emptiness and
silence of the chapel, barely touched by the noise of his classmates out
in the school yard.

Kneeling on the wooden rail, Cipriano obsessively made two prayers: One was for Minervina and the other concerned his future, his life after school. While he prayed, he was serene. It was when he walked out and took holy water from the small font at the door of the chapel when the doubts would well up in him: As he prayed and made the sign of the cross, was he thinking about the sacrifice of Our Lord or was he thinking about the pair of stilts waiting for him in the school yard? His doubts became deeper and deeper and more corrosive. If he set them aside to play, his scruples would not stop bothering him for the rest of the morning. So he decided to go back to the chapel and make the sign of the cross with holy water, very slowly, thinking about what he was doing. But even that gesture failed to calm him. When he went out onto the playground, the doubts about his concentration again came back, so he returned once again to the chapel to use the holy water and to make the sign of the cross slowly, pausing fervently in each of the four essential movements. But, always in accord with the sermons of Father Arnaldo, he reached the conclusion that his requests were inevitably egotistic: He was praying on his own behalf, to solve the problems of his future life and praying for the sake of Minervina, the only being he loved in the entire world.

So he decided to pray as well for the Charger, for him to stop masturbating during their walks, for him to stop forcing the Kid to visit his bed whenever he needed him. He prayed for Tito Alba, for whom he was beginning to feel some affection. Slowly but surely, he added prayers (for the Hick, so his understanding would open to knowledge; for the Scribe, so he would know how to guide the boys wisely; or for Eliseo, the former student working at the Tannery, so his master would conform with the terms of the contract) to the point that his visits to the chapel began to last as long as recess. The result was that Cipriano found no time to let off steam, and on Saturday, in his meetings with Father Toval, who confessed the boys using two face-to-face prie-dieus, covering his face and that of the boy confessing with immaculate white handkerchiefs, he recognized that his prayers to Our Lord were still egotistic for the simple reason that he was not seeking the peace or happiness of his classmates but the tranquility of his own conscience.

Father Toval urged him to persevere, to think less about himself and the causes that moved his acts. Then, one fine day, to help him, he tested Cipriano using the ten commandments. When he reached the fourth, to honor father and mother, Cipriano told the priest that his mother had died giving birth to him and that he hated his father with all his might. Here the confessor found serious matter indeed, and even though Cipriano told him about his father's terrible stare and how he'd mistreated his only son, the priest could not justify his aversion for his father. "Our father engendered us: For that reason, if for none other, he deserves our esteem. How could we love Our Lord in heaven if we didn't love our father on earth?" Cipriano's vague scruples now came into sharper focus: It wasn't so much for the Charger he had to pray but for his father and for his own feelings toward his father.

He left confession with his ears burning and in a state of bewilderment. Thereafter, he would refer to his father during his recess visits to the chapel but only mechanically, not out of love but because Father Toval had told him to do so. His scruples hardened: I can't love and hate the same person at the same time, he told himself. Whenever he thought about his father, he saw his wicked, wounding gaze and understood that it was meaningless to pray for him. He stopped taking communion. His friend Tito Alba noticed the change in him and on a walk through town asked him why. "Ha . . . hating is sinful, isn't that true, Tito?" "Yes it is." "And hating your father is an even more serious sin, correct?" Tito Alba shrugged his shoulders: "I don't know what a father is." "What can I do if hatred wells up in my heart just thinking about him?" "Well," said Tito, "pray for that not to happen." "But if in spite of all that it does happen and I can't fix it, will I burn in hell only because I hate my father and can't love him?" Tito Alba was at a loss for words. His saucer-like eyes with their short lids were warm and gentle, unlike Don Bernardo's. He whispered: "Speak with Father Toval." Cipriano instantly answered: "I do, every Saturday." Tito Alba was overwhelmed by his friend's pain. He found relief in looking at the two classmates directly ahead of them: "Look, he said, there goes that filthy pig Charger jerking off again. You should pray for him." Cipriano waved his hand in the air: "But you just can't take on all the sins of the world, all its filth, isn't that right?"

Father Toval also noticed Cipriano's bewilderment. They spoke about sins that produced no pleasure and only pain, like hatred or envy.

Father Toval even went so far as to tell him to offer the disgust he felt because of his hate to God as an expiation, but he failed to convince the boy. "I . . . it would be like fooling myself, father. I'd be tricking myself and tricking God. Offering him my hatred would mean debasing myself."

Cipriano's third year at school was disturbing for him. Despite his good relations with most of the students, and in spite of how much he was learning in class, he did not feel satisfied. And it wasn't just his conscience that was weighing him down. Human injustice began to torment him, the fact that his father could pay the scholarship of three students who, in adddition to being pour, had no idea who their fathers were, just so he could study; the fact that the Kid had to come when Charger called him even if he didn't want to and had to accept being periodically humiliated because he had no power; the fact that his flesh was beginning to awaken and that he noted a strange force transforming his body, whose demands were taking control of his will. It was then that he began to understand the Charger, even though he detested the violence he used on the Kid in order to satisfy himself. These new thoughts changed his character. He felt attacks of agressivity and lived in permanent unhappiness with himself. Sometimes he surprised himself by taking on the role of protector, a role no one would attribute to him, as he did the night when he stopped the Kid in the halflight of the dormitory as he submissively answered the Charger's summons: "Charger, the Kid's not coming to you tonight."

There was a huge commotion at the other end of the dormitory. By the faint light that rose from the river, Cipriano spied the Charger in his nightshirt running between the two rows of beds. He jumped into Cipriano's bed, and the boy could smell his savage breath, hear his curses, feel his virile hardness and his outsized arms clasping him. With great serenity, Cipriano bent his leg, slammed his knee into the Charger's testicles, and pushed him so hard he ejected him from the bed. For a few minutes they all heard the Charger howling like a beaten dog. The dormitory was possessed by a palpable tension. Slowly, the Charger stood up and, holding his stomach in his hands, said, "Tomorrow during recess I'll find you on the playground."

It was on the playground, at the corner it formed with the school, away from prying eyes, where fights between students were settled. A challenge would gather the entire student body around the fighters. This was the first time the Charger had ever fought in the school. No one had ever dared face up to him before. But the attitude of the two fighters that morning was different. The Charger tried to grab Cipriano by the neck in his long, ungainly arms and throw him to the ground, but the smaller boy waited at a distance, not letting him approach. Cipriano's advantage was his speed. As soon as the Charger raised an arm, Halfpint's little fists, as hard as stones, landed three times on his adversary's nose. The students observed the fight in silence, with only the occasional comment: "Do you see how hard Halfpint hits?" And Claudio, the Fatboy, tried to explain to all of them, one at a time, that Halfpint carried the dead from the Mercy Hospital without anyone's help and had muscles of steel.

Cipriano again landed a right on the Charger's stupid face and his nose began to bleed. The Fatboy again repeated that Halfpint was very strong, while Cipriano danced around the gangling boy, ducking every time he tried to grab him by the neck. The Charger withstood another pair of punches. After a while, it was like watching the unequal struggle between David and Goliath. And David was that small boy, short for his age, but with astonishing agility and the hardness of marble.

The Charger's smock was covered with blood, and between his teeth he tried to provoke his rival, calling him a dwarf and a little bastard, but Halfpint wouldn't fall into the trap, would not throw himself blindly on his rival, and kept his distance. His fists were like the annoying bites of an insect that saps the morale of his victim. And after five minutes, when the Charger dropped his guard and attacked openly, convinced he was fighting a weakling, Cipriano met him with a punch to his right cheek that made him stagger. With the next punch, the Charger went down on one knee, but, ashamed at his own weakness, he got right back up and stuck out his right arm, again trying to catch his enemy. Cipriano dodged him, stepping back just in time, and when the Charger stumbled after his failed effort, he landed two more punches on the Charger's nose. This time the big boy stood back trying to stop the blood with both hands. No one spoke, but since the Charger did not seem to want to start fighting again, Tito Alba stepped in and said: "Charger, go change your smock before the Scribe sees you."

He walked him to the dormitory while Cipriano cleaned himself up. He saw the Charger walk off, helped by Tito Alba, and then his classmates surrounded him, asking him about his strength, feeling his muscle, and he raised the leg of his underwear, stretched his leg, and showed the muscles in his thighs, as tense and taut as cables.

The next Saturday, Halfpint confessed his sin: "Father, I beat a boy until he bled."

"How is that possible, my son? Don't you know that even the most contemptible man is the living temple of the Holy Spirit?"

"He offended the others, father. He's a killer."

"And who is that boy? Is he a student?"

"I must not say anything else."

In the next religious instruction class, Father Arnaldo talked about his work as a teacher and about the obligation of the students to absorb his teachings in order that they might some day help some fellow human being who'd gone astray. They were more or less the same words Minervina had used when she taught Cipriano to pray: "If you go to hell because you don't know things, dearest, I'll go to hell for not having taught you." Those were, twenty years later, the same words used by Don Nicasio Celemín in Santovenia. When he heard Father Arnaldo's admonition, he thought of the Charger, forgot his hatred for his father, and his mind was occupied by the tremendous loneliness of his classmate. No one liked him. He decided to wait for the right moment, approach him as a friend, and try to help him. And one day, during the routine walk, he asked the Hick to walk with Tito Alba and leave the Charger to him.

"What do you want now?"

"To talk to you, Charger. To ask you to forgive me for the other day. I didn't want to hurt you."

"And what do I matter to you? You can move on now!"

"All people matter to me, Charger. We should try to help one another."

Two young women, both carrying shopping baskets, passed through the double file of boys. The Charger took careful note of them and turned his face shamelessly to stare at them from the rear, to stare at their undulating backsides. Then he turned to Cipriano: "Know what I say to you, Halfpint?"

"What?" asked Cipriano, his hopes high.

"Shove it up your ass. I want to jerk off."

Cipriano slowed down, lagging behind the Charger. But even so, he said timidly: "I'll come talk to you again, Charger. If you need me some day, just call me."

The next week the town was crowded with priests; secular and regular; canons; and bishops. The first day, forty or fifty arrived, the next one hundred and sixty, and they continued arriving at that rate until their number reached fifteen hundred. The first meeting to take place between the foundlings and the clerics was talked about for years. The students kept up the pious custom of kissing the hands that consecrated the host as a sign of respect, but on that occasion there were so many hands to kiss and so many lips trying to do just that that there was a traffic jam on Santiago Street that took a long while to clear. Once the boys were back in the school, the Scribe praised their attitude but begged them earnestly to omit those shows of respect as long as the Conference lasted.

That was the hundredth time they'd heard the Conference mentioned. The Conference was the topic of the day. Observing the large groups of clerics who fluttered about everywhere, passersby would say: "They're on their way to the Conference," or "They're coming from the Conference." That was self-evident. And in truth there were so many meetings and the number of committees was so large, that the bands of clerics striding along the streets at all hours had to be part of the to-ing an fro-ing involved in the Conference. For months, the Conference was the only news item. Three was no more room, not even for one more priest, in any of the monasteries in and around the town.

The theological controversies generated in San Pablo, San Benito, or San Gregorio stretched out until late at night, or as the townspeople put it, never ended. The arguments in the Plaza del Mercado between peasants and artisans became heated easily. And at the center of all that polemicizing and argument, all the chatter and hubbub, was the controversial figure of Erasmus of Rotterdam, an angel for some, a demon for the others. Erasmus's writings had divided the Christian world, and, logically, because of the Conference, two sides formed in the town: erasmists and antierasmists. But this division manifested itself not only in schools and convents but in all the institutions, industries, businesses, and families in the city—wherever more than two people congregated.

The Foundling Hospital was not exempt from this schism, and it appeared not only among the teachers but among the students as well. Although they all took exquisite care not to show their predilections, it was common knowledge that Father Arnaldo was antierasmist and Father Toval erasmist. The first said: "Luther was nurtured at the breasts of Erasmus," that without him, the world wouldn't find itself in its current mess. Father Toval on the other hand asserted that Erasmus of Rotterdam was exactly the reformer the Church needed. But there was never the slightest friction between the two. They carried out their tasks with the same zeal as ever, but they never argued face to face. This difference of opinion about Erasmus's ideas, which divided the adults, ultimately replicated itself among the students, who a week earlier didn't know Erasmus existed. But during the Conference, it seemed Fathers Arnaldo and Toval were those delegated to bring the latest news about it to the school, each discreetly arguing his own position.

"The antierasmists have put spies in the book shops so they can accuse the readers of being heretics."

"At the Conference Virués said that both the inquisitor Manrique and the Emperor are on the side of Erasmus."

The town, the setting of the Conference, was divided; the townspeople argued, and became angry, and, in the Plaza del Mercado, next to the vegetable stands, alongside the space where they conducted their arguments, other meeting places sprang up, filled with wildly gesturing, excited intellectuals. The Court, temporarily lodged in the city, made the erasmists feel protected. On their afternoon walks, the foundlings crossed paths with groups of priests, large groups commenting the events of the Conference in raised voices, carrying the controversies along with them right out into the street. One morning, Father Arnaldo imprudently asked the students to pray for the conversion of Erasmus. The erasmists protested, and Father Arnaldo changed the objective of the prayer: "that Our Lord illuminate all those participating in the Conference."

Cipriano, instinctively sympathetic to Erasmus, took an active part in his defense. Leaving the chapel, Claudio the Fatboy asked him: "Who is this Erasmus?"

"A theologian, a writer who thinks the Church should be reformed."

At the other end of the playground, the Hick was screaming: "Burn Erasmus at the stake!" In general, the antierasmus theses all hinged on the idea that without Erasmus there would be no Luther.

Halfway through the Conference, the foundlings believed the erasmists were winning and that their adversaries, Master Margalho, Brother Franciso del Castillo, and Brother Antonio de Guevara, were in full retreat. A few days later, Father Arnaldo announced that divorce was being discussed, that Erasmus defended it, and that both the Conference and the people had lined up on his side. But then Master Ciruelo leapt into the argument; he was a man who, for his point of view and for his name, which meant "cherry tree," had become popular, saying that he admitted Erasmus of Rotterdam had made some mistakes but that his books, all in all, had helped to illuminate the four gospels and the Apostles's epistles. A war was brewing at the Conference, and the town seemed like an enormous sounding board. Erasmus's principal adversaries were the religious orders, which he had ridiculed in his *Enchiridion*. Merely reading it made the monks see red, and protests from their pulpits proliferated, with the result that with each passing day the agitation of the people grew more intense, until they demanded that Erasmus's works be burned. The dispute reached the level of violence when Master Margalho one morning complained that Virués was in contact with Erasmus and that he sent him daily letters about the status of the Conference. Virués defended his right to communicate with the Dutch theologian who was the subject of this controversy. And because of that honest statement, tempers flared.

Among the students, the two sides came to blows one morning during recess when each group cursed the other, demanding that either Erasmus or his enemies be burned at the stake. The fight was very violent, and three students had to be taken to the infirmary with head wounds. Father Arnaldo and the Scribe lectured the boys the next day on respect for and understanding of their fellow men and gave them a thorough dressing down. The general impression, however, was that the controversy was tilting in Erasmus's favor and against Luther, and that this result was satisfactory to the Pope and the Emperor. And when the erasmists, especially Carranza de Miranda, brilliantly refuted the proposition made by the monks on the subject of free will and indulgences, basing their opposition on the work of Erasmus, on the Bible, and the texts of the Holy Fathers, the argument was settled.

At the same time the Conference was going on, Valladolid was horrified by a concern of another kind: A servant of the marshall of Frómista was passing through, and he suffered from the swollen glands typical of plague. It was indeed plague, and he infected three of the marshall's maids, all young, and the four died within a few days. Simultaneously, health officials reported a man sick with plague in Herrera de Duero and a woman in Dueñas. A few hours later, there were bonfires on the street corners burning thyme, rosemary, and red lavender to sanitize the area. Even so, people started walking around handkerchiefs tied over their mouths. The Council named a special committee to gather information about the health status of the city and the surrounding towns and appropriated the money raised through the wine and bread tax to organize defenses against the sickness. Then they published a proclamation read by all the town criers requiring cleanliness in the streets, prohibiting the consumption of melons, gourds, and cucumbers ("easily contaminated by malignant exhalations"). Their next step was to organize a system of medical attention, pharmacies, and food for the poor, since hunger helped the spread of contagion.

The rich hurriedly gathered their effects and valuable objects and furtively abandoned the town by night in their carriages. They went to their riverside country houses to wait for the epidemic to pass. The plague had come again: the city prepared for a long siege, and a papal brief from Clement VII closed *sine dia* the famous Conference after its various months of debate. At the same time, the Court moved to Palencia and the chancery to Olmedo. At first, the instances of plague in Valladolid were few in number: six dead. The Special Committee, in order not to spread alarm, reported that six people dying of plague was "an insignificant figure," that this epidemic must be of another kind because "plague always killed many people." Others recalled the high number of people who came down with measles over the course of the past fortnight, and from that fact drew their own conclusions: It wasn't plague but measles that people were suffering, although measles were always a prelude to plague.

In fact, the sickness was growing stronger and extending quickly. There were not enough doctors to attend to so many victims, just as there were not enough priests to provide them with spiritual attention. The dead, piled on carts, were driven to the cemeteries near churches to be buried. The Council opened four new hospitals on the right bank of the Pisuerga, two of them, San Lázaro and the Homeless, for those seriously ill. They also mobilized active forces, among them the students at the Foundling Hospital. The boys were practically children, barely adolescents, but their legal status made them exempt from any family protests. It was during the hardest days of the epidemic that the students carried out their most selfless tasks—burying the dead, moving the ill, making sure the town was isolated, regulating traffic on bridges, and quarantining buildings where there were many victims of plague. The students themselves nailed up signs to seal the doors of infected houses, and Cipriano specialized in the delicate job of pushing apart the tiles on roofs to drop food to those locked within. With the school cart, pulled by Blas, the diminutive ass, Cipriano went from one place to another, distributing sacks of food among those in need or regulating the barges from Herrera de Duero, the source of many immigrants from the south. The boy interrogated these people about where they'd been and the health conditions in the towns they'd passed through, after which Cipriano immediately dispatched them to detention centers on the other side of the river.

A few months later, temperatures fell and people breathed a sigh of relief. It was commonly believed that plague was the result of heat, and that cold and rain lessened its effects. A few days later, the temperature went up and the plague reappeared in the towns and cities of Castile. During this second wave, people began to talk about the plague of the year 1506, more serious than the one in 1518. The banker Domenico Nelli calmed his colleagues in Medina, telling them that in general those who died from plague were poor and, therefore, devoid of interest. But others insisted that the plague could remain dormant, like the one in 1506. It was worse than the 1518 plague, they asserted.

Then they began to organize prayers in the churches of San Roque and of the Virgin of San Llorente to ask for the autumn rains.

Instead of shrinking, the poor population increased, and the city council was forced to take two radical measures: first, they separated the drifters from the merely poverty stricken and expel the vagabonds, and, second, they required all prostitutes not born in Valladolid to leave. But the expulsion of social groups was no solution. To the contrary, the immigrants began to outnumber the emigrants, and the council found itself having to provide lodging for them on the other side of the river. But the avalanche of needy people grew and the plague spread further, with the result that the mayor instantly sent all the healthy poor to the other side of the bridge. It was his intention to have some of gentlemen council members expel them after providing them with sufficient food for the journey. But the poor refused to gather at the bridge. In town, they were receiving free medication, half a pound of lamb, and half a pound of bread per person, per day, and no one could guarantee them that kind of help in the neighboring towns. Besides, they had no idea what the sanitary situation was in those places. So they hid in the corners of the Paseo del Prado, and at night, with some of the inhabitants of the quarantines, they would cross the Pisuerga in boats, by swimming, or by fords they knew, where they could then wade across and avoid the town wall.

Cipriano and the foundlings redoubled their efforts to help their fellow citizens. At times, if there were no urgent tasks to tend to, they lit bonfires of thyme, rosemary, and red lavender to counter the noxious emanations and continued feeding those quarantined in their homes through holes in their roofs. Sometimes, a sick person in a sealed house would die, and it would be necessary to open the doors to bring out the dead for burial.

It was during the days of the final phase of the epidemic when Cipriano's uncle Ignacio appeared at the school. He'd come to say good-bye, before moving to Olmedo with the chancery. Halfway through their talk, he revealed that Bernardo was gravely ill. Days ago, he'd come down with plague even though he always thought the disease only attacked the poor. From childhood, Bernardo had always had a horror of disgusting diseases, and now he was suffering this one in its most virulent form, his body covered by open, running sores, the kind common during the plague of 1506. There was nothing Ignacio could do but leave him in the care of the maids and Doctor Benito Huidobro. He wasn't going to ask Cipriano to visit him, first out of fear for the boy's safety and second in order not to humiliate his brother. However, he did ask him to be one of the company of foundlings accompanying his brother to his grave, if in fact he died. When it was time to leave, Ignacio hesitated as he did the previous time and ended up shaking Cipriano's hand, giving him pats on the shoulder, and telling him that, should his brother pass away, they would speak about his future education.

Cipriano was not saddened by the news. He felt not the slightest spark of love for his father. At the same time, his routine was so demanding he barely had a moment to think about him. The drought continued—it hadn't rained for almost a year—and lately the authorities had taken to burning the houses most affected after carting the inhabitants off to hospitals outside the city. Nine months after beginning their participation in the emergency, the foundlings suffered two losses: Tito Alba and Beggarbread. It was Cipriano himself who brought them in the school cart to the Mercy Hospital. He wept as he whipped the mule. Tito Alba died a week later, and Beggarbread during the first days of the next month.

Sometime between Tito Alba and Beggarbread, Bernardo Salcedo gave up the ghost. Cipriano put on his least shabby smock and cape and gathered with his schoolmates at the entryway to Corredera de San Pablo 5. He himself helped Juan Dueñas put the corpse in the coach and later to put it in the winding sheet. Then he accompanied his father in silence, with his torch ablaze, listening to the chanting of the chorus. Immediately after, in the church, he witnessed the funeral, and the sacristans began the last response: *Libera me, Domine, de morte aeterna . . .*

It was then he spied Minervina kneeling and tried to go over to her. But the Scribe made him walk out to stand next to the grave, where the boys were to intone the litany of the Saints. By the end, Minervina had left, and the Scribe ceremoniously shook his hand and said: "On my behalf and on the behalf of all your schoolmates, we express our deepest sympathy."

The feverish activity and the chores did not allow Cipriano to reflect on being an orphan. Back at the school, he was ordered to

Herrera de Duero to find a group of refugees. They spoke about seeing corpses in gardens and in ditches along the road, about the lack of doctors in the small towns, where the sick were taken care of by amateur healers and barbers, if not by their neighbors. It was everyday reality.

So many long months had passed since the epidemic began that the people of Valladolid came to think about the possibility of a permanent plague. They saw no way out. The months went by without there being any encouraging news from the Special Committee, while the figures related to the dead were repeated over and over again. Unexpectedly, at the outset of the new autumn, after an awful harvest and harsh weather, the Special Committee announced that in the preceding month only twenty persons had died out of the two thousand in the hospitals. In November, there were only twelve, with 493 the number discharged from the hospitals. It was like coming out from under a dark cloud after a year and a half without seeing the sun. People began to appear on the streets in order to breath the aromas of thyme and red lavender and ventilate their lungs. They came to Espolón Nuevo once again to chat and laugh. The miracle had taken place! And when, in January, the number of patients released from the hospitals reached 843 and the deaths from plague fell to 2, the town exploded in joy. Processions to the hermitage of San Roque were organized, and the Council announced that in spring there would be jousting and bullfights. The plague was over.

On a holiday during the spring, Uncle Ignacio appeared at the school. His skin, because of life in town, was even redder than usual. The first words out of his mouth were a compliment: He congratulated Cipriano for what he'd done during the plague. Among the medals awarded by the town council, there was one for the students at the Foundling Hospital. That was his only reference to the past. He instantly began speaking about Cipriano's future. The boy accepted the idea of a doctorate in Law and also the idea of living with his uncle and aunt until he was of age and could come into possession of his property. He did not, however, accept the idea of being adopted by his uncle. His estrangement from the human race, his sad experience as a son inclined him to the idea of his uncle's being his guardian. Ignacio then told him that as soon as the chancery returned to Valladolid, he would come for him at the school, that because of his important position he'd resolved the bureaucratic mess beforehand.

His uncle's house, his aunt Gabriela, the maids, and family life constituted a not especially comforting innovation for Cipriano. He missed his classmates, their walks, the classes, the games, the talk, the habits he'd acquired. Being told he would have a tutor, Don Gabriel de Salas, did not improve the situation. The memory of his first tutor back in his father's house, his phobia about who lurked on the other side of the wall, all came back automatically. Gabriela bent over backwards to attend to his needs, to make his life more agreeable. Following her own acute female instincts, she asked one day if he didn't miss Minervina. Cipriano said he did. The absence of Minervina, the only person he'd ever loved, the one in whom he'd always found a refuge, made his return home even emptier.

At the same time, getting to know his uncle's house raised Cipriano's spirits. It wasn't, as anyone might have thought, the pretentious house of a grand bourgeois, but the attractive and serene refuge of an intellectual. Cipriano spent hours in the library where more than five hundred volumes were shelved, some actually published in Valladolid—translations of Juvenal, Sallust, and the *Iliad*. The Latin poets were practically all there, and, step by step, Cipriano began discovering the pleasure of reading, the intimate and silent act of deflowering a book. There were also good paintings in the house, high-quality copies of famous works along with some attempts at sculpture. The recent arrival of Alonso de Berruguete at Valladolid gave Ignacio the opportunity to commission from him a wood panel in relief, what the artist called a bulk panel, that represented Doña Gabriela. It was a piece of notable quality, more for the technique than the resemblance. It was hung in the small anteroom to the library, and Ignacio, a very religious man, very respectful with art, took his hat off when he walked by it as if it were the consecrated Host. These new subjects—art and good taste—stimulated Cipriano. He'd taken well to Don Ignacio, and his progress in Latin, grammar, and law was striking.

One morning as he left class, he found himself face to face with Minervina in the sitting room. She still had her elasticity of four years earlier, the same flexible waist, the same long, delicate neck, the same mouth with its full lips. A smiling Gabriela was with her, and Cipriano had no idea what to do or say. It was Minervina who spoke first, to tell him he'd grown that he was becoming a man, and that she was saddened by it.

Days went by, but the old, intimate relationship did not start up again between Minervina and Cipriano. Something like a paralyzing barrier of modesty sprang up between them. Until one Thursday afternoon, when his aunt and uncle were out and Minervina's fellow servants had the day off: when Cipriano saw her sitting up straight on the sofa in the grand salon, her small bosoms barely a hint under her overdress with its square neckline. He felt the same overwhelming and naive attraction he'd felt as a child. He went to her, embraced her, and kissed her, saying "He . . . hello there, Minervina . . . I love you a lot, do you know that?" Minervina melted when she discovered her breasts in the palms of his hands, while his burning lips passionately worked their way over her decollete: "Oh, darling, don't lose your head!"

"I love you, I love you. You're the only person I've ever loved in my life."

Minervina, dazed, smiled and gave herself: "Your whiskers are scratching me. You're a man now, Cipriano."

They wrestled as they did when he was a child, they hugged and kissed, but the boy noticed that a new element had entered their relationship. As they rolled around on the thick carpet and he pulled open the buttons on her smock, Minervina tried to resist. But it was useless.

The next day, Cipriano went to Father Toval: "I . . . I've lain with my wet nurse, Father, with the woman who fed me at her breast."

Father Toval reproached him harshly: "Doing such a thing is like lying with your own mother, Cipriano. She didn't give you life, but she gave you part of hers when you couldn't survive on your own."

Now Cipriano wandered the house like a sleepwalker. He barely dared look Minervina in the face in the presence of his aunt and uncle. All he could think about was his confession. He hadn't been completely sincere with Father Toval. Besides, it disturbed him to have to give an account of such intimate feelings. He could Father Toval ever understand his relationship with the girl? And if he couldn't understand it, how could he judge it?

The next Thursday, alone again, Minervina and Cipriano took refuge in each other as if it were the most natural thing in the world. Without confessing it, they'd both been impatiently waiting for this moment. Instinctively, she again gave herself to him, nurtured him, and he clung to her as if she were a life preserver. They were together, naked, in her narrow bed, and Minervina's timid reservations made the consummation of the act even more precious. He took her three times, and, when he was finished, experienced something like a disgust with himself, thinking that he was prostituting the girl. His love for her, the purity of his feelings for her were clear to him, but, behind it all, he could not help but see the sordid adventure of the young master who takes advantage of the maid. He sought out an other confessor in San Gregorio, one he did not know: "I . . . I confess, Father, that I possessed my wet nurse, but I'm not sorry I did it. My love is stronger than my will."

"Do you love her or desire her?"

"If I desire her, Father, it is because I love her. I've never loved anyone in my life as I love her."

"But you're still a boy. You're certainly not going to marry her."

"I'm fourteen years old, Father. My guardian would not understand."

The priest hesitated. Finally he said: "If there is no repentance, my son, I cannot absolve you."

"I understand, Father. I'll return to you soon."

Thursdays became the obligatory day for the lovers's trysts. It was an inevitable meeting, and with sex added, the living reproduction of the affection between the boy and his wet nurse. During the pauses, they talked. He told her about his school years, about the sexual deviation of the Charger, about his loss of innocence. And she talked about her first love for a boy in her Santovenia, her fall, her pregnancy, her giving birth. As she spoke, she wept, and told him, "You're like the child I lost, my darling." But they would immediately become impatient with themselves, and throw themselves into exploring each other, in loving each other. Their lovemaking on Thursdays, now in Cipriano's room, was longer and more complete, and went on for almost four months. It was with the unexpected return home of Doña Gabriela and Don Ignacio one winter night that everything fell apart. Gabriela discovered them naked in bed, making love, and was unable to understand anything: "You've abused the boy and my confidence in you, Minervina. You've dishonored this house, dishonored all of us. Leave and never come back!"

Down in the Plaza del Mercado, Minervina took Jesús Revilla's coach back to Santovenia the next morning. All she carried were the same two bags she had when she came to Ignacio's house five months earlier.

# BOOK II
# THE HERESY

# VII

WHEN he came of age, Cipriano Salcedo became a doctor of law and took possession of the warehouse in the Ghetto along with the Pedrosa properties. He moved back into his father's house on Corredora de San Pablo, which had been shut up since Bernardo's death. With these objectives attained, he took on another three, all very well defined and ambitious: He intended to find Minervina, achieve social prominence, and raise his economic position in order to be at the same level as the great merchants of the country. The first objective, which he thought would be the easiest—finding Minervina—failed. In Santovenia, he could barely find anyone who remembered her. Her parents were dead, and she—people said—had left the village. "Married" said one, but another corrected that notion: "Minervina never married; she left with her sister for Mojados, where an old aunt of theirs lived."

Cipriano went to Mojados on his new horse, Lightning. No one there knew anything about the girl; they'd never even heard such a strange name before. He insisted: Minervina, Minervina Capa. but no one reacted. In the whole of the area, no one knew a girl by that name. Cipriano Salcedo, who could not comprehend life without her, searched through all the neighboring villages. It was useless. Not knowing what became of Blasa and Modesta after his father's death, he initiated the search again, starting back at the beginning: Santovenia. He connected with Olvido Lanuza, one of the *illuminati*, who'd gone slightly mad, and she told him Minervina had become a servant in the house of Bernardo Salcedo in Valladolid. No one gave him any leads to follow except

Leonor Vaquero, an infirm lady a hundred years old. She told him
Minervina had married a manufacturer from Segovia. Lightning carried
Cipriano to Segovia in two stages. But where should he begin his
search? He asked, one by one, at all the weaving centers in the city, but
people would always ask the name of the husband, since the wife's
maiden name figured on none of their pay lists. Salcedo, desolate,
returned to Valladolid. His last hopes were fading. Finding Minervina,
which had always seemed an easy task to him, now seemed an unattain-
able utopia. He decided to stop, to dedicate himself to routine, and only
to start looking again when he found reliable information that would
give him some guarantee of success.

Dionisio Manrique, who for ten years had kept the warehouse
going under the supervision of Don Ignacio, was relieved to see
Cipriano incorporated into the work. The building, naked and empty
most of the year, with no one else there but the mute Federico, had
become odious and unbearable to him. Small wonder Manrique saw the
arrival of Don Cipriano as a gift from heaven. Cipriano's first act in the
Ghetto was to read all the correspondence with the Maluendas, first
that of Néstor, the famous merchant, and now that of Gonzalo, the son
who followed in his footsteps. Cipriano thought that his first step in the
business should be to get in touch with Burgos, meet the new head of
operations, and see if he couldn't improve the conditions of his contract
with him, which involved his supplying Maluenda with six hundred
thousand fleeces from Old Castile each year.

Cipriano loved to ride, and he needed no excuse to mount
Lightning, so at the outset of October he crossed the Puente Mayor,
passed through Cohorcos and Dueñas in the morning, and met with
Gonzalo Maluenda two days later in his establishment at Las Huelgas.
Gonzalo received him in good spirits. He talked without stopping, with
the pretensions of an ingenious man, repeatedly patting Cipriano on the
back, and just as frequently referring to his father, Don Néstor: "He
gave your father the first birth stool to enter Spain. Your mother was the
first to use it."

"E . . . exactly," admitted Cipriano. "Things didn't go well, so
Doctor Almenara, the most eminent physician of the time, had to take
a hand in things."

Gonzalo Maluenda burst out laughing and slapped Cipriano's shoulders: "So you are the first Spaniard to be a child of the stool."

Cipriano did not like the young Maluenda. His insinuations mortified Cipriano, as did his vulgar jokes, his backslapping: "In point of fact, I'm my mother's son. The Flemish chair did nothing but help her bring me into the world."

Seeing that his witticisms were meeting with little success, Gonzalo left off the frivolities. He was an insecure man without a well-defined personality: Cipriano did not think he was the right person to be in charge of wool commerce with Flanders. He seemed to be typical of the third generation in merchant families, the kind who quickly waste the fortune their grandfathers accumulated with so much work. He wasn't surprised that Gonzalo Maluenda would again laugh out of turn as he told him that two ships from the wool fleet had been captured by pirates. It was as if he thought it a funny anecdote.

"They strayed from the rest of the fleet and didn't sail with the convoy."

"B . . . but they must have been insured."

"They were, but because they left the convoy, the insurer said the contract was null and void. It's only natural. We all want to defend our own."

Cipriano returned to Valladolid depressed. The new head of operations in Burgos simply could not deal with the circumstances at hand. He seemed like a mere pup, and the capture of two ships was a warning he would have to take into account in the future. He was fully aware that Gonzalo Maluenda's errors would inevitably drag him down as well. He connected that idea with his intention to visit Segovia, the cloth-making center of Old Castile. When he saw it for the first time months back, he'd been surprised by its activity and, even though Minervina occupied all his thoughts at that moment, he could not help but notice that Segovia, a small textile city, was developing by using its own resources. The city was transforming its own raw material into finished products, so the capital invested always stayed right there.

Why not try the same thing in Valladolid? Why didn't Valladolid turn the seven hundred thousand fleeces it annually exported to Flanders into wool cloth in the same way they were doing it in Segovia? Might it not be possible that he, Cipriano Salcedo, was the man to bring that about? The wind in his face, strengthened by Lightning's cantering, stimulated his imagination. Valladolid: the Court of Spain, resigned to its status as a service town, he thought, was a sleepy place where the highest aspiration of the poor was to fill their stomachs and the highest aspiration of the rich was to live off their rents. Nothing moved there.

He reported his thoughts to Dionisio Manrique when he returned. He did not like Gonzalo Maluenda. He was a young fool who thought it was funny that two ships were captured by pirates. They were going to have to be careful. A blunder by Maluenda could seriously affect Castile's wool trade. Why not try in Valladolid what they were already doing in Segovia? Dionisio's eyes opened wide with greed. He agreed. It was clear that the Maluenda era had passed. Don Gonzalo was both lazy and a gambler, bad vices in a merchant. It was time to think in a new way about the business of the fleece: Strengthen the fleets or, perhaps, attempt to transport them by land through Navarra. Cipriano was stimulated when he saw Manrique supporting him. They agreed to think it over. Meanwhile, Cipriano decided to visit Pedrosa: He wanted to give his name some luster. His doctorate in law meant little if it was not accompanied by a patent of nobility. To enter the aristocracy at the lowest rank—as an *hidalgo*—would be an astute move that would embellish his career and reinforce his personal prestige.

Cipriano had met Martín Martín, his new sharecropper, the son of Benjamín Martín. He knew Teresa, his wife, and his eight children, as small and light as rats. His uncle Ignacio had accompanied him there on an earlier trip. The house, naked and poor, with a dirt floor, had caught his notice. As did, in violent contrast, the canopy of embossed leather that adorned the matrimonial bed. "It's the only inheritance I received from my poor father, may he rest in peace," said Martín Martín by way of explanation.

Ignacio and Cipriano had gone out to Pedrosa by the well-trodden road that passed through Arroyo, Simancas, and Tordesillas, the same one Bernardo had taken, but on that trip, Cipriano, who loved adventure, conceived the idea of skirting the hills, crossing the lands of Geria, Ciguñuela, Simancas, Villavieja, and Villalar. There was no well-defined road there, but Lightning was marking it out now, in his second trip, with his canter, trampling down the furze in the low areas. Cipriano managed the horse with expertise; he dominated him, and in each long ride he made him learn something new. It was June, and the male and female partridges were flying with their young from the vineyards to the hills with a metallic flutter that made the horse tremble.

For months, Cipriano had been taking the steps to acquire a patent of nobility. Martín Martín, to whom he'd ceded a third part of the harvest, would support him unconditionally. And he'd heard the elders of the community speak well of Don Bernardo, the last defender of oxen for agricultural work, and also of Don Aquilino Salcedo, Cipriano's grandfather, who'd spent the last years of the previous century in Pedrosa. None of the locals had either a good or bad notion of their masters, but they did have a vague idea that in life it was better to be friends with a rich man than a poor one. Besides, Don Domingo, the old parish priest, had in the church archives papers concerning the Salcedos, where there were records of the charity and the donations made to the town during difficult times, like the plague of the year 1506 or the storms in the year 1490, which made threshing impossible and caused the grain to sprout on the threshing floor. As if that weren't enough, Cipriano Salcedo was prepared to prove his family's purity of blood for seven generations.

As soon as he arrived, Salcedo talked the matter over with Martín Martín. Thirty-seven neighbors out of thirty-nine were ready to vote that the Salcedos had been considered nobles in Pedrosa for two centuries. Don Domingo would add to the dossier copies of the documents in the parish archive, which would attest to the generous patronage doled out to the town by the family. Cipriano was fully aware that his title of doctor, linked to a patent of nobility, not only exempted him from contributions and taxes but also made him eligible to be a member of the administration. He also knew that it was easier for a landowner than a merchant to enter the nobility, and that the old maxim "nobles are born, not made" had no meaning whatsoever. He was ready to prove it. Martín Martín promised him that as soon as he had the statements by the neighbors and the copies of Don Domingo's documents, he would have them sent by courier. To add merit to merit, and taking advantage of the new laws concerning the opening of unused land to farming, Cipriano took note of the boundary of the lands near the Villavendimio stream with the intention of soliciting permission to cultivate them and authorization to add them to his properties.

Two weeks later, a courier came to Valladolid with the papers from Pedrosa, and Cipriano delivered them to his uncle, the judge, who, in turn, presented them, with a polite request, to the Chamber of Nobility in the Chancery. A few months later, Cipriano obtained the title of "doctor-*hidalgo*" and became exempt from taxes. A fast courier communicated the good news to Don Domingo and Martín Martín in Pedrosa and urged the sharecropper to sacrifice on July 3 a dozen lambs and have ready two barrels of Rueda wine to celebrate Cipriano's change of status. Only two people were excluded from the celebration, Victorino Cleofás and Eleuterio Llorente, two farmers who, far from considering the Salcedos magnanimous, disinterested beings, judged them to be exploiters. The feast was celebrated in the yard behind the house at nightfall, and, according to the old chronicles, not even the town of Toro, of which Pedrosa was a suburb, ever knew, in its best years, a party like that, so joyous and wild, one in which even the dogs and farm animals participated. Tomás Galván's female mule, Torera, drank a bucket of Rueda wine and spent the night braying and kicking in the streets of the town until, at dawn, she dropped dead.

Established now in his adult life, his title of hidalgo achieved, and his affairs in Pedrosa in order, Cipriano focused all his attention on his business with Burgos. And even though he didn't like Gonzalo Maluenda, or precisely for that reason, he decided to accompany the autumn shipment himself, just as his father had a few months after he was born.

It took several days to load the five huge iron-wheeled wagons in the warehouse, while the forty mules hired from Argimiro Rodicio were being prepared for the trip. Dozens of temporary workers were busy in the yard, and, when the day came, Cipriano took his place at the lead and went along the dusty Santander road. At that instant, after having taken all the pertinent precautions, Cipriano felt important and happy. Warned that the bandit Diego Bernal was roaming the area, he was armed, as were the other drivers, while squads sent out by the rural police, the Holy Brotherhood, put on notice about the importance of the convoy, patrolled the route.

The road, with its ruts and potholes, did not make the trip easier, but that caravan of five massive wagons dragged by eight mules each was a sight enjoyed by mule drivers and passersby loitering along the roadside. Cipriano led the long caravan, never taking his eyes off the horizon, fearful that the gang of thieves, whose leader Diego Bernal, the only thief famous in both Old and New Castile, might appear along some ridge. The wagons formed an austere procession, frequently changing speed but adhering to a preconceived plan: They were to cover six leagues each day, so that the trip, with the required stops for mule changes at the stage houses at Dueñas and Quintana del Puente and the inns of Moral and Villamanco, would take about four days.

Once they arrived at Burgos, the unloading would take place, which was even more complicated than the loading, even though Maluenda, forewarned, hired experienced temporary workers who shortened the operation. Relieved of their cargo, the wagons made the return trip in three and a half days, and as soon as they arrived, Cipriano gathered up the weapons and returned them to the Holy Brotherhood. Conscious of having done his duty, he returned to his routine.

The huge warehouse in the old Ghetto, a few days ago packed with fleeces and now looking frightfully empty, would fill up again, slowly but surely over the coming months. And when July came, a new caravan would be put together to go to the same destination. Cipriano, usually cautious and timid, rose to these grand moments whenever they presented themselves. Storing seven hundred thousand fleeces and transporting them to Burgos in two annual expeditions seemed to him an accomplishment fit for great men, so when he was sitting at the dining room table and Crisanta the maid was serving him his first meal after the trip, he made no attempt to hide his hairy little hands, which he now saw as strong and masculine, fully up to the task when it came to dealing with large-scale enterprises. And in those moments, he saw himself closer to Néstor Maluenda, the great merchant, who with only his talent and courage had made Burgos into a great commercial emporium while he was still young.

His uncle and guardian, Ignacio, with whom he usually met once a week, and especially, Gabriela, his wife, were pleased to see that their nephew idolized Don Néstor. For Gabriela, there was nothing more admirable than a powerful merchant, even if her husband pointed out that she admired the great merchants more for their income than for their social status. Cipriano's adoration of the grandfather Maluenda, whom he never met, did not attenuate his contempt for his son Gonzalo —it simply amplified it. Following the lead of such a runt, such an ingenious pretender to a commercial throne, would not satisfy his desire to rise in the world.

At the same time, receiving merchandise with his left hand and handing it over to a third party with his right in exchange for a stipend came to be an ignoble activity in his eyes. Cipriano, rather than admiring the merchant made rich by his perseverance and effort, admired the man who, thanks to his brains, introduced an innovation into the product, so that, without knowing why or why not, he soon came to modify the buying habits of the clients. This innovating will led him, step by step, to a better understanding of himself, which in turn led him to intuit his creative initiative and the reasons for his personal dissatisfaction. His eagerness to discover new methods grew a few months later, when another two ships from the Flanders fleet were taken by the pirates, while a third had to take refuge in the port of Pasajes after suffering severe damage.

If this news was accurate, the risks of the fleet increased with each year that passed, with cargos and shipments growing more and more expensive. The alarm of those in the wool business grew, while Salcedo's idea of taking things in a new direction took shape. The very idea of shipments no longer functioned on its own as a means to get Castilian wool out into the world and make a good profit. It was at that stage when, in the mysterious way these things develop, Cipriano was struck one day by the idea of ennobling a piece of clothing as popular and humble as the sheepskin jacket. An overcoat ideal for shepherding or crossing the Páramo in winter could be transformed by three slight alterations into an article of clothing for higher social classes. Success, as always happens in the world of fashion, depended on inspiration, on a touch of genius, on, in this case, breaking the flatness of the back and the cuffs with some daring yoking, which gave the garments a new drape. By means of this alteration, this coat, typical peasant-wear, acquired an indefinable urban grace that made it perfect for ladies and gentlemen.

The tailor Fermín Gutiérrez was the first to approve Salcedo's innovation. And Cipriano was so clever at praising the virtues of the new coat that Gutiérrez became enthusiastic about the project. He was immediately hired to work at home for a salary that could be changed in the future: seventy two *reales* per month. For his part, Salcedo agreed to supply him with all the sheepskins necessary. During the first year, *The yoking revolution*, as Cipriano called it, aroused curiosity in the town. But it was during the second when an unexpected enthusiasm manifested itself and forced Salcedo to send two caravans of coats made in his new style to the fairs in Segovia and Medina del Campo. The coat conquered the market, and the demand was so high Cipriano had to set up, in the basement floor of his house on Corredera de San Pablo, an establishment whose name evoked the novelty and its creator in an ambiguous rubric: "Cipriano's overcoat." He'd taken the first step toward fame. But Cipriano noticed that even though the coat was well received by the middle class it was still not penetrating the highest social sectors. Then he conceived two modifications: for the lamb's wool lining he substituted finer pelts. He also turned up the cuffs. These additions tripled the price of the coat, but for the nobles they would constitute surefire lures. He didn't use exotic skins but those of animals from out in the mountains, animals high society knew nothing about—sable, stone marten, nutria, lynx, and genet. And he made a hit. What he hadn't achieved with his yoking, he won with his new lining and his turned-up cuffs. What especially attracted the nobles was the variety of skins: It was possible to have more than one option. After that last innovation, Cipriano's overcoat came into all homes, became a fashion at the Valladolid Court, and spread to all the capitals in the kingdom.

Once he was convinced he was on the right path, Cipriano hired the services of a knowledgeable man from the country, Tiburcio Guillén, who organized a network of pelt suppliers, who in turn created other networks of trappers and a team of expert tanners who treated the skins with birch oil. This way, Fermín and his provisional shop had their supplies guaranteed all year round. At the same time, Fermín was allowed to hire a staff—cutters and seamstresses, "principally," as Cipriano demanded, "among the young widows in town who in general had more need than other women."

When he reorganized the business, he decided to pay Gutiérrez for each finished coat instead of paying him at a monthly rate. This change accidently familiarized him with the world of numbers: The manufacture of a coat cost three *reales*, and half a *real* for transportation; treating a dozen skins with birch oil cost 120 *maravedíes*, and so on. Using those numbers as a base, he was able to determine precisely the commercial margins that were enhancing his fortune day after day.

Months later, under the direction of Dionisio Manrique, dazzled by his master's success, Cipriano imposed a final deadline on the tanners: The skins would have to be ready by the first of May so the business could continue producing all year round in a regular rhythm. The skins Tiburcio Guillén delivered to Dionisio Manrique, and which he delivered to Fermín Gutiérrez were handed over on fixed and foreseeable dates, after the animals's molting period was over. The number of tanners was also increased, and, with the avalanche of fleeces piling up, Salcedo decided not to limit their use exclusively to lining overcoats. He expanded the business to include winter clothing for men and women. "Fine clothing lined with light and dark fur" was the subtitle added to the sign outside the shop on Corredera de San Pablo.

But the trappers, who for the first time saw their skins held in esteem, overwhelmed the mule drivers with their deliveries, so Salcedo had to make one of the most important decisions of his life: to sell his products abroad, at first with reputable merchants in Antwerp, with the world-famous Bonterfoesen, all of which gave the overcoats and the "fine clothing lined" a universal extension. The well-known merchant David de Nique made a comment that appealed to Salcedo's vanity: "Never did a simple yoke cause such a revolution in fashion. That's real ingenuity." By now, the lamb-lined overcoats were losing prestige despite the yoking, and city people, especially rich Spaniards, preferred their linings to be made from the fur of wild Spanish animals, not only because they were prettier but because they were less bulky and warmer.

Over all, however, demand was not going down, and Salcedo decided, after considerable lucubration, to convert half of the Ghetto warehouse into a tailor shop. The vast hall was divided in half, one still used to store fleeces, while the other became a huge workshop where

Fermín Gutiérrez reigned supreme. Without noticing it, Salcedo was beginning to walk down the path of incipient capitalism. The huge factory never stopped working, winter or summer, and to counteract the intense cold of the Castilian winter, he installed a ceiling and brought in huge braziers that burned fine oak charcoal which he placed between the worktables to help the workers hampered by chilblains.

As was only logical, Salcedo's relationship with Gonzalo Maluenda and Burgos weakened. The two annual caravans became one and the ten wagons became four. Maluenda secretly admired Salcedo's enterprising spirit and was mortified by his successes. Publicly, he would say that putting an article of clothing as vulgar as overcoats before commerce with central Europe was in itself a symptom of Cipriano Salcedo's bad taste and low social class, no matter how large the words "doctor-*hidalgo*" were printed on his visiting cards. Deep down, Maluenda envied the fact that Salcedo had foreseen the decline of the wool trade and had found an elegant means of marketing his merchandise.

But after some years, nature had the final say. The wild animals could no longer outbreed the devastation of the hunters, and their numbers began to decline. But Salcedo, by now a rich and experienced man of business, was already aware of that situation, which coincided with the decline of sales of the new overcoat. That is, by the time demand began to shrink, he'd already cut his orders so that he did not have to experience the bitter plight of the redundant workers. Five years after the product was introduced, sales of the yoked overcoat had settled to the point that only one shift of workers was necessary in the Ghetto warehouse to supply the market. But by that time, Cipriano's fortune was estimated at fifteen thousand ducats, one of the strongest and economically sound in Valladolid.

It was in the third year of the business when Cipriano Salcedo, brimming over with joy at the happy results at his good luck, sent a communication to Estacio del Valle in Villanubla asking for more fleeces. Estacio answered with an urgent letter explaining that except for a new sheep rancher in Peñaflor, Don Segundo Centeno, who had more than ten thousand sheep and a few small-time ranchers in other places, Cipriano already had all the wool in the Páramo. When good weather came, Salcedo rode up to Villanubla along the old road so

familiar to Lightning. He found Estacio old and haggard, but still lucid
and cunning.

Don Segundo Centeno, a man who'd made a fortune in the New
World, had established himself in the wilds of La Manga some two years
earlier. He was from Sevilla, and the sheep ranchers from the
Guadalquivir recommended he set himself up in the Páramo, near
Valladolid. He was a primitive, rough individual who lived with the
sheep on the hillsides and dressed like a peasant. He was, however, a
man of wealth, though no one knew exactly how much he had. He had
contracts to sell his wool to the Moriscos, Christianized Moors, who
were weavers in Segovia, complicated arrangements whereby the
weavers themselves provided the teams for transporting the wool. He
was tightfisted and not especially sociable and had barely any ties with
the people of the Páramo, sheepherders, or farmers.

He had a solid, white-skinned daughter named Teodomira, who for
her skill at sheep shearing was nicknamed "the Queen of the Páramo."
The girl never left La Manga: Tall, extremely hard working, she always
wore a smock of rough cloth and a strange headdress that made her
head look larger. She walked through the mire and garbage in the yard
and corrals, wearing galoshes to protect her feet. The inhabitants of
Peñaflor and Wamba swore that even if her father considered
Teodomira the Queen of the Páramo, she worked like a pack mule for
him, because when the time came to shear sheep the two maids always
managed to disappear.

Teodomira herself would drive the sheep into the sheepfold and,
seated at the gate on a chopping block, shear them one after another,
then locking the bare animals in the adjacent corral. The Queen of the
Páramo never tore a fleece. She got them off intact, in one piece, and hot.
No one ever challenged Teodomira, but it was well known in the vicinity
that she could shear a hundred sheep in under a day. Don Segundo, who
helped her from afternoon until midnight, also had an affinity for the job,
so that in seven weeks they would have the shipment ready for the
Moriscos to come up and cart it off. It was Estacio del Valle's opinion that
Salcedo could try to get hold of Don Segundo's wool, even if the man's
manners when making deals left a great deal to be desired.

In these matters, Segundo was a lout from the top of his head to

the tips of his toes, a man who could only be found—Thursdays except-
ed—out in the fields with his sheep. He was never at home. Estacio
pointed Cipriano in the direction of the hills: He was to take the
Peñaflor highway and after perhaps half a league, next to the highest
watchtower, he would see the start of a red, clay road, half effaced by
the flocks, that led right up to the house. In a clearing in the woods, as
round as a bullring, there it was: a structure of adobes with a slate roof,
large and ramshackle, only one story, surrounded by sheepfolds, corrals,
and farmyards where a few sheep were bleating. Opposite the facade
was a well made of limestone, a pulley, and four drinking troughs for the
sheep, also made of limestone. The maid who greeted him told him in
which direction he might find Don Segundo. He was out in the fields,
at the foot of the mountain over toward Wamba, with the sheep.

Sure enough, Salcedo found Don Segundo with a large flock
exactly where she said he'd be. He was slovenly, with short hair and a
face unshaven for many days. On his head he wore a crazy hat, which in
front was a grease stain and which behind was nothing but tatters. It was
an old-fashioned toque that matched his short, sleeveless jacket. On his
legs were buttoned leggings and on his feet crude sandals. The barking
of two mastiffs wearing spiked collars put Cipriano Salcedo on guard,
while Lightning, a coward, would not go near them until Centeno qui-
eted them down. Salcedo dismounted, but before he could say a word,
Don Segundo raised his hand, abruptly turned his back on him, and
said: "Hold on a moment."

He was carrying a staff in his right hand that he held up high as he
walked. And without any hesitation he made his way toward a small
space that had opened in the herd. His approach scattered the sheep,
but when he came to the right place, a hare jumped out, dodging away.
Before it could escape, Don Segundo threw his staff, which spun
through the air. The stick hit the hind legs of the hare, knocking it
senseless on the grass, making spasmodic movements. Don Segundo
ran over to capture it, so Salcedo could see: "Just look at that. It's a big
as a dog," he laughed.

The sheep had gone back to their peaceful grazing, and Salcedo in
the meantime tried to introduce himself, explaining his relationship
with Burgos and the wool market. But Segundo Centeno, cut him off

with an ironic question: "Now, you wouldn't be, by any chance, the overcoat Cipriano, would you?"

While he talked, he squeezed the hare's stomach so it would urinate, concentrating so attentively, so oblivious of Salcedo's presence that Cipriano, after nodding, decided to win him over with praise: "I've heard down in the town that even with ten thousand head of sheep, you don't need extra help shearing them, that you can do it alone with the help of your daughter."

A golden stream poured out from between the hind legs of the hare, and Centeno passed his huge, heavy hand over its immaculate, white stomach to help it: "She's pregnant. These hares are always ready for sex. April's just the same as January for them. They never rest. At sunrise, from my window I see them going at it in the cobwebs every day of the year, hot or cold."

Salcedo tried to introduce his reason for being there into the conversation, but, aside from the emotion of the moment, nothing seemed to matter to Segundo Centeno. But that was mere appearance, since after a minute, he picked up the thread Salcedo had tossed to him earlier and started up the dialogue again as if nothing had interrupted it: "Well, people may say I work alone out here in the fields, but it's not true. I've got five shepherds—two in Wamba, another two in Castrodeza, and one in Ciguñuela. They tend the flocks, and when the time comes, help us to shear them. It is true that my daughter Teodomira is second to none in shearing. In the time it takes the others to peel one sheep, she peels two. That's why I call her 'the Queen of the Páramo.'"

The endless plain, barely interrupted by four oaks and some piles of stones lined up as markers, stretched out before Salcedo's surprised eyes. "The Páramo, in general, has little grass, but what it has is good. Of course, some places are just bare. Look over there. To plough two fields, we had to clear enough rocks to make a monument." He used his stick to point to the closest pile of stones, made up of rocks that weighed up to ten pounds. Three sheep wandered off, and Segundo gestured to his mastiffs, who were sleeping at his feet, to bring them back to the herd. Segundo had stuffed the hare into his knapsack, and Salcedo once again tried to get his attention by talking about the Moriscos in Segovia, but Segundo ignored the theme. After a while, however, he stated that the Moriscos were hard-working, self-sacrificing people, and that he was very satisfied with them. They charged less than other carters, and, as if that weren't enough, they absorbed the cost of the mule teams. So his wool was already spoken for. The Maluendas in Burgos, who took up practically all the wool in Castile, would have to do without Segundo Centeno's wool. On the other hand, he could offer him rabbit pelts for his overcoats, thousands of them. Because you line coats with all kinds of fur, but you've forgotten about rabbit."

"Rabbit is too common," Salcedo replied sincerely. "Here in Castile, maybe because there are so many, no one cares much for it."

Segundo gathered his flock, and with the help of his dogs, drove it by degrees toward the hills. He called out to one of the dogs by name: Lucifer. He didn't like the dog, cursing it and throwing stones at it.

Then he said, point blank: "That's because you make overcoats for rich city people. But you should think a bit about the peasants in the Páramo. For them, we have coats lined with lamb's wool you say, but rabbit would be cheaper and maybe warmer."

The sun was going down on the plain just as it does at sea. It was sinking over the horizon line, which was just now beginning to eat away at its perfect circle. It would be a brilliant sunset until the horizon devoured the setting sun. The clouds, white until then, became apricot colored as the sun set. "We'll have good weather tomorrow, yes sir," said Segundo sententiously. "Let's head for home. It's time to bring in the sheep."

Salcedo was leading Lightning by the bridle. The spectacle of the setting sun over the immense sea of land had overwhelmed him. He really didn't know what to make of Segundo Centeno. He most certainly was one of those tight-fisted peasants who end up amassing a fortune by practicing austerity, by depriving themselves even of necessities. All for the useless pleasure of dying rich. The shadows of the oaks crept along the ground, and in a few minutes the whole countryside was in a silent twilight. Now Segundo was scratching his head, putting a black fingernail under his hat. Suddenly he said: "Today, a rabbit, its pelt I mean, could cost you twenty maravedíes. How many pelts do you need to line an overcoat? Ten, fifteen? And even if that were true, lined with wool, and calculating the cost at its lowest, it would still cost you double."

Cipriano let him ramble on. To begin with, he didn't believe that the Moriscos of Segovia absorbed the cost of the mule teams. He also thought that Segundo Centeno could easily end up, without forcing the issue, as a new client in the Páramo. They could now make out the house through the bushes, and in a space that had to be a window, shone a candle. Cipriano pretended to be interested in the rabbit pelts: "And how could you catch so many rabbits when they run so fast?"

"I'll make you a bet," said a jovial Centeno. "I bet I can catch a dozen rabbits in an hour without moving a muscle. And if I could get some help from Avelino, the trapper from Peñaflor, I'd get four dozen. What do you think of that?"

"You'd catch them with nooses."

"Not a chance. Nooses take too long. Ten today, fifteen tomorrow. I couldn't use nooses to get the numbers I'd need. You've got to get rabbits moving, find out their ways. Here in La Manga there are millions of them. But with some good ferrets, you could make a slaughter in four days."

They'd reached the clearing, and Segundo drove the sheep into the folds. Over in Wamba and Peñaflor, the flocks spent nights out in the open during the hot months. Once the sheep were secured, the mastiffs slowly made their way toward the house, in one of whose windows—the kitchen no doubt—a light danced. Over the front entry, there was a grape vine from which hung bunches of green grapes. "Come on in for a while."

The furnishings were as austere as those in a convent. Just a large pine table in the hall, two benches, some wicker armchairs, a cupboard, and on both sides the usual earthenware pots. But Salcedo had no time to sit. The sheep erased the path, and it was easy to get lost: He'd have to take advantage of the last light. He'd come back another day to continue their conversation. A Thursday? Agreed, it would be a Thursday. Lunch? He'd appreciate that kind of attention from the Queen of the Páramo. Also, he, Segundo, would show him how to catch forty rabbits in one hour. If you send me a message giving me enough warning, you'll meet Mr. Avelino, the Peñaflor trapper, doing his job. And who knows?

Maybe the idea of using rabbit fur for linings will capture your fancy and we'll become partners, what do you think?

Cipriano was getting ready to leave, when the Queen of the Páramo entered the room. She was a tall, strong redhead, dressed like a peasant from the region—short skirt, wide, old-fashioned sleeves. She made noise as she walked because of the galoshes on her feet. Segundo Centeno's face brightened: Here you have my daughter Teodomira, the Queen of the Páramo, a title she justly deserves. Her expression didn't change. She said hello curtly. The flame of the candle illuminated her face, a face much too big for the size of her features. But what surprised Salcedo most was the pallor of her flesh, especially odd in a peasant woman. A white face, not the white of flour but that of marble, like that of an ancient statue. There wasn't the slightest trace of even downy hair on that face, and her eyebrows were very fine, almost nonexistent.

Since her hair was mahogany colored, her eyelashes stood out, shading very vivacious eyes the color of honey. The girl moved gracefully despite her bulk, and when Segundo introduced his guest as Don Cipriano Salcedo, the man who makes the overcoats, she congratulated him, saying he'd ennobled an article of clothing no one respected. Then he looked her right in the eye, and she looked back. Under her intense, sweet, affable gaze, his heart melted. Nothing like that had ever happened to Salcedo before, and he was even more surprised because, objectively speaking, aside from the expressive nature of her eyes and her protective presence, he could discover no special charm in the girl. Then he was happy he'd promised to come back.

And when the girl held out her hand to him to say good-by and he clasped it, he noticed that her hand too was as white and hard as marble. But then Centeno repeated that rabbit fur might capture his fancy and that the two of them might enter into a partnership. By then, Cipriano had already mounted Lighting, and after circling the well and the troughs at a trot, he disappeared in the shadows of the scrub oak, waving his left hand in farewell.

# VIII

❧

THE next Thursday Cipriano Salcedo appeared in the wilds of
La Manga at four o'clock in the afternoon, even though
Segundo had warned him that it wasn't the best time to hunt
rabbits. And there he found father and daughter together at the well,
enjoying the afternoon sun, accompanied by a short individual with
sun-bronzed skin, wearing a striped doublet; wide, full leggings; and
work boots. This gentleman Segundo introduced as Mister Avelino,
the Peñaflor trapper.

Segundo was wearing his usual outfit—short, sleeveless coat, buttoned leggings, and his old-fashioned toque on his head. The girl, on the
other hand, even though this was a country affair, had dressed up for
the event, a fact that pleased Cipriano because of the old saying, "A
dressed-up woman is an interested woman." He was so used to being
unnoticed that this detail actually moved him. Even so, he reaffirmed
his conclusion that the Queen of the Páramo was too much woman to
be beautiful, but no sooner had he dismounted and clasped her hand
than he was caught by the charm of her honey-colored, hot, and protective eyes, a feeling that stayed with him all afternoon.

Then, next to the corral, down on his knees watching the trapper
in action, he caught a glimpse of the fine, red Moroccan leather short
boots worn by the girl, whose presence enveloped him. Her father
paced back and forth, uselessly bustling about, making obvious suggestions to the trapper who, while pretending to follow his instructions,
went around placing nets over the rabbit holes. From time to time, he
would reproachfully tap his knuckles against an old wooden box inside

of which something was moving around: "Calm down! Go to sleep!" he would say from time to time.

"B . . . but what do you have in there?

"The animals, of course."

"What animals, if you don't mind my asking?"

"The ferrets. What animals would you think I'd be carrying?"

They had a sharp, rat-like muzzle and were long and thin, like hairy snakes. Mister Avelino moved about diligently and treated his ferrets with deference, spoke sweet, affectionate words to them, and every so often spit into the palm of his hand, letting a ferret drink up the saliva with delight. And when more than half the rabbit holes in the yard were covered with nets, he placed two ferrets in two holes far from each other. Then he waited a while, relaxed. There was a muted drumming underground: "Can you hear that? There's a riot going on down there."

"A riot?"

"The animals are going after the rabbits. They get them all excited. Can't you hear them? Finally, there's nothing they can do but get out."

He'd barely finished speaking when a net jumped up with a rabbit caught in it, and Segundo gave a grunt of satisfaction. "The party's started," he said.

He grabbed the net, pulled out the rabbit, held its hind legs in his left hand and with the edge of his right gave it a dull-sounding blow on the nape of the neck. Then he tossed it on the ground to die. The noise of running grew louder underground. "Watch out now. There are cartloads of rabbits down there," warned Avelino.

The rabbits in flight, caught in the nets, began to jump everywhere. Segundo and Teodomira untangled the animals and covered the holes again. The sheepherder felt a bit like the hero of the performance. "Well? What do you think of the show?"

But Cipriano was now observing Teodomira, her skill at killing rabbits, the lethal blow she laid on the back of the animal's neck, the absolute coolness with which she delivered it.

"Don't you feel sorry for them?"

Her gaze, warm and understanding, banished any suspicion of cruelty: "Why should I feel sorry? I love animals," she smiled.

They conducted their hunt in six enclosed yards, and on the way back, gathered together the sacks with their prizes: ninety eight rabbits. Segundo was exultant: "You could line ten coats with what we have here. Thirty fleeces wouldn't do you a better service."

After dinner, when Salcedo was pushing the Queen of the Páramo in a swing hung between two oaks that grew on one side of the house, she rocked with laughter and asked him to push her more slowly, because she couldn't stand the dizziness. But he pushed her with all the strength of his muscular little arms. But in one push his hand slipped from the seat and fell against Teodomira's backside. He was shocked. It wasn't the mushy flesh her size suggested but a solid body that did not yield to his touch. He was perplexed. She too seemed disconcerted: Had he done that intentionally? In any case, Salcedo gave in to her pleas, and his pushes became less forceful.

Then she spoke in praise of fine clothing lines, and confessed to having visited the shop on Corredera de San Pablo several times. Salcedo smiled with embarrassment. He was pleased by the profitability of the business, but it would never have gratified his ego that it would be the delight of plebeian vulgarity. He was even ashamed at the presence of certain people. But Teodomira, taking advantage of the fact that the swinging had moderated, went on speaking: More than any other, she liked the coats lined with nutria, even though she couldn't understand how anyone could kill such a beautiful animal.

He reminded her of the cold sacrifice of the rabbits, but she argued that it was necessary to make a distinction between animals that humans used as food and others. He asked it in that case animals people used to keep warm shouldn't be treated in the same way, to which she retorted that killing through intermediaries, as he did, was even more unforgivable than doing it oneself. She thought the person who ordered the act was worse than the one who executed his orders. Cipriano began to feel a boyish joy in carrying on that argument. He realized that he hadn't argued with anyone since his school days, that in his life not a single person had ever verbally fought with him. Then, when the girl said she loved animals, especially sheep, who always smiled, Salcedo, just to take the opposite side, mentioned horses and dogs, but she rejected his preferences: Dogs were incapable of love, were egotistic sycophants; horses, on the other hand, were fearful and conceited, animals so self-interested that they could never arouse affection.

Salcedo returned to the high country the next week with an overcoat lined in nutria two sizes larger than his own. Teodomira, who again had changed her costume, thanked him for being so thoughtful. Then they rode out together on horseback through the hills. They talked about the periodic tree harvests carried out by the charcoal makers, which yielded Segundo as much money as his sheep. The Queen of the Páramo was riding sidesaddle on a gentle horse, Obstinate, who looked like a cow. Salcedo asked her if she'd learned to ride in the New World, but she informed him that the only one to go there was her father, that she'd lived in Sevilla the ten years Segundo had been away. Then Cipriano told her she'd picked up the grace of Andalusia, and she shot him a look of such thankfulness that he became flustered.

Cipriano had bad nights. The incident with the swing and the memory of his furtive contact with the girl's body excited him. The next day, barely after sunrise, he ran in search of Father Esteban, whom he'd chosen, a bit blindly, as his confessor after his sad separation from Minervina, now more than fifteen years ago: "Fa . . . father, I touched the body of a woman and felt pleasure."

"How many times, son, how many times?"

"Just once, father, but I don't know if I did it intentionally."

"Do you mean that you don't even know if you did so deliberately or not?"

"It was a matter of seconds father. I was pushing her on a swing, and my hand slipped or I made it slip. I still have my doubts. That's the problem."

"On a swing? Do you mean, my son, that you touched her posterior parts?"

"That's it, father, exactly, her posterior parts. That's how it was."

Strictly speaking, his attitude was not new. His economic ease had only exacerbated his lack of self-confidence. Also, despite the years that had passed, he was still a man gnawed by scruples, and the more his piety increased the more his scruples plagued him. There were holy days of obligation when he would attend three consecutive masses, overwhelmed by the sensation he'd been distracted in the first. And on

one occasion, he accosted an older man who'd come into the church
after the elevation of the Host and told him his being there was superfluous. He tried to tell him diplomatically so he wouldn't hurt him, but
the man became annoyed: Who was he to interfere with his conscience?
He would tolerate no invasions of his privacy by insolent fops. Cipriano
asked the man to forgive him, recognizing that if he hadn't intervened,
he, Cipriano, would have felt responsible for the man's sin, and that his
warning, apparently impertinent, was inspired in a desire to save the
man's soul. Completely out of control, the man grabbed Cipriano's
jerkin and shook him. At the climax of his rage, the man blasphemed
against God. Cipriano came to Father Esteban desolate: "Father, I
accuse myself of the fact that I caused a man to blaspheme."

The priest listened to him attentively and made him see the limits of propagating the faith, the respect due the conscience of others,
but Cipriano observed that in school he'd been taught that we must
make an effort not only to save ourselves—an egotistical act when all's
said and done—but to help others to save themselves. Father Esteban
simply pointed out to him that while it was a Christian's duty to love his
fellow man, this did not extend either to humiliating or verbally attacking him.

The coat business was yet another cause of Salcedo's conscience
problems. In these matters of fairness, he would usually consult with his
uncle and guardian Ignacio, a religious man of sound judgment. The
instruction about giving preference to widows in the selection of seamstresses in the factory was dictated by the fact that the widows raised
the poverty index in the town, and many people took advantage of that
to exploit them. Cipriano did nothing but mull these matters over. So
one day he got out of bed obsessed with idea that it was necessary to
raise the amount of money he paid the trappers or the salary of the tanners. His uncle was making calculations, adding, subtracting, and dividing, all to come to the conclusion that, taking into account the prices in
the region's market, both groups were well paid. But Cipriano wouldn't
give in: He was making a hundred times more than his workers and with
half the effort. His uncle tried to calm him down, reminding him that it
was he who took all the risks, that what he was earning was compensa-
tion for the risk. Ultimately, Cipriano silenced the reproaches of his

conscience by giving handsome sums to the Orphan School, which had just been established in Valladolid, to benevolent institutions, or, simply, to the poor, the crippled, or the syphilitic who paraded their miseries through the streets of the town.

Despite all that, Cipriano always aspired to moral perfection. He remembered school with nostalgia and had a marked preference for homilies and sermons. He examined them, first, with regard to their content but second to their form. He would have paid a goodly sum for the beautiful exposition of an important religious problem. But, curiously, Salcedo tried to stay away from convents or monasteries. His preferences were for secular priests and not members of religious orders. In this new quest of his, the foreman of his tailor shop, Fermín Gutiérrez, was a decisive influence. Of course, in the opinion of Dionisio Manrqiue, Fermín was nothing but a pious fool. Even so, the tailor made a distinction between the cautious orators and the fiery ones, between the modern and the traditional. It was through him that Salcedo learned of the existence of Doctor Cazalla, man of such penetrating speech that the Emperor had brought him along on his travels through Germany.

Agustín Cazalla was a native of Valladolid, so his return to his hometown aroused a genuine tumult. He would speak on Fridays, in the church of Santiago, which would fill to overflowing. He was a mystic, sensitive, and physically fragile. With a weak constitution, a tormented soul, he had moments of authentic ecstasy, followed by emotional reactions that were rather arbitrary. Despite that, Cipriano listened to him with total absorption, which did not preclude when he'd returned home, his being invaded by a certain uneasiness. He analyzed his soul but could find no cause for his disquiet.

In general, he could follow Cazalla's homilies easily, because they were carefully measured in intonation, brief and well-structured. And when they were over, an idea would remain in his mind, only one, but a very clear one. It was not, then, the essence of Cazalla's sermons that were the cause of his disquiet. The cause wasn't in what he was saying but perhaps in what he didn't say or in what he suggested in his accessory sentences which were more or less ornamental. He recalled Cazalla's first homily about Christ's redemption, his nimble word play, the emphasis on a God who dies for man as the key to our salvation. Our prayers, our charity were worth little if we forgot the fundamental thing: the merits of Christ's Passion. High up in the pulpit, he evoked Christ, holding his arms out at his side, after a theatrical silence that claimed the attention of the audience.

People left the church commenting the Doctor's words, his gestures, his silences, his insinuations, but Fermín Gutiérrez, sharper and better informed, always alluded to the erasmian element in Cazalla's speeches. Cipriano wondered if that might not be the element that disturbed him. In one of his visits to his uncle Ignacio, he asked about Cazalla. Ignacio knew him well but did not admire him. Cazalla was born in Valladolid early in the century. He was the son of a royal accountant and Doña Leonor de Vivero, in whose house, now that she was a widow, he currently lived. There was a time when people thought the Cazallas were secret Jews. Don Agustín studied Arts, with considerable success, in Saint Paul's School, with Don Bartolomé de Carranza, his confessor. Later, he took his master's degree on the same day as the famous Jesuit Diego Laínez. Ten years later, the emperor, seduced by his oratory, named him royal preacher and chaplain. He traveled with the emperor for several years through Germany and Flanders and now had just moved back to Valladolid after spending a few months in Salamanca. Ignacio thought him haughty and fatuous.

"Cazalla fatuous?" Cipriano asked in perplexity.

"Why not? In my opinion, Cazalla is a man of big words and small ideas. A dangerous combination."

Ignacio's opinion did not satisfy him, although, truth be told, he was surprised that after his objective exposition of Cazalla's life, his uncle would have rounded off his portrait with those disdainful words "haughty" and "fatuous." How could that tiny figure be any such thing, he was so delicate, so dark, he seemed to offer himself up in a holocaust each time he ascended the pulpit? Salcedo said exactly that to his uncle after a brief pause.

"I wasn't referring to appearances," retorted Ignacio. "A well-organized head in a scrawny body, that's what Doctor Cazalla seems to me. I believe the Doctor expected some honorific distinction from the emperor, but it never came. That's the source of his despair."

Cipriano confessed: "I get a lot out of listening to him, but his words leave me with a bitter aftertaste, like ashes."

Ignacio stared at his nephew with a dominating air: "Couldn't it be that he raises problems he doesn't solve?"

That remark, made almost nonchalantly, had a great effect on Cipriano. He'd defined Doctor Cazalla. His cautious approach to the big problems aroused the public's attention, but the orator, in words further and further away from the heart of the matter, never dealt with those problems. He left the solutions behind somewhere. Perhaps he did it intentionally or perhaps he lacked conviction.

In his next visit to La Manga, Cipriano talked about the new preacher with Teodomira and her father. Teodomira had heard nothing about him, and Segundo was suspicious of new voices. The world, as he saw it, was full of saviors, who in truth were consummate heretics. People, especially monks, set themselves up as theologians, but they were frauds devoid of learning. Cipriano pointed out that Cazalla wasn't a monk, that he even avoided convents to spread his doctrines, but Segundo warned him that was no guarantee whatsoever, that it was nothing more than a strategy.

Salcedo looked at Segundo, looked at his crazy hat with its sweat-stained, faded brown brim, the hat he never took off, not even indoors, and did not see a serious adversary for Cazalla. Segundo was a primitive being, and like all simple people, he was ready to rush to judgment. But, despite everything, now that the cold weather and rain had begun, Cipriano began to find himself at home in the sitting room of the adobe house, with the fire crackling in the fireplace, sitting on the hard bench.

The Queen of the Páramo was sitting in the wicker armchair, where she sat every day. In her—she always knitting or sewing—he saw a home-loving, balanced woman of good judgment. On days of obligation, she would mount Obstinate and take herself off to Peñaflor for the eleven o'clock Mass. During the work week, she had no opportunities to foment the pious life, but she did recite an Our Father when she went to sleep and when she awakened. Cipriano listened to her with great pleasure. When Teodomira spoke, he felt a huge interior peace. That woman, overweight and all, was the incarnation of serenity. And her voice, with its caressing inflections, produced in him a sensation of security such as he'd never experienced until then. But what surprised Cipriano most was the discovery of Teodomira as woman—the fact that, at the same time she calmed him, she could also excite him sexually.

The afternoon when the swing event took place and his subsequent confession revealed that the pleasure he'd felt touching her backside was from his point of view a forbidden pleasure. The memory of that fact caused him to consider her volume from another point of view. He recalled his brief adventure with Minervina, analyzed it, and concluded that it had been nothing more than a reminiscence of childhood. Minervina hadn't given him life, but she had nursed him, and he, instinctively, had seen in her his reason for living. He'd embraced that reason the moment it reappeared. There was nothing else. Now he was realizing that Minervina, a creature who was too light, was not exactly what a man needed, that carnal passion required—obviously—flesh as its first ingredient. The result was that his interior peace, the calm with which the Queen of the Páramo saturated him, was accompanied at times by a repressed lasciviousness, a burning desire that attacked him with its ever-growing demand. This mixture of peace, security, and desire drew Cipriano to La Manga with greater and greater frequency.

Lightning's familiarity with the road enabled Cipriano to get there in a little over an hour. And that cold, rainy winter did not discourage him. His leather leggings and his overcoat lined with nutria—like the one he'd given Teodomira—protected him from the weather. They would spend the afternoon indoors or take a walk to see the flocks of wood pigeons or woodcocks just arrived from the north. In the meanwhile, the two maids from Peñaflor prepared the meal. Ordinarily, Segundo would not appear anywhere near the house until then, after locking up the sheep in the folds. He would then join in the conversation, recounting the day's adventures, even from time to time coming back to his old obsession: the coat with the rabbit lining. Cipriano would lead him on, and in turn would insinuate the possibility of his taking charge of the transportation of the fleeces, replacing the Segovian Moriscos. One thing for another was his condition. Segundo would scratch his head in doubt, but his illusion about entering the coat business finally won out: "All right," he said one afternoon. "I'll cede the

transportation and sale of my fleeces to you, provided you sign a contract with me to exploit rabbits for coat linings. Fifty-fifty."

"Agreed," said Salcedo.

Right then and there they signed the contract, according to which
Don Segundo Centeno, born in Sevilla and residing in Peñaflor de
Hornija, ceded the transportation and sale of the fleeces from ten thousand sheep, all on his property, to Don Cipriano Salcedo, Doctor of Law
and Landowner in Valladolid. At the same time, both parties agreed to
exploit the pelts of three thousand rabbits derived from the area of La
Manga, which Don Segundo promised to supply annually to Don Cipriano.
The aforesaid pelts were to be used in the business of coats and fine
garments lined with fur in accord with the prices set by the market.

After signing, Segundo placed a jug of Cigales wine on the table
and the three toasted the hoped-for success of the enterprise. That
night Cipriano dined in La Manga and slept in Florencio's inn. The
news about the purchase of the rabbit pelts surprised Estacio del
Valle, who pointed out to Cipriano that lining coats with rabbit fur was
hardly a new idea. In Segovia, the Moriscos made them, and in the
Páramo, the shepherds and peasants had been using them since time
immemorial.

Salcedo, who hadn't signed the contracts with the intention of
increasing his fortune, retorted that it didn't matter, that the business
would consist in making better and cheaper coats than the competition
and beat them at their own game. Cipriano fell asleep with the supplementary thought that signing the contracts conferred on him some right
over Teodomira. So when Lightning carried him out to the hills the next
morning and he found himself alone with the girl, who was tending the
fire in the house, he drew her close and kissed her on the mouth. She
had full, firm, and demanding lips, and Cipriano felt submerged in an
indefinable sea of pleasure, but when he thought all that could only lead
to one logical conclusion, Teodomira angrily stood up and revealed that
while she too was in love with him, there was a time and place for everything. First, his guardian would have to visit her father. They would
have to speak and agree on the marriage contract. Then if all went well,
they would marry. Cipriano retained at the tips of his fingers the sensation of the hardness of Teodomira's breasts, not softer than her but-

tocks, and then accepted her conditions. He lacked experience in love matters and gave in. He realized that access to the Queen of the Páramo would be a slow process requiring a series of necessary steps.

That same afternoon, he visited his aunt and uncle and announced his intention to marry. Aunt Gabriela expressed interest in the subject: "May we inquire as to who the lucky lady might be?"

Cipriano vacillated. He didn't know where to begin. He realized he'd come to his aunt and uncle in haste, without preparing a speech.

"A . . . a girl from the Páramo. She lives out in the hills of La Manga, in Peñaflor. Her father made his fortune in the New World."

"The Páramo? A fortune made in the New World?" His aunt wrinkled her nose.

He thought that perhaps his words would be more effective if he pretended to share their shock, if from the outset he were to explain things just as they were, even caricaturing them: "He did make his fortune in the New World, and he never takes off his cap, not even to sleep. He's a rustic, but with potential. In reality, he knows nothing about us, but he respects me. Yesterday we signed a contract to manufacture coats lined with rabbit fur, which is what he was after."

Aunt Gabriela stared at him as if he were some strange new species, as if he were joking, while Uncle Ignacio listened without daring to interrupt. Perhaps he needed more information before offering an opinion. So Cipriano added: "She has no education whatsoever. The only work she knows is that of shearing sheep. She does that more quickly than the shepherds, so they gave her the title "Queen of the Páramo." Over the course of her life, she's sheared thousands of sheep without tearing a single fleece."

This was abstruse talk for Gabriela, who gaped at him with growing perplexity. Uncle Ignacio smiled slightly: "And what will our good made-his-fortune-in-the-New-World man do if you deprive him of his best shearer?" There was undeniable logic to his question.

"Well, that's his problem. He must have done his calculations, I suppose, but in order to marry off his daughter, it's possible he'd give his entire fortune. Speaking for myself, I can say I'm in love. I'm not quite certain what that word means, but I think I'm in love because when I'm with her I find I experience both tranquility and excitement at the same time."

Uncle Ignacio cleared his throat: "Getting married is perhaps the most important step in a man's life, Cipriano. And love is something more than tranquility and excitement."

They all fell silent. Cipriano seemed to be reflecting. After a bit, he brought up an extremely important point: "Her father did get rich in the Indies, and as such, he's thrifty and miserly. He wears rags and kills hares by throwing his stick at them so he can eat meat the next day. He normally eats stew for breakfast and cabbage for dinner. She, on the other hand, has never left Spain. When her father sailed off, she stayed with an aunt in Sevilla. She's a well-bred girl, but the only problem I see is her size. She's perhaps a bit big for the likes of me."

Now it was Gabriela who didn't want to speak; she knew she couldn't say anything without hurting him.

"Have you ever heard about the idea that opposites attract?"

"No," Cipriano confessed.

"Sometimes we fall in love with what we don't have, and the same thing happens to the other person. The short man married to the tall woman is a classic example. There are justifying circumstances."

Cipriano became interested: "What might that be in my case?"

Ignacio was off and running: "In your case, you could have seen in her the mother you never knew."

"Would she necessarily have to be a tall woman?"

"That's a supplementary fact, Cipriano. A child seeks shelter from his mother, and it's hard to see how he'd find it in someone physically weaker than himself. It's completely possible that for you the girl represents the protective shield you didn't have as a child."

"But she says she loves me. What could have moved her?"

"The mutual attraction between the short man and the tall woman is a well-studied subject and nothing new. Just as you seek protection in her, she seeks someone to protect in you. Maternal instincts are always at work in women. Maternal instinct is nothing else but that—trying to help a being needier than oneself."

Slowly but surely, Gabriela made her way to the disagreeable detail. She couldn't stop herself: "Sweetheart, is there really such a great difference between you two, physically speaking?"

"An excessive difference. Let's say she weighs about one hundred and sixty pounds, while I weigh one hundred and seven."

Gabriela was sinking in a stormy sea. All that kept her going was talk: "Now Cipriano, tell us what she's like. Is she pretty?"

"I wouldn't use that word, even if perhaps she is pretty. Her complexion is white, and her face is too large for her modestly-sized features. Only her way of looking is special, tender, exciting. Honey-colored eyes that change shade depending on the light. Extremely beautiful eyes. Then there are her coarse lips, and the quality of her flesh. Her size and whiteness would lead you to think she was a soft woman when she's exactly the opposite."

Cipriano was blushing. Suddenly he realized his words had gone too far, that they'd aroused a premature knowledge of his sweetheart. He thought his aunt was about to say something about that, but she was thinking what he was thinking and skillfully changed registers: "What's her name?"

"Teodomira."

"My God! That's horrible." She could no longer hold back and brought her well-tended hands to her eyes. Ignacio stepped in: "Such details are of no importance."

Gabriela smiled, as if asking forgiveness: "We could call her Teo. That wouldn't hurt anything."

The conversation went on in a tense atmosphere, where neither side would give in. But Ignacio's common sense began to dominate the situation. The important thing was to be sure of being in love. Therefore, the prudent course of action would be to wait a couple of months before taking action.

On the seventeenth of February, a cloudless day in early spring, the waiting period was over. Vicente, the servant, had cleaned and prepared the carriage the previous night in order to drive his master Cipriano and Uncle Ignacio out to La Manga. Gabriela decided not to go. Since Teo had no mother, she thought her presence would be unseemly. Actually she was afraid. Cipriano in a brocade and silk suit with rich embroidery and a dangling jewel on his shirtfront, drove to his uncle's house to pick him up. The chancery judge, with puffed sleeves and a doublet of scarlet velvet, looked as if he'd stepped out of a painting, which led Cipriano to think about the clothes his uncle would find in La Manga.

After detouring around the washed-out areas on the road, following the path experience had taught Cipriano, the carriage stopped outside the entryway with the hanging grape vine next to the well. There was no one to be seen. Even the dogs and geese had been removed, and Cipriano did not recognize Octavia, the Peñaflor maid, now wearing a scarf and a skirt, when she opened the door. In the sitting room, sitting next to the fire on a wicker settee as if it were his throne, was Segundo Centeno. He'd dressed his hair and beard and substituted a blue half cap for his usual toque.

Cipriano took a deep breath when he noticed the change from the door. But when Segundo stood up to greet Ignacio, the blood rushed to Cipriano's cheeks as he noticed the slashed stockings Segundo was wearing, a style the German lansquenets had made fashionable in Spain thirty years earlier. He was a bizarre spectacle, which quickly dissolved in his shocking naturalness, a naturalness that clashed with his attempt to use words not habitual to him. The ceremony moved forward with the entrance of Teodomira, wearing an equally improper costume: a black skirt with a short train, an attempt to make her size diminish, a filmy silk cloak. Her size, in any case, was slightly excessive. Ignacio, himself of average height, was a bit shorter than she. But the most curious sight of all were those four characters, wrapped in their festive clothes, moving around in the modest sitting room with its wood fire, as if they were on a stage in a theater.

Segundo proudly showed off his possessions to his guest and went on to speak of the contracts signed with his nephew which, as he said, he hoped would *redound* to their mutual benefit. Then he launched into the theme of country life, whose advantages he sang in an exalted song. He assigned the proper value to the fact that Ignacio was a chancery judge, and they both agreed to sign the marriage agreement after lunch, while the future bride and groom were elsewhere.

When he sat down at the table, force of habit outweighed company manners, and Segundo wolfed down the lamb pie and eggs with spinach with his cap on. He only took it off when he noticed the gestures of his scandalized daughter as Octavia was serving some fried tidbits. Finally, having eaten and drunk a bit more than his fill, Segundo sat back in his chair, immobile, his face bright red, his hands over his stomach. Then he let out a belch which he himself cheered with a "Thank God!" of relief and a proverb that once again exalted the virtues of the country over the city and the excellence of his food. "As you yourself know, sir, in fancy houses we get fancy plates, fancy glasses, but not enough food to fatten our asses."

When they were alone, Segundo adopted a more ceremonious manner to deal with Ignacio, addressing him as "judge," or "Don Salcedo." He gave the impression of having studied the subject and that he was so willing to marry off his daughter he'd actually part company with his prize cap. For his part, the judge, overwhelmed by the crudity of the shepherd, wanted to end a meeting that from the moment of his arrival had made him uncomfortable. Following his desire, the agreements were signed without any objections. Don Segundo Centeno would provide his daughter Teodomira with a mere thousand ducats, and Don Ignacio Salcedo would turn over to Don Segundo Centeno as security the sum of five hundred.

From that moment on, Segundo began to speak more loudly and to pat Ignacio on the back as if they were old pals whenever he spoke. It appeared that the sum announced for the purchase of his daughter had surprised him favorably. The judge was just as pleased about the dowry. Segundo was not, it seemed, a confirmed skinflint. Now that the matrimonial contract had been agreed upon, Segundo added, as a matter where there was no room for discussion, that the wedding would be celebrated in the parish church of Peñaflor de Hornija, as long as *Don Salcedo*, did not oppose the idea, on the fifth of June at nine o'clock in the morning. And the banquet, given the fact that he had few relatives, would be a family dinner in the front yard of his farm house, next to the sheep folds that were his life. Ignacio agreed, but once they were in the coach on the way to Villanubla at nightfall, he tried to convince his nephew of the disparity of the union: "A question Cipriano. Does your father-in-law just let his beard grow like that or is it that he doesn't shave? Those would seem to be the same thing, but they aren't."

Cipriano burst out laughing. The Cigales claret had had an effect on him, and his uncle's reaction amused him: "T . . . today he was quite the dandy. I like his lansquenet stockings. I hope my aunt will appreciate them at the wedding."

His nephew's ironic tone disarmed him. He'd gotten into the carriage with the hope of making him reflect, since, by his lights, the two families were irreconcilable. He said exactly that, but Cipriano answered by saying that his uncle's bourgeois prejudices did not affect him. Ignacio cruelly referred to his fiancee by saying that the girl was something larger than a bourgeois prejudice, but Cipriano dodged the issue by arguing that a luncheon was not enough time to judge Teo. In a final, desperate attempt, the judge asked him if the attraction he said he felt for Segundo's daughter was nothing more than a case of love sickness.

"Love sickness? What's that?"

"A carnal desire that overwhelms all reason."

"And it's a sickness?"

The horizon of the Páramo was blazing in the west, so the oaks they were driving toward seemed gigantic.

"Don't take it as a joke, Cipriano. It's an illness with a documented diagnosis and a treatment. You could pay a visit to Doctor Galache—not necessarily for medical treatment but simply to have a talk with him."

Cipriano's smile was forced. He put his hand on his uncle's knee: "As far as that's concerned, sir, you may rest easy. I'm not sick, I'm not suffering love sickness, and I'm going to get married."

On the fifth of June, in the Peñaflor church, decorated with wild flowers, the controversial marriage took place. Gabriela, taken with a sudden indisposition, could not attend. But Ignacio, Dionisio Manrique, the tailor Fermín Gutiérrez, Estacio del Valle, Mister Avelino the Peñaflor trapper, Martín Martín, and Segundo's shepherds from Wamba, Castrodeza, and Ciguñuela did. The nuptial banquet, in the front yard of the big house, was very jolly, and, after dessert, Segundo, with his slashed tights and his half cap on his head, awkwardly stood on top of the table and delivered a sentimental speech in which he cheered the bride and groom, the priest, and the company. He finished off his performance with a nervous jig.

On the way back, the newlyweds had their first squabble. Teodomira insisted on bringing Obstinate, her gentle horse, down to Valladolid, and Cipriano asked her what kind of figure she planned to cut in the

Court with such a worthless beast. In a fury, the Queen of the Páramo retorted that if Obstinate didn't go, she wouldn't go either, and he could consider the marriage null and void. Cipriano tried to put up a fight, but seeing his bride's intransigence, he ultimately gave in. Vicente the servant rode Obstinate down, while the newlyweds shared the carriage, which rolled along side by side with Ignacio's.

In the house, after presenting his bride to the servants, Cipriano put himself to the test he'd been preparing himself for during the past two months. In his muscular little arms, he lifted the lady who was now his legal wife, pushed open the bedroom door with his foot, marched to the nuptial bed, and softly deposited her on the huge wool comforter Segundo had given them. Teodomira stared up at him, her round eyes brimming over with astonishment: "You could have fooled me, sonny. Where do you get all that strength?"

# IX

THE first months of marriage were pleasurable and tranquil for Cipriano Salcedo. Teodomira Centeno, now called Teo, had breakfast in bed at ten o'clock, dressed, and then spent a short time in the shop on the ground floor of the house. Some afternoons, she would take a ride on Obstinate all the way to Simancas or Herrera, or go up to La Manga for a while to see her father. Cipriano, aware that his wife's old nag was unacceptable in Valladolid, the seat of the Royal Court after all, gave her a handsome young chestnut stallion, but Don Segundo's daughter rejected it in a rage, declaring that she preferred the horse she'd had all her life to that pretentious pureblood. The Queen of the Páramo often erupted spontaneously. Usually easy to get along with, she would suddenly throw a fit for no good reason and rave, shout, becoming irascible and aggressive.

To her face, Cipriano told her that the only reason she acted that way was to contradict him, while she would retort that Cipriano was ashamed of her, but that now that they were married, he'd have to suffer the consequences. Once again, Cipriano gave in, and after that, whenever they went out on horseback, they took different routes. If they were visiting Segundo, Teo would wait for him on her spotted horse on the other side of the Puente Mayor. It only took a few weeks for Cipriano to notice something important: He'd organized his life around Teo's indolence and the attacks of rage he was beginning to observe in her. But since the trips to La Manga were infrequent, Cipriano could dedicate his mornings to the warehouse, his afternoons to the shop downstairs, and his free time at home to answering letters and reading.

After he left school, he found his uncle's great library, and now, established in his own home, he was going back to his old habit. After the wedding trip through Avila and Segovia, cities Teo had never seen, Cipriano felt the need to visit Pedrosa, where he hadn't been for two years. Martín Martín had only been able to give him some bits of news on his wedding day in Peñaflor—items such as the passing away of Don Domingo, the old parish priest who'd helped Cipriano get his *hidalgo* title, that the fields at the Villavendimio stream had been incorporated into his property to reinforce his status as landowner when he applied for the title. The fields unfortunately yielded more thistles than grapes. It seemed the current harvest was at normal levels, but it still hadn't been easy to get the farmers to pay their rents. Guided by the maxim that the captain never abandons his ship, Cipriano had decided to visit Pedrosa more frequently.

With regard to sex, the matrimony functioned. Teo's indolence had no effect on it. Nor did she ever try to hire a maid, since Crisanta and Jacoba were sufficient to take care of the house, and Fidela took care of things in the kitchen. Teo had arrived at Corredora de San Pablo 5 like a lady. It was another matter entirely that the conjugal life of Cipriano and Teo corresponded in no way to the impatience and lust of newlyweds. As Crisanta the maid said, you'd think that the master and Madam Teo had already been married for a dozen years.

This was all true when the couple was viewed externally, but internally it was completely false. Cipriano, when he made love to Teo, was discovering surprising peculiarities about her, like the fact that there was absolutely no hair on her body. The white, firm, and appetizing flesh of his wife was totally hairless; there was no hair even in the places that would seem to require it—armpits, pubis. The first time he saw her naked he could barely cover up his perplexity, but in fact what surprised him at first now became a new stimulus. Possessing Teo, he said to himself, was like possessing a marble Venus full of hot water. Teo might be white and robust, but she was not cold.

In their sex play, he called her "my passionate statue," a name that did not seem to disturb her. In any case, Teo behaved like a sensual woman who knew what she was doing, not at all coquettish. Her agile, sheep-shearing hands played an important role in lovemaking. From the first day, she learned to search in the dark for his "little thing," and whenever she found it, she would burst into little shrieks of admiration and enthusiasm. In this way, which was the way it had to be, the "little thing" became the axis of the couple's intimate life. But once she found it, Cipriano assumed the active part in the conquest. He struggled to get on top of her, though it was almost impossible, and once he was on high, he played, lost in Teo's generous mountain range, as hard and solid as he'd surmised it would be during their courtship. Teo quickly metamorphosed into Obstinate, and he joyfully rode her. But because his body lacked the surface area to posses her totally, his little hands had to go into action. She felt him on top of her like some furtive parasite. She received him with enjoyment and in the culminating moment she choked in a boisterous, shameless, and salacious laugh that disconcerted Cipriano the first time but which came to constitute over time the apotheosis of their carnal festivity. It was the sonorous accompaniment to her orgasm.

Giving pleasure to a woman that big appealed to the vanity of little Cipriano. And when she, moments before her guffaw, exclaimed during her paroxysm: "You charge like a bull, little man!," he, who for obvious reasons, detested references to his height, accepted the warm "little man" as a homage to his virile aggressivity. But there were nights when Teo, tired or simply unwilling, remained passive in bed, did not reach for his "little thing." Cipriano would wait expectantly, but the search would never take place, which obliged him to take the initiative on his own, and after some impatient moments, he would begin to climb up his wife's side toward the conquest of those protective protuberances. She would pretend to put up with his siege, but when she found him on top of her, she would whisper provocatively: "What are you looking for, my love?"

The question was a signal that the game they played every night should begin, though from another direction. In any case, after repeated acts of lovemaking, Teo would be left in a faint, her left arm abandoned on top of the pillow, away from her body. Cipriano, always eager for a protective nest, got used to resting his little head in Teo's warm, hairless armpit. Once he was in that safe refuge, he would fall asleep.

During the sultry days of their first summer together, Cipriano made another surprising discovery: Teo did not perspire. She felt the heat, became breathless, got tired, but her pores never opened. In the face of a phenomenon as inexplicable as that, Cipriano became even more reverential. His physical aversion to sweaty armpits, to body odor, found nothing offensive in his wife. Not even on the hot wedding trip, in stuffy inns or on their strolls through old cities did Teo sweat. Meanwhile, Cipriano's reduced anatomy, with little fat to burn, melted like butter on hot days. At first, he explained the anomaly by theorizing that Teo would perspire under other conditions, but she dispelled his notions: "Not even after shearing a hundred lambs has a drop of sweat fallen from my brow."

That was another novelty that enlivened Salcedo's sexuality. He tried to find a reason to explain it all and finally thought he did: The absence of sweat and of body hair were aspects of the same phenomenon. Teo's flesh was so solid that water could not escape it. But despite all that, despite everything, Cipriano, during the first year of married life, was far from considering those strange phenomena defects. To the contrary, he considered them exciting. They were libidinal stimuli. Teo too made extraordinary discoveries about her husband's body. Cipriano was not only a beautiful human being, though small and muscular, but, totally unlike her, exceptionally hairy. Body hair not only grew abundantly in his armpits and pubis but in places that seemed not at all favorable to follicles—his feet, his shoulders, his waist. In the face of such a huge display of masculinity, on some nights (after her explosive laugh) she would wildly shout: "You make me crazy, little man. You've got more hair than a monkey."

Cipriano, who loved the hard, smooth, perfectly regular flesh of his wife was thinking: the attraction of opposites. But between this exclamation by Teo and his own muscular demonstration on the first night, he felt validated, distinguished as a real man, which contributed to the creation of a healthy reciprocity between them. She seemed satisfied with him and he—aside from Obstinate—satisfied with her.

Fearful that Aunt Gabriela might allow their family relationship to cool, Teo and Cipriano invited Ignacio and Gabriela frequently. The result was that eight months after the wedding, Gabriela, as refined and well-dressed as she was, had as much fun with Teo as she did with any of her female friends in town. Actually more, because Teo could transport her to an unknown world, the world of the country and of work, where for her everything was new: personal hygiene, small rituals, living with animals. She could not, for instance, understand that a flock of geese could be more effective in protecting a house than guard dogs, which Teo declared to be the case. Ducks, for Gabriela, were domestic animals devoid of aggressivity. Gabriela asked Teo about her clothing, the household furniture, her jewelry. She could not understand how Teo could live for years with one smock for work and one outfit for festive occasions. The girl admitted that her father was rich, but she added that he'd worked hard to earn it, so wasting money pained him. The fact that Segundo had given her a dowry of a thousand ducats proved that he lived only for her. This thought moved Teo, and she went into the hills of Peñaflor practically every month just to give him a hug. She even nurtured the idea of spending a couple of weeks with him each spring to help with the shearing.

But before she could put her plan into practice, Segundo remarried. Estacio del Valle came down from Villanubla on his mule to notify Cipriano. Segundo Centeno had proposed to Petronila, the eldest daughter of Telesforo Mozo, one of the Castrodeza shepherds. To Estacio's way of thinking, this was a perfect union because in a single stroke, Segundo acquired a bedfellow and a worker to shear sheep; and now that Teodomira was no longer there, Petronila was the best shearer in the district. By the same token, Telesforo Mozo was not deprived either: Segundo authorized him to add to his flock a group of breeding sheep the cost for which would be borne by the master.

As soon as she received this news, Teo told Cipriano to meet her on the far side of the Puente Mayor, so they could ride out to La Manga together. She was in a state, irritated, at the boiling point, incapable of accepting Cipriano's ability to understand her father's decision. But when she reviled her father for the miserable marriage he'd made, Cipriano made her see that Segundo was a slave to his sheep, that with only his own two hands, growing older every day, he could hardly keep things together. In the face of that tacit recognition of how important she'd been to her father, Teo embraced him tightly. For his part, Cipriano asked Segundo if he'd signed any papers with Telesforo Mozo.

Segundo said he hadn't because out in the country papers were superfluous, while a handshake was binding.

But the next month, Telesforo said he was taking double the number of breeding sheep because having ten was like having nothing at all.
Segundo visited his daughter in Valladolid, and when he left the house
reeked of sheep manure, a smell that didn't dissipate for several days.
Segundo wanted the help of Ignacio, but his son-in-law told him that
out in the country, despite his earlier opinion, a handshake was as fragile as it was in town, that Segundo had handed Telesforo Mozo a
weapon he could use to squeeze sheep out of him until Judgment Day.
Hearing that, Segundo abandoned the project of soliciting Ignacio's
help and went back out to the hills, with his stench of excrement, hanging his head, and very down in the mouth.

When April came, Cipriano found the time to visit Pedrosa. As
usual, he crossed the Puente Mayor and galloped along the slopes of the
hills until he came to Villalar. He found his farmer having breakfast, and
they rode out together to the Villavendimio fields. The young vines had
barely begun to sprout leaves, and the lanes between them hadn't been
raked clean. Cipriano suggested to Martín Martín the possibility of plant-
ing wheat there, but Martín rejected the idea, because grain just wouldn't
grow in such poor ground. They spent the morning visiting the other
vineyards, and Lucrecia, a very old woman now, served them lunch just
as she had during the lifetime of the deceased Don Bernardo.

Later that afternoon, Salcedo took a room in the inn, which now
belonged to Baruque's daughter, in the Plaza de la Iglesia. As he was
closing the shutters to nap during siesta, he caught sight of a priest sitting on a stone bench at the church reading a book. He was so absorbed
that neither the flocks of pigeons flying over his head nor the peasants
crossing the plaza singing as they spurred on their mules could distract
him. After sleeping a while, Cipriano opened the shutters and found the
priest still in the same place. He was so fixed in his place he looked like
a straw man, but when Salcedo came out to say hello, the new priest,
who replaced the deceased Don Domingo, courteously stood up.

Cipriano introduced himself, but the priest already knew who he
was. The townspeople had spoken about him, about his rise to *hidalgo*
status, and the party that followed, but he was curious about one detail:

Was the chancery judge, Don Ignacio Salcedo, a relative? "My uncle, he's my uncle," Cipriano clarified, adding that he was also his guardian. Then the priest spoke of Ignacio as one of the most cultured and well-informed men in Valladolid. His library, if not the first, was certainly the second in number of volumes. He then introduced himself: "Pedro Cazalla," he said humbly. In turn, Cipriano asked him if he were related to Doctor Cazalla, the preacher: "We're brothers. For a few months, he lived in Salamanca, but now he lives with my mother in Valladolid."

Salcedo confessed he always attended the Doctor's sermons. "Yes, he's got an easy style," said Cazalla without giving the matter much importance.

He seemed to be younger than the Doctor, with his thick, black hair gray at the temples, his suntanned masculine face, and his dark eyes with their scrutinizing gaze.

"Something more than an easy style," retorted Salcedo. "I'd say he's the best sacred orator we have at the moment. He constructs his sermons the way a good architect designs a building."

Pedro Cazalla shrugged his shoulders. Excessive praise of his brother embarrassed him. He accepted his expressive facility, his spirituality. The emperor had brought him to Germany for a few years precisely for that reason, for his spirituality. That was an honor and an experience his brother would never forget, now that Charles V was preparing to retire to Yuste.

Cipriano asked Cazalla why his brother systematically preached outside of convents. Cazalla again shrugged his shoulders: "That way, he's freer. A community of monks generates many kinds of criticism, and the results, it they find something to criticize, are not always healthy."

Salcedo could feel his curiosity about the new parish priest intensifying. His passion for reading, the newness of his ideas, an absence of paternalism (so common among rural priests), surprised him. Night had already fallen when he said goodbye to him. It was the priest who suggested the possibility of their meeting the next afternoon, an invitation Cipriano—who'd planned to return to Valladolid the next morning—did not decline. At ten, after breakfast, the priest was still reading in the atrium, in the same position he'd been in the previous afternoon. When Cipriano passed by to get him after lunch, he was still

motionless on the stone bench by the church. He closed his book as
Cipriano approached and stood up: "May I ask what you're reading
with such zeal, Father?"

"I'm rereading Erasmus. It's impossible to exhaust his thinking."

"There was a time when I was a veteran Erasmist," said Cipriano
mockingly.

The priest was surprised: "Were you really interested in Erasmus?"

"Let me explain, father. I'm talking about my childhood, about the
Erasmus Conference. In my school, two sides formed, and I was with
the Erasmists. And even though neither group knew who Erasmus was,
we actually fought because of him."

They'd walked across the town without any preconceived plan and
now found themselves on the road to Villavendimio, walking toward
Toro. Cazalla made comments about the animals and birds, revealing
his expertise in country matters. He said the spotted starlings were
more quarrelsome and better nest-builders than the black ones, more
talkative and musical as well.

But the priest was interested in Cipriano's school days. He asked
him where he'd studied. "The Foundling Hospital," said Salcedo.

"But you weren't one, weren't a foundling, I mean."

"I wasn't, but my father subjected me to that hard discipline. He
didn't believe in my intelligence, and several tutors had failed with me."

"Wasn't Father Arnaldo at that school?"

"Father Arnaldo and Father Toval, on opposite sides in the mat-
ter of Erasmus. Erasmus inspired Luther, according to Father Arnaldo.
Without him, the Reformation would never have taken place. Father
Toval, to the contrary, believed in the Dutchman's good faith."

Cazalla's eyes seemed to focus on something remote: "Those were
days of hope," he said suddenly. "The emperor was on Erasmus's side.
He supported him, as did the inquisitor Manrique. Those who attacked
him were nothing more than pesky mosquitoes. It was around that time
that Erasmus published the second part of his *Hyperaspistes*, rebutting
some of Luther's assertions. That consolidated his prestige with the
King, who wrote to him, using "honored, devout, and beloved by us" as
his greeting."

Cazalla's words had a shaken, nostalgic tone. "And what," asked

Salcedo, "ruined that zeal?" Everything turned upside down. It was fate. Manrique, the inquisitor, stopped supporting Erasmus, and the king went to Italy and forgot him. The monks took advantage of the opportunity to attack him from the pulpit. Carvajal made a bitter response to the *Hyperaspistes*, and Erasmus, instead of remaining silent and aloof, answered him violently. The situation had reversed itself. From that moment on, Erasmus and Luther were, for the Inquisition, branches on the same tree."

They'd reached Old Man's Bend, near where the rushes grew, and a magpie was holding forth insolently. The priest contemplated the bird with curiosity but without stopping. The sun widened and grew redder as it sank behind the gray hills to the west. Pedro Cazalla stopped and asked: "Have you ever noticed these Castilian sunsets?"

"I enjoy them very often. The sunsets here in the highlands are frequently overwhelming."

By then, they'd turned around, and the afternoon was beginning to grow cooler. In the distance they could see the little adobe houses lorded over by the church. The storks and their chicks were walking around; they stood out in the rushes like schematic drawings. Father Cazalla again looked at the setting sun. The half-light of sunset fascinated him. Then in the still air, a bell tolled. Cazalla had to hurry. He fixed his deep eyes on Salcedo: "Yesterday, Erasmus was a hope, and today his books are prohibited. Nothing of that keeps some of us from believing in the Reform he proposed. The Council of Trent will contribute nothing substantial."

The next morning, the sky was marred by some white clouds, but Lightning flew along the Villavieja road over the hills at a full gallop. Cipriano enjoyed the speed, the cool wind on his face, but all the while he thought about the Cazalla brothers, their melancholy, and their reforming anxieties. Now he understood better the sensation of emptiness the Doctor's sermons produced in him. Erasmianism was being purged out of Castile, and because of that, Erasmus's cause was a lost cause. Even so, twenty years earlier, Father Arnaldo had ordered the boys to pray for the Church, for the disappearance of Erasmus's doctrines. How was it possible to reconcile such disparate responses to the same phenomenon? Lightning left the town of Tordesillas behind, and when he reached Simancas, made for the main road and crossed the Roman bridge a league and a half from the village.

Teo welcomed him as if they hadn't seen each other for a month. That had been their first separation, and she missed him. After dinner, the Passionate Statue cut the dessert short, and to the surprise of Crisanta, at ten o'clock the couple was in bed. Teo hugged him close, and he liked feeling protected, in the fortress, safe from any traps. Then, she reached for *the little thing* and commented in honeyed tones how wonderful it was her husband hadn't forgotten about her out in Pedrosa, while Salcedo labored to climb up on the plateau of protuberances. He felt the choked guffaw of his wife, vibrant and prolonged, but that did not stop her from starting all over again a few seconds later. Cipriano was surprised at her eagerness. It seemed Teo was linking together her contacts in a compulsive attitude, as if she were testing his resistance. And after a fourth time, when her pursuit stopped, Cipriano, extenuated, sought refuge in her armpit. Out in Pedrosa he'd missed her warmth and had to sleep with his cap on. Back in his own house, he felt secure and happy, even if Teo's attitude was still undefined.

When he awakened, he found his wife agitated, inquisitive, pressing. There was another stumbling block, apparently insignificant, in their marriage: "Why don't we have a child, Cipriano? We've been married for ten months, and nothing ever happens to me."

Salcedo caressed her the deep red curls on the back of her neck, winding them around his fingers, but still not calming her: "Oh darling, these things don't work by a schedule! They don't follow our will. Also, the Salcedos were never very fertile. You shouldn't get impatient over this. It will happen."

It was easy to see that Teo had thought about the situation: "Every woman who gets married has a child, Cipriano. Why didn't you tell me beforehand that your family had difficulties? Every time you leave your seed in me I think that this time it will take hold. But it never does."

She was bristling with anger, resentful, but he treated the matter as unimportant: "Don't worry about it, darling. We Salcedos reproduce in small numbers. My great-grandfather only had one child and my grandfather two, but with eight years between them. Uncle Ignacio has no children, and don't forget that my mother, may she rest in peace, spent five years treating her supposed sterility. And do you think the treatment helped? Not at all. My mother became pregnant four years after stopping, when God willed it, and when she'd already forgotten about her obsession. There are astral influences that to a certain degree determine these things. The body needs time to ripen."

"How long did your mother's need?"

"Exactly nine years and seven days. Maybe the gestation of the Salcedos expresses itself in years rather than months. All that aside, the number is curious."

Teo hesitated: "Could . . . could your *little thing* be sick?"

"You know it works perfectly well. Now, I talked about the low fertility of the Salcedos, but the problem may be on your side. Doctor Almenara, who was famous in his time, used to say that two out of three instances of infertility derived from the wives."

Teo's impatience translated itself into a frenetic sexual eagerness. She thought, doubtless, that frequency would increase the possibilities. Cipriano tried to instruct her every night: "Darling, more important than the number of times is your receptive condition. When I enter you, try to be relaxed, receptive. Don't forget that every time we do it, I introduce into your vagina hundreds or thousands of seeds that try to find a place to take root. But fertility does not depend on the number of seeds but on the ground you prepare to receive them."

Outwardly, Teo seemed calm, but she was actually obsessed. She thought about nothing else and would use even the flimsiest pretext to trot it out. He'd told her: Many problems are resolved by waiting, by forgetting about them. She tried to follow his advice, but instead of thoughts, it was her anguish about how to purge her mind of those thoughts that tortured her. She confided to her husband: "All I ever think about is that I shouldn't be thinking about it. I'm beginning to believe this obsession will drive me crazy."

"Why don't you give me a time period by the end of which you have to be pregnant? Why don't you wait for a few years before making any decisions? In four years, you'll be twenty seven, the ideal age to have children."

Teo said nothing. She tacitly gave him the time period, but little by little she lost faith in him and in losing her faith lost her sexual fire.

She hardly ever searched for *the little thing*, and when she did, it was halfheartedly, without the ardor of earlier times. She knew that the child had to come through that means, but she'd now spent more than a year trying without success. Salcedo was fully aware of his wife's disheartenment and tried to distract her by having her work in the shop, but Teo was bored there. Then he thought that since shearing time was approaching, Teo could spend a long time in La Manga helping her father. But before the shearing began, the news reached them: Telesforo Mozo intended to divide the flock he tended fifty-fifty with Segundo. This was no longer a matter of his taking possession of a fairly large number of sheep but of taking half his master's flock. Segundo rejected the idea out of hand. He fired Telesforo, took Benita, the daughter of his Wamba shepherd—Gildardo Albarrán—as his mistress, and relegated his legal wife, Petronila, to the condition of maid and shearer at the salary of six reales a month.

Given the gravity of the situation, Teo went to live in La Manga. She immediately noticed Petronila's resentment, though she never said a word and spent the day walking around the house with her eyes averted, making faces and melodramatic gestures. For his part, Segundo made sure the problem would never be solved: He ordered Petronila to make the adulterous bed while it was still warm and wash his and his mistress's underwear. Petronila spent the rest of the day shearing sheep. She said nothing. She would sit down to shear on a stool and wouldn't open her mouth no matter how hard the Queen of the Páramo tried to engage her in conversation.

One night, Teo took a walk and seemed to see between two lights the furtive silhouette of a man hiding in the oaks. She spoke seriously to her father: He shouldn't take such chances. He should change his attitude. No man would simply accept being fired and seeing his daughter repeatedly humiliated that way. For his part, Gildardo strolled around the farm as freely as if it were his own property. He met with Segundo in the sitting room, walked through the front door of the house, and chatted with him as an equal. At the same time, Gildardo asked for nothing. Having seen how Segundo had treated Telesforo, having learned from his failure, he knew that it was better to be on Segundo's good side than on his bad side.

With things as they were, Teo's old aspiration faded. She was less concerned about becoming a mother than she was about keeping her father alive. And when Cipriano visited her once a week, she had time to chat with him as she did during their courtship: strolling over the hills, rousing flocks of wild pigeons out of the oaks, their crops stuffed with acorns, or seeing partridges scuttle across the clearings. Cipriano believed distraction was a kind of therapy and was sure Teo would return to her normal life and allow him a reasonable period of time before declaring their marriage a failure. But he slept badly. When Teo denied him the shelter of her armpit, his head became cold, turned in odd directions during the night while he slept, so that when he woke up he had a stiff neck.

He went back to being the abandoned child he'd been. He used caps, hats, and even hoods lined with fur as replacements for Teo's armpit. At the same time, he tried to attenuate Teo's prolonged absence with frequent visits to his aunt and uncle. Gabriela, very satisfied with being childless, could not understand Teo's attitude. There are other things in life—institutions, the sick, hungry children, charity schools. To want at all costs a being of our own blood on whom to pour our affection is egoistic. In his heart, Cipriano agreed, but at the same time he never stopped understanding that giving birth was the highest aspiration of all women in the world.

One morning, before he left for the Ghetto, a urgent message from Peñaflor informed Cipriano that his father-in-law had been murdered. His throat had been slit with a sickle. Telesforo Mozo, the murderer, had turned himself over to the authorities in Valladolid, and when asked what his reason for committing the crime was, he said: "He threw me out into the street like a dog and ruined my daughter. He didn't deserve to live."

Cipriano instantly went out to La Manga. He took the time to bury his father-in-law in the atrium of the Peñaflor church and to take possession of the papers Segundo had in his desk. Petronila, terrified, had fled the house; Gildardo Albarrán, on the other hand, appeared on behalf of his daughter, not because he expected the law to help him, but because he had witnesses that Don Segundo had made a kept woman of his daughter without his consent. Teo's composure was admirable.

The shearing was finished, and that gave her a sense of relief. Also, her father's bloody death seemed horrible to her, but at least he didn't suffer, which was a consolation.

Cipriano foresaw serious complications and an increase in work until it could all be straightened out, but his Uncle Ignacio, as usual, simplified matters. Mister Centeno's will was clear. Teo was the only heir; Petronila would have the use of a small farm and a lease on the house as long as the time of the contract allowed; Benita, the mistress, went back to Wamba with her father, and Estacio del Valle was left to resolve the problem of the shepherds, since Segundo's herds, as Cipriano told him in his letter, had become the property of Teodomira Centeno, his wife.

# X

TEO lost a few pounds when she went into mourning, a distinguished and respectful mourning that caused her to wear over her bosom a necklace of black pearls that contrasted with the pallor of her skin. Cipriano also shrank, dressed in a sleeveless leather coat, black—as was the fashion—and wearing a collar that was so high it covered half his neck. Above the collar appeared the ruffled boarder of his shirt. But mourning did not resolve the difficulties in the couple's relationship. Teo's hopes for motherhood returned, while Cipriano maintained she should give him a period of time and be sensible. In his eagerness to convince her, Cipriano brought up the fact that his father was eight years older than his Uncle Ignacio, that she should realize that his grandparents had probably had the same intimate relations both before and after their first child.

Even so, one afternoon, certain he'd never convince her, he made a private visit to Doctor Galache. He would have preferred to see the doctor who'd help bring him into the world, Doctor Almenara, but he'd died eleven years earlier. Doctor Galache examined Cipriano and said everything was fine, but that he could enrich the quality of his sperm by drinking an infusion of verbena and honeysuckle after each meal. Salcedo admitted he felt physically strong, and that the sterility did not seem to derive from his side. It was then Doctor Galache made the request he feared most: "Why don't you bring your wife to see me? Wives are often the cause of matrimonial sterility."

Salcedo told him that she wasn't prepared for such a visit, but that perhaps with time she might decide to come. Cipriano said nothing to

Teo about seeing Galache; nor did he start drinking the infusion.

The next morning he left for Pedrosa. It was a calm day with white clouds and high temperature. Cipriano's lightness, the speed of his horse, and the maze of shortcuts and side roads he'd come to know allowed him to reach Pedrosa in a little over two hours. He began skirting the hills, then turned on the Geria path, and from there rode in a straight line through the young vines crossed Villavieja and Villalar, reaching Pedrosa through the fields of wheat without having to make any detours. Seated outside some shack, there would be a man; then a rat terrier would bark when the horse passed. Sometimes children would wave.

He took a room in the Baruque's daughter's inn and immediately went to see his farmer. Days earlier he'd had a luminous idea: Pull up the vines from Villavendimio and replace them with a stand of pines. No one had ever dared plant pines on the right bank of the Duero, but the quality of the soil, thin and sandy, simply demanded it. Besides, Martín Martín was an expert in pines. He'd cultivated white pine with his uncle over in Olmedo, knew how to tend trees, and even knew the fluctuations of pine nuts in the market: "The advantage of pine over other plantings," he said, "is that with pines you can predict the harvest two years in advance."

"How can you do that?" asked Cipriano.

"Look, sir, today you harvest the ripe nuts, but on the tree you can see the bud, that is, next year's nut. It's a tiny thing about this big," he said pointing to half of the first joint on his finger, "but it's the nut for the next year."

Cipriano Salcedo felt satisfied about his project, and Martín Martín agreed to hire a team of farmhands to remove the vines from the Villavendimio acreage. With Cazalla, Cipriano showed off as an expert landowner. He'd thought it over a great deal. After incorporating that land into his property he just couldn't let it lay fallow. He would plant white pines, which produced pine nuts and indicated beforehand the next two harvests. Which was to say, it was the only crop from which no surprises were expected. For his part, Pedro Cazalla invited him to go partridge hunting with him the next morning at the foot of the La Gallarita hills. Cipriano burst into laughter: "You, father, are much more surprising than white pines."

First light found them at the salt marshes of Cenegal, a long league from Casasola. Cazalla was carrying a short shotgun over his left shoulder and in his right hand a cage containing a male partridge. It was covered with sackcloth. Just when the sun was coming up, they came to the blind, a huge, hollowed out thicket with an opening cut into it for shooting. Cazalla put the uncovered cage on a kind of pedestal, weighing it down with four stones, and then he and Cipriano went into the blind and sat on a bench. It was growing brighter, and while the male partridge was making its first screech of the morning, Pedro Cazalla very proudly showed Cipriano his shotgun, which he'd brought from the Basque master armorer Juan Ibáñez. It probably measured a bit more than three feet in length. Cazalla, who was very handy, had made the walnut butt himself and inserted the iron barrel at the other end. The gun was loaded through the muzzle, by the tamping down of powder with a bit of wadding and then adding a handful of shot. Cazalla showed him the lead shot some friends had sent him from Germany.

Showing Cipriano the firing mechanism, he became almost childishly excited. It had a serpentine shape, like an "s." On top, the hunter would place the burning match, while the lower part was the trigger. When the hunter squeezed the trigger, the match would touch the hole in the barrel, and when it touched the powder, there would be an explosion. But the hunter would have to hold the weapon on target for four or five seconds, until the charge ignited, if he wanted to knock down his prey.

It grew lighter, and the caged partridge filled the field with his ardent and persuasive calls. From the hills, echoed a remote response: "Did you hear that? The fields are answering."

"Are the other birds coming to set the prisoner free?"

Cazalla grinned, the indulgent smile of the expert toward the novice: "It isn't like that. It's mating season, and one male comes to the call of another to fight over the females with him. He's coming to fight. Sometimes he comes alone, and sometimes he brings his mate so she can witness his victory."

The fields were responding with greater and greater insistence, and the caged partridge stretched out his neck, broadcasting his cries throughout the Páramo. Cazalla carefully extended the muzzle of his shotgun through the viewing hole and warned Salcedo: "Keep silent."

The male changed tone, substituting the harsh shriek of the beginning with a inextricable chatter, a confidential jabber.

"Careful now, they're on their way."

Salcedo stretched forward until he could just see the caged partridge. He was walking around in circles, pecking at the cage, never ceasing his prattling, while another partridge, at the foot of the pedestal, clucked in a lower tone. Cazalla then whispered, as he fixed the butt against his shoulder: "The fool has come. See him?"

Salcedo nodded. The free partridge straightened his neck and stared angrily up at the caged bird. The priest added: "Here comes his mate behind him."

Salcedo peered through he hole, and, indeed, a smaller partridge was following the first one. Cazalla squeezed his cheek against the weapon and aimed at the male. He was about sixty feet away, next to the pedestal, and he opened his wings slightly in a challenging way. Cazalla squeezed the lower part of the "s," nervously followed the path of the free male through his sights until the explosion startled him. When the smoke cleared, Salcedo saw the partridge flapping weakly on the ground while three blue feathers rose in the air. The female slowly walked away from the scene of the tragedy. Cazalla rested his shotgun on its butt. He was smiling: "Everything went perfectly, don't you think?"

Salcedo wrinkled his lips in disgust. He did not approve of ambushes, that treacherous waiting, the intervention of his friend in the sentimental life of the birds. But Cazalla, insensible to all that, was again packing powder into the barrel of his shotgun.

"You didn't like it? It's a clean, almost scientific way to hunt."

Salcedo shook his head: "Games with love seem dishonest to me. Why did you fire?"

Cazalla shrugged his shoulders. Through the opening, they could see the caged bird fluff up his wings, proud of his accomplishment: "I had to. If I didn't shoot, the caged bird would be ruined and never sing again. Death is necessary for the prisoner to go on inciting the countryside."

Silence returned. Through the sighting hole, the Páramo, full of light, disclosed itself. A pile of stones on the right produced a dark, slim shadow. The grass was black and cool, and Salcedo said to himself that a good-sized flock wouldn't be a bad idea in Pedrosa. He'd speak with Martín Martín. As in La Manga, the soil here was full of rocks. Cazalla unwrapped a small package and handed a meat pie to Salcedo. His sister Beatriz had made them. The partridge in the cage seemed fully rested. He'd forgotten his former adversary and went back to showing off and serenading the fields. The initial scene repeated itself half an hour later, but now a solitary male appeared, a widower or perhaps a bachelor without a partner. Cazalla, made nervous by the long lapse of time between his pulling the trigger and the powder igniting, missed when the bird jumped up on the cage. But contrary to what Salcedo expected, he did not get angry. The matchlock shotgun was a very tricky weapon, he said calmly, and his friend, the Basque Juan Ibáñez, was not making anything better.

They could hear the harsh cries of the magpies, the peeps of the larks, and the raucous caws of the crows. It was hot inside the blind. The caged partridge walked around in circles and from time to time gave out a weak screech that lacked his earlier brio. The bird himself was surprised when a response came. A flaccid dialogue took place between the two birds, who barely paused to let each other sing. Despite his feeble response, he had to be an enraged male because his approach to the cage was more rapid than that of the first two. In effect, he walked into the open space with his coquettish mate behind and responded to the confidential prattle of the caged bird with a fierce attack, his wings half-open. Pedro Cazalla brought him down with a perfect shot. He was about six feet from the pedestal, and again the caged bird trumpeted his victory by stretching his neck as far as it would go.

Cazalla got up from the bench smiling. It was midday, time to return. He hung the two partridges from the perch and put the cover over the cage when his own bird began to raise a racket. Salcedo carried the shotgun when he left the blind. He stared at the weapon with curiosity and doubt, but Cazalla, who was not wearing his priest's cassock, but buttoned leggings noted: "The shotgun is not a well-designed weapon. My friend Juan Ibáñez will make something better one of these days."

The sun was baking the road, and Salcedo noted the moist heat of his hat on his forehead. When the salt marshes of Cenegal came into sight, Cazalla went over to the first, sat down on the shore, took off his shoes, and put his feet in the water. When Salcedo imitated him, a pair of wild ducks flew out of the reeds. "They're always here," said Cazalla. "They always make love here."

"Might they be nesting?"

"It's late in the day for that. That duck's an early riser and likes his sex early too."

The reeds broke as he marched through them, and Salcedo felt a rare pleasure as he sensed the oozing mire between his toes. Then he spied an enormous frog swimming among the bulrushes. It was swimming slowly without disturbing the water, its bulging, cold, and indifferent eyes fixed on something. He pointed the repugnant creature out to Cazalla.

"That's the female," he said with curiosity. "She's copulating right now. Did you notice?"

Just when he heard him, Salcedo discovered the male, a diminutive, fearless frog on the female's wide back. His stomach turned. He felt a kind of blow, then nausea. He stared at the two coupling animals but did not see them. He saw a barge with Teo's face and breasts like a figurehead and himself rowing alone on the stern. He felt disgust with himself, such an overwhelming repugnance that he hastily got out of the water. But before he could reach the road, he vomited. Cazalla walked behind him:

"Are you getting sick? All the color's drained from your face."

"Those animals, those animals," Salcedo repeated.

"The frogs, you mean?" He laughed: "The female is ten times larger than the male. Funny, isn't it? The male is barely anything more than a device for injecting sperm. He's just a little sack of sperm."

"Don't say any more, father, I beg you."

The murky image wouldn't leave his head, even though he tortured Lightning with his spurs; it was as if the grotesque vision were related to his speed. The Teo-frog allowing herself to be climbed by the Cipriano-frog, and, once he'd conquered her, sailing on her around the great lake—it was a scene that again turned his stomach. Would he have the courage to have sex with Teo again?

The Queen of the Páramo welcomed him home with an exaggerated show of relief: "Oh, you're finally here, little boy! My God, I thought you'd never come home! I found myself alone, Cipriano, and I said to myself: Alone I can't have a child. I need my husband's *little thing*."

But that night, Cipriano made no attempt to approach her. And Teo, as if she sensed something, did not grope for the *little thing*. And the next night the same scene repeated itself, each one waited for the other to start things. But for Cipriano, the image of the huge female frog swimming in the Cenegal salt marsh was stopping him dead. Teo's unfruitful wait went on for a whole week. Cipriano kept seeing in her the authoritarian, capricious, and possessive frog. And the complementary image disgusted him even more: the servile, accommodating, and diligent attitude of the little inseminating male clinging to her back. A little bag of sperm, is what Cazalla had said.

Never as in those days was Cipriano so distanced from any sensual inclination. The mere idea of attacking his wife's flank made him nauseous. Teo finally grew angry, overcome by an intense anxiety, the prelude to an attack of hysteria. Her husband didn't want a child. She even disdained his *little thing*, lamenting that she lacked the ability to inseminate herself. The *little thing* was the essential element for reproduction, but she could no longer count on it. Her husband had made it disappear as if by magic. She wept over him, wearing mourning— unlikely to change Cipriano's mood. Every time he embraced her without being able to get his arms around her, he saw her as the frog, enormous and absorbent, swimming in the salt marsh, demanding he make her pregnant.

Things went from bad to worse. Cipriano couldn't leave the house. Teo moaned and shrieked for no reason, stopped eating and sleeping. Finally, one morning Cipriano suggested they visit Doctor Galache, the most sought-after physician in town at the moment. They would set out the problem before him. Cipriano did not conceal the fact that he'd visited the doctor before or the fact that the doctor had given a good opinion of his reproductive possibilities and expressed an interest in seeing her.

Cipriano found Galache as solemn and open as the first time. He was dressed luxuriously in velvet, his hands very well manicured and bare. He thought that forty years earlier, his parents had made a similar visit without results. And that he'd been born after his mother had abandoned treatment for four years. He was about to mention it, but he kept silent. His impertinence would most certainly have wiped out his wife's incipient optimism. He therefore made no reference to that fact in his statement about his family history and the meager fertility of the Salcedos. Doctor Galache listened gravely. Then he said: "Excuse me. I'm going to examine your wife."

Teo stretched out on a table. And for a few moments, the room was silent, until Galache straightened up: "There's nothing out of the ordinary. This lady's reproductive mechanism is fine, perfect for conception."

He sat them both down in a gallery with the table and white chairs.

"I'll be frank. Our grandparents, in a case like this, when both parties seem perfectly capable of procreation, would have had recourse to superstitious tests, tests we know today are useless—the garlic test for instance. But I know, without any need to insert garlic in this lady's vagina—since there is no communication between the vagina and the mouth—that my patient is not blocked up. Let's move on to practical matters."

Cipriano became nervous: "Do you think we'll be able to do it?"

The doctor joined the fingers of his bare hands: "The two of you have come to me because you have confidence in me. And I am going to try to resolve your problem. In the first place, the history of the Salcedo family is important: The males are not excessively fertile. But neither are they sterile. They require time. There are couples who need only nine months to have a family, but not the Salcedos. They've needed six, even nine years to reproduce. Theirs is a slow reproduction which is part of their nature. With regard to you, madam, you are going to have to remain calm. Let yourself go on living, keep yourself occupied, don't think, and I assure you that when the Salcedo reproductive time is over, you will be pregnant. I solemnly promise you that, as long as you know how to wait and you welcome your husband's embraces enthusiastically, with the idea of conceiving. No woman has gotten pregnant, at least as far as I know, with sobs and tears. Make an effort."

Doctor Galache stood up. He rapidly scrawled some enigmatic words in his prescription book. Then he added: "The men in the Salcedo family suffer a peculiarity we physicians today refer to as reluctant semen. Against it, the best medicine is patience. Don't hurry things, just wait for the necessary time to pass. But, just to try something, I am going to help you. Every night, Mister Salcedo is to take a preparation of silver and steel scoria to augment ejaculation. It works, and there are no side effects. And you, madam, will do me this favor: Mark out a period of four consecutive days each month for sexual abstinence. On the fifth night, at the approximate time you would be making love, do not do so. Instead, drink a hot cup of salvia with salt. It's the best way to prepare the body for conception."

Teo walked out of the examining room, rejuvenated. The doctor's advice eradicated all her apprehensions. It had been a year and a half since her father's death, so when she reached home, Teo sewed a white border along her bodice. It might not have seemed it, but that little ribbon softened her mourning, made it less rigid and sterilizing. And it animated Teo. Later, in the days that followed the examination, she followed the doctor's advice very carefully. She brought the mix of silver and steel scoria for Cipriano, and each month she punctually called a four-day halt to their physical relations. On the fifth, she drank a hot mix of salvia and salt. Cipriano, who'd finally managed to banish the grim image of the mating frog, was no longer sexually nullified. He even experienced certain pressing desires every time the prescribed days of abstinence came up.

"Are you crazy? Don't you remember Galache's recommendation?"

She would turn her back on him, and he would be left alone, unprotected, as he was every night. Teo still denied him the warm shelter of her armpit he needed to fall asleep, so Cipriano found a substitute: He would fold a pillow and place his head inside the fold. He eventually got used to the innovation, so now they slept back-to-back. Of course, whenever Teo rolled over, she would pull all the covers off Cipriano, who shivered. But he thought it was all fine, seeing that his wife was back to normal.

As if that weren't enough, Teo decided to begin a more active life. She would get up early and go down to the shop to help Elvira Esteban at the counter. Autumn was moving along, so Valladolid made ready to face the hard Castilian winter by buying coats and other fur-lined articles of clothing. It was curious to note that once their novelty had worn off, fur-lined clothing had become indispensable in Castile. At night, Teo would give Cipriano the day's sales report and the condition of their finances. She got used to business and started taking pleasure in accounting.

Domestic peace restored Cipriano's freedom, so a month later, at the end of September, he attended a new sermon by Doctor Cazalla, this one on Catholic egoism as opposed to the unconditional giving of Himself by Christ in His passion. The Doctor was very hard that afternoon. He talked about how scandalous it was that monasteries could make use of vassals, about prelates who thought they were aristocrats, about gluttonous, lascivious bishops. For once, Cazalla went straight to the point and didn't mince words. There was a murmur of protest and disbelief among those present, but just then, the Doctor wisely referred to Cisneros, the confessor of Queen Isabella the Catholic, a man who in his day had spoken out against those excesses, a man whose conduct we believers should imitate.

Cipriano passed by his Uncle Ignacio's house and borrowed a copy of Erasmus's *Enchiridion*. He suspected that the Doctor had deliberately refrained from mentioning Erasmus and had used Cisneros as a kind of screen, for the simple reason that the people had good memories of him. He opened the book after dinner and read it slowly, trying to wring all the meaning out of each line. When the light in his lamp was waning, Cipriano closed it. He'd finished it. He felt discouraged. He was aware that he was ill-prepared to debate the work's essential points: the efficacy of baptism, heard confession, or free will. But he noted the initial disquiet of the dissident, his unquiet spirit, his need to ask questions. He slept badly. He was unsettled, knowing there existed another world, different from the one in which he was living, a world he perhaps had the obligation to know.

Early the next morning he left for Pedrosa. He left Teo with Aunt Gabriela. She would stay with his wife during his absence. He'd been thinking about Pedro Cazalla for several nights, and now that he had no spiritual director, he told himself that Cazalla might be the right person for that job. He loathed bland directors who loved confessional secrets, and Pedro Cazalla looked like a solid, open man who wouldn't have to be asked to take charge of his spiritual life.

For the first time, they took the Villalar road, through the flat-tened stubble fields. The vista lacked the geometric accompaniment of the vineyards, and Cipriano wondered if the priest would have a prop-er road for each situation. As it was, the ruined appearance of the bare fields, their desolation, paralleled his own disturbed soul. Salcedo con-fessed to the priest that he'd read the *Enchiridion* after listening to his brother's harsh sermon against clerical abuses.

"The one led to the other?"

"Something like that. I wanted to know the source of his inspiration."

"And you found the source?"

"Your brother used Cisneros as a screen, but in reality he'd drunk at the fountain of Erasmus. It was clear. It's likely he referred to Cisneros to quiet the muttering and protests of those present."

Pedro Cazalla scrutinized Salcedo's diminutive profile: "And what was your impression of the *Enchiridion*?"

"It was weak. As you know, the book is immature."

"Which edition did you read?"

"The one done by the canon of Palencia, Fernández Madrid."

"What?" exclaimed Cazalla in surprise. "The *Enchiridion* is much harsher than all that. Alonso Fernández declawed it, made it pretty. He made it into a sweet little book for family reading."

Encouraged by the silence and the solitude, Cipriano confided his scruples and doubts to Cazalla. He'd always suffered from them. From the time he was a child, he'd had doubts about good works. He repeat-ed his prayers over and over again because he feared he was falling into routine, that he wasn't thinking about what he was doing.

"Why do you torture yourself that way? Have faith in Christ, in the merits of His passion. What value can our acts have compared to that?"

Cazalla's words, his deep gaze, the persuasive tone of his voice calmed Cipriano: "I'd like to believe it's that way," he murmured.

"Why this lack of faith? If Christ died for our sins, Why would he demand reparation for them?"

The wheat stubble was growing lighter, turning almost white in the fading light. Salcedo thought the words of this Cazalla were also sounding like Erasmus, and he told him so. Pedro Cazalla smiled and shrugged his shoulders: "You should worry less about the source of the ideas and more about the ideas themselves, whether they're moral and just or not."

"Father, do you mean that our sacrifices, our suffering, our prayers are useless, that they lack meaning?"

Cazalla delicately rested a hand on Cipriano's arm: "No good work is useless. Neither is it absolutely necessary to enter the kingdom of heaven. But you only speak to me about works. Don't you have faith?"

They sat down on the side of the road, and Cazalla rested his elbows on his knees, which covered by his cassock. He held his head in his hands. Cipriano's voice was strained with emotion: "I have faith. A lot. I believe in Christ and that Christ is the son of God."

Cazalla barely let him finish: "Well? Christ came to the world to redeem us. His passion made us free."

Salcedo looked at him but was self-absorbed. It seemed he was giving form in his own mind to the ideas the other was formulating. Even so, he intuited that he'd just made a rare discovery: "That's true. Christ said he that believes in me shall be saved; he will not die forever. If you consider it carefully, he only asked faith of us."

"Do you know a wonderful little book titled *The Beneficence of Christ*?"

Cipriano shook his head. Cazalla added: "I'll lend it to you. The book hasn't been printed in Spain, but I have a manuscript copy. Don Carlos brought the original from Italy."

Cipriano began to believe that something was beginning to glow within him. It was as if he could make out a spark of light on a totally dark horizon. The priest seemed to showing him a new dimension in religious life: confidence in the face of fear.

"Who is this Don Carlos you just mentioned?"

"Don Carlos de Seso, a gentleman from Verona who's settled in Castile, a man as elegant physically as he is refined spiritually. He lives in Logroño now. In 1550, he traveled to Italy and brought back books and new ideas. Then he attended the Council of Trent with the bishop of Calahorra. Some people say Don Carlos is seductive if you know him slightly, but that he's disappointing when you know him well. In sum, a small dose of him is enough. I don't know. Perhaps you'll have the chance to meet him and then you'll be able to judge for yourself."

Cipriano Salcedo realized he was moving into deep water, that he was getting involved in a highly important and crucial conversation. He had the vague idea that he'd heard Don Carlos de Seso mentioned in his Uncle Ignacio's house. And even though he was quite comfortable there, sitting on the ridge along the roadside, he was beginning to feel a chill.

He stood up and walked down to the road. Cazalla followed him. They walked along in silence for a bit, and then Cipriano asked: "Didn't Don Carlos de Seso have Lutheran connections at one time?"

"Oh! Forget your prejudices now. The Church needs a reform, and no opinion is out of order in these circumstances. We must understand one another. Those who come back from Trent say they don't think everything about Lutheranism is evil."

Salcedo's spirit became calm. He enjoyed hearing Cazalla's tranquil and convinced voice. The priest then added, as if putting the finishing touch on his disquisition: "The Dominican Juan de la Peña said, and quite rightly: "Why should I conceal the fact that I put my faith in the Passion of Christ, because through His mercy, I have found my own?" That idea comes from the Church Fathers. The Lutherans have appropriated it, and refer to it constantly as if it were theirs, but the Church Fathers said it first. Fear keeps us from accepting from the protestants truths we recognized long beforehand."

In the fading light, the little village blended in with the earth around it, and if it hadn't been for the tenuous light of the odd oil lamp, it would have been all but invisible. Suddenly, with no preamble, Pedro Cazalla invited him to dinner. That way they could go on chatting. His sister Beatriz gave Salcedo a warm welcome. She was a jolly girl with a big smile. The furniture in the house was as plain as it was in Martín Martín's: a kitchen with a table and two benches. Hassocks in the living room, wicker armchairs, and a book case. And on either side of the hall, two bedrooms with iron beds and gilding on the head board. Beatriz cooked and served in silence. Her respect for her brother was such that while he spoke she didn't dare move a finger. She remained still, her back to the hearth, staring at the table, her hands folded over her waist. Only during pauses did she pour wine or move a plate. Pedro Cazalla, despite the fact that it had been half an hour since they'd finished their walk, went back to his speech naturally, exactly the way Salcedo's deceased father-in-law had done, as if the conversation had never been interrupted.

"I've known Don Carlos for almost fourteen years. Back then he was an elegant and refined young man who dressed well, so much so that the last thing you'd expect him to talk about was theology. In Toro, he had several friends, and one afternoon he made us see that Christ had simply said that he who believed in Him would have eternal life. All He asked of us was to have faith. He imposed no other conditions."

They ate mechanically, served by Beatriz. Cazalla talked, and Cipriano silently allowed himself to be indoctrinated. During dinner, the priest went more deeply into the same subjects they'd touch on during their walk, and at the end, everything went back to the book *The Beneficence of Christ*: "It's a simple book of great depth, an impassioned exaltation of justification by faith. After reading it, the Marquis of Alcañices was swept away. The same thing has happened to many other people."

Once dinner was over, they moved to the living room. In the corner book case stood several dozen bound books. Cazalla picked one up without hesitating and handed it to Salcedo. It was a manuscript, and Cipriano leafed through it, praising the grace of its calligraphy: "Did you write it out, father?"

"Yes, I translated it," Cazalla said modestly.

The next morning, Cipriano attended nine o'clock Mass in Pedrosa. There were barely two dozen people in the church, mostly women. When it was over, Cipriano said good by to the priest in the sacristy and returned the book. Pedro Cazalla shot him a questioning glance with his somber eyes, which were distantly hopeful. Salcedo nodded with a smile: "Reading it did me a lot of good," he said simply. "We'll go on talking."

# XI

L IKE many of Valladolid's citizens in the middle of the sixteenth
century, Cipriano Salcedo assumed the Court would remain there
forever. Valladolid overflowed with competent artisans and aristocrats of the first quality, and the courts of law and political life gave no
sign they were temporary. To the contrary, once mid-century arrived,
progress in the town manifested itself in all orders.

Valladolid was growing. Housing sprawled beyond the old city limits, and the population grew at a regular rate. "We no longer fit within
the walls," said the citizens with pride. And they themselves answered:
"We'll build another wall even greater to protect us all." A Flemish visitor, Laurent Vidal, said: "Valladolid is as large as Brussels," and the
Spanish essayist Pedro de Medina measured the beauty of the Plaza
Mayor by the openings it offered to the outside: "What is there to say,"
he wrote, "about a plaza with five hundred doors and six thousand windows?" After 1550, construction, an active industry since 1540, accelerated. The Tanneries, opposite the Puerta del Campo were urbanized,
and important buildings were erected beyond the gates of Teresa Gil,
San Juan, and the Magdalena. The gardens of Santa Clara lost their
agricultural nature and became building sites, only to be covered by
multi-storied buildings with wrought iron balconies. A neighborhood in
its own right, it ran parallel to the Pisuerga River.

The frenetic rhythm of new construction caused new blocks of
houses to spring up everywhere. Already enclosed spaces—patios and
gardens for example—as well as open land on the outskirts were
pressed into service. Cipriano Salcedo and his neighbors were proud to

see the transformation of their part of town, from the Corredera de San Pablo all the way to the Ghetto next to the Puente Mayor. Three dozen new houses were raised on Lechería, Tahona, and Sinagoga Streets, and a similar number—though more solidly built—in the garden of the San Pablo Convent, which was ceded to that end. To provide access for the new housing, Imperial Street was expanded, connecting the new neighborhood with the town. Other permits for major construction were granted on Francos Street and in the garden of the Convent of Santa María de Belén, located between the Colegio de Santa Cruz and the Plaza del Duque.

But the most spectacular expansion took place in the parishes outside the city walls: San Pedro, San Andrés, and Santiago. The ceding of the property of the Pesquera brothers, which facilitated the construction of sixty-two new structures, turned out to be beneficial even for the donors, and that, in turn, induced other property owners to exchange their farms for a life-time annual rent in specific places such as Zurradores Street, the end of the Renedo road, and the end of the Laguna road, to the left of the Puerta del Campo. Halfway through the decade Valladolid was one huge construction site, and the years went by without any decrease in the febrile activity.

At the same time the new buildings were going up, there arose among the well-to-do classes the need to outfit their houses, to furnish them in conformity with the most demanding European aesthetic norms. Interior decorating began to be considered an art. The Court and its demands stimulated the citizens of Valladolid's propensity for consumption, and its first manifestation was fashion. Even Teodomira Centeno, who for years had managed to survive without spending money, was swept along by this fever of sumptuousness which had seized her neighbors. For Cipriano, his wife's wild spending revealed, on the one hand, a social contagion, and, on the other, her unstable character.

Teo explained this weakness in an expressive way: "The day I don't spend a hundred ducats I consider a day wasted." This obsession with spending, together with her rigorous following of Doctor Galache's therapy, filled her life in those days. There was one peculiarity: Aunt Gabriela, so resistant years earlier to Cipriano's marrying Teo, suddenly became her most faithful friend and ally. The proverbial good taste of the aunt united with the niece's fabulous fortune. Teo was not only docile, but actually accepted with thanks Gabriela's suggestions. The Queen of the Páramo knew her limitations; she knew she was a better sheep shearer than her aunt would ever be, but she also knew she lacked her superb taste. As if all that weren't enough, Aunt Gabriela, who was approaching sixty, found in the frenetic spending of someone else's money a rejuvenating activity.

And as for Cipriano, so loosely attached to material things and focused now on transcendent problems, his wife's tendency to hedonism barely affected him. Actually, he encouraged it. At this stage in his life he was happy to have a busy, distracted wife since Teo had ceased to be a factor in his tranquility. He'd made a mistake with her. Her size, her statue-like whiteness, her lack of body hair and perspiration were defects that his fantasies as a suitor had turned into charms. That fleshy, solid, and milky figure no longer said much to him as a woman and said nothing to him as a safe harbor. Their relationship was simple: each night, Teo would serve him the silver and steel preparation, and in exchange for that she would demand five days of respect each month. Teo was buoyed by the hope of being a mother. She absolutely believed Doctor Galache's promise and followed his instructions to the letter. One fine day she might be made pregnant by Cipriano, and then the doctor's prognostications would come true.

Cipriano, on the other hand, drank the nocturnal concoction simply to keep her happy. He had not the slightest confidence in it and was sure Galache had used the remedy to rid himself of a hysteric. Once the five or six years in the plan had gone by, he'd figure out a new way to extend her expectations. But Teo never wavered. For her, their intimate relations had the same goal as the iron and steel infusion or her own ingestion of salvia and salt after the four days of abstinence. She no longer sought out *the little thing*. That game was now part of history, along with Cipriano's climb to the plateau with the two protuberances. Having by then forgotten the frog and her disturbing copulation, Cipriano accepted his obligation without hesitation or enthusiasm, just as she did, but while he didn't believe in the doctor's fertility therapy as she did. Bereft of the original physical protection Teo granted him, he had nothing but the folded-over pillow into which he placed his little head each night to fall asleep.

None of this prohibited Teo from enthusiastically showing him the latest progress in the decoration of the house. The pine furniture was disappearing, substituted by other, more noble woods, principally oak, walnut, and mahogany. His office, for example, was rising in quality and richness: on the grand walnut table reposed a writing desk of hazel, alongside of which there was a book stand, and against the opposite wall an oak bookcase packed with books. Below the window Teo had placed a Venetian cassone made of ebony with ivory inlay work showing scenes from the Bible. An authentic gem. Even benches were being relegated to the poor. They were replaced by leather chairs or others in the French style.

But the transformation of the house did not stop there. The master bedroom passed from practicality to daintiness. The old iron-bed was replaced by another, covered with scarlet damask and a canopy of gold brocade. Facing the bed Teo installed a mahogany dressing table whose hardware was made of silver, and next to the door a huge chest lined in calf-skin where the bedclothes were stored. The copies of paintings she distributed throughout the principal part of house did not enter the matrimonial sanctuary where the walls were covered with gold-trimmed leather hangings. But presiding over the entire room, above the bed, was a crucifixion commissioned from Don Alonso de Berruguete. In the same style, enriching doors and windows and bringing in tapestries and rugs, Teo decorated the drawing and dining rooms. Only the attic rooms on the upper floor, the store rooms, and the room of Vicente the servant, next to the stables on the ground floor, remained in their original state.

But the most important change the house on Corredera Street experienced related to sheets and towels: the towels were embroidered, the sheets came from Flanders, the handkerchiefs and face cloths came from Holland, the pillows from Germany, and all sorts of clothing, including intimate apparel, stuffed the gigantic armoirs. And on shelves and corner cabinets were tea sets, vases, and candelabras in gold and silver from the New World. The cutlery, the cruets, the nutcrackers, the sugar and salt bowls arranged on the sideboard were also made of silver and gold, and opposite them in the Venetian display case were porcelains and Bohemian goblets in exquisite forms and tones.

Cipriano could not help being moved by Teo's will to overcome her sheep-shearing past without forgetting it—aside from Obstinate, the broken-down nag she fed until it died, she kept in her personal armoir, like a relic, along with sumptuous linens, the whip, the knives, and the scissors, thanks to which she once upon a time won the title "Queen of the Páramo." Cipriano let things move along at their own speed. He wasn't displeased by either the luxury involved in the transformation of his, nor by the passion Teo invested in it. From time to time, Teo and Aunt Gabriela would walk in loaded down with knick-knacks just as afternoon was beginning; Crisanta would serve pastries and cool drinks, and the three of them would chat for a long while about new projects and the most recent acquisitions.

Usually, however, Cipriano was not terribly concerned about these novelties. He was increasingly consumed with books and trips. His visits to Pedrosa were more frequent because the words of Pedro Cazalla, his company, and his indoctrination had become absolutely necessary to him. Sometimes, as he waited for him to return home, Cipriano would talk with his sister Beatriz, who was very subtle and intelligent with a strange angelic aura in her face: She was simultaneously luminous and stubborn. Her confidence in the theory of Christ's beneficence, about which she brooked no discussion, was itself edifying. The Lord's Passion had been a perfect work, and it was grotesque that some believers with their miserable inventions actually thought they could surpass the Redeemer. She led an active life with the women of the town, and with three of them she kept up the parish church.

Every so often, Cristóbal de Padilla and Juan Sánchez would turn up in Pedrosa. Padilla was a servant of the Marquis of Alcañices, and Sánchez had been servant to Doña Leonor de Vivero first, and then to Pedro Cazalla in Pedrosa. Cazalla ended up sending him back to his mother because of his meddling. Padilla was a strange person—tall, ungainly, with a long mane of red hair that made him look like a character from a fairy tale. Juan Sánchez, conversely, was a short boy with a big head and dry, parchment-like skin. He was, nevertheless, very active and nosy. Riding an old mule, alone or accompanied by Cristóbal de Padilla, he'd spontaneously become the liaison between the community in Valladolid, and the groups in Zamora and Logroño.

In Zamora, Padilla ran the show, organizing catechism groups to facilitate the search for new adepts, though he frequently revealed himself as too bold, too prone to taking risks. Despite orders to the contrary, Juan Sánchez would accompany him from time to time. Beatriz Cazalla, on the other hand, was cautious and discreet, and supplied them with ideas and expressions for their future evangelizing. Sometimes they would argue about the Sacraments or whether priests should marry: it was then that Pedro Cazalla felt obliged to intervene and shut them up.

Conversations between Pedro Cazalla and Cipriano Salcedo usually took place during walks. They would take the path to Casasola, with the Cenegal salt marshes and La Gallarita woods for a background, but halfway along they would sit down on top of Cerro Picado, the hill closest to town, and go on talking there as they contemplated the tiny houses grouped on one side of the church, among the acacias, and the common, with its straw, the well, and the remains of wagons and demolished threshing machines. On some afternoons, they would stroll toward Toro, among sewn fields and vineyards, until they reached the road to Zamora. Or they would go instead toward Villavendimio, on whose barren, sandy lands the pine grove planted by Martín Martín was starting to develop. In spring, they would hike up at dawn, with the caged partridge, inevitably going to the edge of La Gallarita. Little by little, Cipriano had become quite a bird expert. He could pick out the voice of Antón, their caged lure, among the screeches of all the other querulous males, and faultlessly distinguished the calls of the birds in the wild. Hardened by a thousand hunting forays, he no longer criticized Cazalla for all the spilled blood. He lived the duel between man and bird passionately, and, acquiescent to the priest, ended up accepting, sooner or later, everything he said.

One day in April, while Antón was blaring out an ardent screech from the top of the little pedestal despite the stubborn silence of the surrounding fields, Pedro Cazalla brutally, with no preparation whatsoever, told Cipriano there was no purgatory. Even though he was seated, Salcedo reacted to Cazalla's harshness with a strange weakness in the knees and a vertigo in the pit of his stomach. The priest looked carefully at him out of the corner of his eye, waiting for his reaction. He saw Cipriano turn pale, as he did the day they saw the frog, and then try to straighten his legs in the tight space of the hunting blind. Finally he muttered: "Th . . . this I cannot accept, Pedro. It's part of my childhood faith."

They were inside the blind, sitting on the bench, one next to the other, Cazalla with his loaded shotgun between his legs, both oblivious to the partridge. Cazalla spoke sweetly, shrugging his shoulders: "It's very hard, Cipriano, I understand that, but we must be coherent within our faith. If we observe the commandments, there is nothing for which we are not forgiven thanks to Christ's Passion."

Salcedo looked as if he were going to burst into tears, such was his desolation: "You are right, father," he said at last, "but with that revelation, you leave me forsaken."

Cazalla put his hand on Cipriano's shoulder: "The day Don Carlos de Seso told me, I suffered as much as you. Darkness surrounded me, and I felt fear. I was so afflicted, I thought about denouncing Don Carlos to the Holy Office."

"And how did you overcome your anguish?"

"I suffered a lot," he repeated. "I felt myself to be a man of sin. In the following days, I could not say mass. So, one morning I saddled my mule and went to Valladolid. I had to see that virtuous theologian Don Bartolomé Carranza. Do you know him?"

"He's known to be a holy and wise man."

Cazalla removed his hand from Salcedo's shoulder and went on: "I confided in him. I opened my soul to him. Don Bartolomé looked at me as though he had an intuition and asked me: 'Who told you that about purgatory?' I didn't want to tell him, so he added: 'If I guess correctly, will you confirm it?' And since I answered in the affirmative, he spoke the name of Don Carlos de Seso, and I nodded yes."

Cazalla paused as if expecting an immediate reaction from Salcedo, but Cipriano's mouth was dry, and it was hard for him to say anything: "And what did Don Bartolomé tell you?" he finally asked.

"It was I who put him on notice that I felt obliged to report to the Holy Office, to denounce Don Carlos. But he calmed me down, telling me to take my time, to denounce no one, to return to my parish and say mass as I did every day. I followed his advice, and he, meanwhile, sent a message to Logroño begging Don Carlos to travel to Valladolid, that it was a matter of great importance. Don Carlos came immediately and went directly to the Colegio de San Gregorio to speak with Don Bartolomé Carranza. But I met him in the patio, and he embraced me, kissing me on the cheek, something he'd never done before. That moved me. Together we went up to the theologian's cell, but he told me to wait outside, that my presence wasn't necessary. Then, according to Don Carlos's account, Don Bartolomé asked him if it was true that he'd told me there was no purgatory and if so, what was he basing his statement on? Seso answered that he based his statement on the superabundant payment Our Lord had given for our sins with His Passion and death. Then Don Bartolomé warned him that no good reason was sufficient in itself to depart from the teachings of the Church, since not all men left this world as full of faith as he was. Then he warned him that he was just about to leave for England with the King, our master, but that as soon as he returned he would try to listen to him and to satisfy him in all particulars. Before they parted company, he again praised Don Carlos's faith and went on without condemning his words. All he did was urge him to keep their meeting a secret. He said these exact words: "Make sure that what's transpired here stays buried. Under no circumstance are you to talk about it."

The interest with which Salcedo listened to the story distracted him momentarily from the reason for his affliction. When Cazalla paused, Cipriano immediately asked: "And did you ever talk again about all that?"

Cazalla shrugged his shoulders. With a certain bitterness he said: "Don Bartolomé has yet to finish his affairs."

Antón went hoarse in his last screech. The bird seemed bored and depressed; the countryside was deserted. Cazalla stood up in the blind, his hands on his hips. His tone changed: "There's no way to lure game. If no one's home, better to leave it for another day."

That night at the inn, Cipriano suffered mortal anguish. He couldn't sleep. His spirit was confused, afflicted. Back in the hunting blind, he'd had a violent jolt, like an amputation. Now he realized his whole world seemed changed because of Cazalla's words. And in the mass of ideas mixed up in his head, only one seemed clear: the need to modify his thinking, to turn everything upside down in order to set the foundations of his belief in tranquility. He rose before dawn, and daybreak found him in Villavieja. Back in Valladolid, he frenetically searched through his books, there he found what he sought. Melchor Cano's statement calmed him momentarily: "Carranza's intentions have always been orthodox," he said. But Don Bartolomé identified himself with Seso, which was the reason Cazalla didn't denounce him. Bartolomé Carranza most certainly did not believe purgatory existed, but he was fully aware of how risky it would be to say it openly without knowing the level of education of the person to whom he spoke. The great theologian was, no doubt, a scrupulous and prudent man.

Even before the week was out, Cipriano's disquiet brought him back to Pedrosa. He was surprised that Cazalla—doubtless in a burst of humility—had called him "brother." The priest had no doubts about the relationship between Seso and Carranza. Between the two there was a clear analogy of thought. Melchor Cano was right on that point. They were walking along the path to Toro, on a peaceful afternoon, when they saw a svelte charger enveloped in a cloud of dust coming toward them. Pedro Cazalla did not show any emotion when he said: "Unless I'm mistaken, here comes Don Carlos de Seso in person."

The horse—pliable, with a white blaze on his forehead, and fine legs—was the first thing to catch Salcedo's attention. It was obvious at first sight that this was no ordinary horse, but one carefully chosen: a bay, impatient, who snorted elegantly when it reached the two men. The rider greeted them before dismounting. He was a thin man with a steady gaze, a few years older than Cipriano. Blond, with a short beard and short hair, wearing an Italian cap, his costume—plain sleeves in the Turkish style, his shirt collars visible, piquéd, full-length breeches—seemed perfectly designed for riding. He gave the impression of being a man of the world, a dandy, haughty even without making the effort to seem so.

He was coming from Toro. He was going to be named governor or *corregidor* and had visited the town to say hello to his old friends. He was eloquent, able to strike many tones, a man whose ease made him attractive. He was leading his horse, Veronese, by the bridle, walking between Cipriano and Cazalla, completely at home. With no preamble whatsoever, he turned to Salcedo: he'd met an uncle of his many years before, in Olmedo, during the plague, a learned man, well-known, and, with good reason, an open man. He'd heard about him from Pedro, he knew that Cipriano was a land-owner and a spiritually disquiet man. They'd talk later. He planned to sleep in Baruque's inn and leave early for Logroño.

Beatriz Cazalla received them with great affection and ease. She invited them to dinner. She didn't have enough for everyone, but she'd fix that by getting a ham. Don Carlos treated Beatriz with a mixture of familiarity and respect. He would tease her, and she couldn't stop laughing. During dinner and dessert they chatted about trivial subjects: Pedro's love of hunting, the vineyards, the whitewashing of the church, but as soon as the three were alone with a pitcher of wine in the inn's sitting room, Salcedo did not hesitate to bring up the subject of purgatory. The sudden appearance of Don Carlos seemed so opportune, that Salcedo had no doubt that Cazalla had sent him a note demanding his presence. Above a chest hung a huge crucifix, and as soon as he noticed it, Seso pointed to it theatrically and said: "There you have my purgatory. That's my purgatory."

He looked like a visionary. In slippers, his gray eyes fixed on Cipriano, wearing his traveling robe, it would seem his personality had changed. Salcedo looked imploringly at him, manifesting his suffering during the previous few days.

"You Spaniards give a lot of importance to this purgatory business," Don Carlos commented with a smile. "In my county, people accept the fact that it doesn't exist as a logical consequence of the new doctrine. Don Bartolomé Carranza didn't want to listen when I tried to give him the reasons. He considered them known."

Baruque's daughter had withdrawn after feeding the oil lamp and tossing some logs on the fire. While Don Carlos poured himself another glass of wine, Cipriano pulled himself together long enough to say: "And . . . and could you tell me what makes you so convinced? I lack both your knowledge and your holiness."

Don Carlos's metamorphosis was now complete. The apparent ease he'd shown on the road had disappeared, and despite his handsome face and short, blond hair, he seemed more a man of the church, ready to begin a sermon than a gentleman. His light eyes stared willfully at Cipriano's small, hairy hands: "Well, I don't want to bore you," he said with a protective air, "but as far as I'm concerned, there are three powerful arguments to demonstrate that purgatory doesn't exist . . ."

He left his arguments hanging in midair, and Cipriano brought his face close to Don Carlos's lips, fearing the man would never state them: "I'm all ears," he said impatiently, pressing him.

Don Carlos drove his eyes like daggers into Cipriano's face, and went on with his exposition: "In the first place, when we accept the fact that there is no purgatory, we are actually recognizing that we've received the greatest mercy from Christ. To that, add the fact that the Evangelists and Saint Peter never mention it in their writings. Finally, and this for me is also essential, we have the position taken by Don Bartolomé de Carranza, the saintliest of men, a man of great wisdom. Do you need more and greater proof?"

Cipriano blinked repeatedly as if he were bedazzled. A kind of supernatural power was working on him, a power that seemed to emanate from that man. His arguments, all three, convinced him, especially the second: Why was it the Evangelists did not allude to purgatory when they did speak of heaven and hell? But Don Carlos gave him no time to reflect. He spoke and spoke beyond all measure. He drove the nail home. To face up to his new faith, Don Carlos suggested he visit Cazalla, the Doctor, and speak with him. He should frequent the meetings of their small groups, exchange impressions with the brothers. "Don't put it off. Our strength isn't great, but it isn't despicable either. Don't just sit back. Get moving. Open your spirit, don't resist grace. There are secret groups in Valladolid, Toro, Zamora, in many places." Cipriano made certain to make a mental note of his advice, of the names of people and places he recommended. Suddenly, Don Carlos changed the course of his lecture. He spoke about Trent, he'd been there, and the Council had not aroused any great hopes in him. He also mentioned Juan Valdés, who'd died a few years back, as his true teacher, and in this way he went on linking themes until fatigue and drowsiness overwhelmed them.

Very early the next morning, they rode together to Valladolid. Don Carlos was going to Logroño, to Villamediana, where he lived. For the first time, Salcedo admired qualities in another horse he didn't find in his own: Veronese sprang to a gallop from a slow trot without any transition and was able to stop in two body-lengths, something Lightning and he had never achieved. This was a spirited and well-trained horse. Don Carlos said he'd bought Veronese in Granada and that more than half his blood was Arabian.

Cipriano found Teo on the verge of a new crisis. Ever since she'd stopped constituting for him a refuge or a carnal incentive, Salcedo only aspired to one thing: that she leave him in peace. He didn't believe in Doctor Galache's words, nor in the timetable Teo observed with such rigorous precision. He merely pretended he did to maintain conjugal tranquility. Whenever he was away from home, he had in his luggage a little sack of silver and steel slag which his wife prepared for him. The sack always came back unopened, but Teo never noticed. She thought Cipriano was living the doctor's instructions with the same conviction she was. In this way, the marriage survived, but this time the return was desolating.

Teodomira did not come out to meet him at the door. He found her in her room completely self-absorbed, staring through the window and seeing nothing. She mechanically returned the kiss he planted on her cheek, but in such a cold way that Cipriano wondered what novelty awaited him this morning. Sometimes it had been her old horse Obstinate, others his disdain or his infertility, but it was clear that her alienation meant something. She accompanied him to the bedroom so he could change clothes. Cipriano still hadn't gotten used to the new tapestries, the curtains, the canopied bed . . . He was overwhelmed by them. But with no warning Teo declared in dominating tones: "Cipriano, I think this business of sleeping together in the same bed is disgusting."

"Disgusting? It's what married people usually do, isn't it?"

She was, slowly but surely, becoming enraged.

"Do you really think it's normal for us to spend nine of the twenty-four hours in a day exchanging our effluvia, our breath, continuously smelling each other like two dogs?"

"Since you put it that way," agreed Cipriano on the spot, "perhaps you're right. Maybe we should put another bed in this room."

Teo's huge figure moved lightly from one place in the room to another. She seized one of the columns of the bed and shook it violently.

The canopy above trembled: "Two beds here? Is that all you can come up with after I've racked my brains trying to make this into a decent bedroom? To destroy it with another bed? Well! This is the great man's suggestion!"

Teo was like an avalanche: the steeper the slope the stronger and bigger she became. Having reached this extreme, Cipriano hesitated: Should he accept her suggestion or disagree? He was not ignorant of the fact that if he accepted without a fight, the initial theme of their confrontation—generally minor—could easily mutate into something more personal and explosive. And if he were to opt for confrontation, it was possible that his wife's exasperation, in a foreseeable escalation, could end up moving from words to acts. Cipriano hadn't forgotten that in the crisis that preceded their visit to Doctor Galache, Teo one night had threatened him in bed, that she'd started to strangle him with her powerful white hands. From that moment on, he'd adopted an ambiguous attitude toward her, one not innocent of self-defense. That's what he'd done this morning when he noticed how distanced she was: neither to accept blindly nor to disagree totally, but to wait for things to mature in their own time. He tried to tame her with friendly words, but she went on being irascible. The confrontation only diminished when Teo led him to an old storeroom next to the bedroom which she'd transformed into a bedroom: "What do you think? Crisanta and I fixed it up for you."

In distress, Cipriano stared at the wretched little window, the ottoman in a corner next to the chest that would serve as his night table, where for the moment a silver candelabra reposed. A little mat, a pine armoir, two leather chairs, and a rack where he could hang his clothes constituted the furnishings. Cipriano thought he'd been expelled from paradise, but at the same time, he had the immediate solution to his problem within his grasp. He hesitated: "It's just fine, it's sufficient. After all, ostentatious display in a bedroom is superfluous."

Teo smiled. Cipriano was wise enough to praise her efforts. She led him to the door. To the right of the frame, attached to the wall there was a sheet of paper where she'd drawn a kind of calendar. The four days of abstinence recommended by Doctor Galache were marked in red. She smiled in a remotely lascivious way: "Don't try to fool me now.

I have an outline just like this at the head of my bed."

The flood waters had receded. Teo was exultant. She didn't realize she'd been beaten. For his part, once he'd recovered his freedom,
Cipriano, following Seso's instructions, decided to visit Doctor Cazalla.
He wasn't at home, but Cipriano was received by his mother, Doña
Leonor de Vivero, a lady advanced in years who nevertheless conserved
a vigorous freshness. A smooth complexion, her blue, lively eyes, the
serene coordination of her movements, her thick white hair all com-
bined to banish any idea of old age. A full-length brocade skirt and a
white ruff outlined her figure. She smiled when she spoke, showing her
teeth as if she'd known him all her life. Pedro had spoken about him,
his devotion, his probity, his good will toward his fellow man. Agustín
would be returning late; he had a meeting with the town council. The
small receiving room where they were chatting gave an idea of the rest
of the house, low-ceilinged and dark, where the heavy, outsized furniture occupied most of the available space. Only the meeting room, the
oratory, which Doña Leonor kindly showed him, was different. It was
spacious, but at the expense of the rest of the house, with exposed
beams and no furniture other than a small platform with a table and two
chairs and a long row of benches: "It's here we hold our monthly meetings," explained Doña Leonor. "I hope you'll honor us with your presence at the next one. Agustín will give you precise instructions."

The chapel had no ventilation except for a narrow opening on the
west, its shutters padded to reduce noise and light.

Cipriano returned to Doña Leonor de Vivero's house frequently.
She was such an open and jolly woman that it didn't matter if the
Doctor were late. She also welcomed him happily and listened without
even blinking to his amusing anecdotes. Cipriano had never felt so
flattered, and for the first time in his life he delayed the ending of his
stories, which, because of his innate timidity, he'd always tended to
cut short.

Doña Leonor laughed easily but discretely, without noise, without
explosive guffaws. Despite her restraint, she laughed until she wept,
and her tears spurred on Cipriano, who'd never been esteemed for his
sense of humor. He would connect one story with another, and by his
fourth visit he'd used up his repertoire of tales about others, so, since

there was no other way, he began his collection of stories about himself or those he knew. The stories about Don Segundo, *the man who made his fortune in America,* or about his wife, *the Queen of the Páramo,* sent Doña Leonor into gales of laughter. She split her sides laughing but without making a spectacle of herself, elegantly, with a light clucking, delicately holding her stomach with her small, well-cared-for hands.

And once Cipriano began there was no stopping him: his wife's nickname, *the Queen of the Páramo,* came from the fact that she sheared lambs with greater speed and skill than the shepherds of Torozos. And her father received visitors wearing the slashed stockings the lanzquenets had made popular around 1525 in Valladolid. Doña Leonor laughed and laughed, and Cipriano, drunk with success, told her with good humor that Doctor Galache had recommended a mixture of silver and steel slag to augment his fertility.

One afternoon, animated by Doña Leonor's attention, he confided his little secret to her: "Did you know I was born the same day as the Reformation?"

"I don't understand, Salcedo."

"I mean I was born in Valladolid at the same time Luther was nailing his theses to the door of the castle church in Wittenberg."

"Is that possible, or are you just joking?"

"October 31, 1517. My uncle told me."

"In that case, were you predestined?"

"There have been times when I've been on the verge of believing that hoax."

Doña Leonor gazed at him with an admiring intellectual tenderness, her teeth peeking through her pink lips: "I'm going to propose something to you," she said after a pause, "and it's that we celebrate your next birthday here in this house along with the Doctor and the rest of my children. A thanksgiving dinner. What do you think?"

Doña Leonor and Cipriano Salcedo became absolutely necessary to each other. He often thought that after his sentimental failure with Teo, Doña Leonor had come to replace the mother he'd hoped to find in her. The fact is that whenever he had a meeting with the Doctor, he came early to his house only for the pleasure of talking awhile with Doña Leonor. And there, sitting in the leather chairs in the small vestibule, they would chat and laugh. From time to time, she would invite him to a light dinner. But as soon as the Doctor appeared, she would rise, rein in her spontaneity, even if her authority would still show without words. That house, without a doubt, had been a matriarchy that the sons had recognized and spontaneously encouraged.

In the little office on the other side of the wall from the chapel, Cipriano and the Doctor would talk sitting around a table under which a brazier was placed because the theologian felt cold even in the month of August. The room was lined with books, and aside from them and a small engraving of Luther that presided over the pine table next to the window, it had no other decoration. Day after day, Cipriano took note of the Doctor's fragility, his hypochondria, and, at the same time, his sharp wit, and his admirable mental order.

The Doctor had taken Cipriano in as if he were his brother's son, such was the passion Pedro Cazalla expressed in introducing him. They spent long sessions together, and the Doctor, extremely proud of his great ability as a teacher, progressively inculcated Salcedo with the principles of the new doctrine. His persuasive accent, his easily comprehended arguments all helped support his efforts. And for Cipriano, the mere fact of having at his disposal the words of the great preacher, venerated in the city, constituted in itself a reason for feeling proud.

After having admitted that purgatory didn't exist, it was relatively easy for Cipriano to accept the uselessness of nuns, of priestly celibacy, or to reject the monkish pharisees. Christ never imposed celibacy on the apostles. Saint Peter, specifically, was a married man. Salcedo agreed and went on agreeing. He never doubted. He even swallowed unreasonable truths, which the Doctor expounded. With similar ease, he found reasons to reject the cult of the saints, images, relics, the tithes whereby the Church exploited the people and the institutional clergy. He rejected transubstantiation, which was a logical thing to do given the Gospels. Everything was simple for Cipriano now. He didn't question the value of mental confession. He'd never felt any aversion toward reciting his sins in a confessional, but doing it now directly to Our Lord left him more tranquil and satisfied. It actually seemed to him a more complete and emotional act than spoken confession. Alone in the darkest corner of the church, in silence, fascinated by the tiny flame that burned in the tabernacle, Cipriano would concentrate and come to feel very close to the real presence of Christ in the temple. Once he even thought he saw Him at his side, sitting on the bench, his tunic glittering, the white space of his face framed by his hair and his pointy, rabbinical beard.

It was Cipriano's opinion that none of the Doctor's teachings deeply affected belief. He usually spoke slowly and softly, but the grimace of bitterness never disappeared from his mouth. Perhaps that rictus expressed the disquiet and fears the Doctor kept to himself. There was only one new teaching Cipriano balked at: the omission of mass. No matter how hard he tried, he couldn't come to think of Sunday as just another day in the week. If he didn't attend mass, which he did perhaps more out of habit than devotion, he thought he was missing something essential. Thirty-six years of carrying out that precept had created in him a second nature. He felt unable to betray it. He said so in just those terms to the Doctor, who, contrary to what he expected, did not become angry: "I understand what you mean, son. Attend mass and pray for us. I too find myself obliged to do things in which I don't believe. Sometimes it's even advisable to continue with old practices so we don't arouse the suspicion of the Holy Office. Someday we'll be able to bring our faith into the light."

"Are there that many of us new Christians, your reverence?"

The bitter grimace became more accentuated on his mouth, but nevertheless he said: "Look, son. If they were to wait four months before persecuting us, our numbers would be equal to theirs. And if they were to wait six months, we'd be able to do with them what they want to do with us."

The Doctor's answer impressed Cipriano. Was he trying to suggest that half the city was infected with the *leprosy*? Did he mean that the great mass of the faithful who attended his sermons were in accord with the Reformation? For Salcedo, the Cazalla brothers and Don Carlos de Seso were three indisputable authorities, more lucid than the rest of humanity. Whenever he found himself alone, he would thank Our Lord for having put them in his path. Their teaching had cemented his faith, which had been dissipated by his old scruples: his serenity had been restored. He was no longer anguished by doubts or by an impatience to carry out good works. Even so, sometimes, when he was thanking God for having met such virtuous people, he wondered—the idea passed through his mind like a lightning bolt—if those three people, all so outwardly different, were not linked by pride. He shook his head violently to banish such a sinful thought. The Evil One never rested; the Doctor had warned him about that. It was necessary to live with one's spirit on full alert.

But this had to be a matter of accidental apprehensions, he thought, since he respected the voice of his masters and venerated them. Their intelligence was so far above his own that it was a rare privilege to be able to take hold of their hand, close his eyes, and let himself be led.

It was January, the 29th. The Doctor stood up from the old chair and vigorously rang a small silver bell he took out of his portable writing desk. Juan Sánchez, the servant, as scrawny as ever, his face like parchment, as yellow as old paper: "Juan," said the Doctor, "you already know Don Cipriano Salcedo. He will attend our group on Friday. Summon the others for eleven o'clock at night. The password is *Torozos* and the countersign is *Liberty*. As always, be very careful."

Juan Sánchez lowered his head, nodding agreement: "Whatever your eminence orders."

# XII

ENSCONCED in the store room, Cipriano heard his wife's banal coughing in the next room, sat up in bed, and waited a few minutes. The maids were probably in bed up in the attic as the house was silent. Not even Vicente was moving around in his room on the ground floor, next to the stables. He felt his heart pounding when he got out of bed. He took a deep breath. He'd oiled the hinges so the doors wouldn't squeak. Carrying a candle, he made his way downstairs on tiptoe. In the entry, he snuffed the candle out and left it on the chest. He'd never been much of a night owl, but tonight he was excited, and by more than the strangeness of the situation. He was excited by the memory of Pedro Cazalla's words in Pedrosa: the small groups had to be clandestine. Secretive and complicitous, he thought, were one translation of other, more inflammatory words, such as fearful and mysterious. Only they should know of the existence of these meetings; should someone find out about them, the Holy Office would implacably fall on everyone. At the front door, he made the sign of the cross. He did not feel terror, but was indeed anxious.

The night was cold but calm. In his bones he felt a moist chill; the weather out of character for Castile. The silence disconcerted him; he heard nothing but the noise of his own footsteps, which put him on the alert, and the hooves of the horses on the stable floors, the distant passage of a patrol . . . He walked tentatively, though above, where the houses drew close to one another, it was possible to make out a diffuse, milky clarity. Lamps winked timidly in a few windows, but they were so veiled that their light did not reach the street. He heard, very far off, the voice of a drunk and the kick of a horse or mule against a wooden door. He made his nervous way along De la Cuadra Street until he came to Estrecha.

On that especially narrow avenue, flanked by noble palaces, the nervousness of the horses was even more noticeable. They stamped the ground and snorted in their impatient sleep. Cipriano concealed his face with his hood. His fear intensified the cold. At the corner, he turned right. There he could see the vague whiteness of the buildings and the blackness of the empty spaces. He walked almost down the middle of the street, to the left of the gutter, and the imperceptible echo of his footsteps bouncing off the buildings oriented him, as if he were a bat. Very soon he saw the wooden house that came before Doña Leonor's, and he drew close to the buildings. His heartbeat, under his hood, were now very pronounced.

Cipriano hesitated. The Doctor had warned him: "Don't use the knocker; it would make too much noise." He approached the door but, didn't knock. All he did was say *Juan* twice in a low voice. He knew that Juan Sánchez was in charge of receiving the participants, but he heard no answer. He raised his arm out of his cloak and knocked twice with his knuckles. Even before the second knock, he heard the scratchy voice of Juan Sánchez in muffled tones: "Torozos."

"Liberty," answered Cipriano.

The door opened noiselessly; he entered, and Juan greeted him. Juan spoke in whispers, and without raising his voice asked if Cipriano knew the way. Cipriano told him he knew how to get to the chapel at the rear of the narrow corridor. As he walked down the hall, he remembered once again Pedro Cazalla's mysterious words: secretive and complicitous. He was trembling.

Doña Leonor and Doctor Cazalla were already seated on the chairs at the table on the raised dais. The table was covered with a purple cloth and faced directly toward the eight large benches. The small window at the rear had a pillow attached to its shutter to keep light and voices from leaking out. Cipriano greeted the Cazallas with a nod of his head. Pedro was there as well, sitting on the second bench, and Cipriano shot him a conspiratorial look before sitting down. The room was timidly illuminated by one candle burning on the Doctor's table and another in a wall sconce near Cipriano. It was then he noticed in the man alongside Pedro the unmistakable traits of the family: it had to be Juan Cazalla, one of the Doctor's other brothers. Next to him sat Juana Silva, his sister-in-law. Scattered around on the benches, Cipriano identified Beatriz Cazalla, Don Carlos de Seso, Doña Francisca de Zúñiga, and the jeweler Juan García. In a barely audible whisper, he asked García who the people were on the fourth bench, to the left of the Doctor's table. It was Herrezuelo, the university graduate from Toro, Catalina Ortega, daughter of the prosecutor Hernando Díaz, Brother Domingo de Rojas, and his nephew Luis.

Just before the meeting was called to order, a tall, graceful woman of extraordinary beauty entered wearing a close-fitting shift and a turban. She aroused a light murmur among those present. Juan García turned to him and confirmed his suspicion: Doña Ana Enríquez, daughter of the Marquises of Alcañices. Moments before Doña Ana entered, a carriage rumbled by but did not stop until the next corner. Doña Ana Enríquez was afraid of the dark, but was prudent enough not to want to give away the location of the clandestine meeting. Finally, closing the door behind him, the helpful Juan Sánchez entered, with his big head and skin wrinkled like old parchment. He sat in front of Cipriano, at the left end of the first bench.

Everyone stared expectantly at the Doctor and his mother up on the dais. Once the whispers ceased, Doña Leonor cleared her throat and announced that the meeting would begin with the reading of a beautiful psalm that the brothers in Wittenberg sang daily, a psalm they would have to be content, for now, with simply reciting. Doña Leonor spoke in her slow, well-modulated, powerful, but restrained voice. Cipriano looked over at Doña Ana, whose long neck emerged from her blouse decorated with a pearl necklace, and he saw her bow her head and devoutly join her hands.

Cipriano attempted to find prohibited references in the psalm:

> Bless the Lord at all times,
> His praise shall forever be on my lips.
> My soul glories in the praise of the Lord,
> Let the wretched of the earth hear it and rejoice.

At the outset of the second stanza, Doña Leonor, who probably found the first one cold, heightened the emphases, but the Doctor discreetly nudged her with his elbow, and she lowered her tone:

> Praise the Lord with me.
> Let us all together exalt His name;
> Because I sought the Lord, and He answered me;
> He has freed me of all my fears.

Ana Enríquez raised her head, cleared her throat, and smiled sweetly. The Doctor leaned toward his mother and briefly exchanged glances with her. Doña Leonor followed the agenda, and, he, like all stars, reserved the end of the meeting for himself. Silence reigned in the chapel, when Doña Leonor announced that the group would discuss relics and other superstitions. To start things off, she would read one of the dialogues between Latancio and Arcidiano in Alfonso de Valdés's book *Dialogues on Things that Transpired in Rome.* "The text," she said, "will make you laugh out loud, but I beg you to do so with some discretion, given the hour and the place."

Cipriano glanced over at Ana Enríquez, her erect head, her white neck rising out of her garnet-colored shift, her right hand, very well manicured, clinging to the back of the bench in front of her. Before beginning the reading, Doña Leonor pointed out that more than a few of these absurd beliefs still held sway in our churches and convents and were respected as articles of faith. She opened the book at a place marked by a ribbon and read: "Latancio." Then, after a brief pause, went on:

> You've said a great truth, but God, for reasons best known to Himself, has allowed this: the hoaxes perpetrated with these relics which are used to drain money from fools. You will find that the same relic will be shown to you in two or three places. If you go to Dura, in Germany, they will show you the head of Saint Anne, mother of Our Lady. And they'll show you the same thing in Lyons, in France. The fact is that either one or the other is false, unless they mean that Our Lady had two mothers or Saint Anne had two heads. And since it is a lie; isn't it a great evil that they want to fool people by wanting them to venerate a dead body which may

be that of a criminal who's been hung? Which would they take to be the greater problem: That the body of Saint Anne not be found or that in its place the body of just any woman be venerated?

### Arcidiano
I'd rather neither one be the case, since I wouldn't want someone have me worship a sinner instead of a saint.

Cipriano nodded assent to Doña Leonor's words, and lowered his head affirmatively at Arcidiano's witty response.
Doña Leonor's voice went on:

### Latancio
Wouldn't you prefer that the body of Saint Anne that, as they say, is in Dura and in Lyon be buried in a grave and never shown rather than seeing so many people fooled by one of them?

### Arcidiano
Yes, indeed.

### Latancio
That being the case, you will find infinite relics all over the world, and very little would be lost if there were none. If only God would remedy the situation. I've seen the foreskin of Our Lord in Rome and in Burgos and also in Our Lady of Auvergne (the noise of laughter here). And the head of John the Baptist—in Rome and in Amiens, in France (whispers and laughter). There are twelve apostles if you'd care to count them, and even though there were no more than twelve, we could find twenty four in various places on earth. There were three nails in the cross, Eusebius writes, and Saint Helena threw one into the Adriatic to calm a tempest, and used another to make a helmet for her son, and made yet another into the bit for his horse . . .

Suddenly, footsteps and the noise of voices could be heard in the street. The muffled laughter was instantly silenced. Doña Leonor stopped reading and raised her head. No one spoke. Those listening, waiting for those on the dais to react, held their breath. Doctor Cazalla raised his thin,

white hand and hid the flame of the candle. Cipriano did the same with
the one in the sconce next to him. The voices came closer. Doña Leonor
looked at each one, as if trying to reassure them. The group outside
seemed to stop in front of the house, and suddenly, a powerful voice
rang out: *They thought they'd go together*, said the voice.

Cipriano was certain they'd been discovered, that someone had
informed on them. He tensely awaited the sound of the door knocker,
but it never came. But another word rang out at the far end of the
house: *mercenaries*. Then came the noise of footsteps and intertwined
conversations again. Every face was pale, and all eyes showed fear. But,
little by little, as the footsteps and the voices began to move off, they all
regained their normal color. All except the Doctor, who evinced a transparent, glassy whiteness. The group in the street kept moving, and once
their voices became nothing but a whisper, the Doctor uncloaked the
candle. Doña Leonor, serene at all times, picked up the book and said
simply *we'll go on* And she went back to the reading:

> . . . and made yet another into the bit for his horse—she repeated—; and
> now there's one in Rome, and another in Milan, and another in Cologne,
> and another in Paris, and another in Lyons, and infinite others elsewhere
> (the spirited laughter returned). And about the wood of the Cross, I tell
> you truly that if all of it they say is legitimate were so it would fill a cart
> with wood. The baby teeth of Our Lord from when he was a child exceed
> the five hundred shown today only in France. The milk of Our Lady,
> Mary Magdalene's hair, Saint Christopher's molars—there's no counting
> them. And beyond the uncertainty that surrounds all this, it's a great
> shame to see what in some places is told to the people. The other day, in
> an ancient monastery, they showed me the records of the relics they had,
> and I saw among other things that it said: "A piece of the Kidron brook."
> I asked if it was the water or the stones from that creek, and they told me
> not to mock the relics. There was another entry that said: "Some of the
> earth where the angel appeared to the shepherds." I didn't dare ask them
> what they understood that to be. You'd laugh yourself to death if I told
> you about other more ridiculous and impious things people tell you they
> have, like the wing of the angel Gabriel, the shadow of Saint James's
> staff, the feathers of the Holy Spirit, the doublet worn by the Trinity and

myriad other things like that. Let me just say that a few days ago in a collegiate church they showed me a rib from Saint Savior. If there was another Savior beside Jesus Christ and if he left behind a rib or not, they can show it to you.

Arcidiano

Truly, it is, as you say, more to be laughed at than wept over.

The final paragraphs had illuminated Doña Leonor's face, with her toothy smile. She closed the book and observed the audience with obvious pleasure. Meanwhile, the Doctor, who had barely recovered his normal color, pushed the writing desk aside and crossed his arms over the table as he usually did in the pulpit during crucial moments. There were a few coughs and throat-clearings in the audience during the pause, but when everyone noticed the Doctor's preparations, silence once again prevailed. Cazalla's voice, clear and faint as it was in his sermons, seemed more accessible and confidential here than in church. He referred to the famous dialogue between Latancio and Arcidiano, part of which they'd just heard, and said that it was in itself so expressive and humorous that commentary was almost superfluous. But, attracted, as always, by routine and order, he said he would take the reading as an opportunity to say a few words on the subject at hand: relics.

The audience had become slightly distracted. They were looking at one another, saying hello with nods. Cipriano noticed that Don Carlos de Seso often turned toward Ana Enríquez. And that Herrezuelo had a mark, perhaps a scar, that began on his upper lip, giving him a permanent grimace Cipriano couldn't decide was of gaiety or repugnance.

For its part, the Cazalla family had relaxed. For some, the words spoken by the mother were more attractive than those of the Doctor, and several had laughed aloud during the reading of the Latancio and Arcidiano dialogue. The Doctor began a short commentary on the text. He mentioned again Valdés's caustic humor and pointed out the that cult of relics usually involved fabrications involving Christ or the saints which, as Luther might say, "made the devil laugh." Over the course of a few minutes, he tried to prove that relics were unnecessary and not only useless but prejudicial for the Church. We should, he said, make an effort to extirpate that puerile cult from our religious customs.

With that innate ability the Doctor had to slip two threads through the eye of one needle, he ended up speaking about the problem of indulgences, as he did so frequently in his sermons. Indulgences, he said, for the living and the dead, were inevitably produced by means of money. He concluded asserting that this kind of traffic not only lacked any scriptural validity but that the fallacies they provoked were all too obvious.

His final words fell on an already fatigued audience. Cipriano paid close attention the progress of the agenda, but was embarrassed when Doña Leonor, smiled at him from the dais and welcomed him aloud once the Doctor had finished his lecture. "This is a generous and devout man," she said, "whose collaboration will be of great utility to us." Everyone turned toward him and nodded. Then Doña Ana Enríquez said that to the good news of Mister Salcedo's joining their group, she could add more: two people very close to the Crown, with great political influence, were in contact with one of the brothers and would be joining in the fellowship in short order.

Pedro Cazalla, visibly annoyed at this inappropriate show of optimism, retorted that it was necessary to move with prudence and caution, that haste made waste, and that if in principle it was to their advantage to incorporate influential people into their sect, they should not forget the risk implied. Doña Catalina Ortega, for her part, said she'd learned from a good source that the number of Lutherans in Spain was in excess of six thousand, and that a rumor was circulating in Court that Princess María and the King of Bohemia himself sympathized with their cause. The urge to talk was contagious and Juana de Silva, Juan Cazalla's wife, usually quite withdrawn, said at that point that the King of Spain himself looked on the reform movement sympathetically, but that Court commitments would not allow him to express it. Euphoria, as usually happened in small group meetings like that, spread rapidly. So in order to bring matters back to plain, everyday reality, Mister Herrezuelo took the floor and pointed out that all these chimerical victories were typical of clandestine situations like the one they were living and led to nothing practical. They only produced false illusions that would demoralize the group when they collapsed. The Doctor heatedly supported Herrezuelo's observations and announced that they would proceed now to celebrating the Eucharist, the culminating moment of the meeting.

Fervently, but without changing into clerical robes, using a large crystal goblet and a silver tray, with the congregation kneeling, Don Agustín Cazalla consecrated the bread and wine and then distributed them among those present, who filed by him. One by one, they returned to their places in serenity, and the Doctor ended the ceremony by inviting his mother to take communion on the dais. After giving thanks, the Doctor, standing up, had everyone swear on the Bible that they would never reveal to anyone the secret of the groups, that they would never inform on a brother—not even in time of persecution. After the energetic "we do so swear" with which they all responded, the assembly dissolved. However, some remained behind at the dais, commenting on the recent events.

For a few minutes, Cipriano Salcedo was the main attraction, shaking hands and receiving congratulations. The diligent Juan Sánchez organized the discreet dispersal, accomplished by sending people out in pairs every two minutes. After the first couple left, he returned to the chapel to announce that it was snowing.

But no one paid him any attention. The group was trying to limber up after an hour and a half of immobility. Cipriano Salcedo asked Ana Enríquez where she lived, and she told him that part of the year she lived in Zamora and part in a summer house her father had in Valladolid on the left bank of the Pisuerga River, just where it joined the Duero. She encouraged him to visit her so they could discuss doctrine and comfort each other. For his part, Herrezuelo expressed his doubts about the efficacy of the small groups and if, in any case, their supposed efficacy in any way compensated the risks they all ran, and if it might not be more useful and less dangerous if they maintained communication among the members by means of monthly newsletters. The Doctor admitted that it would not be a bad idea to do just that, but he defended the group meetings as the only possible means to create a community and to share the Eucharist. Juan Sánchez, fully aware that his first announcement fell on dead ears and that the second couple was delaying their departure, repeated: "It's snowing."

Only then did comments, worries, and a collective haste arise.

They all left the house two by two, and when Cipriano, finely alone, stepped out onto the street, he detected in the snowflakes a certain luminosity. It was easier to see now than it was two hours earlier, the streets seemed brighter, and the snow on the ground enhanced that impression. He wrapped himself up in his hood and smiled intimately. He felt content and protected. He puffed up with pride. But even more than the flattery of being welcomed, he'd been moved by the meeting itself. He searched his confused mind for the proper word to define it, and when he did, he smiled openly and rubbed his hands together under his cloak. Fraternity: that was the perfect word and just the thing he'd hoped to find among his fellow-believers.

That clandestine meeting was a gathering of brothers encouraged by faith and fear. They were exactly like the early Christians in the catacombs, like the apostles after Christ's resurrection. He felt something, an undefinable emotion, that more than once became a tiny serpent slithering up his spine. He was aware he was at the beginning of something, that he'd entered a brotherhood where no one asked you who you were before helping you. From the servant Juan Sánchez to the aristocratic Ana Enríquez, they all seemed to enjoy the same privileges. Fraternity without classes, he told himself. In a moment of cordial euphoria, he considered the possibility of having his friends and employees, Martín Martín, Dionisio Manrique, even his aunt and uncle Gabriela and Ignacio, participate in his happiness. He thought he wasn't far from the fraternal world he'd dreamed about since being a child.

In an ineffable idealization, he saw himself as an apostle spreading the good news, organizing a multitudinous group, perhaps in his shop over in the Ghetto, where shepherds, tanners, tailors, seamstresses, trappers, and mule drivers would all praise Our Lord together. And, should it come about, thousands of Valladolid's citizens would congregate in the Plaza del Mercado to chant, with no opposition whatsoever, the psalms that Doña Leonor furtively whispered at the beginning of the meetings.

The next afternoon, he visited Doña Leonor and her son. From Pedro Cazalla and Carlos de Seso, he'd learned that in Avila, Zamora, and Toro there existed small Christian groups, satellites of the more important nucleus in Valladolid, and that Cristóbal de Padilla, servant of the Marquis of Alcañices, and Juan Sánchez had contact with them. But the movements of Padilla and Sánchez, their crude and rudimentary intellectual baggage, their lack of tact, were a serious concern for the Doctor. Those contacts should be taken more seriously, and Cipriano could be just the person to do so. The Doctor was satisfied with his good will. He overflowed with discretion and talent, and he had the money to take on such a task.

And then there was Andalusia. They were separated, increasingly so, from Sevilla, from the Lutherans in the south, and exchanges of ideas, given the vigilance of the Holy Office, were very precarious. The Sevillians were not ignorant of the fact that a communication inter-cepted at the right moment could simultaneously destroy both Protestant centers in a few hours. The result was the almost total isolation of both groups. Don Agustín Cazalla looked favorably on Salcedo's offer and his availability. Cipriano could begin in Castile and end in Andalusia. He was a good horseman and not pressed for time or money. He began by visiting the three convents in the town, where they had adepts with whom they hadn't communicated in months: Santa Clara, Santa Catalina, and Santa María de Belén. He carried letters of introduction to the nuns and enjoyed visiting room chats with the mother superiors: Eufrosina Ríos, María de Rojas, and Catalina de Reinoso. Those three were staunch supporters, but the Doctor wanted to know if the new ideas were making any progress among the novices or not.

Propagating doctrine in convents was risky, as the Doctor said, because there were always fanatics ready to tell tales to the Inquisition. Eufrosina Ríos confirmed the Doctor's fears in the convent of Santa Clara. It had been a novice, Ildefonsa Muñiz, who was deeply commit-ted to Reform, who'd introduced Lutheranism into the convent Luther's short treatise *The Freedom of the Christian* and who studied the best ways of making it known. Things were worse among the nuns of Saint Catherine where, despite María de Rojas's fervor, nothing had changed and where, given the circumstances, as the mother superior reported, it would be better for the moment not to attempt anything.

The surprise came from the Belén monastery, and it was related by Catalina de Reinoso, the prioress. Through the convent's revolving window, in her nasal, very monastic voice, Catalina told him of the advance of the new ideas taking place within. There were many nuns who embraced the theory of Christ's beneficence, and she provided a list: Margarita de Santisteban, Marina de Guevara, María de Miranda, Francisca de Zúñiga, Felipa de Heredia, and Catalina de Alcázar. The rest of the community was well disposed; all she asked of the Doctor were two things: simple books and a bit of patience. Cipriano wrote down the names of the new Christians and incorporated them into the file he kept in his desk, a file that grew day by day.

Before traveling to Avila and Zamora, Cipriano commissioned the printer Agustín Becerril to make a one-hundred copy edition of *The Beneficence of Christ* based on Pedro Cazalla's manuscript. A somewhat greedy man, Becerril took on the job in exchange for a hefty sum. Weighing pros and cons, he agreed to publish the pamphlet on condition that no one know about the operation. He did the work, with no help, and one night a month later, Cipriano picked up the bundle in his coach at the rear of the print shop. The possibility of having a hundred copies of *The Beneficence of Christ* at his disposal was discussed and celebrated at the group meeting on February 16. Now, he'd have to distribute the books with tact, without haste, trying to do so to the greatest effect.

In Avila, he connected with Doña Guiomar de Ulloa, a lady of ancient lineage, who from time to time held Christian meetings in a palace built into the city's famous walls. She possessed great dignity, which increased when she addressed the group. Her activity was very limited and could only be that way: a routine catholicism prevailed in the city, she said, neither open nor given to reflection. On the other hand, the small group was famous for the high quality of both their members and the topics they discussed. Her house had been visited by Brother Pedro de Alcántara, Brother Domingo de Rojas, Teresa de Cepeda and even more eminent people. Cipriano listened to her in a rapture, sitting back on the ottoman, surrounded by cushions like a sultan. Even Doctor Cazalla passed through here shortly after his return from Germany. Taking his visit as an opportunity, she'd convoked the brothers from all over the province, Luis de Frutos, the Piedrahita barber, Mercadal the jeweler, from Peñaranda de Bracamonte, as well as his nephew Vicente Carretero. The Doctor listened to all of them one by one and left a good memory of his stay, even if he, personally, was disillusioned when he departed. It was a difficult, harsh province, he said, and Doña Guiomar agreed. Cipriano was now drinking from the same sources, exchanging opinions with the same characters. Luciano de Mercadal, the jeweler, as not as pessimistic as Doña Guiomar. It was true that Avila, the provincial capital, was extremely traditionalist, but in Peñaranda and Piedrahita there were factions in the process of organizing, and he was involved with it. Now, in Peñaranda, he could be absolutely sure of Doña María Dolores Rebolledo, Mauro Rodríguez, and Don Rafael Velasco, and in Piedrahita there was the carpenter Pedro Burgueño, who led an interesting group of three.

From there, Cipriano dashed to Zamora, to Aldea del Palo. On the road, he noticed for the first time that his horse Lightning was showing weaknesses that concerned him. Lightning had never been sick, and these symptoms seemed serious. He'd suddenly stopped being the indefatigable charger, able to make the run from Valladolid to Pedrosa at the gallop and without stopping. Now he needed rest, either walking or a slow trot. But those symptoms that had suddenly cropped up, followed by noisy asthmatic choking, were something new and proved that Lightning had aged, that he was no longer a horse for fast travel, a horse he could count on. When he got back to Valladolid, Cipriano would consult Aniano Domingo, the Rioseco horse dealer who knew all there was to know about horses. As he patted Lightning's neck, Cipriano realized the animal was perspiring copiously.

Even so, he arrived on time for the meeting chaired by Pedro Sotelo, in whose house the proselytizer Cristóbal de Padilla had not only a safe refuge but an appropriate place for clandestine gatherings. Sotelo was a slovenly man with thick cheeks, clean shaven. He and Padilla constituted a comic pair: Sotelo with his bulging backside, short, potbellied, and Padilla, with his red locks, slack and unkempt, as thin as a spindle. Despite their physical differences, each had confidence in the other, and they seemed inseparable. What concerned Cipriano was the audacity of their public behavior. At their meetings, which they held in broad daylight, they used neither passwords nor countersigns. Anyone could enter the house, with the result that the gatherings were excessively lively and aggressive without the appropriate devotion.

When Cipriano arrived, they were already there with the organizers, Don Juan de Acuña, son of Blasco the Viceroy, who'd just arrived from Germany, Antonia del Aguila, a novice from the Convent of the Incarnation, Herrezuelo, and another half dozen unknowns. But before Acuña could joke with the nun, two Jesuits entered and sat on the last bench. It was just at that point that Don Juan de Acuña was saying, ironically, to Antonia del Aguila that God had done her the favor of making her a nun because she'd be useless as a wife, to which the novice, very moderately, responded that she wasn't yet a nun, but that she thought she would become on if the Holy Father granted her a dispensation.

Acuña imprudently commented that dispensations with regard to vows of chastity were no longer in the hands of the Pope. Just then, the younger and more battle-proven of the Jesuits stood up and intervened, without coming to the point that he'd just returned from Germany where he'd observed that the Lutherans lived extremely dissolute lives, providing a bad example, while the Catholic priests did so in secret and honesty. It was clearly a provocation, but Don Juan, now also standing and gesticulating vehemently, accepted the challenge and declared that he too had been in Germany, and what he'd seen did not coincide with his reverence's observations. The young Jesuit asked him what conclusions he'd derived from his trip, and Acuña, without the slightest hesitation, declared there were, essentially, three: the devout nature of the Lutheran preachers, their efforts to be and to appear honorable, and the fact that they had their own wives and not mistresses.

The other, older Jesuit tried to interrupt, but Don Juan stopped him: "Just a moment, your reverence," he said, "I haven't finished." And, throwing precaution to the wind, he immediately launched into a condemnation of the German Catholic clerics who, he said, ate and drank immoderately, kept their concubines in their houses, and, what was even worse, were proud of themselves and showed off. Cipriano became increasingly exasperated because the controversy concentrated on religious life in Central Europe. He glanced first at Sotelo and then at Padilla, but neither seemed disposed to interrupt the debate and change its course. He concluded that this must be the habitual tone of the group meetings in Aldea del Palo and trembled at the idea. But Don

Juan de Acuña was still shouting that it was public knowledge that one of the reasons the Germans were moved to close convents was the licentious life that went on within them and that, at least in that aspect, the least evil sect wa that of luther.

Cipriano could see that the argument had gone too far and that it was no longer going to be easy to divert it in other directions. The older Jesuit, in a voice that feigned serenity, tried to show those present that Luther had died raving and had been carried to his grave by demons. Don Juan de Acuña, made with anger, asked him how he knew that, and when the Jesuit answered that he'd read it in a book published in Germany, Don Juan pointed out in ironic tones that Germany was a free country, so people could publish things that were true and things that weren't especially true, that according to his sources, the death of Luther had been edifying.

The younger Jesuit then brought up Luther's marriage, his free union with a cloistered nun, a sacrilegious act, he said, because both had taken vows of chastity. Acuña refuted that idea by pointing out that the rule prohibiting clerics from marrying was established by law, that is, a law passed by a Council and that, therefore, another Council could authorize it, as had the Greek Church. The arguments grew more and more bitter, and the subjects began to fuse with one another without anyone's noticing. Acuña alluded to the fallibility of the Pope, exemplified in the attempt of Paul IV to declare the Emperor schismatic, and it was at that moment when Cipriano, fully aware that Acuña had fired directly at the heart of the Jesuit order, moved to the dais, and, shouting more loudly than the others, begged the polemicists to change the subject and their tone, that those present did not like either the form or the content of the discussion. After all, they'd come to listen to a doctrinal lesson and not to put up with a lamentable exchange of insults.

There was some timid applause, but to the astonishment of everyone present, Don Juan de Acuña, perhaps conscious of his excesses and shocked at his own behavior, suddenly stood up, stepped down from the dais where he'd been sitting, walked over to the Jesuits and begged their pardon. His change in attitude didn't stop there, because he went on to explain that he had a brother in the Company and that while he was in the habit of exercising with him in these verbal duels, he in no

way fomented heretical ideas. He did not believe in the point of view
he'd upheld, and everything had begun when he'd allowed himself to
make an innocent joke with the novice Antonia del Aguila. They knew
each other well, and he felt an old affection for her. The novice nodded
her head and smiled, while the Jesuits, not to be outdone in that unforeseen battle of good manners, stood up, accepted his explanations and
praised the work of his brother in the Society of Jesus. He was *a great
theologian*, they said in one voice, and, expressing the hope that Don
Juan would never repeat in public what he'd said this morning, they
considered the matter closed.

Cipriano cut his tour short. Depressed by the scenes he'd witnessed
and concerned about the condition of his horse—he'd had another choking fit going up a low hill—he returned to Valladolid, leaving his visits to
Toro and Pedrosa for a better moment. He immediately reported to the
Doctor the results of his trip. Cristóbal de Padilla was, after all was said
and done, a servant and could not, in Cipriano's opinion, act under his
own initiative. Nor could they permit his explosive alliance with Pedro
Sotelo. The events in Aldea del Palo constituted a serious warning. If it
hadn't been for the Jesuits's discretion, the Inquisition would be on
their trail even now. They'd run a totally unnecessary risk. At the same
time, the Doctor should make contact with Don Juan de Acuña as soon
as possible and silence his fiery mouth, which was exposing the entire
organization. His imprudent speechifying in Aldea del Palo would more
than justify the intervention of the Holy Office. Many others, more discreet and measured than he, were awaiting sentence in secret jails.

Don Pedro Sotelo, who was much too naïve, should stop those
insane meetings immediately. The members of the Society of Jesus moved
through the world in twos, and the commands of the order usually compensated the intransigence of one with the tolerance of his companion.
The attitude of the pair in Aldea del Palo had been, it had to be said,
strangely unanimous and understanding given the fact that the Society,
with its military character, had been founded expressly to defend
Catholicism. One favorable factor they should take into account was the
militancy in the Society of Don Juan's brother. Without that factor, it was
more than probable that the pair of Jesuits would not have behaved so
obligingly. The very violence with which Acuña expressed himself, togeth-

er with his own youth and his brother's record, induced the two Jesuits not to take his words too seriously and, as well, to accept his explanations.

In any case, the scene had been so imprudent that Salcedo mounted his horse as soon as it was over and—disdaining Pedro Sotelo's invitation to lunch—went back to Valladolid without saying good-by to Acuña or Cristóbal de Padilla. The brusque statements exchanged in the polemic had burned his stomach. He couldn't wait to speak with the Doctor, and when he saw the castle of Simancas from the top of a hill, he breathed a sigh of relief. However in that very instant, the horse tripped or, because of his weakness, unexpectedly flexed his forelegs, bent his back legs and stood there, stock still, on the thyme, his eyes sad, his dewlaps dripping foam, choking.

Alarmed, Cipriano dismounted and gave Lightning a few friendly pats on the back. The horse sweated and panted, stared indifferently, and did not react. A few harsh, guttural noises now came out of his mouth along with the foam. Cipriano sat down at his side next to some furze to wait for him to recover. He had the impression that the horse was very sick. He thought about Valiant, stretched out and bloody among the vines in Cigales, according to his Uncle Ignacio's tale. Lightning bowed his head and whinnied long and low. That's the death rattle, thought Cipriano. But, instants later, the animal made an effort and stood up. Salcedo led him by the bridle to Simancas, gave him water, and, at the old bridge, remounted him. The horse was able to carry his light load to Valladolid. Vicente was cleaning the stable when they arrived, and as soon as he saw him, realized the horse was sick. He's been weak, asthmatic, and without appetite for three days, Cipriano reported. Then he added: "Tomorrow, after he's rested, take him over to Aniano Domingo in Rioseco. Find out for certain if he can be cured. Spend the night in La Mudarra, taking care he doesn't wear himself out. I don't want him to suffer."

Vicente looked into Lightning's eyes, constantly patting his neck. He saw his master was hesitating, that he opened his mouth, and closed it again. He couldn't decide. Finally Vicente heard him say: "If Aniano says there's no hope, put him out of his misery. A bullet, that's right, in the white spot between his eyes. And the coup de grace in his heart. Before you bury him, make sure he's dead."

# XIII

H E was shocked by the way Teo received him: her tense cheeks, her shouting, tears, the harshness of her gestures. Things were moving at an oppressive speed, a gathering crescendo that passed through various phases, depending on his wife's level of agitation. At first, he couldn't understand a word: she muttered disconnected, long paragraphs, a melange of words, incoherent sentences he couldn't comprehend. The fact was, Teo was not interested in being understood. They withdrew to the bedroom, where she remained standing, pacing back and forth, articulating indecipherable words, among them some few that did have some meaning for Cipriano: slag, forgotten, last chance.

She was charging him with some crime, but he still couldn't define it. Step by step, as in a slow labor of apprenticeship, Teo began to link one word with another, focusing her discourse a bit. Her eyes were hard, like glass, still human even if her gaze had not even a spark of lucidity. But her words, when they finally began to cohere, became expressive, speaking of his having forgotten the silver and steel slag, of his indifference to the doctor's treatment, the flaccidity of *the little thing*, of her useless efforts in the face of his passivity.

She went on without resorting to violence, as if trying to reason, and Cipriano too went on connecting one sentence with another, piecing together her thoughts as if they were parts of a puzzle. Finally a moment came when everything became clear to him: Teo had forgotten to include the little sack of silver and steel scoria in his baggage, perhaps involuntarily, perhaps—and this seemed more likely—to test him.

When he returned, she immediately checked his bag and confirmed that he hadn't replaced the metal shavings. Therefore, Cipriano had gone four days without his medicine. He'd deliberately interrupted Doctor Galache's therapy.

Now her words were becoming a kind of lamentation, of heart-broken but still comprehensible whining. He'd stopped four years of medication before it could take effect, and now she was too old and too disillusioned to start over. Cipriano made an effort to avoid an overflow, to keep his wife's disenchantment within reasonable limits: nothing that had happened was of critical importance; a four-day interruption was insignificant in such a long treatment. They would both start again with renewed rigor, two doses a day instead of one, whatever Teo wanted. But she drowned out his arguments with her ranting. She had lived for nothing else but to have a child, and now she would never achieve that goal, and it was his fault. She'd had fun shearing lambs until she felt herself marriageable, mature. But if she married it was only in order to become a mother, but he, just like that, had ruined everything. Over the course of her life, everything had spoken to her of maternity: the dolls she played with as a little girl, the places out in the hills where the sheep gave birth, the nests the magpie made in the oak outside the front door, *the little thing*. To reproduce had been her only reason for being, but he did not want that, he'd destroyed everything when only a few months remained in the term fixed by the doctor.

When she reached that point in her tirade, Teo became unusually violent. Perhaps it was Cipriano's attempt to calm her, his gesture of appeasement that caused her to lose all control. Her words again became indecipherable, her fury increased, she ran to the windows and ripped down curtains and drapes, swept all of the silver items from the dressing table to the floor and launched into a string of cut-off words that sounded like barks. Cipriano suddenly understood. She was calling him something he didn't at first understand, a "billy-goat bastard." Teo had never used obscenities, and Cipriano thought it might be a reminiscence of her past as a sheep-shearer, when each flock of sheep had by law to include two females ready to breed and one male.

He made another attempt to calm her, but it had the opposite effect. Teo was screaming like a woman possessed, pushing him toward the door, screeching, while he tried to search in her eyes and find a spark of light. But her eyes were cloudy and empty: she was completely out of her mind. And the more he tried to get her under control, the filthier became the repertory of insults, which she was now mixing with filthy scatological terms, throwing in his face his inability, the small size and uselessness of his "little thing." Cipriano was trembling. He tried to cover her mouth with his hand, but she bit him and went on with her flood of insults.

She collapsed onto the bed and with her rapacious nails tore the delicate counterpane and the pillow cases. Then she abruptly stood up and tried to swing on the canopy, which promptly collapsed. She seemed to be enjoying her destructive fury, her indecency, not concerned in the slightest that her verbal outbursts could pass through partitions and walls. In the naked windows, the decaying shine of the street was being replaced by the ashen, matte light that announced nightfall.

Teo had collapsed on the bed once again, panting, and Cipriano, making a desperate effort, tried to immobilize her, to hold her wide shoulders to the mattress. She rolled her eyes and squinted while he again and again told her to be calm, that there was a cure for everything, that he would go back to the medication, twice a day instead of once, but her crossed eyes were sinking more and more behind her cheekbones, in an oblique and inexpressive stare. Those eyes were occluded, incapable of seeing and understanding. They struggled again, and Teo managed to turn herself over. She was stronger than Cipriano had ever imagined. This sickness, this kind of sickness made its victims stronger, he told himself. He managed to turn her face up and clasped her wrists against the mattress.

When she found herself immobilized, Teo again unleashed her torrent of invectives, more and more insulting. Suddenly, she mentioned her dowry, her inheritance, her fortune. Where had Cipriano hidden *her* money? This factor added new reasons for her to feel offended, so she ransacked her confused mind for words that would be even more wounding and went on offending him in her general disintegration. Cipriano noticed that after two hours of struggle, his wife's tension began to diminish. Once again, he tried to caress her forehead, but once again her furious mouth turned on his small hand.

Nevertheless, after the third attempt, she accepted the caress and allowed herself to be touched.

He began flattering her again, whispering sweet words of affection, and she remained still, attentively listening to his voice, probably without understanding a word. Teo was panting, her eyes closed as they would be after an arduous physical effort, while he went on caressing her. He twisted her hair into ringlets, but she neither thanked him nor protested. She'd reached that neutral, limp point when some nervous crises resolve themselves. She began to weep gently. The hot, silent tears were pouring down her cheeks, and he, with infinite tenderness, dried them with the fold of the sheet. He did not love this person, but he was sorry for her.

He evoked the days out in La Manga, their strolls over the hills, holding hands while flocks of wood pigeons took flight from the oaks with their craws stuffed with acorns, or while the woodcocks at dusk flew toward the clearings. In reality, Teo for him had been like those pigeons or woodcocks, one more fruit of nature, alive and spontaneous.

He'd barely had any relations with women, and the simplicity of the Queen of the Páramo had disarmed him. He was even pleased by the fact that she sheared sheep out in the open in the same way that bourgeois ladies would knit in salons. He'd always admired practical work and disdained pastimes, which he considered dissimulated tedium. Sitting on the bed, he stared at her. She'd closed her eyes, and her breathing was becoming deeper and slower. He carefully stood up and walked out on tiptoe, trying to place his feet only on carpets. He lit a candle, and, holding it his hand, rummaged through the medicine chest. He took several and with them, adding a good dose of wine, he prepared a julep in the kitchen. Aunt Gabriela always said that juleps were one remedy that never let her down; not only did she sleep deeply after drinking one but she didn't wake up until late the next morning.

He went back to Teo. She was still lying there, breathing regularly. He sat down at the head of the bed and for the first time noticed, in desolation, the destruction of the room: the torn canopy, the drapes pulled down, the two pillows with their wool stuffing pouring out. What would he say to Crisanta? But, why say anything when the servants, even if they were invisible, had to be witnesses to his wife's paroxysm? Teo began to stir nervously, muttering unintelligible words. She opened her eyes and shut them without actually seeing him. Suddenly she changed position, turned, and rolled onto her right side, facing him. She began to nod her head, whispering confused words. Very carefully, Cipriano picked up the potion in his right hand and delicately raised his wife's head with his left: "Drink this," he said in an imperative tone.

And she drank. She was thirsty. She drank without stopping, avidly, choking on the last drops and suffering a mild coughing attack. Outside, night had fallen, and the street was silent. With the candle at his back, Cipriano could see the shadow of his head moving over Teo's white face. He sat there without moving until three in the morning. Teo stirred several times, changing position each time she moved. Sometimes she muttered words in a low vice, but they were like rockets that never exploded. She was probably dreaming. When Cipriano got up from the bed, she looked calm, her breathing was regular, but despite all, he left open both the door between his room and Teo's as well as the door to his room. He undressed by lamp light and, in bed, picked up one of the copies of *Christ's Beneficence*, in which he usually took refuge in moments of tribulation. Without his realizing it, he was overcome by sleep, and the book fell out of his hands. It was only for an instant, or so it seemed to him. Teo's slamming the armoir drawer shut awakened him, along with a kind of inarticulate scream and the voluminous silhouette of his wife in the frame of the doorway. She was still wearing the torn shift she'd fallen asleep in, but in her raised right hand she was carrying her large sheep-shearing scissors. Cipriano tried to stop her, tried to say something to her, but all that could be heard in the little storeroom was the approaching menace of Teo as she burst in: "I'm going to skin that damned monkey body of yours!" she shrieked.

Cipriano took the precaution of leaning his back against the headboard of the bed while simultaneously pulling his legs back, so when Teo dove onto him, he unbent his knees and held her momentarily with his feet. Finally Teo fell to one side of the small cot and they immediately became entangled in a muted struggle. She was waving the shears around while Cipriano simply dodged her wild slashes while grasping her hands without hurting her. "Listen," he said, "listen to me, Teo, please," but she grew wilder, hemming him in. Cipriano noted a deep scratch on his right arm, which he'd been using to try to contain her, at the same time that he heard his wife's concrete threats: "I'm going to geld you like a hog," she was saying, "I'm going to cut off that *little thing* because it's useless to both of us." There was a moment when, in spite of the wound or perhaps stimulated by the pain, Cipriano held Teo by both her arms, but with a vicious movement she freed herself, and her armed hand dove under the covers and began a blind journey. Cipriano screamed when she wounded him in the right thigh, but just then he managed to grab Teo by the neck and flip her over.

His position was that of his nights of love, riding his wife's protuberances, but this time struggling with her for possession of the shears. Teo tossed around, insulted him again, "I'm going to skin that damned monkey body of yours," she repeated, but Salcedo had her under control. He let her vent her fury in useless movement and sordid threats. He saw the emptiness in her eyes, her sunken, merciless pupils, and in that instant he understood that he'd lost Teodomira, that his wife was gone forever.

After one more vain attempt, Teo gave up. She dropped the shears and burst into a gentle sob of defeat, which went on and on until it intensified without being as violent as before. She went on in that way until she placidly fell asleep. Cipriano made a second trip to the medicine chest, but this time skipped the julep and instead administered a strong dose of an opiate, Roman philonium. Then he went to his office and wrote a note to his Uncle Ignacio: "I'm afraid Teo's lost her mind. I can't leave the house. Could you bring the most knowledgeable person you know in matters of mental illness?" He awakened Vicente and gave him the letter to his uncle. The mistress was ill. The visit to Aniano Domingo with Lightning would have to be postponed.

Two hours later, Don Ignacio Salcedo, proceeding with characteristic diligence, came to his nephew's house accompanied by the young Doctor Mercado. Cipriano welcomed the doctor. Mercado was an eminence in the making. Doctor of the Monastery of the Conception and of the House of the Marquis of Denia, he was beginning to be respected in the Court. People swore that on the day of his wedding he brought with him nothing but the clothing he was wearing, a mule, and two dozen books. In any case, the five hundred-ducat dowry his bride brought constituted the foundation of his later fortune. Currently, he owned just a few vineyards in Valdestillas and a house on Cantarranas Street. Even so, the good citizens of Valladolid never stopped talking about his clinical eye, about the efficacy of his treatment, about his growing prestige. He was the first doctor in the city to stop wearing the dark clothing all doctors wore. Instead, he dressed elegantly, like a gentleman. Externally, nothing broadcast his profession. He walked into the room and with a single glance made note of the drapes on the floor, the torn bed clothes, Cipriano's bloody arm, and the general disorder in the house: "Sir, did she attack you?"

Cipriano nodded.

"Is it the first time she's ever done that?"

Cipriano again nodded. The doctor glanced at his wounded arm: "We'll dress that shortly." He turned toward Teo, who was sleeping: "What did you give her?"

"A julep and Roman philonium, doctor. I didn't dare give her anything stronger."

Doctor Mercado smiled smugly: "Slim defense against a cyclone."

Now he took her pulse and put his hand very carefully on her left breast: "No fever," he added after a short while. "My examination is necessarily superficial, but there isn't much doubt about the situation. Any obsessions?"

"One huge obsession, doctor. Being a mother. She married to have children, but I haven't been able to give her any. The Salcedos—he glanced over his shoulder at his uncle—are not prodigies in the fertility business."

He hastily told Doctor Mercado about his visits to Galache, the regimen to which he'd subjected them and the unjustified interruption of his doses of silver and steel slag during his last trip as the reason for the unleashing of the crisis. The doctor smiled again.

"Did he really think he was going to cure your infecundity with bits of silver and steel?"

Cipriano held up his wounded arm with his left hand: "I took it to be the doctor's strategy to distract my wife."

"Quite right."

He'd removed a German magnifying glass from his calfskin bag and walked over to the sick woman holding it in his hand. Turning his head, he said to the two men: "Be ready to hold her down. She could wake up at any moment."

He raised the lid of her right eye and carefully scrutinized her pupil. Then he repeated the same operation with the other eye. Again he took her pulse: "It will be necessary to intern this lady. On Orates Street, there's the Innocents Hospital. Not a luxury hotel, but it isn't easy to find anything better in this city. The treatment is primitive. The sick are tied to the bars on the bed or put in ankle chains so they won't run away. Of course with a little money, paying two attendants so they keep an eye on her, you may avoid that humiliation.

Don Ignacio, who'd remained silent until now, asked the doctor if it might not be possible to place the lady in a normal hospital and pay for the extra nursing. The doctor nodded: "Money is a very good thing. With it you can get almost anything you want in this world."

Accompanied by Uncle Ignacio, they temporarily lodged Teo to the Innocents Hospital on Orates Street. Then, at the door of the hospital, when two attendants tried to manacle her, Teo twisted like a panther, with such force that one of the attendants was thrown to the ground. The passersby, attracted by the spectacle, gathered at the foot of the stairs, where the fallen attendant had landed, but a few minutes later, Teo was installed in the mad house under the care of two hired peasant women, apparently strong, who, if the occasion arose, seemed capable of controlling her.

Even so, at nine that night, Salcedo received a note from the mad house informing him that "because of the guardians's carelessness, the lady had escaped." Cipriano again informed his uncle, who in minutes mobilized the town security forces. On his own, Cipriano, accompanied by Vicente, searched the city from north to south and east to west without finding a trace of the patient, without hearing any reference to her. She'd evaporated. The next morning, they initiated the search again, with no luck. That afternoon, Aquilino Benito, the ferry man, who supplied the service between the Espolón Viejo pier and the small dock on Paseo del Prado, informed the Chancery that he'd found the fugitive in the reeds along the shore, unconscious and in a very bad way, looking like a beggar. During the crossing toward Espolón, Aquilino managed to return the patient to consciousness, but she was exhausted.

Meanwhile, Don Ignacio had made the relevant inquiries, so once Teodomira had recovered, she was transferred, in her husband's coach, to Medina del Campo. During the journey, she remained silent. In Medina, she was housed in the Hospital of Saint Mary del Castillo, under the auspices of the Guild of Our Lady of Mercy, just a step away from the Monastery of Saint Bartholomew. It was a dilapidated but noble mansion, with a stable number of inmates, and Doña Teodomira was placed in the care of two male nurses on permanent guard and a peasant woman to see to Teo's purely feminine needs. The bill came to forty-five *reales* per diem, but they could depend on the benevolence of the organization—someone would be there to look in on the woman from time to time.

Once his wife was hospitalized, Cipriano felt relieved, but returning home depressed him deeply. Habituated to Teo's presence, he missed her, despite the fact that she no was no longer an essential element in his life. He went back to his old routines. Very early in the morning, he would visit the shop and the storage area where he would chat with Fermín Gutiérrez and Gerardo Manrique about the news of the day. There were two important problems: giving up rabbit in the manufacture of coats and the progressive scarcity of wild animals because of the relentless hunting that went on out in the country. They'd just settled the rabbit issue, when an unexpected letter arrived from Burgos communicating the death of Gonzalo Maluenda, who, though young, had died of typhoid fever. His half brother, Ciriaco, the son of Don Néstor and his third wife, had taken charge of the business.

The new impresario said an armed galley would accompany the wool fleets, so they would again enjoy relative security. The costs, logically, went up, but so did the safety, so no wool-purveyor thought twice about supporting the measure. Cipriano's business with the Maluendas had declined from the ten annual cartloads it had reached during the best times with Don Bernardo, to the three that had survived peak of the coat business. Now, he thought, the moment had come to raise the number of cartloads to five. To negotiate those details and to meet the new executive, Cipriano made a trip to Burgos. So once again an urgent letter from Burgos had come to rouse a Salcedo from lethargy. Life repeated itself.

He mounted his new horse, *Pispás*, bought for him by his friend Seso in Andalucía. But even the expertise of Don Carlos in these matters could not keep Cipriano from missing his old horse, and he was taken aback by the reactions of the new one, his innate vices, his nervousness, his size. Vicente had sacrificed Lightning out on Illera mountain, in Villanubla, with a bullet through his forehead. Estacio del Valle had lent him the pistol and a pair of powerful mules to facilitate the burial. The servant had placed a large, flat stone on top of the gravesite to identify the place.

Even though the new Maluenda was not a Don Néstor, not by a country mile, he did not make a bad impression on Cipriano. Ciraco Maluenda's diligence and probity made him vastly superior to the deceased Don Gonzalo. He happily accepted the increase in fleeces Cipriano announced, because even though it was only half the number the Salcedos had once sent, it almost doubled the number of recent shipments. Relations with the Maluendas again became friendly.

Taking time out from his various activities, Cipriano would visit Teo in Medina. Sedated with philonium, she lived calmly, with no desire to fight. Actually, she was vegetating, allowing herself to dry up. Cipriano was saddened by those eyes with their empty stare, eyes that had once been so beautiful. He never knew if she recognized him, if his visits had any effect on her because whenever he came she stared at him blankly, in the same way she gazed at her nurses as they walked around the room. Day by day, she shrank, ceasing to be the strong woman he'd met out in La Manga. Her body diminished at the same time that her features grew larger, occupying more and more of her shrunken face, once so wide and florid.

She didn't speak, didn't eat, only opened her mouth to drink; she had no interest in life, he guardians told him, but she doesn't suffer. That relieved him. The barred window of her room opened onto the countryside, and from there it was possible to see the castle, which seemed to hypnotize her. Cipriano tried to find something that might stimulate her, but his presents—little jewels, flowers, sweets—aroused not the slightest reaction. Each time he visited her, he came home more depressed than the previous time: she hadn't recognized him; it wouldn't matter if he never returned. Sometimes the guards themselves would become excited: she'd eaten a bit, taken a little walk around the room, but in her face there was no sign of any progress of that kind. With his habitual generosity, Cipriano gave Teo's guards tips that he himself never considered sufficient. At this point, he thought, it was the only thing he could do for his sick wife: bribe her guards so they would be happy to take care of her, so they'd bestow a touch of affection on her, so some day they'd make her smile.

His afternoons he dedicated to the Cazallas, the Doctor and his mother. Doña Leonor de Vivero never lost her joy or her ease in dealing with people. He spent time with her in her small study, silent, staring at the wall with nothing amusing to tell her. Even so, she would receive him with her toothy smile, her conversation, her usual good humor. During the first days, she made an effort to console him: "You look sad, Salcedo. Do you love her a lot?"

Cipriano's reply was concise and convincing: "She was a habit in my life, Doña Leonor."

"Don't torture yourself. In the face of madness and death, we often feel responsible for no reason."

But his report about the verbal confrontation in Aldea del Palo deeply depressed both Doña Leonor and the Doctor. They endured agonizing days because they felt unable to control the group. They considered it absolutely necessary that Padilla be reigned in, that he be stripped of the authority he arrogated and that those small-town meetings, open and improvised be stopped. The Doctor wasted no time sending him a letter calling him to order, warning him that what happened in Aldea del Palo could never happen again. He also wrote to Don Juan de Acuña, urging prudence, making him see the risk of his verbal excesses in view of the fact that the Holy Office was constantly on guard.

Despite his rapid reaction, the Doctor could not restrain his own dismay. He spoke to Salcedo from the heart, calling him his closest adviser. He admitted that while Cipriano had only recently become a member, he'd acted without hesitation, with enthusiasm and resolve. *Motu proprio* he'd attained important objectives, and the Doctor hoped he'd continue with his organizing efforts, work temporarily interrupted because of his wife's illness. Salcedo was deeply moved by the Doctor's favor, the obvious fact that he considered him his beloved disciple.

One foggy afternoon, when night fell prematurely, Cazalla confessed to Cipriano that they'd never gone through a time of such isolation as the one they were now suffering—they had no books, no supporters, no news from Germany. When Luther died, Melanchthon was faced with a difficult panorama. The Doctor was leaning his head over, as if he couldn't bear its weight. They were alone, and Cipriano tried to cheer him up: these were unfortunately hours of tribulation; one day they would pass. But the Doctor, instead of calming down, mixed together disparate sorts of problems, piling them up. For a moment, he forgot the group's isolation and went back to the Padilla business. He was a gossip; he hadn't answered his letter; it was as if the Doctor didn't exist or that Padilla didn't recognize his authority.

One day, he suggested to Cipriano that he visit Doña Ana Enríquez at The Confluence, her father's country house at the point where the Duero and the Pisuerga met, a leafy, park of elms, lime trees, and horse chestnut trees. A beautiful house, the Doctor said, among the many the aristocrats had built along the riverbanks when the Court came. It would be a good thing if Doña Ana who, despite her youth, was a woman of character, would urge her servant Cristóbal de Padilla to behave properly and to take the matter of group meetings with all the seriousness it deserved.

Cipriano was delighted to carry out the Doctor's orders. Doña Ana's beauty and her attractive profile had distracted him from religion during the last group meeting, which concerned the sacraments. A perfect profile, suggestive, regular, and willful, a perfection heightened by the elegant simplicity of her clothing, which left exposed a long neck decorated with a pearl necklace. But what was most notable in Doña Ana's profile was the toque she wore outdoors: it was long and tight, and she skillfully wrapped like a turban on the top of her head. While Cipriano was contemplating her so attentively, he could not be sure whether she sensed she was being watched. He preferred to think she didn't, that she was just that way—spontaneous and natural, both when she listened to the Doctor's homilies, when she devoutly kneeled during the opening psalm, or when she timidly raised her hand to ask permission to speak during the discussions. Doña Ana's presence at the meetings was absolutely relaxed but she clearly wanted to take part in things.

When the Doctor told him to visit her with the intention of finding out what was behind Padilla's silence, Cipriano did not hesitate. She answered his urgent note, sending the messenger right back to him: she'd expect him two days later at eleven in the morning. On the road toward Medina, Salcedo thought of his wife, but he quickly concentrated on the motive of this trip: Ana Enríquez, her warm, melodic voice that carried so far, her being unmarried, her well-defined personality, something extraordinary in a girl barely twenty years old.

Cipriano's legs were adapting to the reduced girth of Pispás, a horse who allowed himself to be governed more by pressure from the knees than by the reins. He was as well a pureblood, as fast as the wind, but less corpulent and prudent than Lightning. One day, he'd ride up to Illera to visit Lightning's grave, a necessary act of respect.

Once past Puente Duero, Pispás took a sandy road to the right among stands of pines. Finally, when he heard the booming sound of the water, the violent clash of the two rivers, he stopped. The road ended there, and on the left among the trees, rose the great, two-story house, surrounded by a garden whose paths were covered with dry leaves. The flower beds had been left untended, but there were autumn flowers: marigolds, still brilliant, and roses, discolored and dying. A very young maid, wearing a toque, led him to Ana Enríquez, who was dressed all in green. Quite easily, simply, barely noticing what was happening, he found himself strolling at her side through the garden. He noted how her short Morocco leather boots dragged along the leaves, as if she were playing a game. The Doctor, she said, shouldn't be concerned about Cristóbal Padilla's delay; he was lazy when it came to writing. He might even be ill. In any event, she would send him a note warning him to follow the Doctor's instructions. In the sect, there existed a hierarchy, and it was necessary to avoid endangering it with foolish gatherings.

Her warm, sumptuous chatter under the noble, centenarian trees enchanted Cipriano. For her part, she began to enjoy his conversation and spoke to him openly, in a perhaps imprudent way, about Don Carlos de Seso, whom she called a *big trickster*, about Beatriz Cazalla, *his perverter*, and about Brother Domingo de Rojas, a great friend of the family, who calmed her down after her initial confusion.

Before lunch, Salcedo left for Pedrosa and Toro under a leaden sky and with a light rain falling. Beatriz Cazalla and her brother Pedro brought the three village women who took care of the church into the group, while Don Carlos de Seso, in Toro, gave Cipriano a piece of good news for the Doctor: Bartolomé Carranza's famous *Catechism* was infiltrating Spain from Flanders in loose, unbound notebooks, and it was beginning to spread in the north. The Marquess of Alcañices had been the first to receive it, and both she and all those who'd read it were in agreement about its erasmist spirit.

He slept in Toro and returned to Valladolid by way of Medina del Campo. He hadn't visited his wife in almost a month, and with each day that passed his guilt weighed more heavily on him. He'd never understood Teo and had never made any effort to do so. He supplied her with comfort and some slight attention, but he never shared much less understood her anxieties or her desire to be a mother. But that desire had grown, had become an obsession, and had ended by devouring her. He found her worse than she'd been four weeks earlier, just as vacant but more emaciated. When he met her, the size of her face surprised him because it was excessively large for the size of her features. But now, as her face grew thinner, her features grew more pronounced, and her thin nose hung over a pugnacious chin, which had never been one of her good points. Also, those empty, static eyes, bounded by two livid shadows, that had once filled the upper part of her face were now sinking into it. He found her pacing the corridor, actually dragged along by the two strong guards who accompanied her. With her hair a mess, her shoulders bent over, and her laborious walking she looked like a little old lady about a thousand years old, a ghost who'd arisen from the dark depths of the hallway. Cipriano stopped in front of her and observed her carefully. In her flat eyes, he detected not even a spark of consciousness. They seemed to look either within or a long way off. Nevertheless, when he tried to take her by the arm and she made a brusque gesture as if to free herself, he thought he spied, deep in her eyes, a flicker of lucidity.

When they went back into her room, Cipriano insisted on helping

her. He again took her by her fleshless arm, and this time she did not
resist. She passively let herself be put to bed and lay there staring at the
castle visible through the barred window. The guards and the female
attendant, perhaps hoping for a tip, agreed that she was better. She was
eating solid food, walked a little bit each day, and her thin eyes revealed
something that wasn't there before. Cipriano sat at her side and took
her hand in his. He tenderly called her by her name, but she stared over
his shoulder at the castle's battlements. A moment came when she shifted her gaze and stared at him, so fixedly, so insistently that Cipriano
could not stand it and looked away.

When he looked back, he found Teo's eyes still focused on him,
imperturbably, as if she were scrutinizing the depths of his soul. But he
saw her so alienated, so helpless, that his own eyes filled with tears. He
again spoke her name, squeezing her hand between his, and suddenly
the wonder occurred: her eyes grew lively, acquired the old and missed
honey color, her thick mouth formed a slight smile, and her fingers
became animated for an instant. Then she murmured two, perfectly
audible words: *La Manga.* Cipriano burst into tears; for a few seconds
their eyes met, they understood each other, but he, even though he
tried to hold on to that moment, was unable to prolong it. Teo again
became vacant, shifted her eyes away from his, and freed her hand from
his. She again became the passive and remote being she'd been for the
past eight months.

At nightfall, Cipriano passed through Serrada and La Seca at a full
gallop. His visit to Teo had left a painful mark on him, and he was saying to himself that his behavior toward her, the fact that he'd removed
her from her world and later abandoned her, demanded reparation.
The more he tried to repress it, the more his sense of guilt grew, and he
thought that even a long life of sacrifice would not be enough to excuse
a responsibility that would last for years. He found no consolation, and
as soon as he reached Valladolid, he left Pispás in the hands of his servant and went to the church of San Benito.

The size of the deserted temple magnified his sensation of loneliness and accentuated the silence of the place, even though the little
light in the sanctuary, so tenuous and hesitant, communicated a pale
impression of company. Salcedo sought the darkest corner in the church,

a bench off to one side, behind one of the thick pillars, and once he was there, seated, gathered into himself, his hands joined, he again wept, imploring the presence of Our Lord to reconcile him, to relieve him, once again, of his sins. He was so concentrated in himself, enveloped to such a high mystical degree, to focused and ethereal, that he felt in a very lively way the presence of Christ at his side, sitting in the pew. In the half light, blurred by tears, he glimpsed His face, His white, shining tunic, but each time he tried to look directly at Him, at His eyes, the figure of Christ faded.

He tried several times without success and then decided to be satisfied with feeling Him at his side, His shoulder against his shoulder, and to glimpse out of the corner of his eye His peace-giving gaze, the diffuse white stain of His face framed by His hair and His rabbinical beard. He was overwhelmed by the awareness of his sin, the systematic destruction of his wife, his terrible egoism. He confessed it to Christ submissively, speaking to him familiarly, confiding in him humbly. And, because it was impossible to un-do the evil he'd done, he had recourse to his old desire for reparation. He had the absolute security that Our Lord was listening to him, observing him with a remote air of complicity. Then, humbled, in complete ecstasy, Cipriano Salcedo formulated the two offerings that he'd been mulling over on the road: his sexuality and his money. Intimate commitments of chastity and poverty. He would definitively renounce all carnal contact and divide his wealth with those who'd helped create it. He'd never felt any special attraction for money, but the firm intention to dispose of it produced in him a new sensation of power.

That night he slept badly, fully clothed, stretched out on top of the bed. Very early the next morning Crisanta handed him an urgent letter from Medina del Campo. It was from the director of the hospital who informed him that his wife, Teodomira Centeno, had died at midnight, hours after his visit. They'd found the body in bed, smiling, as if at the last moment Our Lord had visited her. They awaited his instructions for the burial.

# XIV

**D**EPRESSED, his spirits low, Cipriano Salcedo left for Pedrosa along the only road there was, the road the old Don Bernardo, not much given to adventure, had followed thirty years earlier: Arroyo, Simancas, Tordesillas, flanking the Pisuerga and the Duero. Three days ago, his wife had been buried next to her father, Don Segundo Centeno, in the atrium of the church in Peñaflor de Hornija, the same church where Cipriano and Teo had been married eleven years earlier. He made the decision about where to bury Teo after discussing with his uncle Ignacio the possible meaning of the enigmatic words Teo muttered on her last visit, during the only moment when her eyes seemed alive: *La Manga*, she'd said.

What was Teo thinking when she mentioned the place where she'd spent her early years shearing lambs? Was it perhaps the only place she remembered with nostalgia? Or was it their short courtship out in the wild that she treasured more than any other moment in her life? Or did she mean, simply and plainly, that she wanted to rest there, under the strong, red earth of the Páramo, next to her father, "the man who made his fortune in the New World?" Before he made his decision, and before he transported his wife's body to Valladolid, Cipriano had spent a few hours in the Medina hospital conversing with the people who'd been with Teo during her final moments. The peasant woman denied that the scene which took place that afternoon during his visit had ever taken place again. Moreover, Mrs. Teo was left prostrate after her words, she said, and when it was time to administer the Roman philonium so she would sleep, they'd had to pry open her jaws with the handles of two silver spoons, doing so with such force that they broke two teeth.

Cipriano was horrified and asked if that procedure, which seemed so violent, was common. The peasant woman answered that they used it whenever a patient fought taking something the doctor considered indispensable. The two male guards had also spoken with the same crudity and openness. Doña Teodomira had died in her sleep, with no repetition of the *visions* she'd had that afternoon. Nevertheless, she did smile, something they hadn't seen her do during the two months they'd been taking care of her. With regard to the spoons, that was the usual method of feeding patients who refused to eat. In the case of Doña Teodomira, who clenched her teeth and only opened her mouth to drink water, there was nothing else to do but resort to the spoons. There were even days, when she was still strong, when her resistance was such that they had to chain her hands to the headboard to keep her down.

For Cipriano all that was painful news, and he spoke about his wife with the doctor and the director of the hospital. They were surprised at his surprise. If they hadn't used the spoons, the patient wouldn't have lived eight months. She would have died immediately. He could have imagined it for himself. Administering doses of Roman philonium, fruit juice, or bouillon was only possible if they overcame her resistance. She instantly knew when they were trying to give her something other than water and would then shut her mouth so tightly that only by prying could they open it. From the first day, the patient had refused to ingest anything but water, and in the face of such a negative attitude, they had no choice but to resort to force. In the Hospital of Santa María del Castillo suicide was forbidden, as was helping someone commit suicide. The director declared that the conduct of his subordinates had been proper, and when Cipriano tried to make him see that subjecting a patient to such violent treatment was something that had to be cleared first with the family, he laughed out loud. Cipriano, he said, was mistaken, things were not like that, they'd sworn a Hippocratic oath, and applied it rigorously whether or not the patient's family agreed.

Trembling with rage, Cipriano went down to the basement to see the body which, in effect, was serene and smiling. That smile, about which they'd all spoken so much, was genuine, and not only reflected

peace but even well-being. That was Cipriano's only consolation, a satisfaction that ultimately overcame his crushing pain. Something at the
last moment had induced Teo to smile. A few hours earlier, she'd
named La Manga in a moment of lucidity, he told himself it was logical
to imagine that she was dreaming or thinking about La Manga when
that farewell smile appeared. Uncle Ignacio was of the same opinion,
and after prolonged conversations they agreed that when Teo mentioned La Manga, she was referring to the place where she hoped to
rest forever. The Queen of the Páramo wanted to return to the Páramo,
and there was no reason to thwart her desire.

Cipriano was deeply moved when the four carriages that accompanied the funeral coach stopped on the esplanade outside the Peñaflor
church. He was accompanied by his old friends Gerardo Manrique,
Fermín Gutiérrez, Estacio del Valle Jr., and his new friends, Doctor
Cazalla, his brother Francisco, and the jeweler Juan García. Uncle
Ignacio rounded out the party. The sky was overcast, but it didn't rain,
but even so, the group of laborers and shepherds who awaited the body
took shelter on the church porch. It was as if they were in uniform: the
farm workers with their smocks and their short breeches which left
their hairy calves visible, and the shepherds, old and young, wearing
rabbit coats and buttoned breeches.

They all left their refuge and surrounded the coffin when Don
Honorino Verdejo, the parish priest, recited a prayer for the dead at the
church door. For these rough Castilians, the woman they were about to
bury constituted a symbol, since she not only worked with her hands as
they did, but did so with more spirit and profit than the men. For that
reason, it was only proper she be given the nickname "Queen of the
Páramo." "She was a shearer, like us," said an old shepherd in a tremu-
lous voice, for whom manual labor erased the sin of her being well-off.
Manrique and Estacio del Valle, Jr. had some relation to the peasants,
who looked at the outsiders with a mix of stupor and curiosity, as if they
were beings of another race or inhabitants of another planet.

But everyone became astonished when they dug the grave for the
*Queen of the Páramo*: her father's body lay intact at the bottom of the
pit, with his gray hair and naked body, not at all decomposed, his penis
erect, and his eyes open, bloodshot, and full of dirt. One peasant

declared that to be a prodigy, but Don Honorino, an honest and well-informed man, nipped that chimera in the bud: he of course made no reference to the incomprehensible autonomy of Don Segundo's member, but he did explain the properties of certain soils to slow the rotting of bodies. "Specifically," he said, "in Gallosa, the town where I was born, no corpse rotted before being four years in the ground."

Later, when they left Peñaflor, Cipriano told his uncle that he felt affection for Don Segundo, that the fact that his body had remained intact and his sex alive, as if he'd died with his appetites, had moved him a great deal. A short time later, as they were crossing the wild part of La Manga, Cipriano spied the large mound of stones and the red road half rubbed out by the sheep, the bushes cut back by the charcoal burners, and, way back, the slate roof of the house, he leaned forward and asked his servant to slow down. He leaned his forehead against the window and for a few minutes remained silent, his eyes half closed, evoking his walks with Teo in the clearings and odd corners of that familiar place.

When they drew near to Pedrosa, Cipriano left the coach and road Pispás on the last section of the road. The pale stubble, the black, recently-plowed earth, the furrows in the road all reminded him of his itinerant chats with Cazalla. A tightly grouped flock of partridges noisily took off from the ditch and spooked Cipriano's horse, who snorted and reared several times before calming down again. Martín Martín, who was waiting for him, told him as soon as he came into sight that the grape harvest had been magnificent but that the grain crop was poor. He held the same opinion as his father: the money was in the vines.

Riding a robust mare, the farmer followed him at a short distance through the various divisions of the property: the shoots, the skimpy young vines behind the hills, the parcel of land at Villavendimio with its flourishing stand of pine. On the way back to the house, Cipriano notified Martín Martín that Teodomira had died. It was then that the scene which occurred thirty-seven years earlier between their fathers took place again. Hearing the bad news, Martín Martín took off his hat and made the sign of the cross: may God give you strength to commit her soul to Him.

Later, they ate alone, served by the aged Lucrecia and her daughter-in-law. Cipriano then communicated to his farmer that because of

his wife's death, he'd thought things over and was inclined to share the
property with him. Martín would work the land, and he, Cipriano,
would pay the expenses involved. It was such an unheard-of and generous offer that the farmer dropped his spoon onto his plate. "I'm not sure
I really understand . . ." he stuttered, but Cipriano interrupted him:
"What you've understood is what I just said, we'll share the ownership
of the land between us. You will supply your sweat, and I'll supply my
money. The profits we'll split fifty-fifty." He ended his little speech with
a lie: "It was my deceased wife's wish."

Martín Martín tried to thank him but couldn't get the words out.
Cipriano, one step ahead of him, said his uncle, the judge, would formalize the new contract, but that it was his desire also to better the
salaries of the farm hands, so at what rate was he paying a day's work in
the Pedrosa vineyards. The farmer became serious: low; the salaries were
low. A worker could demand fifty maravedíes, but a harvest worker
wouldn't get half that. It was necessary to raise their wages, it was essential to raise the standard of living in Pedrosa, and he, Cipriano, as the
largest landowner, had to set an example. He talked about doubling the
salaries of the day laborers, of the odd-job workers, but the farmer
clasped his hands to his head: "But have you thought your plan
through? The small landowners won't be able to compete. No one in
Pedrosa will want to work for less than what we're paying. The entire
region will collapse."

Cipriano began to intuit that his donation constituted another
problem, but at the same time he did not want to renounce his largess.
Things would have to be studied, deliberately, with competent people
and lawyers. He realized that his decision, in the simple way in which
he'd conceived it, would be popular among the day laborers but unpopular among the landowners. He would have to reflect and then act
methodically, with a clear mind.

That same afternoon, he went out for a walk with Pedro Cazalla,
who praised his decision to make a new contract with Martín Martín.
The region was in a critical state and those who lived off it faced misery.
They earned little, and the taxes and the Church, with its obligatory
donations and tithes, ruined them completely. Any plan to remedy rural
incomes would be insufficient. The problem Martín Martín pointed out

was a fact, but the Chancery judges, the high administrators in the Court, had more than sufficient means to find the proper solution. As for himself, he would talk the matter over with Don Carlos de Seso, who, as a rural administrator, would be fully informed on these matters. Back in Cazalla's house, Cipriano gave him three hundred ducats to cover the town's most urgent needs, even, he pointed out in passing, paving the streets, but Pedro Cazalla said that idea was out of the question because horses and mules would slip on the cobblestones and break their legs. They would have to think about another, less risky, use for the money.

Cipriano entered into a phase of feverish activity. Solitude horrified him, because he was afraid to be alone with his thoughts. He simply did not know how to be by himself or idle, and aside from his habitual work in the warehouse or the tailor shop, he had to find ways to be busy for the rest of the day resolving other issues. Uncle Ignacio, who approved of his good intention to give away half his fortune, assured him he would take charge of the contract with Martín Martín. But, given the way the world was organized, doubling the wages of farm workers and day laborers would be a provocation. Even so, there had to be a solution to this problem, and he would find it. In the Chancery, there were prominent people willing to help. On the other hand, the idea of stimulating manufactures filled his uncle with joy. Don Ignacio Salcedo, from the time he'd gotten his degree, has specialized in juridic and economic subjects. He read a great deal, with authentic avidity, not only cases and matters of jurisprudence but French and German publications and books sent him by his friends in central Europe.

By that means, he found out that the organization of production in guilds was slowly but surely becoming old fashioned. In France and Germany new kinds of labor organizations were forming that in Spain were still unknown, structures in which not only men, but also capital joined together to make themselves stronger. Bringing Valladolid into modern times was one of his secret aspirations. The guilds were declining, and when his nephew asked him for new methods to organize the wool trade with Burgos and to reorganize the business of manufacturing coats and fine apparel, Don Ignacio thought that perhaps limited partnerships could resolve both issues.

Both Dionisio Manrique and Fermín Gutiérrez would cease to be employees and become partners instead, their labor being valued in terms of capital. That is, they would supply their labor and he the capital. They would create two mixed companies in which capital and labor would earn similar profits. But here, as in the country, a prickly problem arose: What was to be done with the skinners, the trappers, the leather makers, the mule drivers and all the others who had no expertise in the warehouse or the workshop? Don Ignacio immediately saw the solution: incorporate untrained labor into the benefits. For him, the novelty of the concept constituted an authentic economic revolution, especially in Valladolid, which made it seem even more just to him, with more potential. Manrique and Gutiérrez would be equal partners with him, but the wage earning workers, instead of having their salaries raised—which would cause a war with the competition—would receive, on a seasonal basis, extra income derived from the profits. That money, to be divided among skinners, trappers, cutters, mule drivers, and leather makers, would be a percentage of the profits or from the part owed to Cipriano Salcedo. It all depended on how much he would release. In any case, neither the transportation of wool to the Low Countries nor the coat business created insurmountable problems.

The uncle and the nephew spent entire afternoons conversing to such a degree that after Teo died, Cipriano's mind never again had a moment of repose. It was strange, but in recent years, when communication with Teo hadn't existed, all Cipriano had to know was that she was there, in the house, to hear her moving from one room to another for him to feel accompanied. As he said once to Doña Leonor, Teo had come to be a habit for him.

The more Cipriano delegated the transformation of his businesses to his uncle, the more intense became his relationship with the Cazalla family. Doña Leonor lamented his being a widower with a beautiful expression of solidarity and said she understood his wife perfectly. She had given birth to ten children, but she'd celebrated each one as if it were the first. Even so, she also understood Cipriano, because the life of a man went way beyond the family circle, just as his egoism was greater than that of a woman. For his part, the Doctor once again reaffirmed his confidence in Cipriano. He felt weak and fearful, and Cipriano's collaboration was indispensable for him. He'd finished making his list, but the reduced Castilian community needed constant attention. Small problems cropped up everywhere. Ana Enríquez had assured them that Cristóbal de Padilla would be under their control, that he would not go his own way again, but reality was something very different. Antonia de Mella, the wife of Pedro Sotelo, told the Doctor that Cristóbal had paid her a visit to read her a letter, as he said from Master Avila. A very dangerous letter, which he offered to leave with her so she could study it. A few days later, Padilla came back with another letter, also apparently from Master Avila, but this time he read it to Robledo's wife. It concerned God's mercy, and when he finished reading it, he told her to advise her husband to abandon his penitence, because Our Lord had done it for all of us. The next day, he convoked a meeting of women in Sotelo's house and offered them a little book, where they could study the articles of faith oriented toward the doctrine of justification.

When some of the women expressed their outrage, he confessed that the book had been written by Brother Domingo de Rojas, though to others he said he was the author of the book. Cipriano had to make two trips to Zamora to convince Pedro Sotelo not to supply Padilla with meeting places since the man, according to the Doctor, who was growing more frightened with each day that passed, was sowing discord wherever he went. For the moment the Doctor was satisfied, but each day brought its new problem, and one afternoon he informed Cipriano that the jeweler Juan García had told him he was having serious family problems and that Cipriano should get in touch with him as soon as possible. Cipriano visited the stall where Juan worked, and he, without raising his eyes from the bracelet he was repairing, told him that the next day at seven in the evening he would visit him at his home, because it was not advisable to speak in the shop.

When they were together, Juan García began whimpering that he was one of the earliest members of the sect, one of the most firmly convinced, but his wife, Paula Rupérez, a fanatical catholic, suspicious of his nocturnal adventures, had followed him through the dark streets on a meeting night. Fortunately, he noticed in time and hid in the entryway to some business and watched her pass by. Then he was transformed from one being followed to one doing the following, and for an

hour walked in circles along the old streets of the San Pablo neighborhood, he on the lookout and she lost. The next day, Paula asked him
where he'd gone so late at night, and he said he'd suffered one of his
frequent attacks of seeing spots before his eyes and had gone out to
clear his head. Juan García eventually calmed down, but he pointed out
that his wife had informed her confessor of her suspicions, and that
there was every good reason to fear that his wife's confessor, if he
became aware of even one hint of heresy, would immediately denounce
them to the Inquisition.

Cipriano tried to calm the jeweler. He told him that for the time
being he should stay away from the group meetings, that every month,
on the day after the meetings he should visit so that Cipriano could give
him a summary of what had gone on. That way, he wouldn't feel left out.
For greater security, he should accompany his wife to religious services
and do whatever he saw her doing. The jeweler wept gain; he was disgusted by the thought of becoming another Nicodemus, pretending to
believe in something he didn't, but Cipriano told him that all of them,
to a greater or lesser degree, did just that, that he himself attended mass
on holidays, because in times of persecution the best defense was dis-
simulation if not outright duplicity.

Seven days before Christmas, Doña Leonor suddenly died.
During the morning, she'd felt a vague tremor in her heart, and after
eating she'd died in her rocking chair without anyone's noticing. The
Doctor discovered her still warm, her chair still moving back and forth
slightly. Her decease was the culmination of this *annus horribilis*, as
Doctor Cazalla termed it. It became necessary to prepare the funerary
honors with all the pomp and circumstance the Doctor's fame and the
fact that three of her sons were clergymen required. The burial was set
for the chapel of the Fuensaldaña family, in the Monastery of Saint
Benedict. Ten maidens, practically children, accompanied the coffin
carrying blue ribbons, and the chorus of the College of the Orphans,
founded just a few years earlier in the city, intoned the usual litanies.
Cipriano imagined he was seeing in those boys the Foundlings of his
own boyhood, his schoolmates, and responded to the appeals to the
saints with devotion and respect: *ora pro nobis, ora pro nobis, ora pro
nobis*, he said to himself, and when they came to the *Dies irae* in the

epistle he prostrated himself on the church floor and repeated the words in a low voice, deeply movied: *Solvet saeclum in favilla: teste David cum Sibylla*.

The entire city attended the Mass for the burial of Doña Leonor. The Doctor's reputation and the fact that three of her sons participated in the funeral Mass stirred religious feeling among the people. As large as the church was, it could not hold everyone. Many stood at the door and at the entrance in devout silence. The voices of the orphans echoed in the diminutive Rinconada plaza, and passersby devoutly made the sign of the Cross as they passed in front of the church. When the ceremony was over, the company gathered in the atrium to accept condolences, but in the moment when most people were present and emotion was at its highest, a manly voice, well-toned and powerful, exploded over the noise of those present: "Burn Doña Leonor de Vivero at the stake!"

People hissed to demand silence, and the insult was not repeated. The ceremony went on at the same rhythm, the crowd filed by the Cazalla brothers, and some, closer acquaintances or simply more daring, approached and gave them the kiss of sympathy.

For the Doctor, the death of his mother brought him to the lowest point in his depression. In life, Doña Leonor had represented authority, calm, order, an obligatory reference point. And despite having left two daughters, Constanza y Beatriz, her solid matriarchy was now left in ruins. The Doctor's face deteriorated even more, growing thin, becoming wrinkled. He lost his hair. Even his voice lost its tone and revealed the great moral suffering that weighed on him. In the gatherings arranged to allow people to pay their respects, which were attended by many admirers, he barely spoke. People left the house disoriented, saying the Doctor would not survive this disaster. At night, when the visitors left, he locked himself away with Cipriano in his mother's small study where they spoke of her, reconstructing her past and her meaning within the family and their sect.

Constanza now ran the household, but nothing was the same. Poor Constanza was merely a simple apprentice, the Doctor said, demoralized. For the lack of a more direct comfort, the friendship between the two men became stronger in this difficult time: "You heard it," the Doctor said one night. "And you can help me identify that voice."

The voice demanding his mother be burned at the stake was eating away at him, allowing him no rest. Behind it he saw the entire city, the whole world. And no matter what he and Cipriano might discuss, the conversation always ended up returning to the same subject: the virile and echoing voice calling for the dead woman to be burned. Cipriano tried to calm him down: a madman, your reverence, any gathering of those proportions inevitably includes some lunatic. But Cazalla insisted that it was no madman, that the voice was firm, cultured, and educated. It's tone was not vile. Cipriano, eager to do his bidding, spoke in the tailor shop with Fermín Gutiérrez, an old admirer of the Doctor. Yes, he too had heard the voice, and, in his opinion and in the opinion of his friends, it had come from a corner where a group of officers from the Royal Guard were standing. The Doctor energetically shook his head: the command voice of a soldier could be identified at a distance of ten leagues. They'd have to think of someone more distinguished, someone familiar with the inner workings of the Cazalla family, someone of sordid soul but courteous in his manners.

After two weeks of useless suppositions and conjectures about the mysterious voice, the Doctor opened his heart one afternoon and spoke sincerely. He revealed a secret it was necessary to take into account during the investigation. He spoke about a strange woman, who in an equally strange way had crossed his path and had argued violently with him. He was talking about Catalina de Cardona, nicknamed *the Good Woman*, who in her youth had been the nurse of the emperor's illegitimate son Don Juan of Austria. In the high spheres of society, she was considered a saint and had ended up in Valladolid at the side of the Princess of Salerno, as her lady of honor. The Princess' husband had come to the Court to beg the restitution of properties confiscated because of his presumed participation in a plot against Spaniards.

During the time the Princess of Salerno had lived in Valladolid she'd had the opportunity to establish a friendly relationship with the Doctor. But Catalina, *the Good Woman*, was never pleased by the friendship between her lady and the Doctor because of the way he spoke about God's mercy and Christ's merits seemed to her mistaken and suspicious. Catalina de Cardona, a busybody, decided to name herself guardian angel to the Princess and, in addition to frowning at the Doctor, would tirelessly contradict and reprimand him at afternoon gatherings. One day she said to the Princess that Satan spoke through the Doctor's mouth. Then the Doctor decided to teach the know-it-all a lesson, and in his famous sermon on the Three Mary's on Resurrection Sunday, he ridiculed the impertinence of certain women who disputed with theologians, third-rate pedants, he called them, who would be better off dealing with pots and pans instead of theology. *The Good Woman* waited for the priest to visit, and when he appeared before her lady, she told her she'd seen bubbles of fire surrounded by smoke come out of his mouth and that she smelled brimstone as well. The scandal *the Good Woman* aroused created a tense atmosphere at the gathering, an unexpected violence. The Princess was obliged to intervene and silence both parties just when Cazalla was about to speak. At that point, he stood up in all dignity and left the house offended.

"I never set foot in the Princess' palace again, Cazalla pointed out to Cipriano. But it seems logical that the voice demanding my mother be burned at the stake was formed there in the Princess' gatherings because of my homilies." Cipriano became pensive. He didn't know the Doctor had enemies of such high rank, but once he did he thought it was a good thing that the insult to Doña Leonor had come from that group or another like it.

Two days later Cipriano found the ground floor of the Doctor's house smeared with filthy writing: BURN DOÑA LEONOR AT THE STAKE it said simply. That abject sign written in red pain sent the Doctor into despair. He called a meeting of the group—in broad daylight—in the oratory in his house. "We can't go on living in this self-absorbed isolation," he said. "Even the stones know who we are; we're watched, hated, and any precautions we adopt from this point on will be of little matter." He looked frightened, cornered. With the death of his mother, on whom he'd depended so much and who embodied courage, came this disgusting revenge from Valladolid's upper class. "We have to admit we aren't free," he added, "that we're up against enemies who won't show their faces. Let's be prudent. All meetings are, for the time being, suspended." The Doctor decided the meetings would be replaced by home visits, where members of the sect would be personally informed of any news. Cipriano, following the Doctor's orders, traveled to Toro, Zamora, and Logroño to warn others.

When he returned, he found the Doctor in even lower spirits, in deep thought. The fact that the existence of the group was known or, at least suspected, was driving him mad. He literally felt his back was up against the wall. Cipriano stayed with him until the early hours of the morning. He was afflicted with insomnia and juleps or Roman philonium had barely any effect on him. His fearfulness was leading him to exaggerated extremes, to a morbid cowardice. At the same time, feelings of persecution and isolation were weighing on all the others.

One night, they painted over the red words on the façade, and the Doctor went back into his house more at peace with himself, as if he'd erased all the bad thoughts from the mind of the guilty party. It was on Cipriano's shoulder he wept: "The Reformer at least knew of our existence and encouraged us," he said. With Luther dead, with their group disconnected from its counterparts in Sevilla, the Doctor saw no future for the cause. But Cipriano realized that one day the Doctor thought one thing and the next the opposite, that he was indecisive, changeable, unable to move forward.

On one occasion, they prepared a trip to Sevilla, but a week before leaving the Doctor abandoned the plan. What were they going to do in Sevilla? Were people better informed down south than they were here? It was necessary to go further, much further, to the source. Would Cipriano be willing to travel to Germany for the sake of the group? Salcedo wasn't surprised by the question; in fact he'd been expecting it for months.

He was convinced that only by speaking directly with Melanchthon and his associates, bringing back direct information, books and other publications, the chimerical promise of aid (should it come to that), would he manage to raise the Doctor's spirits. So, he told the Doctor, he would go to Germany and spend the time needed there, making contact with the brain of the organization, and receiving instructions. The mere idea that Cipriano was going to Germany cheered the Doctor. He showed him routes on the map, cities, roads, supplied him with names and addresses, necessary contacts, centers he would definitely have to visit. It was as if his blocked up mind had suddenly begun moving again.

One afternoon he gave him the address of Berger, Heinrich Berger, a sailor by profession, an apostle of the new Christianity, with whom he might return to Spain through the northern ports. As he remembered his time in Germany, the places he'd visited with the Emperor, his old friends, his initial contacts, the Doctor's face began to shine. Putting their heads together, the two men made plans: Cipriano would leave by way of the Pyrenees and return by sea. Or the other way around. Cipriano's coat business, should it become necessary, could be a good cover story, but for now the project should remain a secret. Had Cipriano ever heard of Pablo Echarren, who lived in Cilveti, a small town in the north of Navarra? No, of course not, Salcedo knew nothing about Echarren, didn't even know Cilveti existed. The furthest north he'd ever travelled had been to Miranda de Ebro. He'd never even been to Bilbao.

The Doctor informed him that Echarren guided people to the French border—people on the run, refugees, exiles, smugglers. He was his man, but he had to be dealt with cautiously. The best idea would be to speak with Don Carlos. Seso had known Echarren since his time in Logroño and had used his services on several occasions. Cipriano was to tell him that Don Carlos de Seso was his friend, his very good friend. No, of course not, he had no fixed fees, he made it up on the spot, it all depended on the moment, the risk he'd run with each move, his own needs, but his payment—he said—would be unlikely to be less than twenty-five ducats or more than forty.

Once he reached Echarren's house, Vicente, Cipriano's servant, could return to Valladolid with the horses, since Echarren had mules of his own that knew the way, were silent, and less likely to cause difficulties. Then he gave Cipriano Pablo Echarren's address in Cilveti. But before leaving, Salcedo made a quick trip on Pispás to Toro, where Don Carlos de Seso added to the information given him by the Doctor and warned him that Echarren's manners were a bit brusque and his character changeable. At the same time, he told Cipriano he could rely on him and that he would keep his word. Finally, he gave Cipriano a note of introduction for Echarren.

On the way back to Valladolid, he passed through Pedrosa to give

Martín Martín a copy of the new contract he'd drawn up with his uncle
Ignacio in Chancery. He'd already sent Domingo Manrique and Fermín
Gutiérrez a draft of the agreements about the new limited partnerships.
So once the obligations keeping him in Valladolid were taken care of
and once the Doctor thought the time was right, they fixed the day of
his departure for April 25. Vicente had prepared things with his usual
meticulousness: Don Cipriano would ride Pispás and he Wrinkled, the
tough, auxiliary nag, while the mule Lonely would carry the baggage.
There was no hurry. Taking into account the slow pace of the mule, they
could cover ten leagues per day and reach Cilveti on or about the 29th
or 30th of April. Regarding their stopovers, Vicente calculated—unless
something unforeseen took place—that they could stay in the inns at
Villamanco, Zalduendo, Belorado, Logroño, and Pamplona. After all
this preparation, Cipriano left Valladolid at daybreak on the 25th. His
light baggage consisted of two saddlebags carried on the mule Alone as
packsaddles. His money, his papers, and the letters of introduction he
carried in various pockets. It was a sunny day, with a few fleecy, white
clouds and a mild temperature. Cipriano suddenly thought of Diego
Bernal. Whenever he travelled with money or something of value, he
remembered the old robber, but Vicente calmed his nerves. Bernal was
thinking about retirement, he said, for over half a year, we've heard
nothing about him.

They kept to their schedule precisely on the first two days. On
the third, they were surprised by a rainstorm and reached Belorado
with water running down their legs. The storm had settled over Castile,
so they waited a day before setting out again. On the afternoon of the
30th, after sending Echarren a note by courier, they entered Cilveti, a
mountain village with stone houses and few inhabitants. Cipriano
unloaded his baggage in the Pablo Echarren's entryway, and Vicente,
riding Wrinkled and with Pispás and Alone on leads, returned to
Urtasun without spending the night. There was no reason to be
noticed. For his part, Cipriano found a less irascible Pablo Echarren
than the one Don Carlos had described. He spoke little, not because
he was unpleasant, merely not to waste words: "You already know that
these are difficult times. Today, I couldn't bring you up for less than
fifty ducats."

When they left, the sun had yet to rise, and as it did, the dark line of the mountain chain, crowned with clouds, stood out against the horizon. Echarren's mule, covered with a blanket, opened the way for Cipriano's and for Luminous, the pack mule. They made their way through an oak forest whose floor was covered with winter leaves, not following any visible path. In the thickest part of the woods, two startled birds suddenly took wing: "Woodcocks," said Echarren succinctly.

"In Castile, we see woodcocks in November," Cipriano noted, remembering days in La Manga.

"They're still making their way back," the guide explained. "In any case, those nest around here."

They paused when the way became steep. A small thicket of beech trees, with new leaves, rose on their right hand, behind a bed of rushes, and on their left stood a great mass of fir trees. Echarren pulled bread, cheese, sausages, and a wineskin out of his saddlebag. He drank before eating, lifting his head, swallowing for a long time without spilling a drop: "We've got to keep the pipes clear," he said to justify himself.

At midday, a pair of fish hawks hovered overhead without beating their wings. As they climbed higher, the mules moved painfully and slowly. The grade grew even steeper as they entered a beech grove, a forest of black, mysterious trees. From time to time, Echarren would stop his mule and listen, telling Cipriano to remain silent. In the higher reaches, despite hours of direct sun, it was much cooler. They were scrambling up through fir trees, a sea of them, and on top of the mountain, they could see bare peaks, small, glittering, snowdrifts, and small cataracts, the result of melting. Once, Echarren stopped and silently but urgently ordered Cipriano to hide in a small clearing surrounded by tall trees. He put his index finger over his lips. They could hear words being spoken a short distance away. Echarren dismounted and peered through the foliage. He must have identified the travelers by their clothing or by their mounts, because he turned to Cipriano and whispered: "Smugglers."

Salcedo, still on his mule, stared in vain in the direction indicated by his guide. He heard the conversation come very close, but saw no one. Then whoever it was moved slowly away, and their voices became a faint whisper. When even that faded totally, Echarren got back on his mule and added: "It's Marcos Duro, the best guide in these parts."

"What are they carrying?"

"Possibly amber, beauty creams, perfumes, and aromatic unguents. Luxury items come from France."

The mountain grew steeper when they emerged from the wooded area, and the vegetation grew sparse: bushes, trailing vines, heather, furze, bilberry. Echarren tried to keep as close to the rocks as possible to make them less visible from below. Once, when they turned a corner, they saw a chamois leaping from rock to rock. They became entangled in the rugged terrain of high peaks difficult to negotiate, but deep down in a ravine, still far above the abyss, protected by a small hollow, appeared a man wearing a mantle and wide breeches, leading two tethered mounts. Echarren turned to Cipriano: "Pierre never made me wait," he said smiling.

He whistled softly. The echo repeated it again and again, more and more softly, from the ravines on the French side.

# BOOK III
## THE AUTO-DA-FÉ

# XV

A T Cipriano's suggestion, the Doctor had Beatriz Cazalla replace her sister Constanza in the readings at group meetings. It had been seven months since Cipriano had returned from Germany, and on this night, just at the outset of May, Beatriz read a few pages from *The Christian's Freedom*, with the same toothy smile, the same intonation, and the same discrete lisp that accompanied Doña Leonor's communications. It was as if she'd come back from the dead. During the pauses, Cipriano admired the beautiful profile of Ana Enríquez, so luminous and attractive under the red turban that made her head seem smaller. Her long, bejewelled hands rested on the back of the bench in front of her.

As soon as Beatriz finished, the Doctor glossed the pages she read. His fervor and conviction were identical to what they were when his mother accompanied him. Ever since Cipriano's return with books, reports, and good news, Don Agustín Cazalla seemed like another man. His position with regard to religion had been affirmed, and he'd recovered his proselytizing zeal. But just when the final, general discussion began, they heard the the pounding hooves of a galloping horse coming closer and closer, striking against the pavement. The silence in the hall was so intense that when the horse stopped, they could all hear the rider dismount and take three steps toward the door of the house. Two muted knocks at the door echoed, and when Juan Sánchez ran toward the stairs, the silence among those gathered turned to ice. A few seconds later, Don Carlos de Seso, wearing an improvised riding costume, his hair in a tangle, his cap in his hand, burst into the oratory, leapt onto the

Doctor's dais, and whispered nervously to him. Once the Doctor had given him his consent, Don Carlos spoke to the gathering with a touch of alarm in his voice: "Cristóbal de Padilla was arrested yesterday in Zamora. Pedro Sotelo and his wife Antonia de Melo denounced him to the Holy Office because of the annual edict. He's being held in the Inquisition's secret prison, but it doesn't seem likely there will be other arrests until Padilla is interrogated. Even so, I felt obliged to inform you so you could take the proper measures, get rid of compromising documents, and flee if you think your life is in danger. May Our Lord accompany us."

There was a stampede. Everyone wanted to be the first to abandon the Doctor's house, and Juan Sánchez had serious difficulties in making them depart in orderly fashion, two by two, with a minute between each couple, as they usually did. It seemed that getting far away from the mother house would also get them far away from the risk of arrest. Cipriano saw Ana Enríquez leave and went over to the Doctor and Don Carlos, who from the dais thought they should organize the evacuation. Don Agustín had become pale and was mechanically patting his white, fine hands on the table. He'd lost control of himself. These sudden changes in spirit, justified or not, were habitual in the Doctor. He tried to speak with Cipriano, but the words piled up on his lips, and he couldn't manage to put them in order. It was Don Carlos who gave him the proper instructions: "You should flee immediately. The Emperor, from the monastery at Yuste, had ordered the inquisitor Valdés to carry out a *sudden and terrible punishment*. Run away. You've been an outstanding member of the sect since you entered it, and your recent trip to Germany and your interview with Melanchthon will make you especially vulnerable now. Go far away. You already know the road to Pamplona. You also know Cilveti and the house of Pablo Echarren. Put yourself in his hands, and in a few days you'll be out of Spain."

Tears came to the Doctor's eyes as he clasped Cipriano's hand. Cipriano, by contrast, felt resolute and decided, capable of taking any action. He wasn't tired, and when he was back in his house, he locked himself in his office and opened the large book case. It seemed impossible that in barely three years he'd been able to accumulate such a quantity of papers: note cards, warnings, summaries, advice, small memoranda, group meeting announcements, miscellaneous correspondence with the Doctor, Pedro Cazalla, Carlos de Seso, Domingo de Rojas, Beatriz Cazalla, and Ana Enríquez. Portfolios filled with projects. Fascicles and booklets related to his travels through France and Germany. Maps and itineraries. Addresses of people and centers abroad and books, many books, among them the seventeen copies of *Christ's Beneficence*, all that was left of the edition printed by Agustín Becerril. He piled up wood in the fireplace and set it on fire. First, he threw in the papers, which burned up rapidly after floating around for a few seconds in the flames. Then the booklets, the papers of greater importance, and finally the portfolios and books, one by one, patiently, unhurriedly. Some books had hard bindings, cloth or skin, with corner pieces to make them more durable, so they took longer to be consumed utterly.

As the piles of papers and rows of books on the shelves disappeared, Cipriano felt freed of a weight, as after confession. At four in the morning he went to bed. Not only had he burned everything that could compromise him and the group, but he'd also removed the ashes from the hearth. At eight, he got up, ate a light breakfast, and ordered Vicente to saddle Pispás as quickly as possible. One hour later, dressed in country clothes and with a minimum of baggage, he was ready to leave, when Constanza announced the visit of Ana Enríquez. Cipriano told himself that this was the last thing he needed at the moment.

Ana had just come from her family's country house and asked his forgiveness with regard to the defection of her servant and her own refusal to practice the prudence recommended to her so insistently. Another servant, just arrived from Toro, did not believe that the mass arrest was imminent. According to the inquisitors, Cristóbal de Padilla, through his meetings and the contacts and visits he'd had in prison, had frightened off "the game." "You'll have to hurry," Doña Ana said, taking him by the hands and sitting down at his side on the sofa in the drawing room.

Cipriano was moved by the girl's solicitude and her eagerness to save him. Her father, the marquis, implored him to go to France. He himself did not feel compromised, and the position of the marquess in the Court would work in his favor. But Cipriano should flee, Doña Ana insisted. She gave him a note with an address in Montpelier: Madame Barbouse will take care of you as if you were I myself, she said. She again pressed his hairy little hand between her own impatient hands. Barbouse, don't forget.

But Cipriano was held in place by a concern: What about her? What was to become of her in such difficult circumstances? Ana Enríquez smiled with her full lips, and two dimples formed in her cheeks. "In situations like this, we women can defend ourselves better than you men. A man will always take pity on a woman. Even moreso with Tribunals made up of men, because men reinforce one another. How could the Holy Office hand down a harsh sentence against the nuns in the convent of Belén?" They looked into each other's eyes; they fell silent, and their faces almost touched. "You are in danger," she added. "You recently took on all the responsibilities of the group, you've visited Germany in its name: How could that be justified? King Philip II won't be less inflexible than his father Charles V. Valdés has requested wider powers from the Pope, and Paul IV has not hesitated to grant them. A great punishment is being prepared, believe me."

Cipriano realized that he was letting himself be convinced of something he already believed. But he was gratified by Ana's insistence, by seeing her concerned for his sake, by her eagerness to see him safely away. Is it that he meant something for her? But when she stood up, she took him by the hands and pulled him up, forcing him to stand. Cipriano told her he was ready to leave. When she heard him, Ana suddenly, doing nothing to announce it, leaned over and kissed him softly on the cheek. "Flee," she said in the softest voice. "Don't waste a minute more, and may Our Lord accompany you."

On his way to Burgos, Cipriano thought about her as he spurred Pispás. He would travel as long as he could at a full gallop. When it became necessary to change horses, he would simply sneak into the corral at a post house, take someone else's, and leave some money if he thought he'd gotten the better of the exchange. He planned to rest by day and ride at night. No one would know if Padilla had told all or remained silent, but it seemed obvious that the Inquisition could mount highway patrols at any time. He brought his hand up to his left cheek. The sweet touch of Ana Enríquez's lips was still there, along with its discreet perfume. Was it possible that such a beautiful girl could have taken an interest in him?

He recalled his vows of a few months earlier, his decision to divide his worldly possessions and to live in chastity. He'd confided his plan to the Doctor one afternoon after his return from Germany when they were alone in Doña Leonor's study. "Don't be too hasty. You're still feeling the effect of the death of your wife. You still feel responsible." Cipriano asked him if that feeling of guilt would disappear one day, and the Doctor had no doubt that it would, and that then he'd find himself in the hard dilemma of either being faithful to his vow or loving a woman.

Salcedo pointed out that his decision had been spontaneous and carefully pondered, that he'd reached it before the death of his wife, that more than half his property no longer belonged to him, and that Our Lord had smiled in accepting it. He quickly added that he knew that works were not indispensable for salvation and made it clear that by doing what he did he was not seeking salvation but a way of compensating Teo for his indifference.

The Doctor listened with his head to one side, as if his neck were incapable of bearing so much weight. They spoke a while, and Cipriano naively confessed that Our Lord had appeared at his side, pleased at his generosity. The Doctor smiled. That chimera, he warned, was an indication of Cipriano's disturbed mental state. The time of portents was long past. Cipriano again enjoyed the words of the Doctor, a lucid, intelligent man who'd managed to overcome the death of his mother. It was true that on his return from Germany Cipriano found him different. This was a Doctor he'd never known, conscious of his intellectual primacy, of the importance of his rank in the group. That rather feminine debility he'd evinced a few months before now seemed never to have existed. Cipriano had raised his spirits. He didn't lie about the details of his journey, but he did exaggerate a few episodes, embellishing them. Melanchthon knew about him—Cipriano said. Several Spanish emigrees had talked about him and about the Lutheran center he led in Valladolid. Cipriano's report excited the Doctor and filled him with confidence.

Cipriano took no heed of how fatuous his attitude was. In reality, the change in the Doctor had occurred even before Cipriano had left the country. It was as if a strange pressure had kept him from breathing, and that suddenly, when Cipriano decided to go, someone had relieved him of his burden. During the months Cipriano was away, the Doctor never stopped thinking about him, and the two long letters Cipriano sent from Germany exhilarated him to an incredible degree, as he told Cipriano on his return. Because of those messages, the Doctor was able to set aside the anguish he'd suffered after his mother's funeral. He grew, he returned to his former activity within the sect, to his ambiguous sermons, to the meetings.

Cipriano was thrilled to listen to him. Once again he was on the good path. The Doctor expressed interest in Cipriano's life. He was disconcerted by his giving away so much of his fortune, by his openhandedness. They'd spoken a great deal during the past months, so much that Cipriano began to discover in Cazalla a new man, sober and holy to be sure, but with a touch of presumption in his motives. The Doctor boasted of what he was and what he represented. If his acts were secret, perhaps his behavior would have been different. And it wasn't that Cipriano was attributing duplicity to the Doctor. He did not think the Doctor did things in search of applause, but he was hardly indifferent to praise and admiration.

He took a detour at Quintana del Puente. In the distance, to the left, on the hillside, began the forests, and on the low ground, a sea of wheat, not fully mature, undulated softly in the breeze. In some spots, the barley was turning light, and at the foot of the uplands, before the woods began, he spied a small summer pasturage, cool, of a tender green. The clear water flowed abundantly from the spring and flowed over the meadow. He rode Pispás to the water and let him drink his fill. The water washed away the foam on his dewlaps as his back slowly stopped trembling. When he saw the horse was satisfied, he turned him into the woods. The young rabbits just born that spring ran every which way in terror and disappeared into their warrens. Halfway up the hill, Cipriano dismounted, removed Pispás's saddle, and left him to graze in the clearing.

His servant Vicente trained horses well. Both Lightning and now Pispás were more like dogs than horses. They never lost sight of their master even if they wandered off, and they came as soon as he whistled. That gave the animal great freedom of movement without worrying the master. Out of his saddlebag, Cipriano pulled a huge loaf of bread stuffed with meat and sausages and a wineskin. From where he stood, he could see all of the great plain stretched out between mountains, from where the grain was waving in the breeze to the gray hills in front of him, with the waters of the Arlanzón river flowing toward Quintana and the road following the river. All was still. He found shelter in the dappled sunshine under an oak, stretched out, and in a few minutes fell fast asleep.

When he awakened the sun had already set, and the first thing he saw was Pispás' head. The alarmed horse was two steps away, staring at him. He gave a happy whinny when he saw Cipriano stand up, and docilely allowed himself to be saddled. At twilight, Cipriano rode down to the Burgos road, spurred Pispás and continued his journey. Without his realizing it, the darkness began to envelope him, though the vague phosphorescence of the highway still hadn't disappeared completely. This helped his eyes to get used to the dark, and he could continue galloping safely. A few mule drivers moved to the side of the road when they heard Pispás's galloping, but for the most part the road was empty.

Like a will-o'-the-wisp, Cipriano passed through the city of Burgos and took the Logroño road, a bit narrower, composed of pink earth. His mind was concentrated on the road, thinking about the possible obstacles that could come up, and only from time to time did he think about Cristóbal de Padilla, about whether he might have been interrogated, about whether he might already have denounced everyone. With every passing moment, he felt safer, further away from the forces of the Inquisition, which would be set into motion as soon as the prisoner confessed.

Before reaching Santo Domingo de la Calzada, Cipriano decided to change horses. The foam from Pispás's dewlaps was shinning in the darkness, and from time to time he was taken by a nervous tremor in his flanks. The horse was exhausted. Cipriano had thought he would cover twenty-four leagues on him, and he'd actually ridden more than twenty-seven. He entered Santo Domingo at a slow trot. At the side of the road, he saw the relay station and stopped there. A tiny light glowed in the second window, and he feared someone might still be awake at that hour. He dismounted and walked around to the other side of the building, passing through the muddy entryway. The stable was in the rear, and two horses were spending the night in the first corral.

He moved along with his back to the wall, to avoid being seen if someone happened to took out. Feeling his way blindly, he chose a horse and brought him out to the patio, where he looked him over more carefully. He was a big-headed old hack, but he looked strong and well-rested. He saddled up the nag and locked Pispás in the stable with a little bag around his neck containing two ducats and a note that said: "I'm not paying you for the horse but for the favor."

Just then, he thought he heard noise at one of the windows facing the street, so he hugged the wall. It was his fear, nothing more: the house was asleep. He gave the horse a few affectionate pats on the neck and mounted. In the dim light, he seemed to be a pinto, with a white head and long mane. Not very obedient to the spurs, he set off toward Logroño at a regular gallop. Cipriano covered eight leagues before daybreak, but not at a full gallop as he had on Pispás, but at the regular pace Weary (as Cipriano called him) set for himself, since he was indifferent to his rider's wishes.

Now with the sun in the sky, surrounded by vineyards covered with tender leaves, Cipriano took a path to the right until he came to the floodplain of the Iregua river. There he dismounted, hobbled his horse, ate, and stretched out in the warm morning sun. He woke up at mid-afternoon, ate some more, and took a long look at Weary, relaxing a short distance away, nibbling the grass within reach. Now he realized what a sorry mount he'd chosen. He'd only seen an uglier horse than this one once before: Teo's Obstinate, the shameful companion from the post-wedding party.

He waited until sunset to set out on the road again. Weary resumed the uniform trot of the previous night and maintained it all night long. That was his way of galloping, and Cipriano had to accept it. At the El Aldea relay house, between Logroño and Pamplona, he exchanged Weary for another horse. This time, Cipriano left five ducats in the little sack and asked forgiveness for the exchange. The new horse was stylish and spirited and showed his arrogance especially in his gallop. He was in no way comparable to Pispás, but he was vastly superior to Weary. This time he'd come out ahead on the exchange. He rode all night, and at dawn hid in an oak thicket a few leagues from Pamplona. The end of his journey was within sight, and he thought that the next day he'd have to wait for nightfall to enter Cilveti and speak to Echarren.

When the thought of his comrades in Valladolid assaulted him, Cipriano came to the irrevocable conclusion that Padilla had told all. Having had several experiences of this kind, Cipriano believed that thoughts could be transmitted. The roundup has begun, he told himself. He tried to imagine which members of the group might have tried to escape and instantly thought of Don Carlos de Seso as the most likely. Don Carlos might already be in France, but who else? With regard to the priest Alonso Pérez, he assumed he wouldn't escape; neither would the Cazallas: Don Agustín was too committed, and he considered Pedro would be incapable of embarking on such an adventure. Who then? He knew nothing of the arrests of Rojas, Brother Domingo, and his nephew Luis, and discarded the jeweler Juan García, much too cowardly. Pedro Sarmiento perhaps? Herrezuelo?

Once again, the figure of Ana Enríquez came to his mind. She could have fled with him. Perhaps at this very moment the bailiff of the Inquisition was arresting her at her country home La Confluencia. Ana was not the kind of woman who could go calmly into the secret prison on Pedro Barrueco street, that run-down, lugubrious mansion the mere sight of which inspired terror. In any case, the secret prison could not hold all sixty of the presumed heretics in Valladolid. The law required those accused to be held in isolation, but the jail on Pedro Barrueco did not have sixty individual cells. What decision would the Holy Office make?

Quite a while ago, construction had begun on a new House of the Inquisition opposite the church of San Pedro, but no matter how they accelerated the construction, it wouldn't be done for another year. Possibly they would be locked up in pairs or in groups that had little to do with one another. No matter how great their power was, the inquisitorial authorities would not be able to cut off all communication among the prisoners. The memory of Ana Enríquez caused him to caress his left cheek. After three days of travel his beard had grown, but he still thought he could detect the trace of her lips. What had she meant by kissing him on the face that way? That she'd wait for him? That she wanted to show her joy at his decision to escape? Had it simply been proof that they'd both belonged to the group?

He looked back through the leaves and saw the horse jumping about with his hobbled legs. He did not fall asleep as he had on previous days, but he shut his eyes and attempted to reconcile himself with Our Lord. He thought about Ana Enríquez a great deal; in his heart he admired her beauty and courage, but his decision to remain chaste was above all these weaknesses. He was alone; the silence, except for the distant cawing of crows, was absolute: Why didn't Our Lord come down to his side? Was the light, perhaps, too strong? Did He reserve his appearances for churches? Could the Doctor have been correct when he asserted that the chimera was an indication of his weakened mental state? Had he suffered a hallucination?

The sun was setting when he awoke. The horse, hopping along, was quite far off. He found him at the edge of a grove of trees, drinking water in the stream at a mill. He saddled him up and looked for the main road. Night had by then fallen. He was not in a hurry, so the next day he stopped at Larrasoaña, his last meal and his final siesta. He carefully waited until night fell before entering Cilveti. The town looked deserted, but the door to Echarren's house was open. The back door as well. Cipriano was struck by the number of mules in the corral, but he suspected nothing. He felt he was far from any traps. How could the bailiffs of the Inquisition suspect that one of the men they were looking for would at that moment be in Cilveti? He tied up the horse outside the door and felt his way in. Echarren's wife, with a candle in her hand, accompanied him to the living room, which he already knew. He heard the sound of conversation, of whispering in the next room. Suddenly, a man wearing the insignia of the Order of Saint Dominic, along with two harquebusiers who aimed their weapons at Cipriano burst into the room. Cipriano stood up and retreated in surprise: "In the name of the Inquisition, I order you to give yourself up." said the bailiff.

He put up no resistance. He obeyed the order to be seated before the officer with the two harquebusiers behind him. Then Pablo Echarren, his hair tousled, wearing his doublet, entered accompanied by the secretary, who put some blank sheets of paper down on the table and sat next to the bailiff. The officer looked over at Echarren, who was standing at his side: "Is this the man?"

"That's the man, yes sir."

From the other side of the table, the bailiff studied Cipriano's small, well-proportioned head and his hairy little hands: "You remembered him very well," he said to himself, smiling slightly.

His long, dirty hair hung down and his eyes squinted a bit as he fixed them on Cipriano. He subjected Cipriano to a detailed interrogation. Cipriano came from Valladolid, Wasn't that the case? Cipriano said it was. Some months back, in April of 1557, he'd passed over into France across the Pyrenees accompanied by Pablo Echarren: Was that the case? The bailiff squinted with satisfaction when Cipriano admitted that was true, but he lost his composure when Cipriano added that he'd travelled abroad several times because of the demands of his business. Business? What business? The bailiff did not know Cipriano's profession, and the secretary took note of it. He asked if Cipriano wouldn't mind telling him what his profession was, and Cipriano, annoyed, was obliged to mention the coat and the fur-lined clothing. The bailiff had heard of the coat, of course, everyone knew about the great coat revolution, the Cipriano coat, Isn't that it?

"I'm Cipriano," said Salcedo.

The bailiff listened with interest to his prisoner's revelation. The amount of money Cipriano might presumably possess softened the interrogation. The secretary noted all his statements. Cipriano had commercial relations with Flanders and the Low Countries. The merchants of Antwerp distributed the coats and other items in the north and in the center of Europe. Now it was the squinting bailiff who nodded in satisfaction and pleasure. But his most important contact had been with the famous Bonerfoesen, the most renowned merchant of the age. The bailiff adopted a different tone. He'd left Valladolid three-and-a-half days before. Was he aware of the arrest of Cristóbal de Padilla? And that of the entire Lutheran group in Valladolid? Cipriano knew nothing of it. That must have taken place after his departure. The secretary wrote and wrote. Suddenly, Cipriano stopped speaking freely and began to be evasive. "Do you know Doctor Cazalla?" "I'd rather not answer that question." The bailiff went on questioning him for a few more minutes. He pointed to Pablo Echarren: "Do you know this man?" Naturally Cipriano knew him, knew as well of his ability, of his sense of direction. "Who recommended him to you?" Salcedo glanced at Echarren and saw he was manacled. For a business man who travelled to Europe frequently, Mr. Echarren needed no introduction. When they finished, they manacled Cipriano as well. Then they heard the noise of people in the patio, and when they walked outside, Cipriano, Echarren, and the two harquebusiers entered a coach pulled by two horses. Behind, escorting them, came the bailiff and the secretary mounted on mules as well as two servants of the Inquisition.

It was very late when they reached Pamplona, and Vidal, the bailiff, handed his prisoners over to the warden of the holy jail. It was almost empty. They were led into two cells, and once he'd stretched out on his pallet, Cipriano tried to calm his nerves. He'd been arrested. It had all been too swift and unforeseen. His cell was small, barely room for the sleeping mat, a table, a chair, and a gigantic urinal with a lid over it in one corner. He could hear footsteps on the floor above, martial footsteps, firm, like those of soldiers. Two days and two nights passed. On the third day, at nightfall, he could hear the noise of running feet above. From the guard who brought him food and from Genaro, who emptied the urinals every day, Cipriano learned that there were two other prisoners: Don Carlos de Seso and Brother Domingo de Rojas.

According to the guard, the two of them were caught on the border at Navarra, and Seso had said that he wasn't fleeing at all, that he had no intention of escaping, but that he was going to Italy, to Verona, where his mother and brother had just died. For his part, Brother Domingo de Rojas admitted that he was on his way to meet Archbishop Carranza, that he felt uncomfortable in Castile, and that, above all, he wanted to avoid the dishonor his possible arrest would bring down on his Order. They'd been held prisoner for three days in the house of the Inquisition's commissioner until the Bishop of Pamplona, Don Alvaro de Moscoso ordered their removal to the secret jail. Don Alvaro was shocked by the monk's clothing, a green velvet suit, a plumed hat, and a gold chain around his neck. This is rather a different habit from the one you wore to the Council, the Bishop ironically observed. To which Brother Domingo de Rojas responded: "Your reverence, I wear my habit in my heart." Then Rojas alluded to the attitude of Carranza, Archbishop of Toledo, whom he was seeking, but Don Alvaro de Moscoso simply told him to forget that name, that the archbishop had nothing to do with this matter. Brother Domingo pointed out that the Viceroy of Navarra had given them safe-conduct passes to enable them to travel to Bearne, that they were carrying letters of recommendation to the Princess, and that the acts of the Holy Office were completely unjustified. With them was a thick-set man they referred to as Herrera, the Mayor of Sacas de Logroño, who was also a prisoner. Herrera had helped them emigrate to France. He admitted the accusation, but stated that he had no idea the Inquisition had charges levelled against the two prisoners.

Don Carlos de Seso maintained his elegance and dignity. Through the peephole in his door, Cipriano saw him pass toward the cells with his habitual gallantry, his clothing loose, his gestures vigorous, his expression arrogant and proud. Once he was locked in his cell, Salcedo could hear him pace, four steps in one direction and four in the other. Normally the jailer did not visit them, and both the warden and Genaro, the janitor, would appear during the afternoon and at fixed times. Except for them, practically no one walked those corridors. On the second day after Seso and Rojas were brought in, and taking advantage of the echo in the basement, Cipriano called through the peephole to Don Carlos. Seso heard him immediately and was surprised to find him so close by. Yes, the viceroy had told him that there had been a mass arrest, that there were so many prisoners, they couldn't all fit in the secret jail, that the trials had begun, and that the Doctor was at the center of all of them.

Cipriano told him about his attempted escape, how he rode at night and rested by day until being arrested in Cilveti at the house of the man Seso had recommended, Pablo Echarren, who'd also been taken prisoner. Don Carlos informed him they wouldn't be sent back to Valladolid until he stopped in to see Juan Sánchez, the servant of the Cazallas, the only one of those who fled who actually managed to take refuge in France.

Juan Sánchez was lodged in the secret jail in Pamplona four days later, and the next, Friday, all the prisoners were put on the road to Valladolid. Off they went: squinting Vidal and the other three bailiffs sent out to arrest them on horseback; behind them came the prisoners, on foot, their hands manacled, Brother Domingo de Rojas with his plumed hat on his head. Flanking them were the servants of the Inquisition, and guarding the rear, twelve harquebusiers curiously uniformed, with short smocks, stocking-breeches, visored hats, and ornate shoes. It was a heterogeneous, outlandish party of slightly more than two dozen people, greeted in the towns and villages they passed through with insults and threats.

Vidal, the bailiff who'd arrested Cipriano in Cilveti, seemed to be in command of the detachment. The plan was to cover five or six leagues each day, eat on the road, and sleep in houses or haylofts previously reserved by emissaries of the Inquisition. At first, Cipriano happily welcomed the sunlight, being outdoors, and the chance to move around, but not being used to such exercise, he was exhausted when they reached Puente la Reina on the first night. The next day, at seven in the morning, after eating a tiny piece of cheese, they were back on the road.

Initially, Vidal arranged them in two pairs: Cipriano and Juan Sánchez, the shortest two, out in front, and the Dominican and Don Carlos de Seso behind them. The rule of silence, respected during the first hour of the march, was relaxed later, when the harquebusiers began telling their tales and jokes. Juan Sánchez took advantage of the moment to inform Cipriano of the details of his life and of his adventures since he left Valladolid and was captured at Turlinger. The sun was beating down on them, and at midday the emissaries would be waiting for them in some shady area near the highway, generally on the floodplain of the rivers they followed. The soldiers in the escort would bathe naked, taking turns at guarding the prisoners, who would dangle their feet in the current, to the great relief of the dominican. Then they would eat, the captives, their hands manacled, in a group set apart, but under the eye of the guards. Once lunch was over, they had a siesta while the fiery sun roasted the fields. Then the prisoners could exchange impressions or read compromising papers.

At two, when the heat of the day was most intense, they would start out again in the same order: the four bailiffs on horseback leading the way, the prisoners flanked by servants of the Inquisition, and bringing up the rear, the twelve harquebusiers. As they passed through town, the women and boys would insult them, sometimes emptying buckets of water on them from second-story windows. One day, now in La Rioja, the peasants working in the vineyards burned two dummies made of vine roots at the side of the road, calling the prisoners heretics and plague-ridden swine. The countryside there wrinkled into low, pink-toned hills, and the soft green from the vines gave an attractive plasticity to the landscape. At around seven, they concluded their daily quota, ate dinner in the town chosen by the emissaries, and spent the night in houses chosen by the Inquisition or in haylofts outside the town, forgetting at least for a few hours the scorching sun and the burning of their sore feet.

Having to walk alongside Juan Sánchez gave Cipriano the chance to get to know, at least superficially, the Cazallas's servant. He talked about Astudillo, the town in the province of Palencia where he was born, about Don Andrés Ibáñez, the priest whose altar boy he'd been, about his work as a shepherd and harvester. As a boy, he'd been a servant to the Greek knight commander Hernán Nuñez, who'd taught him to read and write, and how two years later he'd felt the call of God. He wanted to become a monk, but Brother Juan de Villagarcía, his confessor, convinced him otherwise. Then he went to Valladolid, where he served the Cazallas and other masters and assimilated lutheran doctrine.

On other days, Juan Sánchez told Cipriano about his galloping escape to Castro Urdiales the instant he learned Padilla had been arrested. He stole horses at relay houses without worrying about paying the innkeepers. At the coast, he made contact with a Dutchman, owner of a schooner, who took him to Flanders for ten ducats. By the time the hounds of the Inquisition reached the port, Juan Sánchez had already been on the high seas for thirty-eight hours. On board, he wrote to a person very dear to him, Doña Catalina de Ortega, also a Lutheran, a woman for whom he'd worked, telling her about his adventure, and to Beatriz Cazalla, the woman he'd always loved, and to whom he sent an account of the furious storm that almost capsized the schooner, but which he withstood by commending himself to Our Lord, "because he was prepared to live and die as a Christian." When he finished, he confessed the love he'd concealed for six years.

Brother Domingo de Rojas, who'd heard bits and pieces of Sánchez's story, suddenly asked him during the siesta how he'd let himself be caught while abroad, that such a thing would never happen to him, nor to anyone with an ounce of common sense.

"The Mayor of Turlinger ordered my arrest and turned me over to Captain Pedro Menéndez, who was hunting me down," answered Juan humbly.

From there the Dominican launched into a screaming attack on the servant, telling him his senseless preaching had brought down the entire group. He blamed him for having tricked the nuns of Santa Catalina and his sister María. In the face of such a monstrous accusation, Juan Sánchez lost his self-control and began to rant and shout in such a loud voice that two officers of the Inquisition had to come and restore order. When they set out again, Juan confided to Cipriano that the priest, who had aristocratic pretensions and never trusted the missionary ability of the common folk, hated him.

Usually, however, they walked along in silence. Sánchez and Salcedo could hear, behind them, the dragging feet of Brother Domingo and the firm strides of Don Carlos de Seso, who rarely if ever exchanged a word. The Dominican was convinced that only by saving the very last drop of saliva could he ever reach Valladolid alive. He had a strong complexion, but he was soft, and complained about his bunions. Whenever the procession stopped, he would immodestly massage his feet. But setting aside his physical problems, his great concern, as was the case with his companions, was the future. What awaited them? A trial of course, and after that, a punishment. But what kind of punishment?

Don Carlos de Seso had seen the letter from the Inquisitor Valdés to Charles V in his retirement at Yuste where he asked that *this great evil be nipped in the bud and that the guilty be tried and punished with the greatest rigor with no exceptions of any kind.* Seso interpreted that to mean that they were preparing an exemplary lesson without precedents in Spain. The governor of Toro had a great ability to make friends and spoke to one and all without paying attention to rank, both with officers and common soldiers, and, if they joined in, with the servants of the Inquisition. He was up to date on everything. He knew everything. He was afraid both of Philip II and his father Carlos V, and he was convinced that before 1558 the punishments would have been lighter, but that today Paul IV would not hold back, as he said. In their afternoon rest periods, he informed them of these matters, about the letter from the Inquisitor Valdés to the Emperor, about the Emperor's letters to his daughter, who governed in the absence of her brother, and to Philip II, asking *speed, rigor, and hard punishment*. Many of us will not come out of this alive, he said, and he actually formulated a plan to escape, though he never had the chance to put it into practice.

In general, it was the unexpected things, the everyday incidents that gave credence to Seso's concerns and his brief after dinner talks. On day, while they were still in Navarra, a well-organized town attacked the prisoners with stones. They were men and boys armed with slings who charged out of the alleys and stoned them mercilessly. The four officers chased them on horseback, but as soon as they disappeared, another group would materialize at the next corner with new energy and larger stones. A soldier was wounded in the forehead and was knocked unconscious. His comrades fired their harqebuses, shooting at their legs, as the squinting Vidal shouted from his horse. The hostilities intensified.

From balconies, women threw jugs of boiling water and called the prisoners bastards, heretical sons of bitches. Cipriano, in an instinctive reaction, dragged Juan Sánchez against a stone wall, and they watched curtains of steaming water fall in front of them. Then the townspeople began to shout: "Burn them here! Burn them here!" And they surrounded them in the town square, forcing the soldiers once again to fire their harqebuses. A boy fell, wounded in the thigh, and when they saw the blood, the people became even more violent and attacked the detachment with greater fury. A second casualty convinced them a few seconds later that their efforts were useless, and when the officers charged them again, they dispersed.

Another time, near Saldaña de Burgos, some boys set fire to the hayloft where they were all sleeping. A soldier sounded the alarm and thanks to him they escaped unharmed. But from then on, all along the road, straw dummies were burned, and in the light of flaming bales of hay, they could see scarecrows hanging in the elms. The incensed people demanded the auto-da-fé, called them Lutherans, lepers, sons of Satan, and some, in a burst of patriotism, screamed "Long Live the King!" They had to leave town at three in the morning, and sunrise found them out in the country. In Revilla Vallejera, gangs of day laborers, with their

mules and clay pitchers, were already scything the hay that was turning
white amid fields of toasted-yellow wheat. It was a bucolic scene that
contrasted with the noise and fury of the peasants themselves.

Vidal ordered the midday stop to take place at eleven, and the
detachment made camp under some trees on the banks of the Arlanzón.
In a humanitarian gesture, Vidal allowed the prisoners to bathe "without going too far from the bank, because with their hands tied they
could drown." Brother Domingo did not bathe. He sat on the river bank
and let the current caress his sore feet, which were so white that the
sunfish came in small schools to nibble his toes, thinking they were edi-
ble. For Cipriano, the swim, the fact he could feel the warm water on
his skin, was like taking off his old, tired body, as if his fatigue, his fleas,
the heat and the anxiety he felt on the road had never existed. After five
weeks without washing, it was like a resurrection. He swam on his back,
kicking with his feet like a frog, going back and forth, only worried
about the guards, about going too far and provoking them into taking
action against him.

Beginning at Burgos and the closer they got to Valladolid, the hostility toward them grew. Huge bonfires, anticipating the fate of the prisoners, smoked in the fields that had been cleared, the sheaves and stubble being used for fuel. The animosity of the peasants was pitiless: they
insulted the prisoners, throwing vegetables and eggs at them. Cipriano,
however, accepted the situation as soon as they left a town behind, and
let his eyes rejoice at the extensive fields of grain undulating in the
breeze. He recognized the road he'd galloped over on Pispás, the small
identifying traits in the landscape, the juicy summer pasturage where
he'd let the horse drink. It was familiar terrain he was walking, and
when a furious thunderstorm accompanied by hail exploded over them,
he tied the horses and told everyone to lie down in the mud to avoid
being struck by lightning.

They spent the last night on the road in a large house in Cohorcos,
far from the village, on the banks of the Pisuerga four leagues from
Valladolid. That afternoon, a messenger from the Inquisition arrived
and ordered them not to enter the city until after midnight. The mob
was aroused, and they feared the prisoners would be lynched. They
delayed their departure, and at about five in the afternoon camped in

El Cabildo, half a league outside the city, alongside the river. They would have to wait another eight hours. Brother Domingo de Rojas muttered that no matter what they would be killed anyway. He was afraid of his family, of the most exalted members of it. Not only did they reproach him for being an apostate, but also for having perverted his nephew Luis, Marquis of Poza, who from a very early age had been a member of their sect.

At midnight, after ordering the prisoners to wash and clean themselves, Vidal began the departure. The bailiffs had decked out their horses, and the harquebusiers attempted to put what was left of their uniforms in order. When they crossed the Puente Mayor, the only thing anyone could hear was the pounding of the horses's hooves on the pavement. There was a half moon, and the streets were empty. In the violet moonlight, the tower of Santa María de la Antigua looked like a ghost. Behind it loomed the eternally unfinished Greater church. The horses turned into Pedro Barrueco street, where the secret jail was located. The idea of a return, the nearness of members of the group, of Doña Ana Enríquez, dispelled Cipriano's fatigue. For a moment, he thought about his failed escape, about the fact that his situation now was the same or worse than that of those who'd stayed behind, about the uselessness of so many penalties he'd already suffered. Vidal halted the detachment outside the old mansion. A soldier answered his knock at the door, and Vidal asked for the warden. When the warden appeared wearing his long cape, his eyes heavy with sleep, Vidal, in the name of the Holy Office, turned over the four prisoners: Brother Domingo de Rojas, Don Carlos de Seso, Don Cipriano Salcedo, and Juan Sánchez, names the warden wrote down by candle light in a notebook which he then signed.

# XVI

C IPRIANO shared his cell with Brother Domingo de Rojas. He would have preferred a less austere, more open companion, but he had no choice in the matter. Brother Domingo was still wearing his grotesque lay costume, the only part of which he'd given up was the extravagant plumed hat. Slowly, Cipriano learned about the location of the other prisoners. Don Carlos de Seso was with Juan Sánchez; opposite them was the Doctor's cell. Further down the corridor, five of the nuns from the Belén convent shared a large cell, and Ana Enríquez was in a cell with the sixth, Catalina de Reinoso. Just as Salcedo had foreseen, the pairings were inevitable. The secret jail on Pedro Barrueco street, large enough for the occasional roundup of secret Jews or followers of Islam, was short on space for the number of Lutherans in the spring of 1558. The high number of arrests had surprised the Holy Office, which had a lockup with only twenty-five available cells. Valdés had no choice but to forget about solitary confinement and lock up his prisoners in pairs, or by threes, or even, in the case of the nuns, by five in a cell. Nevertheless, Valdés, always a smart man, demanded that the pairings take into account the divergent social and intellectual rank of those arrested, as well as their degree of familiarity beforehand. This was the case, for example, of Don Carlos de Seso and Juan Sánchez and Salcedo with Brother Domingo de Rojas.

With his ability to adapt heightened, Cipriano quickly adjusted to the conditions of his new imprisonment. The cell, twice the size of the one he'd had in Pamplona, possessed only two openings in its stone walls: a barred window about nine feet from the floor that opened onto an interior courtyard, and the one in the door, itself a solid slab of oak as thick as a man's palm was wide. The bolts screeched sharply whenever they were opened or closed. The beds were parallel to each other at opposite sides of the cell, the Dominican's under the window, and in the opposite corner, in the halflight, that of Cipriano. Along with the cots, on a floor of cold stone tiles there was just a small pine table and two benches, a washbasin and a pitcher of water and two covered receptacles for hygienic purposes. Cipriano was able to calculate the time of day by the routine of their obligatory visitors—the jailer's assistant Mamerto, who came at regular times to bring their meals, and the other assistant, named Dato, a man with a filthy mane of albino hair who wore knee-length breeches. He emptied the receptacles of filth every afternoon and sluiced out the cell on Saturday afternoons.

Mamerto was a surly, imperturbable boy who three times a day deposited two iron trays containing their meager rations on the table, trays he removed at his next visit. Given the season of the year, he only wore a doublet, buttoned breeches of light cloth, and rope sandals. He never said good morning or good night, but it couldn't be said he treated them harshly. He simply either delivered or took away the trays with no commentary about the good or poor appetite of the prisoners. Dato, on the other hand, did not adhere to the prison rules with the same rigidity. Whenever he removed or returned their receptacles, he hummed a frivolous tune as if instead of excrement he was delivering a bouquet of flowers. His mouth opened in a moronic, toothless, unchanging grin that never disappeared from his face, not even on Saturdays during his wash-down of the cell. Though the rules prohibited conversing with the prisoners, Dato would greet Salcedo, who was more accessible than his cellmate, and tell him the news or make vague reports that were not especially useful to the prisoner. Less standoffish than Mamerto, he wore a long mantle of loose-knit cord which he only removed on Saturdays to wash out the cell. All he had on then was a doublet and breeches; he was barefoot, but the fact that he'd removed his overcoat did not make him work any more quickly.

Brother Domingo could not stand Dato's familiarity, while Mamerto's laconic coming and going was more to his liking. Dato's nosiness, his idiotic, toothless grin, his locks of albino hair falling over his shoulders

drove him mad. Cipriano, on the other hand, was patient and affectionate with Dato and coaxed information out of him. He asked him about
the prisoners in the neighboring cells, and despite the ambiguous terms
Dato used, he came to the conclusion that to his left were Pedro Cazalla
and Herrezuelo, to his right Juan García, the jeweler, and Cristóbal de
Padilla, the cause of all their trouble, and opposite, as he'd been told, in
solitary confinement, the Doctor. The walls and doors of the prison
were so thick that not the slightest sign of life from the cells around him
filtered through.

Corpulent, with a double chin, wrapped in his green costume, and
a sordid doctoral robe, the Dominican read stretched out on his cot
under the barred window. The day after they arrived he asked for
books, a pen, and paper. That same day, during the afternoon, he was
brought several saint's lives, Gaspar de Tejada's *Treatise on Letters*, a
small volume of Virgil, an inkwell and two pens. Brother Domingo
knew what a prisoner's rights were and exercised them without hesitation. The content of the books did not seem to matter to him. With the
same concentration he could compulsively read a chivalric romance or
the life of Saint John Clímaco, as if the letters worked a kind of pure fascination on him.

Familiar with the intricate, obscure workings of the Inquisition, its
organization and its methods, the Dominican lectured Cipriano every
afternoon when he woke from his siesta about his future possibilities.
There were punishments and there were punishments. The criminal
condemned to death shouldn't be confused with a relapsed or reconciled criminal. The first and the last were usually turned over to the secular arm to be hung before their bodies were delivered to the flames.
Relapses, recidivists, or the merely obstinate were, to the contrary,
burned alive at the stake.

This last punishment had been rare in Spain until now, but the
monk suspected that from this moment on it would become normal. He
told Cipriano about the sanbenitos, sackcloth cloaks painted with
flames and devils for relapses and with Saint Andrew's crosses for those
who were reconciled. The punishments had various degrees and nuances,
but the sentences were usually very precise. These could include life
imprisonment, confiscation of property, exile, being stripped of a habit

for monks or of honors for a gentleman, though these were often attached to more severe punishments.

Brother Domingo enlightened him as well about the structure and functioning of the inquisitorial apparatus and the rights of prisoners. They spoke from bed to bed, the monk with his usual swollen voice, elaborated in the larynx, Cipriano in his humble, curious tone, the same he'd used long ago with the teacher Don Alvaro Cabeza de Vaca with such poor results. These conferences had become absolutely necessary, but aside from them, the two men led separate lives, ignoring each other because forced company could become unbearable, the worst of the prison's tortures in the monk's opinion.

Brother Domingo de Rojas still had a great deal of self-esteem and thought himself an important man and cleric. No doubt his high opinion of himself led him to wear plumes on his hat during his escape. He never hesitated to talk about himself and his participation in the sect, but he was pitiless when it came to some comrades like Juan Sánchez, the perverter of the nuns of Belén, as he called him, and of his imprudent sister María. He was ambiguous about others, like the archbishop of Toledo, Bartolomé Carranza, around whose neck he would say "no one dares to toss a rope." Other times he asserted that Carranza was no Lutheran, even if his language was. An unstable man, he spoke to Cipriano about his vocation and his entry into the Dominican Order as a member of a fervently catholic family. His relationship with the sect, like Cipriano's, had been brief; he was initiated barely four years earlier. An ardent proselytizer, he'd converted one of his brothers and several of his nephews to Protestantism.

When he was captured in Pamplona, he denied nothing. To the contrary, he boasted of being a member of a modern religious order, open to new currents. But no matter which theme he began with, he inevitably ended up talking about Bartolomé de Carranza, his nemesis. That the theologian enjoyed his freedom while his disciples, as he said, rotted in jail, annoyed him more than anything else. But his time would come. Valdés hated him and would ultimately try him. For the moment, the monk clung to his protection, as if his high rank might somehow help him.

Aside from his talks with Brother Domingo, Cipriano, heavily

dressed despite the summer's heat, remained alone, isolated in the half
light, nervous about his situation. For part of the morning, he would try
to get used to walking with leg irons, dragging the chains, but the way
they rubbed his ankles, stripping the flesh off the bones, was torture.
For that reason, his usual place was in bed or seated on the bench, leaning the back of his head against the moist wall. In the afternoon, he
would read for a while, but got no advantage from it, and he often
evoked Christ in order to reconcile himself with Him or to ask Him for
illumination about how to face the Tribunal.

He tried neither to make a show of his past nor to deny his present simply out of fear. He aspired to being sincere, in accordance with
his beliefs, because it was not easy to fool God. With his eyes—he'd
begun to feel an insidious burning on his eyelids—half shut, he'd said
exactly that to Our Lord, trying to concentrate, to forget where he was.
None of the decisions he'd made seemed frivolous. He'd assimilated
the doctrine of the beneficence of Christ in good faith. There was no
pride, no vanity, and no greed in his taking that position. He simply
believed that the passion and death of Jesus were such important things
that they were sufficient to redeem the human race.

Enveloped in his fervor, self-involved, he waited in vain for the
visit of Our Lord, for a sign, however small, that would guide him.
"Show me the road, Lord," he would sob, but the Lord remained aloof,
silent. "Our Lord cannot take sides," he would say, "I'm the one who
must decide, for the sake of my freedom." But he lacked determination,
clarity, the necessary lucidity. And he would remain in that impatient
state of waiting until a comment by Brother Domingo or the high-
pitched screech of the bolts announcing the arrival of Dato jolted him
out of his self-involvement. Then he would stare at the jailer with his
flat and frayed hair peeking out from under his red wool cap, his filthy
breeches covering half his leg. The charm broke, and Cipriano's mind
returned to his routine life without putting up any resistance.

One afternoon, Dato, before taking charge of his latrine, passed
by his side, and without looking at him, placed in his hand a paper folded
over a thousand times. Cipriano was shocked. He made not the slightest
gesture. He knew he wasn't obliged to share news with Brother Domingo
or to communicate to him the guard's greed. Which is why he remained

motionless until Dato changed the receptacles. Then he unfolded the paper and in the half light, straining his eyes, he read:

## CONFESSION OF DOÑA BEATRIZ CAZALLA

Before the tribunal of the Holy Office, Doña Beatriz de Cazalla declared yesterday, August 5, 1558, in the trial summary appended to this document, that she had deceived Brother Domingo de Rojas. In turn, Cristóbal de Padilla, native of Zamora, was deceived by Don Carlos de Seso, while the brother of Beatriz Cazalla, Don Agustín de Cazalla, was the victim of the selfsame Don Carlos de Seso and her other brother Pedro, parish priest of Pedrosa. Juan de Cazalla in turn perverted his wife, just as the Doctor perverted his mother, Doña Leonor, with the result that practically the entire Cazalla family—Constanza would come later—was deeply involved with the Lutheran sect. Continuing with her sincere exposition, Beatriz Cazalla affirmed that Doña Catalina Ortega had cate- chized Juan Sánchez, and the two of them had then instructed the jeweler Juan García. For his part, Brother Domingo de Rojas per- verted his sister María, even if he denies it, and a good part of his family. Cristóbal de Padilla, in turn, perverted the small Zamora group, and his brother Pedro, together with Don Carlos de Seso, perverted the Pedrosa property owner Don Cipriano Salcedo.

Cipriano froze, disconcerted, choked by a strange interior cold. In his stomach, he felt something like the bite of some animal. Never had so few lines caused so much damage. He fell into a depression. Cipriano had imagined everything but a betrayal from within the group. The fra- ternity he'd dreamed of was splintering, turning out to be nothing but a utopian dream. It had never existed; nor was it possible for it ever to exist. He thought about the group meetings, about the solemn, final oath of the congregation, who all promised they would never inform on their brothers in times of tribulation.

Could what that note said be true? Was it possible that the sweet Beatriz had unhesitatingly informed on so many people, beginning with her own brothers? Was her own life so valuable to her that she would perjure

herself and send her family and friends to be burned at the stake just to save
her skin? Tears came to his soft eyes when he reread the paper. Then he
thought about Dato. Fray Domingo had told him that venality and corrup-
tion were firmly established in the lower ranks of the prison personnel, but
the handwriting on the paper was not that of a jailer, not even a Bailiff, but
of some member of the Tribunal, perhaps the secretary, or, more probably,
the scribe. He saw that a means of communication was open, one he initially did not count on. After thinking about it, he decided not to show
Beatriz Cazalla's confession to Brother Domingo. Why make him even
angrier? What would the monk gain by knowing that Beatriz had informed
on him and on practically every member of the group?

The next afternoon, stretched out on his bed, he awaited Dato's
arrival. He walked in humming, as usual, but when he came close,
Cipriano asked him in a whisper how much he owed him. Dato's answer
didn't surprise him: whatever you think it's worth. Cipriano put a ducat
in his hand, which he stared greedily at and scrutinized, first one side,
then the other. Then he asked if Cipriano would be interested in more
information, and Cipriano nodded yes.

He knew he'd set a price, but he didn't consider it either excessive
or badly employed. Ever since the Dominican had told him about the
punishments inflicted on heretics, he'd concluded that his fortune
would be confiscated anyway. It was then he thought that Our Lord had
inspired his decision to divide his goods among his collaborators. No
matter, the money he had with him did not amount to much.
Surprisingly, in Cilveti they'd barely searched him looking for a weapon.
Vidal was interested in nothing except arms and papers. He respected
Cipriano's money. His mission consisted in conveying him unharmed
from Pamplona to Valladolid, and that's what he did. Here he was, at the
disposition of the Tribunal.

August was coming to an end, and he had yet to be called to the
court room on the upper floor of the building. The same was true of
Brother Domingo. On the 27th, however, he received a surprise. Don
Gumersindo, the bailiff, accompanied by the older jailer, announced
that he had a visitor. Clean yourself up, he said, I'll be back for you in
fifteen minutes. Cipriano was astonished: Who would be concerned
about him under these circumstances?

Cipriano entered the visitors's chamber in shock, his feet light, without chains. After almost four months living in the moist half-light of the cell, the sunlight hurt his eyes, dazzling him. Already on the staircase, he'd partially closed his eyes as a precaution, but when he entered the small room, the sun shining through the windows forced him to shut them completely. It was as if he had dirt in them, like the eyes of his father-in-law when they dug him up. He heard the door shut, and now the silence was absolute. Little by little, he opened his eyes, and then he saw standing before him his uncle Ignacio. He was overwhelmed, just as he'd been as an adolescent when his uncle visited him at the foundling school.

He hadn't expected him. His uncle always surprised him. Both hesitated, but finally they embraced and kissed each other. They then sat down face to face, and his uncle asked him if he were suffering some eye problem. He lived in darkness, he said, but he immediately became more precise, almost in darkness, and the lack of light together with the humidity hurt his eyes. The edges of his eyelids were red and swollen, and his uncle promised to send him some medicine by means of the warden.

Then he gave Cipriano some good news: his uncle was now president of the Chancery Court, a promotion he'd expected because he was the oldest of the seventeen judges. The Chancery and the Holy Office had good relations, so he'd been authorized to visit Cipriano. Smiling, Cipriano fixed his bleary little eyes on him when he congratulated him. He expected a scolding from his uncle; in fact, he hadn't changed position from the instant he sat down so he could brace himself, but his uncle Ignacio didn't seem to notice the situation. He spoke to him as if they were talking in his house, as if nothing had changed since the last time they saw each other.

He'd gone out to Pedrosa and found Martín Martín in an excellent mood and with the farm work well in hand. For the moment the day laborers and farmhands from the neighboring towns hadn't raised a ruckus, which proved that the formula used to divide the property and raise the salaries of the field hands was civilized and did not harm third parties. He was holding for Cipriano his part of the wheat crop, which had been excellent, and expected as well a better-than-average grape crop.

Cipriano stared at him in a daze, his eyes weak. He was moved by the curtains, the shades, the lace doily on which rested the candelabra, the ugly painting of the Assumption of the Virgin over the sofa. It was as if he'd opened his eyes in a different, less hostile, less inhuman world. His uncle went on chatting without stopping, as if each moment of his visit cost money. Now he was talking about the warehouse and the shop. He visited the Ghetto with a certain frequency, twice a month. The new Maluenda did in fact seem hard-working and solvent. He exchanged letters with Dionisio Manrique, who, in  his last letter said that the spring convoy with its escort vessels had reached Amsterdam without incident. With regard to the shop, Fermín Gutiérrez, the tailor, aside from his ability in cutting, had turned out to be a good organizer. The trappers, skinners, leather-makers, seamstresses, and mule-drivers were all satisfied with their new contracts.

Unexpectedly, he changed the subject to say that prison rules did not require those confined to wear rags, that through the warden he would also send Cipriano new clothing. Cipriano was deeply moved by his concern. He tried to thank his uncle, but his voice broke, and his eyes filled with tears. He wanted to ask his forgiveness before he left, to convince him of his own good faith in joining the sect, but when he opened his mouth he could barely enunciate one word: *religion*. When his uncle heard it, he put an effusive hand on his nephew's shoulder: "That's the most intimate corner of our soul. Live according to the dictates of your conscience, and don't worry about the rest. We shall all be judged according to that measure."

Back in his cell, he found that his uncle's visit had left him with a sensation of unreality, as if he'd been dreaming. However, the arrival of new underclothing, a doublet, a cloak, stockings, and medicine for his eyes convinced him his uncle was real and tangible, as were the shades and curtains at the window, the lace doily in the room, or the picture of the Assumption.

That same afternoon, Dato slipped him another folded paper. When he unfolded it, he felt a vertigo that forced him to sit down on a bench to steady his legs. It was an extract of Ana Enríquez's confession before the Tribunal of the Holy Office. As he read it, he could easily guess her suffering, the sea of doubts in which that child had debated for months:

I came to this town from Toro for the Conversion of Saint Paul and met Beatriz Cazalla. She spoke to me about our salvation, about how it would be effected exclusively through the merits of Christ, that all my former life was lost, because works, in themselves, wouldn't be of any use. And I then asked her: "What is all this I hear about heretics?" And she answered: "The Church and the saints are the heretics." And then I asked: "What about the pope?" And she answered: "Each of us holds the pope in the Holy Spirit." And she suggested that what I should do was make my confession to God with regard to my past life, because no man has the power to absolve. And I, shocked at that, asked: "In that case, what about purgatory and penitence?" And she said to me: "There is no purgatory; all we need is faith in Jesus Christ." I did confess, but with a monk, as I'd done before, only as fulfillment of an obligation, but I told him nothing about those conversations. The next day, Beatriz Cazalla told me that priests only gave us half of Christ, the body but not the blood, and that true Communion consisted of bread and wine. I lived weeks of anguish until, because of Lent, Brother Domingo de Rojas, a good friend of my parents, came to our home. So I asked him and he confirmed what Beatriz had told me. I was now calm and really believed him. During those days, Brother Domingo told me that Luther was an extremely saintly man, that he'd only exposed himself to all the dangers in the world in order to speak the truth. He also told me other things, for instance that there were only two sacraments, baptism and the Eucharist, that adoring a crucifix was idolatry, and that after Redemption we'd been freed of all servitude; and that we did not have to fast or make vows of chastity merely because of obligation; nor did we have to do many other things like attend Mass, because during Mass Christ was sacrificed to for money and that "if it weren't for the scandal it would cause, he would throw aside his habits and stop celebrating Mass."

Cipriano shut his eyes. The first thought he had was not about the denunciation, but about the bitterness those words must have produced in Doña Ana's spirit. Then he thought about the plumes on Brother Domingo's hat when he disguised himself to escape. Toward him, he immediately felt a kind of aversion, such a conceited, arrogant, insidious man. His cruelty toward Doña Ana was not exactly a Christian act.

The Dominican had behaved brutally with the girl, had destroyed her spiritual structure with no consideration whatsoever. He turned his eyes toward the window, saw him lazily reading a book, stretched out on his cot taking advantage of the last light of the afternoon, and felt an intense dislike of him. It was only later that Cipriano deplored Ana Enríquez's denunciations, the betrayal of Beatriz Cazalla and the Dominican, her spontaneous perjury. He felt his spirit wilt, felt the augmentation of his loneliness, the anguish lurking in the pit of his stomach, a powerful feeling of ill-being.

But the hours passed quickly during that period in the secret jail. The jailer visited a short time later to announce his appearance before the Tribunal at ten the next morning. On the stairs, with no chains on his feet, he almost flew, but the further he got from the dungeons and the more light there was, the more his eyes stung. He had to half-close them to get some relief. And before entering the courtroom, he spied the little door to the room where he'd met with his uncle. Then he heard a voice speak from somewhere he couldn't identify saying "Bring the prisoner forward," and someone pushed him toward the door made of carved chestnut that stood before him.

He entered with great suspicion. The sun pouring through the windows blinded him; the coffered ceiling and the long red drapery struck fear in him. The jailer who led him by the arm seated him in a chair. Then he saw the Tribunal before him, behind a long table on a dais, there where the bright red carpet that covered the passage from the door. The scene, point by point, replicated what Brother Domingo had told him: the inquisitor in the center, wrapped in a black soutane, his head covered with a four-pointed bonnet, his face long and grave. To his right the secretary, a clergyman also wearing a soutane, also circumspect and lugubrious, and, to the left, wrapped in a severe black robe, the scribe, a layman, many years younger than the two clergymen.

Before the bell rang, Cipriano had just enough time to notice that the inquisitor's ears were translucent and stood out from his head. He immediately leaned forward and felt a strange sensation, as if his body were splitting in half, and that one half of him was listening to the answers the other half gave to the clergyman's questions. But, soon after they began, the silhouettes on the dais, the coffered ceiling, the carpet, and the drapery all disappeared: only the opaque voice of the inquisitor remained. An accusing, intimidating voice that contrasted sharply with the brief, hasty, answers his other self made in a choppy verbal exchange without interruptions, as if the pressured haste of the questions guaranteed the veracity of the answers. Nevertheless, that hard and finely-toned voice did not seem to affect the lucidity of the answers made by his other self, of his other half:

"Who perverted you?"

"F . . . forgive me, sire, but I cannot answer that question. I took an oath."

"Is it true you own an important estate in Pedrosa?"

"It is true, sir."

"Did you not meet there Don Pedro Cazalla, the parish priest?"

"I did meet him and came to know him. We are both fond of the country and would take walks together. He made many curious observations about birds."

"Father Cazalla spoke to you about birds?"

"Not only about birds, sir. Other times, he spoke about toads. I remember a conversation we had about toads in the salt marshes of Cenegal. He's a keen-eyed naturalist."

"And Don Carlos de Seso?" "Did he participate in these divagations?"

"I had barely any dealings with Don Carlos. On one occasion, we ran into him on the road from Toro, but we didn't speak to him about birds or toads. He was going to be appointed governor of the town and had gone there to visit friends."

"Was there a friendship between Don Carlos de Seso and Pedro Cazalla?"

"They knew each other. They spoke. But, if there was friendship between them I couldn't say. By the same token, I couldn't tell you the degree of their friendship."

"Don Pedro never spoke to you about religion on your walks."

"We spoke about all sorts of subjects. Religion was most certainly one of them."

"Do you consider religion an important subject?"

"Religion occupies the most intimate corner of our soul," said Cipriano, recalling his uncle's expression.

"If you believe that, how is it possible you don't remember any of the conversations you had about religion with Don Pedro Cazalla? How is it you can remember what you said about toads but you remember nothing about what you said about God."

"Man is a most complicated animal, sir."

"And what about with Don Carlos de Seso?"

"What about him?"

"Did you two ever speak about religion?"

"I met him, as I told you, on the road from Toro. He was riding, and we were on foot. His horse was a thoroughbred with a lot of spirit. I was more interested in his mount than in him. And that's the truth."

"So you like horses?"

"Thoroughbreds fascinate me."

"Didn't you make a trip to France in 1557 with your horse Pispás?"

"Yes I did."

"Who helped you through the Pyrenees?"

"The guide Pablo Echarren, from Navarra. He was a most knowledgeable man when it came to the mountains, and I suppose he still is."

"Who recommended him to you?"

"Among the people who travel frequently to France, Echarren is a well-known figure. I'd go even further than that: he's an institution."

"On that trip, did you reach Germany?"

"I was in several German cities, yes sir."

"Who induced you to visit Germany?"

"Sir, I'm a merchant, the creator of *Cipriano's Coat*—you may have heard of it. I have friends and business associates abroad with whom I'm in constant contact."

"There were no religious motives in that trip?"

"It seems you'd like to know what my religion is. Isn't that the case? If I tell you that the doctrine of the beneficence of Christ intrigued me, we can save ourselves some words. And if you accept that doctrine, it follows you'll accept other things that derive from it."

"In that case, do you recognize that over the past few years you've been living an error?"

"Sir, error is not the right word. I believe in what I believe in good faith."

"Do you believe what you preach?"

"I was never a proselytizer, sir. I've simply tried to be faithful to my beliefs."

"Is it true that you meet on a monthly basis in small groups in the house of Doña Leonor de Vivero, the mother of the Cazallas?"

"I did meet that lady and the Doctor through my friend Pedro Cazalla, her son and his brother."

Suddenly there was a pause, and the scribe lifted his eyes for the first time. Cipriano's strength was being put to the test. He listened to the answers his double gave with his eyes closed, contentedly. He would have given the same answers if he'd had time to think. His double accused no one, never lied, never informed. He paid close attention to the questions, but his answers did not seem to please the inquisitor. His voice became even more opaque when he said: "You are trying to elude my questions, even though you know I have efficient methods to loosen tongues. Have you ever heard of torture?"

"Unfortunately I have, sir."

"And purgatory?"

"I have heard of it."

"Do you believe in it?"

"If I have faith and admit that Christ suffered and died for my sake, temporal suffering means nothing. If I didn't believe that, I would be doubting His sacrifice."

"And do you believe in the Roman Church?"

"I firmly believe in the Church of the Apostles."

"Don't you repent of having embraced these new doctrines?"

"I didn't accept them out of pride, greed, or vanity, sir. I simply found myself in them. But I would not hesitate to give them up if you were to convince me of my error. By the same token, I would never give them up just to save my life."

"Did you feel no scruples when you took up that doctrine?"

"I felt them before, sir, in my youth. In that sense, the new doctrine calmed my soul."

"Are you so blind that you don't see Luther's excesses?"

"Sir, you and I seek the same God through different means, but I would suppose that in any human interpretation of religion errors are committed."

"For the last time, Mr. Salcedo, before using more persuasive methods, Would you be so kind as to answer these two simple questions? First: Who perverted you? Second: Who induced you to travel to Germany in April of 1557?"

"Sir, I accidentally tripped over the new doctrine the way we accidentally run into the woman who tomorrow will be our bride. With regard to your second question, I repeat that a business man must travel abroad from time to time. The merchants of Antwerp are partners of mine, and I visited them on that trip. If you doubt me, you can ask them."

In bed, stretched out and calm, his arms extended the length of his body, his eyes closed, Cipriano again found himself alone. Now he could detect his own effort to concentrate along with his misgivings when before the Tribunal. Brother Domingo, dragging his chains, had approached him when he returned to the cell and smiled when Cipriano told him that everything had been exactly as he'd described it. He did not go into details about the interrogation when the Dominican asked for particulars. He simply said that there were three judges, that the other two had taken notes. "The president's voice dominated the entire affair, but my mental reserve," Cipriano said, "did not seem to irritate him."

Three days later, very early in the morning, the warden and the jailer came for him. They did not prepare him, explained nothing, and said only one short phrase: "Follow us." And he followed them along the moist paving stones in the entry, along the corridor, and under the roof. Cipriano was concerned about his eyes, but this time the warden took the path to the lower dungeons by means of a stone stairway with irregular steps. Waiting for him there were the inquisitor, with his four-pointed hat and his translucent ears, together with the secretary and the scribe, who was seated at a table before a stack of white paper. Standing next to them, were two other people, and Cipriano deduced, thinking back to Brother Domingo's explanations, that the man with the dark robe was the doctor, and the other, who was barechested, wearing short breeches of rough cloth, the executioner. Before them, in a large dungeon, danced a series of strange devices, like the apparatus connected with a circus.

Before the executioner went into action, the inquisitor again asked him who'd perverted him and who ordered him to travel to Germany in April of 1557. Cipriano, thankful for the semidarkness of the place, said softly that three days earlier, during his interrogation, he'd told all he had to say on those matters. Then the inquisitor ordered the executioner to prepare the pulley hanging from the ceiling. Cipriano was more frightened by the preparations for the torture than the torture itself. Over the course of his life he'd always feared the threat more than the reality, no matter how cruel and demanding that might be. But when the executioner tied his wrists to the pulley, raised him, and left him hanging in the air, he was convinced that in his case the pulley was not going to work.

They'd stripped him bare from the waist up, and the inquisitor made a surprised comment on the disproportionate muscular development of the prisoner. The objective of the pulley was to disarticulate the victim using his own weight, but the executioner hadn't taken into account that Cipriano's body was light, that his arms were strong, so that even if hung he was still able to bend his arms easily and therefore thwart the torture. The executioner consulted the inquisitor with his eyes, and he pointed to a huge weight on the floor, which the executioner immediately tied to Cipriano's feet. Then he again raised him up into the void, so that Cipriano floated in the air, his arms stretched, like an athlete on the rings, swinging back and forth, the useless weight tied to his feet. The inquisitor felt cold and twisted his mouth. He experienced a rare frustration: "The rack," he said laconically.

The executioner untied Cipriano from the pulley and attached him by hands and feet to a kind of stretcher, where four iron drums, when turned, would stretch the body of the victim. During the first turns, Cipriano almost felt pleasure. That apparatus helped him stretch his members, and in that way he escaped the stiffening he'd been experiencing during the past months. But the executioner was not trying to give him pleasure. He went on turning the little handle until the stretching of Cipriano's arms and legs reached a painful point. At that moment, the inquisitor interrupted the torture: "For the last time, can you tell me who converted you to the damned sect of Luther?"

Cipriano remained silent. The inquisitor repeated the question,

but in view of his victim's silence, he nodded to the executioner. The man
wearing the robe approached Cipriano while the executioner turned the
handles, stretching the prisoner's body. The only advantage of this kind
of torture, thought Cipriano, was the slow way one entered it, that
between each turn of the drum there was a kind of rest in his body, time
to habituate himself. But when the tension increased, Cipriano felt an
extremely sharp pain in his armpits and groin. It was as if an overwhelming force, slow but growing, was trying to separate his bones from his
body. But, following his old philosophy, he threw himself suddenly into
his pain, accepted it. He thought that once within it, the pain, no matter
how intense, would become something external, would become futile
and bearable. But to the violent initial pain, others were added in his
spine, elbows, and kneecaps, in all his muscles and nerves.

He half opened his eyes when the executioner interrupted the torture to allow the inquisitor to ask his question again. But in the face of
his obstinate silence, the executioner again turned the handles, and the
result was that all of the different pains transformed into a single pain.
His backbone was breaking; he was being quartered. And the tension of
the nerves, when it reached his brain, produced a horrible pain that
gradually grew in intensity until it reached an unbearable level. At that
moment, Cipriano lost control of his will, howled a terrible scream, and
his head fell on his chest.

Later, in his bed, after the doctor had ministered to him, he recovered consciousness. He had the strange sensation that every bone in his
body was separated from all the others, that they were all out of place.
Every move, no matter how slight, was translated into a dull pain, so
Cipriano opted for immobility, which made the pain more bearable. He
felt an infinite weariness.

In the following days, Brother Domingo revealed a sensitivity
Salcedo never suspected he had. He sat on the bench at the head of
Cipriano's bed and tried to convince him of the madness of his resistance.
The Holy Office, he said, knew only too well that it had been Pedro
Cazalla and Don Carlos de Seso who'd brought him into the group. He
warned him that torture was not limited to a single session, that at first it
was, but that the Inquisition had invented the figure of suspension, where-
by torture could begin again once the criminal had recovered. "That being

the case," he went on, "who's benefitted from your silence?" Why remain silent? One afternoon, when Rojas was insistently repeating these arguments, Cipriano said in the lowest of voices: "A . . . and don't you think that perjury, aside from being a personal failure, is a great sin?"

Brother Domingo did not understand the matter in those terms and was annoyed by large ideas. He immediately tried to evade Cipriano's influence. "A man should adapt to circumstances," he said, "avoid the heroic tone, convince himself that the fact of accepting that someone was attacking our body was a crime more serious than perjury." Cipriano referred to the martyrs, and the Dominican said those times had passed. Christianity was firmly established in the world and no longer needed personal sacrifices.

Two weeks after the torture, Dato slipped Cipriano a note from Doña Ana Enríquez herself:

> My esteemed friend: I'm going to ask a great favor of you. I know you've been tortured for not revealing the name of those who perverted you. Please, do not be obstinate. To place at risk the life Our Lord has given us reveals a disdainful attitude toward the Creator. Saying something to satisfy the inquisitors, telling them something they want to hear, and making them feel momentarily victorious does not mean giving in. Think carefully: your life, even though you don't suspect it, may one day be necessary for someone.
>
> I remember your visit to La Confluencia, my father's estate, on the occasion of Cristóbal de Padilla's follies, for which we are all paying so dearly. Those happy moments of a golden autumn, strolling in your pleasant company through the garden, had a great impact on me. Will we be allowed to re-live those hours some day? Take care of yourself, just think you only have one life to live and that your obligation is to save it. Yours, in respect and esteem,
>
> Ana Enríquez

Cipriano took heart when he read that letter, whose content dissipated the bitter taste of ash left to him by the torture. What did Ana Enríquez mean about the fact that his life might some day be necessary for someone? To whom was she referring? He had paper and pen, and his first impulse was to answer her, but the attempt was a failure because the proper words would not come to him. They all tangled together, and he lacked the necessary lucidity to write a coherent sentence. Days later, now in possession of his faculties, he felt able to put together a few lines. He reread them several times before giving them to Dato:

> My esteemed friend: Thank you for your interest, for honoring me by concerning yourself about my health. I too remember with great emotion that autumnal stroll through the gardens of La Confluencia, just as I remember your profile at group meetings, your fervor, your giving of yourself, that white hand raised, asking permission to speak, and especially, your presence in my house the day of the escape, your farewell, that unforeseen and effusive gesture you made when you said good-by. Believe me, that instant has comforted me a great deal and cheered me in the painful moments I've endured. Will all this pass one day? For now, I urge you not to suffer for me. To carry through with what we think is our obligation holds in itself a reward. With respect and esteem, I remain yours,
>
>                                                   Cipriano Salcedo

A very cold fall ensued, and Cipriano, weaker and weaker, spent his days in bed covered with the prison blanket. The warden had not come for him, and Cipriano wondered if his uncle might not have something to do with the interruption in his torture. At the beginning of November, he received from him a coat lined with genet fur and a Segovian cape. But Uncle Ignacio did not appear. In all likelihood, frequent visits to someone imprisoned for heresy would represent a blot on his career. For his part, Brother Domingo went on reading the books supplied him by the Inquisition. In mid-December, he was called to the Court Room and came back three hours later, unwilling to tell Cipriano the details of his trial. Just what he expected, he said, the usual thing. He stretched out on his bed and went back to his reading as if nothing had happened.

Just at Christmas Eve, when he no longer expected anything, Cipriano received from Dato a few lines from Ana Enríquez, wishing him a merry Christmas. The first part of the letter was flattering: she emphasized Cipriano's probity, his intelligence, the fact that he'd taken on the burden—never asking anything for doing so—of the security of the entire group. "At that moment, I realized that I could not be indifferent to you." Cipriano's heart began to pound and threatened to leap out of his chest. That was too much; it wasn't exactly a declaration of love, but it most certainly proved she'd set him apart from the other members of the sect. But, if there were any doubt, in the next paragraph she went further: "Now perhaps you understand better what my interest in you is." Cipriano was deeply moved.

For the first time, at the age of forty-one, he was living an amorous experience typical of adolescence. He evoked details of Ana's figure, her pearl necklace, her red turban, her white, bejewelled hand, rising like a bird at group meetings, her warm, almost burning voice. Was it possible, Lord, that this singular creature could have set her eye on him? His answer was brief: he wished her happiness and luck, telling her that this Christmas, despite everything, would remain in his life as an unforgettable milestone. Her letter, he said, had the scent of hope, "you feel, madam, the illusion that something is being born." Unfortunately, he could not share her optimism: "The idea that something is ending prevails in me." But he also recognized that he'd never been indifferent to her presence. "I always admired your sagacity, your discretion, your poise, and—of course!—your beauty," he added in a gush of sincerity. And in closing he confirmed his respect and tender feeling toward her.

Dato became the interior mail service between Doña Ana Enríquez and Cipriano Salcedo. The letters passed back and forth between them with greater and greater frequency and put a point of light and hope in the squalor of the dungeons. Ana always led the way in effusiveness and intimacy. "Catalina de Reinoso, one of the Belén nuns, my cellmate, suggests that the difference in our ages is an obstacle between us," Doña Ana said in her letter of February 6. And she added: "But I say, What does age matter in this matter of feelings? Do souls have any age?" Her messages contained, in one way or another, a note of optimism: "Some day they'll let us be happy," she would say. Or: "Our stroll through the garden at La Confluencia will turn out to be the first step in our shared history."

Cipriano was more cautious. A somewhat forgotten promise reappeared and dampened his initial enthusiasm. His conscience began to reproach him for his weakness, the fact that he let himself be carried off by an easy feeling, animating Ana Enríquez to build castles in the air. This time he delayed his response and kept silent. He had no right to encourage the girl's projects when he knew what the outcome was going to be. Things were arranged in such a way that there was no alternative path in his future. The Inquisition would never accept his silence, and he was not disposed to break it just to help himself. He prepared draft after draft, but tore them up one after another. Brother Domingo stared at him from his bed: "Are you preparing your last will and testament?"

Cipriano did not respond to the monk's joke. But in point of fact, what he was trying to write was very much like a will. For that reason, after hearing the dominican's question, he decided to speak clearly, as if this were—was it?—his last will. He loved her; that was essential. He loved her above all things. Even so, between them stood two obstacles impossible to overcome: the vow of chastity he'd made to Our Lord more than a year earlier and his decision not to commit perjury by revealing the names of those who'd converted him. That attitude would never be forgiven by the Holy Office.

As if it were an answer to his message, Dato that afternoon brought him a message from an unforeseen source:

> The emperor Charles V has just died in the Yuste Monastery, lamenting that he did not kill Luther when he had him captive in Worms. In a codicil to his will, he demanded with paternal authority that his son Philip punish heretics with the utmost rigor according to their crimes, without exceptions, without respect for any person. For his part, the new king Philip II has blessed the *holy zeal* of his father.

From that moment on, and as if Dato had been saving up letters until Cipriano's amorous crisis was resolved, papers of all sorts began to arrive—declarations, news, reports, messages about the trials of the Cazalla brothers, Don Carlos de Seso, his cellmate Brother Domingo, a statement by the Archbishop of Toledo, and various other communications that Cipriano arranged in chronological sequence before settling himself in his bed and covering himself up with his Segovian cape. Used to betrayal, he was barely moved by the declarations of his comrades. Disheartened, he read the confession of his friend Pedro Cazalla:

> One day, I ran into Don Carlos de Seso, governor of Toro, in Pedrosa, at the door of my church. I was thinking about the beneficence of Christ, and he said to me out of the blue that there was no purgatory and that he could prove it to me. And he did it so cleverly that he convinced me of it, though my spirit was full of anguish and anxiety (the prisoner here told the episode of the visit of Seso to Carranza in the College of San Gregorio, a scene we won't repeat because all of us know it so well). I then spoke about it with Herrezuelo, not so I could teach him: in fact it was he who transmitted to me the matter of justification by faith without the need of good works and insisted that purgatory did not exist. In the same way, Cristóbal de Padilla visited my house in Pedrosa three times and spoke to me about the same subjects, and I begged him not to do it again. In the same way, a servant I had, Juan Sánchez by name, also lectured me, but I rejected him harshly, and he, in disgust, left my service. And I was happy about that. Finally, I spoke about these matters with my study companion brother Domingo de Rojas, and even before I brought up the subject of purgatory, he himself introduced it in the same terms as the others.

Cipriano's sick eyes oozed as he read all this wretchedness. Carlos de Seso, on the other hand, though he attributed to the recently-appointed archbishop Carranza the origin of the sect, tried to convince the Tribunal of his own innocence in the matter of purgatory. He disguised the truth to his own advantage:

> My intention in speaking to anyone about the non-existence of purgatory was not to lead them away from the Church but to augment their faith in the Passion of Jesus Christ. I never dogmatized, I never held meetings of any kind. If the occasion arose, I gave my opinion about the issue at hand. Seso ended by begging mercy for the scandal he'd caused, defining his ideas about purgatory, about which he said that "it does not exist for those who die united to Christ, serving Him, and confessing their sins." He stated that his

Lutheran ideas were born in Verona during his youth, when he listened to a well-known preacher. In the final sentences of his statement, he expressed his desire to die in the bosom of the Church.

Cipriano was surprised by Don Carlos's tone, his humility and respect. His confession, part of it at least, was not consistent with his conduct. Cipriano attributed his softening to the harsh conditions of the prison, to the sickness the doctors of the secret jail, Bartolomé Gálvez and Miguel Sahagún, had attested to in a separate note:

Doctor Gálvez, physician to the General Council of the Inquisition, found in the prisoner, Don Carlos de Seso, held in the secret jail in Valladolid, a weak and irregular pulse, and significant weakness. With regard to his knees, about which the prisoner complains: no external change was noted, but when I touched them I found them very stiff. And because his suffering has been of such long duration and worsening each day because of the weight of his chains, it seems logical to me to treat him immediately.

Doctor Sahagún confirms: weak pulse, melancholic and sad spirit. Weak knees compared to the body, which is fat. The tendons of the knees are very stiff, for which reason he considers it prudent to remove him from the unhealthy quarters where he is being held.

Doctors Gálvez and Sahagún

For his part, the Doctor, Don Agustín Cazalla, seemed to be collapsing. His cowardice overwhelmed the faith he was supposed to espouse. Reading his declaration increased Cipriano's pessimism about his own future. This is what the report said:

Faced with torture, Doctor Cazalla promised to confess, and that exempted him from torture. Having lost his voice, he made his confession in writing, in his own hand. He declared himself to be a Lutheran but not a dogmatizer. He had not spoken with anyone who did not know beforehand the reformist doctrines. When it was suggested to him that he give information about himself and the others, he answered that he could not do that without incurring false testimony. And he ratified what he said once he was promised mercy. He swore he would be an exemplary catholic if the tribunal respected his life, and at all times he evinced unequivocal signs of repentance.

The longer he read reports and confessions, the more he felt his desolation grow. As spring approached, the number of papers Dato offered him grew. But he was so weak that he felt unable to drag his chains around, so he spent his days and nights in bed, covered by his cape. He grew increasingly disdainful of the documents Dato brought—generally false, foul, and cowardly. The jailer had reached such a high degree of intimacy with him, that he allowed Cipriano to look over the papers he offered before deciding to keep them or not.

In his heart, Cipriano had always expected an answer from Doña Ana to his farewell letter, but it never came. He welcomed two letters of hers with joy, the continuation, even in small doses, of her sweet messages from earlier days, but he himself, with his inflexibility, had put a halt to that correspondence, whose interruption he now lamented. Ana Enríquez, always sensitive with regard to the conscience of others, had respected his vow as well as his desire not to incur perjury. Though Cipriano thought about her frequently, the passage of time and the weakness of his memory made it more difficult with each day that passed to reconstruct her image: the proportions of her profile, the line of her mouth (a bit hard), her hairline, the form of her ears—physical details that were escaping him. The most important question in his mind was whether Ana's silence was caused by respect or by spite. Whenever he considered either alternative, his inflamed yes filled with tears, which he allowed to flow gently in an intimate flood of relief.

Prostrate in his bed, his eyelids half closed, immobile, his eyes sought the rays of the afternoon sun, which came into the cell obliquely through the window. In that light floated myriad motes. While Cipriano was in that frame of mind, Dato, wearing his red cap, walked in like a gnome, carrying the statement of Brother Domingo, also lying on his bed, oblivious to everything. Cipriano took the report:

Unstable character. Late adherence to Lutheranism and proselytizing zeal. A vain man, the prisoner stood before this Holy Tribunal as an old member of the sect and a devotee of the new currents. He attributed his ideas to his master, the archbishop of Toledo, Don Bartolomé Carranza, Lutheran perhaps without knowing it, or—better put—precursor of Lutheranism in Spain. About his epistle *Ad Galathas*, he said that it followed Lutheran language, and about his *Catechism*, he said that it was a hard tough food for simple men, "who don't have the teeth to chew it or the stomach to digest it." These things, he said, should not be put in the hands of the ignorant and were only meant for university graduates and theologians.

When he was called to order by the inquisitor, he insisted that Bartolomé Carranza might be a catholic, but that listening to him express himself, he did not seem to be one. And in a rhetorical pirouette, he enjoyed, Brother Domingo declared that "that was the medicine the archbishop used to win him over to the cause." All told, he left the archbishop of Toledo in a very bad light.

He also informed on Juan Sánchez as the perverter of the Belén nuns and of his own sister, María. In view of his contradictions, he was threatened with torture, but once he was attached to the pulley, he begged to be killed rather than tortured. The Holy Tribunal said it would respect his wish provided he told the truth. At the end, he exonerated several of the people he'd accused but not Archbishop Carranza.

Cipriano folded up the paper with a feeling of disquiet because several of those who'd made declarations had described Carranza as the father of the Lutheran movement in Valladolid. By implicating him, an authority in the Church, they in some way were left free of guilt. Carranza emerged then as a guarantee of life, the scapegoat, the prime target. Without his preaching, without his suggestive ideas, Protestantism would never have taken root in Castile. But for the moment, Carranza seemed to have influential backers.

He heard Brother Domingo's psst, and when he turned, the Dominican asked if he might read that paper. Salcedo became perturbed and asked him if he had any idea what it was. Brother Domingo went right to the point: "My statement. What else could it be? You looked over at my bed twice before you began to read it." Cipriano stood up, stumbled, took two awkward steps toward his bed, and held out the paper in his left hand: "It may be that you won't like what it says."

"And what does that matter? It's important to know not only what we've done but what they say we've done."

The Dominican read the statement in silence, without fussing or commenting. Salcedo, who never took his eyes off him, asked, when Brother Domingo folded up the paper again: "Do you agree with it?"

The Dominican answered in a rather biting tone: "Yes, with what it says, but not with what it doesn't say."

In mid-April, the deafening noise of hammers exploded over the city. It began at first light and did not stop until late at night. It was a hammering in different tones, but in any case dry and brutal, that emanated from the Plaza del Mercado and spread, with differences of intensity, to every neighborhood in the town. That sinister pounding seemed to activate the vitality of the prison, accelerate its rhythm. The routine life of the secret prison suddenly transformed into something very busy and active. Men, alone or in groups, passed back and forth through the entry, along the corridors, outside the cells, bringing in or carrying out objects, giving instructions to the prisoners. A strange agitations seemed to have been unleashed, and it coincided with Dato's haste to provide Cipriano with messages and news. The first night of the deafening hammers, the jailer explained: "They're building the scaffold."

"For the auto?"

"Exactly, sir. In the plaza, for the auto."

The next day, Dato brought him an urgent report that Cipriano paid for with a ducat. The urgency was justified:

#### SESO RETRACTS HIS CONFESSION

said the title. It was clear the summary had been written out in a haste motivated by the gravity of the latest developments, though in the disciplined handwriting of a scribe. It was obvious that the person exploiting this business was in a hurry to put the paper in circulation. Cipriano leaned his head back, trying to find the axis of visibility between his inflamed eyelids. The note was succinct but categoric, indicative as well that the sentences of the prisoners were beginning to be known. Seso had been condemned to the flames, and because of that fact, he was now making a new profession of faith. His excuses, his circumlocutions, his twisting of words, his express desire to die in the bosom of the Church had all been useless. Now he set matters straight. In the new note he now spoke without reservation, convinced that the sentence was fixed, and that there was no appeal possible:

> Now that I've been informed that you gentlemen have condemned me to the flames, something I never believed could happen, I want to make this final statement to give relief to my conscience and help the truth: justification by faith alone is sufficient for salvation. It is Christ who saves us, not our works. For those who die in a state of grace, there is no purgatory, no temporal punishment of any sort: their destiny is heaven. It would not be just that after the Passion of Our Lord, that men should have anything of which to be purged. This means that I retract what I said, that purgatory exists. I have faith and believe in the same thing the apostles believed in, and I believe both in the Catholic Church, true bride of Our Lord Jesus Christ, and in the word of the Church, the Holy Scriptures.

Cipriano read Don Carlos de Seso's brief confession three times. He recalled the arguments that he made so long ago now in Pedrosa to prove there was no purgatory and how he had accepted them with no disagreement. Now he looked at Brother Domingo in his cot and said in a faint voice: "Don Carlos de Seso has been sentenced to burn at the stake."

But events became linked to one another in an inexorable, endless circle, while the hammering in the plaza bellowed in a dull drumming. The next morning, the warden in person announced a visit for Salcedo, but Cipriano could no longer walk. He couldn't move. His joints seemed to have rusted. He was brought a basin of lukewarm, salted water, his chains were removed, and he was made to wash his feet. Even so, around his ankles he had two, unhealed wounds, and his calves were swollen. Stumbling along, he followed the warden, leaning on the arm of the jailer. They moved like a pair of yoked oxen. The light in the stairway blinded him, and he felt something like a strange body inside his eyes. He closed them and let himself be led. His feet, without their usual ballast, ran away with him, but his swollen legs could not carry his weight. He partially opened his eyes when the jailer stopped, and when he heard the knock at the door, he raised his head and peered through the narrow crack left to him by his swollen eyelids. Uncle Ignacio stared at him in disbelief, deeply afflicted as he took him by both hands. It was clear he was in a hurry to speak, not to be silent for even a second in order to prevent Cipriano from asking him something.

"Those eyes of yours are not better, Cipriano. Why didn't you tell the doctor?"

"It's because of the darkness, uncle, the moisture and the cold. My eyelids are inflamed. It's as if I had dirt in them."

"We've got to cure them. There are two doctors in the prison. That's why they're here."

Ignacio immediately began talking, telling Cipriano that Archbishop Carranza had been arraigned and that a long and impassioned trial was in order. It would certainly take more than five years. Cipriano told him that the pressure against Carranza, both inside the jail and outside was huge. He raised his head to see his uncle, sitting on the monastic sofa beneath the naive picture of the Assumption of the Virgin, his elbows resting on his legs, his fingers intertwined, his nails well-manicured. He went on talking about Carranza, pained about the statements made by Seso, Rojas, and Pedro Cazalla, who, in his opinion, were not speaking the truth. He told Cipriano that the Inquisitor General had come to Valladolid and said that if it had been anyone else, he would have arrested him without a second thought.

Cipriano said that the key element had been the meeting between Seso and Carranza after Seso had converted Pedro Cazalla. Uncle Ignacio was well informed and barely gave him enough time to answer. It was clear he wanted to leave no openings for his nephew's questions. Carranza affirmed that Seso had tricked him and the Holy Office had made them believe that their interpretation of things derived from the archbishop. But the precautions of the new president of the chancery were insufficient. When his uncle paused for an instant, Cipriano asked the feared question: "D . . . do you know the sentences, uncle?"

Don Ignacio Salcedo, disarmed, stared at him, his eyes soft, his lower lip trembling. He made an effort and said: "I received them yesterday. Because of my position, I had to be informed."

Cipriano kept his head up so his uncle would not escape from his visual field. He saw Ignacio hesitate, grow pale. Even so, he did not try to weaken his question in any way: "What is my fate?"

Ignacio did not answer immediately. All he could do was stare at his nephew deeply, compassionately, his eyes bloodshot, and when he did try to speak, his voice caught in his throat twice. Cipriano came to his aid: "Will I be burned at the stake?"

His uncle, silent, nodded.

"You and twenty others," he finally said.

Cipriano smiled to relieve the tension in the conversation, to give his uncle the impression that the news hadn't surprised or shocked him, that he expected nothing else: "Would it be an indiscretion on my part to ask who the twenty are?"

Don Ignacio smiled: "That's one small favor I can do for you. Listen: the Cazallas, including the sister Beatriz and the remains of Doña Leonor, Brother Domingo de Rojas, Don Carlos de Seso, Juan García, three women from Pedrosa, Herezuelo, Juan Sánchez . . . Let me think who else . . ."

"That's enough, uncle."

"Anyway, the list isn't final. Tonight, a confessor will visit all of you, and tomorrow, at the auto, you will have the chance to change your fate: instead of the flames, the hangman. Oh yes, one other thing! The remains of Doña Leonor will not only be disinterred, but the property around her house will be sown with salt as a lesson to future generations."

Ignacio seemed calmer. Now he began stressing anecdotal details, trying to distract Cipriano from the fundamental idea. But Cipriano was not thinking about himself. He hesitated. In his vacillation, he lost sight of his uncle's face and had to turn his head to refocus his gaze on him: "A . . . and what will become of Doña Ana Enríquez?" he asked in the slightest of voices.

"She'll be set free after a mild punishment, a few days of fasting, I don't remember how many. She's too beautiful to burn."

Cipriano thought that keeping his uncle there any longer simply meant prolonging his torture. He stumbled to his feet. His uncle was right: Ana was too beautiful to burn. Besides, she'd been tricked: she was very young when Beatriz Cazalla and Brother Domingo perverted her. The hammering of the carpenters in the plaza echoed, a constant, maddening pounding. His uncle too had stood up, and took him apprehensively by the hands, as if he were blind.

"I don't want to make you waste more time, uncle. I thank you for everything you've done for me."

Ignacio drew him close, kissed him on both cheeks, and held him for a moment in his arms: "Some day," he whispered in his ear, "these things will be considered a violation of the freedom Christ brought us. Pray for me, my son."

Cipriano couldn't eat. Mamerto removed his untouched tray. That afternoon, the confessions began. Brother Luis de la Cruz, a Dominican like Brother Domingo, went from cell to cell and reached Cipriano's as the sun was setting. Even so, the monotonous hammering in the plaza went on at full blast. Brother Domingo rejected the aid of his fellow dominican when he accommodatingly approached his bed.

"Father," said Brother Luis when he saw Brother Domingo's gesture, "I'm only praying to God that you die in the same faith in which our glorious Saint Thomas died. I'll be awake all night. You may summon me at any hour."

On his cot, Cipriano welcomed the confessor with affection. He thanked him for coming and told him that in his life there were three sins of which he could not repent enough, and even though he'd confessed them, he wanted to confide them to the priest as proof of his humility: his hatred for his father, the seduction of his wetnurse, taking advantage of her maternal love, and his disaffection toward his wife, his abandonment of her, which led to her dying insane in a hospital. Brother Luis nodded, smiling, telling him his general confession dignified him, but that at his moment, on the eve of the auto-da-fé, he'd hoped for some words of repentance for having subscribed to the doctrine of Luther.

Cipriano, who in the fading light could barely make out the monk's features, answered that he embraced the theory of the beneficence of Christ wholeheartedly, in good faith, that is, he did what he did in good conscience, and that even now his conscience was clear. As if he

gave the matter no importance, Brother Luis asked him who had perverted him, and Cipriano answered that he could not tell him, that he'd
sworn not to, but that he was absolutely sure his teacher had not acted
with any perverse intention. The monk, who was tired, began to show
signs of acrimony. Cipriano's blindness was making him impatient. He
told him he could not absolve him, but that there was still time. After
midnight, Father Tablares, a Jesuit, would be available to the prisoners.
He now humbly recommended Cipriano to reflect, and before leaving
him, he held his hands for a long time, calling him "my brother."

Barely had he left the cell, when in the cell across the corridor,
that of the Doctor, there was a huge uproar. Above the calmer voices
trying to calm him, among which was that of Brother Luis, the Doctor's
imploring screams to God begging His mercy rang out. He beseeched
the Lord to illuminate him with His grace, to help him achieve salvation. They were high-pitched, broken shrieks, and in the brief silences,
it was possible to hear Brother Luis's deliberate voice, the voices as well
of the jailer and the warden, who both came when they heard the ruckus.
But the Doctor, hysterical, would not stop shouting that he accepted the
sentence as just and reasonable, that he would die willingly because he
did not deserve to live even if he were pardoned, because he was con-
victed for not having used his past life properly, so that which remained
to him would be no different.

The hammering in the plaza ceased, so the words of the Doctor,
which he was howling at the top of his lungs, reached the neighboring cells
and with them the attempts to calm him by those responsible: the warden,
the jailer, the doctor. The tension in the first corridor could be felt when
the Doctor went back to his speech about the sanbenito which had just
been delivered to him, the clothing he'd wear with the greatest pleasure,
he said, because it was appropriate to confound his pride and purge his
sins. Then he went back to the idea of repentance, that he renounced all
perverse and erroneous doctrines in which he'd once believed, whether it
was against dogma or against the church, and that he would persuade all
the prisoners to do the same. The Inquisition's doctor must have given
him something, because from the shrieking tone in which the Doctor had
begun his harangue, he passed in a few seconds to a more colloquial level,
and then to a tenuous murmur which also stopped in a short while.

Cipriano did not sleep during his last night in jail. He was oppressed by the idea of the auto-da-fé—not his execution but the ceremony: the light, the crowd, the shouting, the heat. His vital energies were rapidly declining, and a burning urine forced him to visit the covered pot every few minutes. At one, the bells began to ring. Slow, funereal tolling. Brother Domingo had already told him about it. All the churches and convents in the city, which that night did not sleep, summoned the faithful to masses for the souls of the condemned. The bells had taken the place of the hammers, changing voices but equally ominous and terrible. When the tolling ceased, the noise of the gathering people could be heard, the hooves of the horses on the paving stones, the screech of the carriage wheels. Everything seemed ready. The great day, still dark, had begun.

At four in the morning, the prisoners were awakened. Mamerto served them an extraordinary breakfast: garlic soup, bacon and eggs, and Cigales wine. Cipriano ate nothing. His eyes burned, he felt the dirt in his eyesockets, and his loss of energy accelerated. In the jail, there was an extraordinary disorder. People were coming and going, the guards were distributing to the cells the conical hats and the sanbenitos, while servants of the Inquisition, speaking in small groups and wearing their high- domed brown hats waited in the patio for the procession to start. In the moment of greatest confusion, Dato appeared in the cell, handed a folded paper to Cipriano, and whistled when he was given two ducats for his service. The message, as Cipriano had assumed, was from Ana Enríquez, and couldn't have been more laconic: it simply said, courage, and below it was signed Ana.

# XVII

T HE imprisonment of the more than sixty prisoners in the secret jail on Pedro Barrueco street ended definitively at dawn on May 21, 1559, a year, more or less, after it began. Very few of the prisoners would be set free after the auto-da-fé; most would suffer the supreme penalty and be hung or burned at the stake for their religious deviation or their obstinacy. As usually occurs, the collapse of discipline was the first symptom that the end was drawing near.

Servants of the Inquisition chatted in small groups in the prison patio. They wore capes and high, bowler-style hats while they awaited the penitents, while the jailers and their assistants and the warden himself came and went, attending to the final needs of the Inquisition and giving instructions for keeping the procession in proper order. They would leave the jail one hour before dawn. But, aside from those who'd been pardoned, who tried to pluck up their courage and mix with their jailers in a festive way, the rest of the prisoners, overwhelmed by the rigor of the sentence and having endured such a long and severe imprisonment, found themselves so worn-out and lifeless that they awaited the order to leave collapsed on their cots, praying or meditating.

Dato, the foolish assistant jailer, was among those citizens of Valladolid who were absolutely jubilant at the prospect of the grand entertainment about to take place. Grateful to Cipriano for his generosity, and sitting at the foot of his cot, he accompanied him during his final minutes in prison. He talked about the preliminary ceremonies for the auto with such enthusiasm that it was as if he regarded Cipriano not as a victim but as another outsider visiting the city. Like the other jailers,

Dato had put on new clothing, exchanging his filthy leggings for some colorful breeches.

For the assistant jailer everything was a novelty worthy of being talked about, from the criers on horseback, stationed at the corners announcing the auto and urging the attendance of all those over fourteen years of age with the promise of forty days of indulgence, to the prohibiting of anyone's riding a horse or carrying arms—neither edged weapons nor firearms—during the ceremony.

Dato's dull blue eyes sparkled, and his lank albino locks trembled under his red wool cap, when he realized how enormous the number of outsiders who'd come to Valladolid actually was. All of Castile had poured into the town, he said, though there were as well representatives from other provinces and large groups of foreigners speaking strange languages. "More than two hundred thousand people, I swear to you, sir, by the blessed memory of my mother," he said, making the sign of the cross. "There were so many that they couldn't find lodging in any of the rooming houses or inns, and thousands of them had to spend the night in nearby villages and farms, or, taking advantage of the mild weather, outdoors, in the gardens and vineyards on the outskirts of the city or on the little-visited or distant streets of the town. Accompanied by the Princes and the Court, our master the King had come in person to preside over the ceremony."

Dato was raving about how the Plaza Mayor had been transformed into an enormous wooden circus with seating for more than two thousand spectators. The prices for seats ranged from ten to twenty reales. A squad of halberdiers, reinforced at night, had been ordered to guard the structure, because there had already been two attempts to set it on fire by subversive elements.

With his eyes closed, and an intense pounding in the upper part of his eyelids, Cipriano commended his soul to Our Lord, asking Him for illumination so he could tell error from truth. At the same time, he distractedly listened to the latest news as reported by Dato: the day promised to be blazing hot, more like August than May, and many citizens who were unable to buy bleacher seats set up viewing stands on the roofs under canvas tents held up by strips of lathing. In expectation of the arrival of our master the King and the Princes, more than two thousand people were spending the night in the plaza lit by torches and lanterns. "You just can't imagine; it looks like the last judgment," declared Dato, overcome with amazement.

Right in the middle of the jailer's monologue, there erupted in the corridors the sound of running feet, impatient knocking at cell doors, and voices accustomed to giving orders, shouting, "Fall in! Fall in!" Brother Domingo, serious and circumspect, wearing his new robe, stood up on his own; Cipriano had to be helped by Dato. His chains had been removed, and he could feel that his legs were free, but he lacked sufficient strength to stand upright. At the entryway, Dato turned Cipriano over to two servants of the Inquisition, who were wearing woolen smocks under their capes despite the hot day about to begin. It was there the male prisoners gathered, helping one another to dress and put on their shoes. That meeting was like a mirror image of the group meetings, the same men, but without the feeling of fraternity that had once united them. Now, instead, they were dominated by suspicion and distrust, when not by overt hostility and hatred.

Cipriano looked up, trying to find a line of vision. To his right, frowning, pale to the point of transparency, fearful, shrunken into himself, was the Doctor, and behind him, Don Carlos de Seso, transformed by mistreatment and a year in prison into an old, stumbling beggar. His head ungovernable, his body drained, his shoulders hunched, he clung to the arm of a servant the way a shipwrecked sailor clings to a plank. His legs could not support his weight, and his former elegance, his delicacy, and his nobility had all collapsed. On the other side, two servants wrapped Herrezuelo in the new robe, while they protected his swollen feet with rope sandals. He was gagged, his hands were tied, and his gray eyes under his thick eyebrows darted madly from place to place, never stopping anywhere.

Cipriano approached Juan García, the jeweler, and asked why Herrezuelo was gagged. García, in the dim light of the entry area, barely noticed who was speaking to him and answered that Herrezuelo had gone mad, that ever since he left his cell he'd done nothing else but blaspheme against God. Everyone spoke in a low voice, so the entry area vibrated with a uniform murmuring, a monotonous rumbling with no changes in pitch. Juan Sánchez, from a corner, stared at Cipriano,

who had his head raised and was feeling his way around in a disoriented way, like a blind man. He attentively came to Cipriano and asked if
the darkness of his cell had blinded him. Cipriano made little of his sickness; it was his eyelids. They'd become inflamed, and he had to look
through a tiny slit and could only look straight ahead because that was
the only direction in which he could see anything. They smiled at each
other, and Cipriano noticed that the servant hadn't changed during the
past year: there he was with his big head and his yellow complexion like
wrinkled, old parchment. Juan Sánchez entered prison a hundred years
old and left a century old. That was the advantage of men who were
already emaciated, mummified, and ugly.

They had almost nothing to say to each other, and neither wanted
to poison the atmosphere or sow discord. But then, Juan Sánchez in one
of his untimely witticisms, pointed a finger at Cipriano's sanbenito and
then to his own, and ironically noted they'd both been addressed to the
same hell. His repressed, inopportune laugh heightened the tension.
Many of those there had informed on former friends, committed perjury,
tried to save themselves at the expense of others, and so they avoided
proximity, eye contact, making explanations. Pedro Cazalla stayed away
from Cipriano, seeking a dark corner in the entry patio where he could
remain unnoticed. His declaration, like that of his sister Beatriz, had
been remorseless. They'd denounced at least ten other prisoners. Even
so, Pedro Cazalla was wearing the sanbenito painted with flames and
devils which marked those sentenced to death. In the dark corner,
flanked by his guards, he was alone, his head hanging low, uncomfortable. In all likelihood, he and his brother Agustín, leaders of the sect,
were, in that hell of prejudices and suspicions, the ones most despised
by the others.

Herrezuelo's wild eyes leapt from one to another with infinite disdain. He could neither spit on them nor punch them, but his insane
gaze said everything. His hands were tied behind his back to keep him
from pulling off his gag, so he would snap his head from side to side
every time the servants put the conical hat on his head until it fell off.
One of the Inquisition's more patient and ingenious servants improvised
a chin strap with a ribbon to keep the hat on Herrezuelo's head, but he
went wild, butting his head against the servant until the ruined hat fell

off and landed on the ground. During the struggle, the gag came loose, and Herrezuelo, like a man possessed, began to insult Cazalla and swear against God and the Virgin until the guards shut him up by jumping on top of him.

Things seemed to calm down in the street, when the prisoners lined up two by two, guarded by the Inquisition's staff, began to form the procession. In front of Cipriano, marched Don Carlos de Seso making an effort to stand tall and not lose any more dignity. In front of him, small and hunched over, as if he were carrying a cross on his back, the Doctor moved along. First in line was Brother Domingo de Rojas, showing the same imperturbable indifference he'd evinced during his year in prison.

It was barely five o'clock in the morning, but an uncertain, milky glare announced the day above the rooftops. Heading up the procession, on horseback, the royal prosecutor carried the billowing standard of the Inquisition, with the arms of Saint Dominic embroidered on it. Behind him marched the reconciled prisoners, carrying candles, and wearing sanbenitos with the cross of Saint Andrew. Behind them, two Dominicans carrying the scarlet emblem of the Pope and the mourning-wrapped cross from the church of the Savior. They were followed by prisoners destined for the flames, wearing sanbenitos painted with devils and flames and conical hats. Mixed in with them, in similar costume but tied to tall poles, paraded the effigy dummies of the condemned, burlesque copies of their human originals. One of them represented Doña Leonor de Vivero, whose coffin, containing her disinterred body was being carried by four men: it too would be thrown into the fire.

The rest of the procession, that is, those condemned to lesser punishment, marched behind, preceded by four lancers on horseback announcing the religious communities of Valladolid and the chorus, marching up the street and intoning in a low voice the hymn *Vexilla regis*, appropriate to the solemnity of Holy Week.

Clinging to the arms of his guards, Cipriano Salcedo moved almost blindly. Even though the sun was slowly rising, he could only see when he raised his head and focused straight ahead. He was then able to make out the two dense walls of humanity that marked their path, people usually timid and silent, though, as always happens, the sharp voice of some boy rang out to take advantage of the impunity of the crowd and insult them.

When they left Orates street, the procession had to stop to allow the royal entourage to pass as it made its way along Corredera street. The horse guard with fifes and drums led the way, and behind them came the Council of Castile and the high dignitaries of the Court, with the ladies richly attired in rigorous mourning. Guarding that group were two dozen mace-bearers and four masters-at-arms wearing velvet dalmatics. Immediately following, and proceeding the King—grave, wearing a cape with diamond buttons—and the Princes, applauded by the crowd, appeared the Count of Oropesa, on horseback, his sword in his hand. The final group, led by the Marquis of Astorga, was a large number of nobles, the archbishops of Sevilla and Santiago, and the bishop of Ciudad Rodrigo, the man who'd subdued the conquerors of Peru.

Cipriano, in the first rank, saw all that grandeur pass by and tried to find the best angle to view it: he was smiling, devoid of rancor, like a child watching a military parade. Then the procession of penitents started off again and entered the plaza between two high partitions made of boards. The impatient crowd packed into the square burst into shouts and harsh screams. The criminals, walking in a tired way, bent over, dragging their feet, constituted a pitiful, ragged group, their sanbenitos twisted around, their conical hats askew, always about to fall off. Cipriano turned his gaze on the plaza by turning his head in order not to lose his axis of vision and concluded that Dato's reports were far from the truth.

Half the square had been turned into an enormous amphitheater with stairs and box seats. It was built against the wall of the convent of Saint Francis, facing the Consistory, which was decorated with banners, canopies, and brocades glittering with gold and silver. The other half and the adjacent street entrances were packed with a noisy audience in an angry mood who whistled in chorus as the prisoners filed past the King. Opposite the boxes, in the lower part of the stairs, there were three pulpits, one for the two officers who would read out the sentences, the second for the penitents who would hear them, and the third for Bishop Melchor Cano, who would pronounce a sermon to close the event.

In another section, just slightly lower than the pulpits, the condemned prisoners sat on four benches in the same order in which
they'd marched in, so Don Carlos de Seso was on Cipriano's right and
Juan García, on his left. Overwhelmed with anguish, weak, tense,
Cipriano awaited the arrival of the absolved prisoners. He stared obsessively toward the stairways that went up the structure until he finally
saw Ana Enríquez, her hand in that of the duke of Gandía. Wrapped in
the brown robe, she moved with the same natural grace she had in the
gardens of La Confluencia. Prison did not seem to have touched her—
perhaps she was a bit thinner, which emphasized her slenderness, but it
didn't ruin the freshness and splendor of her face. She walked up the
steps arrogantly, and as she passed before the first bench of prisoners,
she looked at each one anxiously, Her incredulous eyes stopped for an
instant on those of Cipriano. She seemed to doubt, looked again at the
others, and turned back to him, immobile, his little head raised, his eyes
half shut, half blind. Then she moved forward to the fourth level of the
tribunal, leaving Cipriano in doubt as to whether she'd recognized him.

The blinding, brutal sunlight had taken possession of the plaza,
hurting his eyes even more. After contemplating Ana, he closed them
for a long time to protect them. A hushed murmur of conversations
reached his ears while the bishop of Palencia, Melchor Cano, launched
into his sermon on false prophets and the unity of the Church. And
when Cipriano opened his eyes again, he was overwhelmed by the huge
crowd before him, an immense mass of people, so tightly jammed
together and riled up that it had immobilized against the fence two luxurious coaches occupied by people of rank.

During the sermon, the people had kept silent even thought the
slightly broken and tired voice of the speaker did not seem to reach
them. But shortly after he finished, when one of the officers swore in
the King, the nobles, and the people, enjoining them to defend the
Holy Office and its representatives even at the cost of their lives, a deafening roar chorused the final *amen*. Then silence was restored when the
officer summoned the first of the condemned, Doctor Cazalla, who,
even with the help of guards, could barely reach the little pulpit. His
prostration, the pallor of his face, his sunken cheeks, his extremely thin
body, seemed to predispose the public in his favor. Cipriano stared at

him as if he were a stranger, and when the officer enumerated the charges against him and announced in his stentorian voice the sentence of death by garrote before being cast into the flames, the Doctor burst into tears, and looked toward the Royal box trying to speak. However he was immediately surrounded by guards and bailiffs who stopped him. The two officers, Ortega and Vergara, alternately read the sentences, while the condemned, walking on their own or helped by guards, stumbled to the pulpit to hear them. Despite being horrifying and atrocious, the ceremony degenerated into a tedious routine, barely interrupted by the jeers or applause with which the crowd bade farewell to the prisoners condemned to death as they went back to their seats:

*Beatriz Cazalla*: confiscation of property, death by garrote, and consignment to the flames.

*Juan Cazalla*: confiscation of property, sentenced to life imprisonment and the perpetual wearing of the sanbenito, together with the obligation to take Communion on Christmas, Easter, and Pentecost.

*Constanza Cazalla*: confiscation of property, life imprisonment and perpetual wearing of the sanbenito.

*Alonso Pérez*: degradation, death by garrote, and consignment to the flames.

*Juan Sánchez*: to be burned at the stake.

*Cristóbal Padilla*: confiscation of property, death by garrote, and consignment to the flames.

*Isabel de Castilla*: sanbenito in perpetuity and life imprisonment; confiscation of property.

*Pedro Cazalla*: degradation, confiscation of property, death by garrote, and consignment to the flames.

*Ana Enríquez*:

Before the girl reached the pulpit, the officer hesitated, and an expectant hush came over the crowd. Fearing she would faint, or simply seeking support in her isolation, she'd climbed the stairs holding the duke of Gandía's hand. But, against all expectations, once she was there, she faced the officer with resolve and a challenging look in her eye. Impassive, she heard Juan Ortega repeat her name and the symbolic punishment to which she was sentenced:

> *Ana Enríquez*: will leave the prison wearing the sanbenito and carrying a candle; she will fast for three days and nights; she will return to the prison and, once there, be set free.

A mocking boo rose from the plaza, descended from the rooftops and balconies, and climbed the stairs. The people could not abide the insignificance of the punishment, the penitent's air of superiority, her rank, beauty, and self-sufficiency. Trembling, Cipriano, his head erect, his eyes burning, stared at her. The reaction of the mob enraged him, as did the solicitude of the duke of Gandía, his protective air, his closeness. He saw her descend from the pulpit with feigned haughtiness, her right hand in that of the duke, gathering her skirts, apparently oblivious to the jeers of the people. Officer Vergara hastily summoned another prisoner in an attempt to quiet down the protests of the crowd, which, when it saw Herrezuelo's gag, his hands tied behind his back, his defenselessnes, returned to an expectant silence:

> *Antonio Herrezuelo*—trumpeted the officer—: confiscation of property, burned at the stake.

> *Juan García*: confiscation of property, death by garrote, and consignment to the flames.

> *Francisca de Zúñiga*: sanbenito in perpetuity and life imprisonment.

> *Cipriano Salcedo*:

Suddenly the rapid succession of prisoners appearing at the pulpit ceased. Cipriano, his head raised, his eyelids pounding, was helped to his feet by a guard. Even though the guard was supporting him, he could not take the first step. His swollen feet weren't weighing him down; they simply would not obey him. There was a tense pause in the plaza. Faced with the prisoner's inability to move, the guard looked over at the bailiff, and a second guard joined them. Passive, light, Cipriano allowed himself to be lifted, still wearing the twisted, grotesque, and inane conical hat, by the two guards wearing their bowler-style caps. A pitiless sun wounded the penitent's eyes, which he instantly shut, visibly squeezing his lids together. He swayed. He was a man destroyed, and the sympathetic muttering of the crowd grew. The officer shouted as he repeated his name:

*Cipriano Salcedo*: confiscation of property, burned at the stake.

The noise from the crowd was now growing and coming in gusts, like the roar of the sea. The prisoner seemed unaffected by the sentence. He gave the impression that even if he were pardoned he could never return to life. He remained motionless, his eyes shut, leaning on the guard's arm, blurred and insignificant. Once again, the second guard stood up, and between the two of them they lifted Cipriano over the railing and carried him back to his place on the bench. His eyelids remained closed, but his cowardly eyes were full of tears. He felt humiliated, confused, degraded. "Lord, slay me now," he begged.

But his humiliation activated the morbid curiosity of the mob. It was incidents like his that breathed life into the festival, and in reality they were just beginning. Cipriano heard Brother Domingo de Rojas summoned and envied his strength, his physical integrity. The officer said:

*Brother Domingo de Rojas*: degradation and to be burned at the stake.

The public seethed, nervous and expectant. Step by step, the auto had entered the dramatic phase all were eagerly awaiting. The officers summoned *Eufrosina Ríos*, condemned to be garroted and *Catalina de Castilla*, perpetual wearing of sanbenito and life imprisonment. Then he called Don Carlos de Seso. The governor of Toro, with his indomitable will, walked up the steps to the pulpit under his own power, with difficulty because of the weakness of his legs, but erect and noble:

*Carlos de Seso*—said Officer Vergara—: confiscation of property and to be burned at the stake.

Don Carlos made a gesture of acceptance with a deferential bow and pretended to step down with his guard. But once he was level with the royal box, he faced the King, made another small bow, and said, with a touch of irony: "Sire, how can you permit this attack on the life of your subject?"

To which His Majesty instantly replied, furrowing his brow: "If my own son were as evil as you, I would pile up the wood to burn him with my own hands."

More because of his manners than his words—which did not reach the ears of the majority—the mob, who hated dignity, booed and insulted the prisoner, while the guards, not fond of remarks and comments, led him away and increased the number of halberdiers in front of the royal box to impede other outbursts. The officers went on shouting names and punishments, but the people, who by then were eager for more original contributions to the program, stopped paying attention, dulled by the tedium and the blazing heat.

Immediately after that, with a brighter and brighter sun pouring down on the plaza, the bishop of Palencia degraded the condemned clerics, which once again aroused the expectations of the mob. Standing before the royal box, wearing surplice, stole, and cope, as well as a white mitre, the bishop approached the five kneeling prisoners, who were covered with black velvet chasubles, with chalices and patens in their hands as if they were saying Mass. He stripped them one by one of those objects, exchanging them for sanbenitos painted with flames and devils as he said: "By the power invested in me by the Holy Church, I eradicate the signs of your priestly state, which you have dishonored with the crime of heresy."

Then he proceeded to rub their mouths, fingers, and the palms of their hands with a moist cloth and ordered a barber to shave their heads so they could be fitted with conical caps. On his knees, pale, thin, and unkempt, with the hood of his chasuble for a hat, Doctor Cazalla, pulling together whatever strength remained to him, shouted three times: "Blessed be God, blessed be God, blessed be God!" And after a bailiff dashed over and pushed him back toward the bench, the Doctor, weeping, his nose running, went on shouting: "May it please the heavens and all men to hear me. May Our Lord rejoice, and may all of you be witnesses to the fact that I, a repentant sinner, have returned to God. I promise to die in His faith, now that he has had the mercy to show me the true path!"

The Doctor's words and tears produced two different reactions in the mob: the more sensitive sobbed with him, while the harder ones, standing on the stairs in a rage, insulted him, calling him a leper, an illuminato. When things calmed down, the bishop of Palencia returned to the pulpit and said that since the sentences had been read and the priests degraded, he declared the auto-da-fé concluded, now, at four o'clock on May 21, 1559. The prisoners sentenced to jail would, he added, be lead in a procession to the Royal and Inquisitorial prisons to serve their sentences, while the others would be transported on donkeys to the burning place, set up behind the Puerta del Campo, where they would be executed.

The mob careened down the stairs, their faces red and sweaty, commenting at the top of their lungs the various aspects of the auto, the women with their heads bowed and their eyes red, the men with kerchiefs around their necks, wineskins held high, drinking according to the rite of the threshing floor. At the moment of greatest confusion, there was a fight among the prisoners that attracted many spectators. Herrezuelo, free of his gag, turned toward the upper stairs, where his wife, Leonor de Cisneros was standing, wearing the sanbenito of those who were reconciled. He insulted her in the worst way, calling her a felon, a whore, and the daughter of a whore, and since no one reacted, he leapt the stairs separating them in three jumps and punched her twice. The guards and bailiffs finally interceded and got him under control. Once again they gagged him, while Doctor Cazalla, overcome once again by his oratorical fever, counselled him to think, to reflect, and to listen "because I've studied more books than you and was fooled into the same error." He went on in those terms, sermonizing the enraged Herrezuelo, who still did not have his hands tied behind his back. He managed to pull the gag out of his mouth and answered the Doctor in a mocking tone those listening adored: "Doctor, Doctor, I'd like to have the spirit now that you showed on other occasions."

Once Herrezuelo was bound and gagged, the penitents, divided into two groups which separated at the bench. Those forgiven, lined up and flanked by guards, began their return to jail, walking between the partitions, wearing sanbenitos marked with the cross of Saint Andrew and carrying burning, green candles. Those sentenced to death, with defamatory cords around their necks, as a symbol of disdain, mounted, one by one, small donkeys especially prepared for them. They stood on the lowest step, got on, and made their way to the scaffold, along the narrow path soldiers opened in the crowd by holding their halberds in horizontal position.

The first to mount was the Doctor, then Brother Domingo de Rojas, and when Cipriano made ready to follow, he glimpsed his uncle Ignacio, in mourning, speaking with guards and bailiffs at the foot of the stairs. Cipriano hesitated when he saw him so close. With his head held high, smiling, he wanted to greet his uncle, but Ignacio spoke to the guard leading the donkey and paid no attention to him. He took the guard aside and replaced him with a woman of a certain age, wearing a charming German bonnet. She was simple and slender with a pleasing face. The woman came to Cipriano, her eyes filled with tears, and caressed his bearded cheek tenderly: "My child, what have they done to you?"

Cipriano raised his head, found the visual axis, and, despite all the time that had passed, recognized her immediately. He could not speak, but he did try to take her hand, to show her his love in some way, but a sudden undulation of the mob separated them. Two powerful guards put him on the back of a roan donkey, while the Doctor and Brother Domingo began riding along the narrow path between the soldiers. A guard patted the donkey's rump, and Cipriano pressed his knees against his mount. He was swaying, but from his elevated position, he looked fondly toward the sweet figure ahead of him. Submissively, Minervina pulled on the halter and wept silently, trying to catch up to Brother Domingo and the Doctor.

The plaza was a seething mass, an uncontrolled sea. On both sides, the mob stretched out, fluctuating and indecisive, angry men arguing with others who blocked their way, sympathetic and teary-eyed women, children running back and forth between the sweet stands which had been set up here and there. The suffocating heat was so humid, and the stench rising from the plaza so overwhelming that overheated men and women with sweat-stained armpits stripped off their holiday clothes.

They stood around in doublets or in shirts, unable to bear the afternoon sun.

Cipriano, lulled by the motion of the donkey, did not feel the heat. Seeing Minervina tugging on the halter, he felt curiously tranquil, protected, just as he had as a child. She was moving forward in such an elegant and confident way, that no one would have thought she was bringing him to his death. Among those leading donkeys, she was the only woman, and despite her age, her figure was so graceful that half-drunk peasants who'd come to town for the party, made passes at her and shouted filthy remarks. But the procession of the donkeys, though slow, moved forward without stopping, threading its way through the mob. Twenty-eight donkeys in a row, ridden by twenty-eight outlandish beings, with sanbenitos covered with devils and conical hats on their heads. A grotesque procession.

But once Cipriano caught up to Brother Domingo, he began to hear the Doctor's preaching, his shrieks of repentance, his appeals for compassion. Cipriano stared at his broken, hunched-over figure, his hat tilted to one side, swaying on his donkey, and he asked himself what he had in common with that man, with that other man who just a few months earlier had instructed him energetically about his journey to Germany. He heard his exhortations and pleas with a great deal of skepticism, disinterest, and with no emotion: "Listen to me and understand that on this earth the Church is not invisible but visible. And the visible Church is the Catholic, Roman, and Universal Church. Christ founded it with His blood and passion, and His vicar is none other than the Pope. And rest assured that even if all the sins and abominations of the world had taken place, if the Vicar of Christ resides there, so does the Holy Spirit."

He was called heretic, scarecrow, mad old man, but he wept and, occasionally, smiled when he alluded to his fate as a liberation. Women made the sign of the cross, whimpered, and sobbed with him, but some men spit on him, saying: "Now he's afraid, he's shit himself the bastard." A few steps behind, Cipriano noted all the insults and curses the Doctor's words aroused in the mob. In that way, they entered Santiago street, where the crowd was even denser, almost impenetrable, and the donkeys slowly made their way between rows of halberdiers.

Groups of women in their Sunday best, with smart outfits, appeared at the windows and balconies to watch the procession pass and comment at the top of their lungs to their neighbors on what was happening. There were children everywhere, playing, hampering the already difficult movement of the animals. They kept everyone in a dazed state by blowing whistles or empty apricot pits. Despite the uproar, bits and pieces of the Doctor's interminable soliloquy reached him. But his attention, though he himself was barely aware of it, was focused in another direction. His debilitated mind drifted toward Minervina, toward her graceful, decisive figure, the halter in her right hand as she opened the way through the crowd.

He delighted in her elegance, and as he looked at her, his eyes filled with tears. There was no doubt that Minervina was the only person who'd ever loved him in this life, the only person he'd ever loved, with whom he'd carried out the divine order of loving one another. He closed his eyes, lulled by the undulations of the little donkey and evoked the crucial moments of his time with her: her warmth against his father's icy stare; his strolls through Espolón, the Santonvenia coach, the tenderness with which she watched over his dreams, her spontaneous giving of herself when he returned to his uncle's house.

When she was fired, Minervina disappeared from his life. She vanished. All his attempts to find her were useless. And now, twenty years later, she mysteriously reappeared like a guardian angel to accompany him in his final moments. But was Mina really the only person he'd ever loved? He thought about Ana Enríquez, a barely outlined project, about his uncle Ignacio, a slave to convention, about his great failure with Teo, about the army of phantoms that had crossed his life and then vanished as he thought he'd found fraternity in the sect. But what remained of that brotherhood he'd dreamed of? Did fraternity really exist somewhere in the world? Who still remained his brother in his moment of tribulation? Certainly not the Doctor, not Pedro Cazalla, not Beatriz. Who? Perhaps Don Carlos de Seso despite his contradictions? Why not Juan Sánchez, the poorest, most humble, and deteriorated of the brothers? The idea of perjury and the easy path of denunciation continued to torment him. A life without warmth mine has been, he said to himself.

As surprising as it might seem, the dying activity of his brain avoided the idea of death to reflect on the tremendous mystery of human limitations. When he accepted the beneficence of Christ, he was not vain nor proud and did not want to be that way now when he would have to persevere. He should either persevere in his new faith or in that of his fathers, one of the two, but in any case in the certainty of finding himself ultimately in the way of truth. But how to find that certitude? He mentally asked Our Lord for some small help: a word, a gesture, a sign. But Our Lord remained silent and in doing so respected Cipriano's freedom. But was human intelligence sufficient to resolve this arduous problem? He'd felt divine inspiration reading *Christ's Beneficence*, but over time, everything, beginning with the words of the Cazallas, had collapsed. So, was it the case then that nothing of all he'd done mattered? Oh Lord, he said in his grief, give me a sign. He was afflicted by the prolonged silence of God, the limitations of his brain, the terrible need he felt to have to decide for himself, alone, the vital question.

The rhythm of the donkey in that undulating sea was putting him to sleep. When he opened his eyes, he observed that dozens of clerical robes were fluttering like flies around Brother Domingo de Rojas, marching at the same pace as his donkey. Voices spoke to him, making their way passed the pikes of the soldiers. They too were tying to get a word out of him, perhaps only a gesture, and they pursued him. But what was moving them in fact? The salvation of his soul or the prestige of the Dominican order? Why this confused company in contrast tot he desolate isolation of the other prisoners? The Dominican remained his own man; no, no he repeated, and those accompanying him, mixed in with the spectators told one another the bad news: he said no, he remains obstinate, but we must save him. And they redoubled their pleas, and one came over and touched him, insisting he die in the same faith as *our* glorious Saint Thomas, but Brother Domingo showed a formidable integrity, no, no he repeated until Brother Antonio de Carreras, who'd spent the night at his side, confessed him, and helped him onto his donkey, chased away the pests, stationed himself at his side, and protected him, talking to him until they reached the burning ground.

Outside the Puerta del Campo, the throng was even larger, but the open field allowed for a more fluid movement. Mixed in with the people were luxurious carriages, tricked out mules carrying married artisans, and even a well-to-do lady with a plumed hat and a golden mantilla spurred her donkey to keep pace with the prisoners and insult them. But as they began arriving at the field, the uproar and expectation grew. The crowning moment of the party was coming. Ladies and women of the people, men carrying toddlers on their shoulders, men on horseback, and even carriages took up positions, wondered who everyone was, whiled away the remaining moments at the trinket stands or playing games of chance. Others had taken places right opposite the tall stakes, which had ladders leaning against them, and defended their positions with all their might. In any case, the smoke from frying crullers and doughnuts spread through the burning ground as the donkeys arrived. The final act was about to begin: the burning of the heretics, their contortions and grimaces among the flames, their screams as they felt the flames on their skin, the pathetic expressions on the faces of those who could now glimpse the road to hell.

From his vantage point on the donkey, Cipriano caught sight of the rows of stakes, the piles of wood next to the ladders, the manacles to keep the prisoners in place, the nervous comings and goings of guards and executioners. The packed mob broke into shouts the minute the first mules arrived. And, hearing their shouts, those who were amusing themselves at a distance made a dash toward the nearest stakes. One by one, the little donkeys carrying the prisoners dispersed, each seeking its own place.

Cipriano unexpectedly spied Pedro Cazalla at his side. He was gagged, and suffering from such a fit of nausea that the bailiffs pulled him off his donkey to give him some water. He'd have to regain consciousness. Out of respect for the spectators, they'd have to work wonders in order not to burn a dead man. Then Cazalla raised his head and turned his insane eyes toward the burning ground. The stakes were about twenty yards apart, the ones nearest the neighborhood of the tanneries for the reconciled and those at the other end for them, those who would be burned alive in an order previously established: Carlos de Seso, Juan Sánchez, Cipriano Salcedo, Brother Domingo de Rojas, and Antonio Herrezuelo. Don Carlos' stake was next to that of the Doctor, who would be garrotted first. Before the executioner began, he tried to address the people once again, but the mob, who saw his intention, burst into shouts and whistles. These late repentances angered them because they slowed down or eliminated the most attractive part of the spectacle.

While the garrotte was fastened around the Doctor's neck, two guards dismounted Cipriano. Once they had him down, they held him up so he wouldn't collapse. He couldn't stand on his own, but he saw Minervina so close to him that he whispered: "Mina, where did you hide so that I couldn't find you?" But two guards lifted him up and carried him to the stake, where he was tied. At his side, at Brother Domingo's stake, the same flapping of clerical robes was going on, with priests climbing up or down ladders, talking to one another, or running to find more important clerics from his order to help him.

Then the Jesuit Father Tablares reappeared. He scrambled up the ladder and had a long talk with the penitent. The roaring of the mob did not allow their voices to be heard, but Tablares must have said something important to him, because Brother Domingo softened, and Tablares shouted to the priests at the foot of the ladder to find the scribe, who appeared a few minutes later mounted on a black mule. A middle aged man with a short beard who knew his job: he removed a sheet of white paper from his portable writing desk, while a very young monk held his inkwell for him.

Brother Domingo, looked one way then another as if he were disoriented, but when Father Tablares spoke into his ear again, he nodded and proclaimed in a full and well-toned voice that he believed in Christ and the Church and publicly detested all his former errors. The priests and monks welcomed his statement with shouts and signs of enthusiasm and said to one another: he's not obstinate any longer; he's saved himself. Meanwhile, the scribe, still standing at the foot of the stake, wrote an account of everything, and the furious mob protested the intervention of all of them.

Cipriano, tied to the iron ring attached to the stake, his cowardly eyes fixed on Minervina, felt the push of the crowd, the activity of the executioners and bailiffs, their movements and their voices. Where was his, his executioner? Why didn't he come? He was terrified by the howls of the crowd, the dull thud of Brother Domingo's garrotted body as it fell lifeless at his side, the rapid action of the gigantic executioner pushing him into the flames, the initial sparks. The people, cheated when they saw a lifeless body burning, now tried to shift to the left, to stand opposite the four criminals still awaiting execution, but those already there, when they saw them coming, pushed them back. Small fights broke out.

The executioner, oblivious to their problems, had just set fire to the wood around Juan Sánchez, who burned furiously and gave off an acrid stench of burnt meat. But the flames consumed the ropes holding him before they reached his body, and Juan Sánchez, feeling himself free, grabbed hold of the stake and climbed it with the agility of a monkey, shouting at the top of his lungs for mercy. The mob applauded and laughed at his monkey-like position. Juan Sánchez's left side was burned, the skin wrinkled and gray, and holding on to the top of the pole, he listened to the exhortations of a Dominican, which for a moment made him hesitate. But when he turned his head and saw the elegance with which Don Carlos de Seso accepted his torture, he allowed himself to burn without a single gesture of protest. He gave a great leap and threw himself into the flames, jumping up and down until he lost consciousness.

The crowd standing before the poles roared its enthusiasm. Children and some women wept, but many men, incensed by alcohol, laughed at Juan Sánchez's hops and twists, calling him a leper and a bastard, parodying his gestures and pirouettes for the other spectators. The contortions and grimaces of Herrezuelo also aroused the hilarity and the tears of the public. He was still gagged, the flames snaking up between his legs, stretching until they enveloped him, then the inhuman howl that came from his throat once the fire consumed his gag and freed his mouth. Many women shut their eyes in horror, others, with their hands together, prayed, looking down, but some men went on shouting and insulting him.

Cipriano had only the vaguest idea that he'd seen Seso, Juan Sánchez, and Herrezuelo die. The flames had rapidly taken their lives, and the heavy odor of burned flesh settled on the field. He glimpsed the executioner approaching his stake, the smoking torch in his right hand, and he shut his burning eyes again and begged Our Lord for a sign. A priest now ran toward the executioner, his robes pulled up, begging him with violent gestures to delay the execution. It was Father Tablares. He reached the ladder out of breath, raised a hand to his chest, and stopped on the first rung. Then he went all the way up and brought his sympathetic face close to that of the dying Cipriano. He was panting. He waited a few minutes to speak: "Brother Cipriano, there is still time. Confess and declare your faith in the Church."

The men were whistling. Cipriano half opened his swollen eyelids and made a timid smile. His mouth was dry and his mind hazy. He raised his head and looked up: "I . . . I believe in the Holy Church of Christ and the Apostles."

Father Tablares brought his lips to Cipriano's cheek and kissed him: "Brother, just say Roman, that's all, I beg you in the name of the blessed Passion of Our Lord."

The mob was growing impatient. Whistles and curses were flying. Cipriano, his head resting against the pole, recognized Father Tablares. For nothing in the world would he want to commit the sin of arrogance. The executioner stared at both men impatiently, holding his torch, while the scribe, pen in hand, waited below for the criminal's confession. Cipriano closed his eyes again, asking Our Lord for a sign. He felt the painful pounding of his eyelids and whispered humbly, as if excusing himself for his obstinacy: "If the Roman is the Apostolic Church, I believe in it with all my soul."

The rage of the people demanding the fire be started and the desire of the executioner to give them exactly what they wanted were pressuring the priest, who in a paternal impulse raised his right hand and caressed Cipriano's cheek: "Son, son how can you set conditions now?"

Cipriano's anguish grew. He sought a new formula that would not betray him that would express his feelings, and at the same time satisfy the Jesuit. A few tender, ambiguous words: "I believe in Our Lord Jesus Christ and in the Church that represents him," he said in the smallest of voices.

Father Tablares lowered his head in discouragement. There was no more time. The spectators were bellowing their demand for a sacrifice: they screamed, jumped up and down, waved their arms. The children's whistles were deafening. The smoke was making everyone weep.

A thickset woman standing next to Minervina calmly ate crullers. Father Tablares, aware of his failure, slowly descended the ladder, saw Minervina sobbing next to the executioner, and the executioner staring intently at him. Then he made a sign, a small movement of his right hand toward the pile of wood.

The executioner touched his torch to the pyre, and the fire opened like a poppy, flamed up, smoked, surrounded Cipriano in a roar, and overwhelmed him. The mob burst into shouts of joy when the deflagration started and enormous flames enveloped the criminal. "Lord, give me shelter," he murmured. He felt an incredibly intense pain, as if his skin were being torn off in strips, but between his thighs, all over his body, with special intensity in the tips of his fingers. He squeezed his eyelids shut in silence, without moving a muscle, in resignation. The people, taken aback by his self-control, but deep down feeling cheated, had fallen silent. Then the silence was broken by the heartrending sobbing of Minervina. Cipriano's head had fallen to one side, and the tips of the flames licked at his sick eyes.

### DECLARATION OF MINERVINA CAPA

In the city of Valladolid, on May 28, 1559, the inquisitors Don Teodoro Romo and Don Mauricio Labrador, during their afternoon audience, ordered Minervina Capa, fifty-six years of age, to appear before them. She was born in the town of Santovenia de Pisuerga and lives in Tudela. In proper form, she swore to tell the truth.

Asked why she was present at the burning ground on the afternoon of May 21, 1599, and what her relationship with the heretic Cipriano Salcedo, she declared that the deceased had been *her child*, that from the time of his mother's death in 1517 she had nursed him and taken care of his needs. She also declared that once the nursing period was over, she remained in the service of Don Bernardo Salcedo, widower and father of the baby, until he decided to place the boy in the Foundling Hospital to be educated, a decision that pained her a great deal.

Asked why she had led the donkey to the stake, she declared that the criminal had been very sick in his eyes and legs and that the idea that she should lead him came from the uncle and tutor of the deceased, Don Ignacio Salcedo, President of the Royal Chancery. He had ordered a search for her through all the neighboring villages, and when he found her, finally, in Tudela de Duero, where she'd resided since her marriage to the farmer Isabelino Ortega to whom she'd given two sons, now grown. She added that Don Ignacio Salcedo, when he asked her to accompany his nephew to the fire, informed her that if she did not, his nephew would be all alone at that sad moment. It was then she accepted, adding, that she would die in his place if she were asked to do so.

Asked about the people who'd spoken with Cipriano Salcedo at the stake and if she'd been asked to do something when he died, or if she saw or heard anything related to the heresy for which he was held accountable by the Holy Office, she swore in proper form that on the day of the autos, she neither noticed nor saw anything at the burning ground other than what she went on to say. That is, the large number of clerics and student from Santa Cruz who surrounded the most important penitent, a pink-cheeked monk named Brother Domingo, who according to the clerics was obstinate. But that it was only the priest named Father Tablares who exhorted and convinced him. And that once he'd finished with Brother Domingo, the same Father Tablares had moved to *her child's* pole and said, "Brother Cipriano, there is still time. Confess and declare your faith in the Roman Church," but *her child* opened his sick eyes a bit and said: "I believe in the Holy Church of Christ and the Apostles." She insists that the aforementioned Father Tablares insisted the penitent say the word "Roman" to which the penitent responded that if the Roman Church were the church of the Apostles, as it should be, that he believed in it. She adds that the monk must have said something more to *her child* since they had their faces together for a while, but that she had no memory of what was aid or perhaps did not manage to hear it because of all the noise and confusion at the burning ground.

Asked finally if she saw or heard anything else that for any reason whatsoever she thought she should declare to the Holy Office, she said that of all the things she saw that afternoon what moved her most was the courage with which *her child* died, that he'd withstood the flames so rigidly and with such determination that he never moved an inch, never screamed, never shed a single tear, that she was of the opinion that, in view of his imprisonment, Our Lord wanted to do him a favor that day. Asked if she thought in good faith that God Our Lord could do a favor for a heretic, she answered that the eye of Our Lord was not the same as that of men, that the eye of Our Lord did not stick at appearances but went directly to the heart of men, the reason why He was never mistaken. Aside from that, she noticed nothing, saw nothing, heard nothing more than what she declared.

She was told to keep all these presidings secret or suffer excommunication.

I, Julián Acebes, scribe, was present.

*(Declaration of Minervina Capa, of Santovenia de Pisuerga, in the report of those who witnessed the executions of May 21, 1559.)*

In addition to the books and authors mentioned in the novel, the works of historians such as Jesús A. Burgos, Bartolomé Bennassar, Carmen Bernis, Germán Bleiberg, Teófanes Egido, Isidoro González Gallego, Marcelino Menéndez Pelayo, Juan Ortega y Rubio, Anastasio Rojo Vega, Matías Sangrador, J. Ignacio Tellechea, and Federico Wattenberg helped me to reconstruct and give form to an era—the sixteenth century. To all of them I express my thanks.